NICE PEOPLE POISON

MURDER IN ROOM 700

MARY HASTINGS BRADLEY

NICE PEOPLE POISON

MURDER IN ROOM 700

Mary Hastings Bradley

COACHWHIP PUBLICATIONS
Greenville, Ohio

Nice People Poison / *Murder in Room 700*, by Mary
    Hastings Bradley
© 2022 Coachwhip Publications edition

Nice People Poison published 1952
Murder in Room 700 published 1931
Mary Hastings Bradley, 1882-1976
CoachwhipBooks.com

ISBN 1-61646-530-1
ISBN-13 978-1-61646-530-8

NICE PEOPLE
POISON

Chapter One

All afternoon Nicholas Parr had been hunched over a client's income-tax papers and he straightened with relief when the intercom sounded and Miss Miller said that Mrs. King was on the phone. "Mrs. *Roger* King," said Miss Miller instructively.

"Yes, Momma," said Nick meekly. The Roger King estate was the largest the firm handled. Into the telephone he said, "Yes, Mrs. King?"

A clear, clipped voice said, "I understand that Mr. Larrabee is away? And Mr. Loomis?"

"Loomis is in Arizona. Mr. Larrabee will be back tomorrow."

"This can't wait. You're a partner?"

"The junior partner," said Nicholas with a hint of humor. There was no humor, only dubiety, in the "Oh!" that came back. Then, again quick and decided, the voice said, "You'll do. In half an hour?"

"In half an hour."

She sounded as high-strung as he had heard she was. It happened that he had never met Veronica King, Mrs. Roger King, for Larrabee had managed her affairs, but he had heard about her and had read about her often enough in the society columns. The money was all hers. Her first husband, who had been much older, had been in lumber

7

and mines and electricity and he had left her a wad of
money. McKenzie, his name was. A year after his death she
had married King. She had been married now for something over two years.

He stacked his papers and eyed his office critically.
There was a definitely zany effect in the different levels of
the window shades, so he sent them all to the top as the
sun was around the corner now. He pulled a big chair near
the desk and put an ash tray on the stand beside it—Mrs.
King had sounded like a chain smoker. He opened the
door of his washroom and ran a comb through his unruly
dark hair and resettled his tie. He said, "You'll do!" to his
reflection. He was a lean, average tall young man in the
early thirties. He had an air of casual cheerfulness that
often made witnesses overlook the acuteness of his dark
eyes.

Half an hour, she had said. Not telephoning, then,
from her home, for she couldn't get into the city in half an
hour. The King place was on the Ridge. A big place, built
by McKenzie, Nicholas had never seen it, except the roof
from the highway, but he knew what it cost to run it and
pay taxes on it. King was president of a small manufactur-
ing company and what he made wouldn't go far toward the
way they lived.

Within half an hour Miss Miller was showing her in,
shutting the door softly on her own exit. Mrs. King stood
a moment outlined against it, a slimly built, long-legged
young woman in a short; loose-fitting mink coat. She had
very blond hair and a very resplendent sun tan, darker
than the hair, and her eyes were the blue of turquoise.
Definitely a dazzler, Nicholas conceded. The sun tan reminded him that the Kings had recently returned from
Florida.

She was looking at him with the same dubiety that had
been in her voice when she said, "Oh!" and Nicholas was

afraid that her idea of a responsible lawyer was a white-haired chap like Larrabee or a bald egg like Loomis so he came quickly forward and said, "What can I do for you, Mrs. King?" in his best professional voice.

She threw off her coat before he could help her with it as if she couldn't wait to be rid of something that had become a nuisance. She wasn't, Nicholas saw then, as slim as her build indicated. The Kings were to have an heir.

She sat down and said abruptly, "I want to make my will." Her will was in the office safe but he could see reason for a new one. As abruptly as before she demanded, "What do I have to do—to revoke that one I made?"

"Simply revoke it. You merely say, 'I hereby cancel and revoke any and all wills made by me at any former time.'"

"Is it here?"

"It's in the safe."

"I'd like to see it."

He spoke into the intercom and in a moment Miss Miller appeared with the will. She gave it to Mrs. King with a glance at Nicholas that somehow communicated awareness of his smoothed hair and Nicholas thanked her gravely.

She went out and he turned his attention to his client. She was staring at the will in her hand. "This leaves everything to my husband," she said. She added, in that clear, brittle voice, "I don't want him to have a cent," and started, quickly, to tear it up. She tried to tear the whole thing at one time but the pages were too many and she took them one by one, shredding each one, scattering the bits about her, like confetti, not bothering with a wastebasket.

"Not a cent," she repeated, in a dry, bitter voice.

So it was like that, Nicholas thought, watching the quick, nervous fingers. He felt a tug of male sympathy for King. It must be hell to be married to a rich woman. A rich woman with a temper. He knew King very slightly and thought him a likable chap, a bit too good-looking, perhaps, too much the man of distinction type, but definitely likable. . . . Well, they'd probably make it up, and the more wills the merrier for Larrabee, Loomis, and Parr, he thought cheerfully.

At the last page Mrs. King stopped. She tore it carefully in two, shredded the lower part with her signature, and kept the upper part. "This is about some bequests," she said. Then, as if he'd been delaying, "As quickly as you can, please."

He summoned Miss Miller again and she looked down at the bits of paper, then, through her eyelashes, at Mrs. King, and sat down, her notebook on her lap. Nicholas said, "Now, Mrs. King, if you will explain what you want done—"

"I want to leave everything to my sister."

"To your sister?"

"I can do that, can't I? I can keep my husband from getting anything?"

"In this state you can." He made that very detached and impersonal. "You are fortunate in your state. It is not so easy to do. Now if you will tell me exactly what you want—"

"I told you. Everything to my sister. To Jennifer Mitchell." Nicholas looked off toward the windows not to seem to be looking at her. "But if you should have children—"

"I'm not going to have children," she said flatly. His eyes went back quickly to her. Her lips were twisting in a queer smile. "I'm not going to live to have a child."

He thought, *Cancer. Heart.* But she did not look ill, not with that glow of health. She must be imagining something, he told himself. He had heard of fanciful fears during pregnancy.

"I can't believe that," he said. "You—"

She broke in, "It doesn't matter whether you do or not." Her voice was mocking and impatient. "All that matters is this will. I want to see that my sister gets everything that I have."

Her curtness made him curt in turn. "Very well. But I must point out that if you have a child and then die this will you are about to make can be attacked."

She stared down a moment, twisting her gloves in her hand, then she told him, "All right, make it half and half, just in case. But my sister is to have charge of all the money. And of the child, too."

"You can't will away a child."

She looked up and for an instant her eyes were startled, then they were mocking again. "It doesn't matter. It won't happen. But fix it so the will can't be attacked. Put in that provision. Otherwise, everything goes to my sister."

"Very well. I'll dictate it while you're here, then if you will drop in, say about Friday—"

"But I want it done now! Finished today. Can't you do it now?"

"Of course. I—of course." He glanced at Miss Miller who gave him back a carefully expressionless look. "Ready?" he said superfluously to her poised pencil and began to dictate. "I, Veronica King, being of sound and disposing mind—"

Like heck she was, he thought. Veronica King was as tense as if walking a tightrope. But it was her money and she knew what she wanted.

It was a short will. Miss Miller went off to type it and Nicholas offered cigarettes. Mrs. King shook her head. "I've sworn off. I'm not leaving *that* chance. . . ."

She sat staring into space, her eyes empty of everything but waiting. Those blank turquoise eyes in her sun-tanned face made him think of the jeweled eyes in a Mayan mask he had once seen, and her face was like a mask. Behind the mask must be a terrific turmoil. He wished that he could say something sensible and down-to-earth but he couldn't find the words.

Miss Miller came in with the typed pages and Mrs. King read them and asked, "Is this watertight?" She must have got that expression from her first husband, Nicholas thought.

"It's as tight as can be made," he answered, "but it can be attacked, of course." At her quick, defiant glance he explained, "Undue influence, you know. There's that angle."

"Undue? Oh, I see!" For a moment some inner amusement laughed at him through her eyes. "But I've quarreled with my sister. I've come straight from a terrific scrap with her."

This was all cockeyed, he thought, but it was none of his business. His job was to get the will signed and witnessed. He got in Ferguson, from across the hall, and Veronica King signed and Ferguson and Miss Miller signed as witnesses, and they both left, Miss Miller bearing the will to the safe. Mrs. King picked up the half page she had laid on the stand by her.

"This is a list of bequests. None of them amount to very much. If you give it to my sister she'll see to them."

She spoke as if she actually believed she wasn't going to live, and Nicholas looked at her for a moment, then said gravely, "You don't really believe this will happen, do you?"

"Never mind what I believe!" she said, in that sharp, mocking, indifferent voice. She picked up her coat and he held it for her, his dark eyes intent on her. It was simply not possible, he thought, that anyone so vivid and so vigorous-looking could have something fatal the matter. She was imagining things.

Suddenly she twisted and looked up at him. "This is absolutely confidential, isn't it? About the will?"

"Absolutely."

"You're sure that man, that witness, won't tell?"

"Indeed not. And he has no idea what was in the will."

"I don't want my husband even to know that I've made another will. I don't want him to know I've been here."

"He won't hear it from us. Nor from Ferguson. I'll see to that."

"Although—" she was drawing on her gloves, speaking slowly for the first time, frowning, as if thinking it out— "although it might save my life. If I don't manage to. But I've got to prove—"

She broke off and said in a perfectly conventional voice, "Good-by, Mr. Parr."

For a moment he did not move, then he shot forward and caught the doorknob she was turning. "What did you say, Mrs. King?"

She looked at him blankly, as if unaware that she had spoken those words aloud. Then she smiled. It was the smile of a wicked child. She said lightly, "I said, 'Good-by, Mr. Parr.'" She went out quickly.

Nicholas stared at the door that had closed behind her. *Although it might save my life.* That's what she'd said. That sounded as if she thought her husband was going to do her in. *If I don't manage to.* Manage to save it? Why didn't she run like a rabbit? She had the price of plenty of plane tickets. *But I've got to prove*— What had she got to prove? That King was two-timing her?

Perhaps he was and that had given her these ideas about her death. Perhaps it was this pregnancy business that had given her a morbid complex. He'd heard of cases like that. He'd ask Doc Abbey. . . . The queer way she had smiled. As if she was having a hell of a lot of fun about it all. . . .

But he couldn't let it go like this. He ran into the outer office and then into the hall. She had gone. The elevator had just gone down. She'd be in her car before he could get down to her. This was the eleventh floor.

Stupid, to let her get away. But Larrabee could follow this up. Larrabee was an old friend and would know how to handle her. Slowly he went back into the office where Miss Miller was closing the safe.

"She's terrific," said Miss Miller. "The cleaning woman is going to love those papers."

"Open up the safe again. There's another paper to go in." But he didn't move to get it. He asked, as if idly, "What did you make of her saying she wasn't going to live to have a child?"

"Lots of women think they're never going to live through it. My sister was like that."

Miss Miller was unimpressed. But Miss Miller had not heard her say, "Although it might save my life." But that was fantastic. Completely fantastic.

"She's certainly off him, isn't she?" said Miss Miller, conversationally.

"She doesn't want him to know she's made this will. He is not to know that she has been here."

"He won't know it from me," said Miss Miller virtuously.

"I wonder what the trouble is."

"I haven't heard anything. I'll bet he hasn't been giving her enough sympathy. That's why she's off him."

"Could be. I'll get that memo for the safe."

Larrabee was back the next afternoon. Nicholas told him the story. Larrabee merely nodded and adjusted the pince-nez on his fine aquiline nose to read the will. He was a spare, tall, silvery-haired man, and all he lacked, Nicholas thought, to walk on the stage as British counselor-at-law was a black ribbon on the pince-nez, and he'd come to that yet. Every so often he added an extra touch.

But he was astute, and he had his integrity, though how much of his integrity was due to his astuteness, to his awareness of the unwisdom of deviating from rectitude, Nicholas was not quite sure. There was, in Larrabee, a streak of cynicism, wide as a cummerbund.

Now his thin fingers drummed on the pages he had put down. "It's curious. I saw them the other evening at the Forrests' and they seemed as usual. . . . Odd how young women go out these days, even when it's quite evident—"

"But what do you make of her saying what she did? That she might live longer if her husband knew she'd made this will?"

Larrabee glanced at the door and looked relieved that it was shut. "Don't let that get to Miss Miller. She didn't hear any of it, did she?"

"She heard her say she wasn't going to live to have a child. Miss Miller didn't think anything of that. I mean she thought it was nerves. And she heard Mrs. King say she wanted her sister to have the child, if there was one, but that might have meant only a quarrel with King. It was later that Mrs. King came out with that speech about living longer. What do you make of it?" said Nicholas insistently.

"I don't make anything of it," said Larrabee. "When you've been in this office as long as I have you'll think very little of hysterical accusations."

"She wasn't exactly hysterical—"

"Veronica is high-strung. She was talking nonsense. She is tremendously in love with King and any trouble between them would throw her off balance." He smiled and quoted, "'For to be wroth with one we love, Doth work a madness in the brain.'"

Larrabee settled everything with quotations. Nick said stubbornly, "Well, it was a queer thing to say."

"She was in a tantrum. Probably a jealous tantrum. Though I haven't heard any rumors."

"He's good-looking. Too good-looking. He'd be attractive to other women."

"He always was. He was a very popular bachelor but rather—rather aloof," said Larrabee, consideringly. "I had the feeling that he set a high price on himself."

And he'd got it. He'd got a girl—a young widow—with beauty, style, and hard cash. And now she was tearing mad at him. Nicholas persisted, "Something has happened."

"Veronica can make much out of little. . . . You say she had quarreled with her sister?"

"She said she'd come from a terrific quarrel with her."

"You see?" Larrabee smiled. "Veronica throws out words. She speaks of a terrific quarrel, then makes her sister the beneficiary. . . . I wonder if Jennifer knows. She lives with them, you know."

"I didn't know. I didn't know there was a sister."

"She was given an income, though not a large one, in the first will."

"I never read the will."

"It was made just after their marriage. About the time you came in with us. I felt she ought to have been more generous to Jenny but she thought Jenny would marry well."

"And she hasn't?"

"She's still in college. Her last year. Home on spring vacation. Odd you haven't met her."

"Not so odd," said Nick. "She'd be in a younger crowd. I never met Veronica until yesterday. When I was a kid, I didn't play around with the socialites, you know. Dad taught in West Town High and that didn't run to polo ponies. What's this Jennifer like?"

"Like Veronica. Like what Veronica was. There are nine years between them. Veronica was only nineteen when she married McKenzie."

"Nineteen?" Nick cocked a mocking eyebrow. "Knew what she wanted, didn't she?"

"She wanted to get away from her aunt," said Larrabee drily. "The Mitchell girls were orphans, with no money.

Veronica was proud. . . . I think the marriage worked
out very well. Of course McKenzie indulged her. He was
very fond of Jenny, too. Like a father to her. . . . Yes, it
worked out well, except there were no children. McKenzie
blamed himself for that. He'd been married before, as a
young man, and had no children then. He told me, not
long before he died, that he hoped life would make it up
to Veronica."

"Very broad-minded," said Nick. "Did she know King
then?"

"I think not. It was all very sudden, after Mac's death,
but that was understandable. I always thought King was
the right young man for her, and I've no reason to believe
the contrary now, although," he said cautiously, "my loyalty is naturally to my client."

"Then get hold of her and find out what's the matter,"
Nick urged.

"Nicholas, to act as audience to an hysterical woman is
to commit her to believe in her accusations. The kindest
thing to Veronica is not to encourage her by taking her
seriously. However—" He sighed. "I'll make a point of
seeing her soon. I'll drop in on Sunday."

Saturday evening there was a canasta party at the club
but Nicholas Parr decided against it. Canasta can run into
money and through his quickness in reaching for checks
his last month's bills had been sobering. Better, far better,
he decided virtuously, to sharpen his wits at chess with Dr.
Abbey. He called the doctor and made a date.

The doctor was not married. He lived in an old-fashioned house with a housekeeper with whom he had worked
out an effective compromise. The front room was exactly
as Mrs. Siddons felt a front parlor should be kept, and the
back room was as the doctor liked it, things left where he
put them. The walls were lined with shelves and cabinets,

the tables loaded with books and periodicals, the chairs big and comfortable, and the whole room was lighted with a prodigious central light that no wife would have tolerated for an instant.

Abbey, himself, was a short, stocky man with a round, cheerful face and blue eyes that twinkled easily. He looked the chatty type but actually, Nick had discovered, he said very little. He played chess in the quiet, easygoing way he had with everything else, but with a concentration that was like an extrasensory perception.

The first game ended in Nick's checkmate. "Doggone," he said ruefully. "I thought it was in the bag."

"It was—transiently," said Abbey. "Then you took it for granted."

Nick leaned back, smoking, reflecting on his moves, while Abbey set up the pieces. Nick had the white and after a few moments' concentration he made an aggressive opening and they settled down to it again, heads nearly touching as they studied the board. Neither head turned at the sound of a knock and the opening of the door.

"Excuse me, doctor," said Mrs. Siddons. "But Mr. King is here."

"King? King?" The doctor's hand was hovering over the black queen. Then, his voice less absent, "But it's too soon."

"I'm sorry, doctor," said a man's voice. "This is an emergency."

Roger King was in the doorway, a tan coat swinging back from his broad shoulders. There was rain on it and on his light brown, slightly reddish hair and a smear of mud across one sleeve. He was holding one arm awkwardly and Nick thought instantly of an accident, and then he thought that Veronica King might be in it and he sat very still, waiting.

"You hurt?" said Abbey, attentive now but unexcited.

"That's nothing. Twisted my wrist—got off on a soft shoulder coming in. It's my wife."

Nicholas Parr straightened. King glanced his way and, after a moment, gave a nod of delayed recognition. "Sorry to break in on your game like this," he said courteously, "but she's ill." He turned to Abbey. "Will you come right out, doctor? She has some bad pains."

"Labor pains?" said Abbey.

Nicholas relaxed. Labor pains had nothing to do with what he had been thinking.

"I suppose so," King was saying. "I don't know what else—she was all right until after dinner. We were having coffee. Then these pains came on. I tried to get you on the phone but it was out of order. And the chauffeur wasn't there. He had the day off. So I had to come in."

He sounded worried and exasperated. Nick eyed him with curiosity. Roger King, the disinherited. He was about his own age, in the early thirties, tall, broad-shouldered, and handsome. Very regular features, with a sun tan like Veronica's. Slate-gray eyes.

"Could it be something she'd eaten?" Abbey was asking.

"I don't know. No, she thought it was—premature, you know. It seemed to come in spasms."

"Time it?" Abbey was busily taking things from a cabinet, putting them in a black bag.

"No, I never thought—I got her to bed. I don't know how bad it really was—you know Veronica is afraid of pain and she exaggerates—but it was real, whatever it was. She kept drawing up her knees. Would that mean anything?"

"July," said Abbey. It was now only late March. He said over his shoulder, "Why didn't you bring her to the hospital?"

"She wouldn't come. You know she'd decided on going to a hospital in Chicago and she didn't want to get involved here."

"That's nonsense. A hospital is the place for her if—"

"I know. I know. She ought to have come. But I couldn't waste time arguing. You'll follow me out? I want to get right back. She's alone out there—"

"Alone?"

"The maids went out directly after dinner. They had some party on so we had an early dinner. And Jenny's off at a dance, I don't know where. I didn't like leaving her"—he sounded defensive—"but what else could I do? The thing was to get you." He said urgently, to Abbey's back, "You'll be right along, won't you?"

"Hold on. You'll have to drive me out. My car's out of commission."

King swung about as if that were the last straw. Nick said, "I'll drive you, Doc."

"No need. I'm ready now." Abbey closed his bag. "But you'd better come along, Nick, to drive me back. And I may need you for errands if the phone's dead."

"I'll get my car started," said Nick.

He caught up his coat and hurried out. Behind him Abbey was saying, "You know women frequently have false pains. Especially in a first—"

But women do not often say, *I'm not going to live to have a child.* Something must be terribly wrong with her, something she had known about. But why hadn't Abbey known it? Abbey was a shrewd diagnostician. That was his reputation. But maybe Abbey hadn't given her a checkup since her return.

He turned up his coat collar against the rain. It had been pouring since afternoon but it was letting up now. King's engine was running; the wheels of his car were thick with mud. A bad skid. . . . Nick started his engine and lit a cigarette, and in a moment the others came out and started and he followed them.

This side of the city was on the way to the Ridge. For a time there was a steady procession of cars coming into town, their headlights dazzling. Coming for the late movies, he thought, and glanced at his wrist watch— nine-forty. King had certainly lost a lot of time coming in. King wasn't driving fast now, but that was probably Abbey's caution. Abbey was a careful man. There couldn't be anything very wrong with Veronica King or he'd have caught it two months ago, before she went south. No use trying to guess about it. They'd find out when they got there.

Now the houses were farther apart with larger gardens and the traffic more infrequent. Then came swanky places where no houses showed at all, only high hedges or walls with impressive entrances. Occasionally there were stretches of woodland yet unclaimed for residence. At last the car ahead turned in between stone pillars and Nick followed.

He had often driven past the King place but he had never seen the house, for it was back from the road, hidden by trees. Now his headlights gave him a glimpse of a broad white facade, then the drive ran under an old-fashioned porte-cochere at one end of the house. The other car had stopped ahead of him and King and Abbey were already at the door. He jumped out and hurried after them.

The hall was wide and soft-carpeted. King opened the door of a dressing room where they shed their coats quickly, then he led the way toward the stairs. The house was utterly quiet. The silent rooms gave Nicholas the feeling of having wandered into some empty theater set Even their presence did not bring it to life, for their feet made no sound on the thick carpeting.

At the foot of the stairs King said vaguely to Nick, "Make yourself at home," and waved toward the open

doors; he and the doctor, bag in hand, started up the stair-
way. Nick heard King say, his voice lowered, "She's probably asleep—" then, in a faintly apologetic tone, "This may
be all a false alarm. . . ."

Nicholas turned into one of the rooms, the one where
the Kings had been having after-dinner coffee, for a silver
tray and service were on a low table and there were half-
filled cups on smaller tables beside the chairs. Queer, he
thought, four days ago he'd never set eyes on Veronica
King and here he was, wandering about her house. He
glanced about the room. Pale fruitwood paneling and sets
of books in rich bindings looking very unread. Over a
couch a big painting of a girl in gauzy blue.

The girl's eyes were blue as her dress; she was young
and slim, with hair like pale wheat. Veronica, of course,
and, from the young freshness, Veronica McKenzie. The
artist had etherealized her, but she must have been a lovely
thing. Veronica McKenzie. And then Veronica King. And
now this funny business about King. He thought of the
young woman in his office shredding that will—the taut
face and angry fingers.

There had been no sound from upstairs. Now, suddenly, he heard King's voice. "Veronica!" The voice was loud,
urgent and aghast. *"Veronica!"*

Chapter Two

He took the stairs two at a time. The door of a corner room was open and King and the doctor were by a bed, the doctor bending over it, King standing at the foot. Nick could see a tangle of pale silk covers and, beyond Abbey's shoulders, a spill of bright hair on a pillow. The room was full of a sick, sweetish smell.

"Open the windows," said Abbey.

Nick ran to them. He pulled the curtains back, flung open the sash and let in the wet night air. When he turned King was still standing, unmoving, staring down, and Abbey was holding up a big wad of white cotton, holding it at arm's length. He put it down on a nearby chest.

"Chloroform!" he said. Nick had never heard him sound so staggered. "Against her face. She—"

"Do something!" said King in that hard, urgent angry-sounding voice. "For God's sake, *do* something!"

Abbey was already bending over the bed again, and now he had his stethoscope out. Nick looked away as he threw back the sheet. He thought that Abbey would tell him to rush for a pulmotor, for an oxygen tank or something helpful; he insisted to himself that Abbey would speak any instant. Then he looked at the bed—he had to. Abbey was straightening up, and there was something in his movement, a sort of settled finality that ended any hope before he spoke.

"Too late," he said. "Much too late. She's been gone for an hour, at least. There was enough on that cotton . . ."

Nick thought violently, *No!* He could see her, outlined against the door of his office, so vivid, tense, alive. . . .

"The little fool!" That outburst, from King, made both Abbey and Nick turn toward him. "She *was* a fool about pain," said King defensively, as if his own words had shocked him, yet still angry-sounding. "She's done this before—sniffed that stuff to dull pain."

"You think she did it?" said Abbey.

"Of course! What else is there to think?"

"I haven't begun to think yet," Abbey said slowly. "But someone could have broken in . . ."

King looked about the room. Then he marched over to a dressing table, picked up a sparkling bracelet, looked at it a moment, then dropped it. "A thief would have taken that," he said in a dry tone. He went past the bed, not looking down at it, to the table between the two beds, took up a bottle on it, turned it about in his hands, then set it down.

"That's from our druggist," he said. "The stuff was in the house."

"You kept it here?"

"There was always some about—for kittens—for hurt animals. Veronica was fanatic about pain. She couldn't stand the thought of pain."

"She's used this before?"

"I caught her sniffing it one night, when she had a bad tooth. Not very much of it then. But I never thought, to-night—I never thought. I left her some aspirin—"

His voice changed, as if realization was making its way through the first numbing shock. He said, almost inaudibly, "She must have been in great pain."

Nick thought, *I must get the hell out of here.* King ought to be alone. Abbey ought to get out, too. A man had the right to privacy—

But Abbey wasn't getting out. He was telling King to get out. He said there was a chance, an infinitesimal chance, that he could save the child. He said, "I hold out no hope— Couldn't get the heartbeat. But there's the chance."

King looked at him blankly as if he had forgotten about the child. Then he blazed, "I forbid it. I won't have her touched. There's no chance—I won't have her touched." He sounded, Nick thought, as if he hardly knew what he was saying.

"You've no choice," said Abbey. "And I've no choice."

He was hurrying off his coat. King, staring stiffly ahead of him, walked out of the room into an adjoining one, like a man walking in his sleep. Now he *would* get the hell out of there, Nick thought. Of course, if he had the guts that God gave the first angleworm he'd offer to help. But he couldn't do it. No, he couldn't. He was surprised to hear himself saying, "Anything I can do?"

The doctor looked around as if he'd forgotten him. "Oh, no," he said. "I can manage. You clear out. But stay within call."

Nick got out. He took a cigarette, then went hastily farther along the hall, away from that room. Doctors were wonderful. Wonderful and awful. But this was their business. Abbey had been looking on death for twenty-five years.

Veronica King dead. Dead with a wad of cotton soaked in chloroform against her face. . . . That was a crazy thing for her to do. If she had done it. . . . Had she done it purposely? Had she been so angry at King that she wanted to make him sorry for something? Or did she want him blamed for it? Or, perhaps, she had meant only to throw a scare—

No use trying to figure it out. He didn't know those two people well enough to figure out what they might do. But his mind went racing up and down one blind alley after another. King seemed to have had the shock of his life. But he had been right there with the answers. King could have done it—

Nick drew hard on his cigarette and thought of Veronica King in his office saying, "I've sworn off. I'm not leaving *that* chance. . . ."

Whatever you might think of Veronica King, and sorry as he was for the dead girl in the room behind him, he thought she was as batty as they made them; whatever you might think of her, you didn't forget a word she had spoken or the way she had said it.

Something made him look up. On the stairs ahead of him, halfway down from the upper floor, a girl was looking down on him. The sister, he thought, his heart sinking. Home early. How was he to tell her? No, God bless him, it wasn't the sister—Larrabee had said the sister was like Veronica and this girl was dark. Or had Larrabee meant alike in disposition?

She was coming down, and he went to the foot of the stairs. She paused on the step above him looking at him in a puzzled, uncertain way. She had the biggest, darkest eyes that he had ever seen and a skin as white as milk. Beauty was an overworked word, but this girl had beauty. Her dark hair was parted and drawn back, satin smooth; she wore a dark daytime dress.

"Is anything—wrong?" she asked in a hushed, hesitant, yet faintly agitated voice. "I thought I heard—"

She wasn't young enough to be a college girl; she looked more like twenty-five or twenty-six, but Nick wasn't taking chances. He asked, "Are you Miss Mitchell?"

"Oh, no. I'm Nina Barrett," she said quickly, then, as she saw the name meant nothing to him, she said, with a touch of reserve, "Mr. King's secretary."

Nick said the first thing that came into his head. "How long have you been here?"

"How long? Why, I came this afternoon. To do some letters."

"You've been in the house all evening?"

"Why, yes. I was staying all night. It was raining and the chauffeur was off duty and Mrs. King asked me to stay all night." As if she felt she had to go on explaining she repeated, "It was raining. And the station is quite far."

She had been in the house and King had said there was no one in the house. He had said that his wife was alone.

Nick demanded, "Did Mr. King know you were here?"

She stared back at him, and said stiffly, "Of course Mr. King knew. He heard Mrs. King ask me."

"The devil he did!"

"Why, what do you mean—?"

"Mr. King said there was no one here. He needed some-one very badly this evening but he said there was no one in the house."

"He said that?"

"He certainly did."

She looked at him hesitantly a moment. "Oh, well, he forgot." Her voice was very light, as if to cover any betrayal of surprise or chagrin. "That isn't surprising. I wasn't at dinner with them." Then she said, "But what do you mean—that he needed someone very badly—?"

"Mrs. King was taken ill after dinner."

She looked quickly past Nick toward the bedroom door. "Oh, I didn't know. . . . I thought I heard something—but that was only a few minutes ago."

She must have heard King saying "Veronica!" She must have come to the top of the stairs to listen. . . .

"I didn't know," she repeated defensively. "I wasn't at dinner with them. I had a tray in my room. Is she—is she very ill?"

There was no time to soften it. "She died about an hour ago."

"Oh, no!" Her voice held disbelieving horror. She shrank back against the wall, as if hiding from sight of that bedroom door. "Oh, no!"

"It was an accident," Nick said. "She took—she breathed in some chloroform to dull the pain she was having and got too much."

"Pain? But she was all right—"

"It came on after dinner."

"I didn't know. I was up in my room." She sounded tensely defensive. The dark eyes looked at him in a sort of panic, then something wary and calculating came into them. "When did you say she died?"

"An hour ago. Over an hour ago. While Mr. King was getting the doctor. The phone was out of order so he had to go."

She looked more and more frightened. She babbled, "How awful—to take chloroform—"

"She didn't know what she was doing. She ought never to have been left alone. Mr. King should have called you."

She said breathlessly, "But he forgot about me. . . I was up in my room. . . . He forgot about me."

"That isn't your fault," said Nick gently. "He probably thought you'd gone home."

"Yes, he must have. . . . Oh, if I only had!" There was a catch of hysteria in her voice. Then, in a quick change of tone, as if she were seeing him, really seeing him, for the first time, "You're Mr. Parr, aren't you? With Larrabee and Loomis?"

"That's right. I happened to be at the doctor's and came along."

"With them? Or in your own car?"

"In my car."

"Then take me away! Please take me away," she begged, in a low, imploring voice. "I don't want them to know I was here. I don't want to be dragged into this. Please take me away!"

"I can't do that," he said uncomfortably. "You can't run out on it now."

"But no one has seen me. No one but you. Mr. King has forgotten all about me."

"He'll remember, all of a sudden. And the maids—they know you were here, don't they? You had a tray at dinner time."

"They won't know when I left. I might have gone right after dinner. Just let me slip down into your car and you take me away when you can." She besought, "It will be so awful! All the—the publicity."

"But how did you go?" Nick argued. "You didn't take a taxi. They can check up on that. It was raining and you didn't walk to the station and take the electric. They can check up on that, too."

"Oh, no, they can't!"

"And your family will know when you got in."

"I haven't any family. I live alone. No one will know. Oh, please!" Her eyes clung imploringly to him.

"But you'd have to lie about it. You don't want to tell a lot of lies, do you?"

A flash of scorn blazed in her. "I'll tell anything, not to be involved! Can't you see what it means for me to have been here, sitting upstairs reading, while she—while she— Oh, can't you see?" she cried desperately.

Yes, he could see. Headlines. *Secretary Reads While Wife Dies.* But it wouldn't help her to go bolting off. He told her so. He told her, "It was no fault of yours that you weren't called on to help."

"But there'll be talk—"

That was her terror. Perhaps there already had been talk about King and his beautiful secretary. Larrabee hadn't heard it, but Larrabee didn't hear everything. A girl like that was bound to be talked about. She had sounded on the defensive when she said, "Mr. King's secretary." Perhaps she had been the trouble between King and Veronica. Perhaps—

But no. King wouldn't be fool enough to kill his wife while his girl was sitting in the house. If she was important to him, he'd certainly have remembered she was in the house.

Nick gave his head a baffled shake. "It's bad luck but running away won't help you."

"You won't take me?"

"I can't do it. It would be a bad mistake."

She looked as if she were going to blaze out at him, but she didn't. She was suddenly controlled and intent. She said urgently, "But you won't say I was here, will you? You won't tell anyone you saw me?"

"Look! You can't run off in the night—"

"No, no! But just don't say you saw me down here. Let me be found upstairs."

As he hesitated she urged, "No one will ask you. No one knows. Let me get back to my room. You can do that much, can't you?" she said, anger breaking through.

"Look!" said Nick, getting nettled himself. "I'm not wanting to drag you into anything. This evening wasn't my idea. I'm not to blame that you were sitting up there—"

She rushed into penitence. "I know. It was my fault for coming down. Only let me get back to my room. Don't speak of me at all. It will be so much easier, to be up in my room . . ."

She had something there. Better to be up in her room where she belonged and come down in her own time than to have him saying, "Oh, look what I found in the hall!"

"All right," he said. "You go back upstairs and pull yourself together. Then, after a time, you come down and explain how you happened to be here. Now, how's that?"

She looked at him anxiously. "And you won't speak about me?"

"Not unless I'm asked. And, as you say, that isn't likely. You come down and explain yourself. Right?"

She gave him a quick, eager nod. There was a sound of a door opening and she fled up the stairs, and vanished, with a swift, backward look. Nick turned about and walked down the hall to meet Abbey. From the shake of Abbey's head Nick knew before the doctor spoke.

"Maybe it's just as well," was the way Abbey told him. "The good Lord knows that King wouldn't know what to do with a child now." He glanced down the hall, toward the door of the adjoining room. "He hasn't come out, has he?"

"No. I haven't seen him."

"I'll have to tell him. . . . Got a cigarette? Mine are in my coat downstairs."

They lighted up and Abbey said, "Nick, you drive to the nearest house and notify the police. Get Wayland himself if you can. They'd better get here as soon as possible."

The police. It would be up to the police to decide whether this was accident or suicide. King wasn't going to like this.

"Best to get it over with as soon as possible," said Abbey. "If the line is out of order along the road go across the tracks."

"I hope Jensen has gone home."

"Jensen?"

"Police reporter."

"Oh, yes. The papers. Well, it can't be helped."

Nicholas ran downstairs, got his coat and hat, and went out to his car. The rain had stopped and stars were shining through the thinning clouds. He drove out and turned

into an entrance across the way. The drive led to a house
that was dark so he drove out again. The next house he
tried was lighted with cars parked about and guests coming out the door. He hurried to it and asked the maid if he
could use the telephone to report Roger King's phone out
of order. She said, "Right in here," and he stepped into a
study and dialed.

He got Wayland, gave his message quickly and hung up
before Wayland could ask questions. He called the telephone company and reported King's phone out of order.
A newspaper on the desk was open at the social page and
headlines said that the Clarence Deschais were giving a
tea dance for their daughter and he wondered if Jennifer
Mitchell was dancing there. He looked up the Deschais'
number. Maybe this was wrong, he thought, maybe Jennifer Mitchell ought to have those last hours of dancing, but
he wanted very much to see Jennifer Mitchell.

A tired voice told him that Miss Mitchell had been
there but had gone on to the Bolgers'. What Bolgers? Why,
the Edward Bolgers who were giving a supper dance. He
looked up the number and when he got an answer, said,
"Please tell Miss Mitchell, Miss Jennifer Mitchell, that her
sister is not well and she had better come home."

He hung up and got himself out of the house, waving
his hand toward the host who was still in talk with a lin-
gering guest. All the cars but one had gone now. Back at
the King house the doctor let him in.

"This porte-cochere," said Abbey. "That's the only
thing about the place that McKenzie insisted on. I remember that Veronica said they were as dated as the dodo. . . .
I've made some coffee."

Nick followed into the kitchen where the dishes in the
sink were a reminder that the maids had left in a hurry. They reminded him, too, of dinner on a tray and he
looked for a tray and saw it off in a corner. He wondered

if Abbey had noticed it. He wondered if that frightened girl was still hiding in her upstairs room.

He said casually, sipping his hot coffee, "I suppose no one has come in?"

"No. King doesn't know where Jenny—"

"It was in the paper," said Nick. He told Abbey what he had done and the doctor nodded. "Yes, she ought to be here."

"How's King?"

"He's shut himself up. I'll take him some coffee. You let the police in."

They were not long in getting there. There was Lieutenant Wayland, big and affable, looking about curiously, and Nolan, a sandy-haired, stubborn-jawed little sergeant, and the medical chap, Petorsky, with his black bag, and Lewis, the fingerprint man. Abbey came down and gave them his account and they went upstairs, single file, looking very solemn and self-conscious and hush-hush. Nick heard King greeting them, his voice controlled and quiet.

Nick began restively walking up and down the hall, his lean shoulders hunched, his hands deep in his pockets. Upstairs he could hear heavy steps and the opening and shutting of doors. Suddenly he heard the front door open and a girl's voice saying breathlessly, "It can't be anything! It's just some upset—" and there was a rustling of silk and he turned to see a girl in a short wrap and ankle-length skirts come hurrying along the hall, a young man behind her.

It was Jennifer Mitchell, all right. A younger Veronica, younger and slighter and even more fair—a girl done in pastels, Nick thought, stepping out in front of her. But there was nothing wishy-washy about her. She had a very spirited-looking face. Her voice had said, "It can't be anything!" but her face was worried.

Nick said, "Miss Mitchell—"

She gave him a quick look. "You're a doctor?" She had Veronica's sudden, abrupt way of speech.

"No, I came with the doctor. I'm Nicholas Parr—"

"He's here, then? Dr. Abbey?"

She started past him, up the stairs, but Nick made a rush and caught her arm. "Wait a moment. I'll get him down here."

She tried to shake off his hand, her blue eyes blazing at him. "Let go of me!" she said in an edged voice. "I live here."

"Please! A moment!" He couldn't, he thought, he couldn't have her go rushing, unprepared, into whatever was going on upstairs. "Let me get Abbey."

She stared at him, panic beginning in her eyes. He bolted up the stairs, and after a moment, he heard her coming behind him. He called "Abbey!" loudly, and Abbey came out in time to meet her at the top of the stairs. She must know then, Nick thought. He didn't look at her as he went down.

Jennifer's young man was standing in the hall, staring up after her. He was gripping the ends of a white scarf that dangled out from his open topcoat. He was older, Nick saw now, than he had thought at first; he wasn't the college boy he'd expected Jennifer to be out with—he looked in the middle or late thirties.

"How is she? What's the matter?" he shot at Nicholas.

Nick walked into the nearest room, the library with the coffee cups sitting about, and the young man came after him.

Nick said, "She's dead. Her sister's dead."

He opened a silver box and took out a cigarette, then turned. The other man was staring at him. Blankly. Disbelievingly. "What nonsense!" he said in a flat, hard voice. "She was all right at cocktails."

He had very light gray eyes in a brown face and he had a white scar on one cheek. Suddenly the scar twitched. "Say that again," he said slowly.

Nick said it again. It was his bad luck, he thought, to have to tell everyone he met that Veronica King was dead. He said, "It was very sudden. She was taken ill after dinner. She was dead when King got back with the doctor."

He had never seen anything hit a man as that hit this man. His face changed fast. His mouth sagged and then it tightened and he swallowed hard and those light eyes of his seemed on fire with a sort of horror and fury. Nick looked away quickly, wondering what the devil this fellow was to Veronica King.

The young man walked across the room, picked up a book and put it carefully on top of another book. He said, his back to Nick, "What did she die of?"

Nick didn't want to talk about it. "I don't know. She was taken ill after dinner."

The young man made no comment He marched over toward the fireplace, opened a door in the paneling, took out a bottle and a glass, and poured himself a stiff drink. He put the things back and turned about. "Who are you?"

Nick gave his name and told him how he happened to be in the house. The young man said mechanically, "My name's Burton. Tod Burton."

There were Burtons out on Old Kent Road, so to keep things going Nick asked if he were one of them.

"No. Never heard of them. Never been here before. I met her—met them—in Florida, so I stopped over. Staying at the Country Club. They got me a card."

Nick had a feeling that he was making an immense effort to pull himself together. He had an air of utter shock. Nick's mind came up with the thought, "I wonder if it was his child?" because minds can think of anything.

King might have been suspicious, have talked of a divorce, and Veronica might have rushed to change her will because of that.

But no, there was the time factor. The Kings had gone south only a little over two months ago.

Tod Burton turned and got out the bottle again and this time he remembered Nicholas was there and offered him a shot and Nick took it. It was superlative Scotch. Burton tossed down half of his, then said, his voice very detached, "Everyone else all right?"

"As right as can be," said Nick drily.

"That's fine." His tone held mordant mockery. "Fine to have everything else all right. . . . Tell Jennifer it will all be the same a thousand years from now."

He walked out.

Nick looked after him thoughtfully. Florida. He'd met the Kings in Florida, he'd said. Jennifer Mitchell hadn't been in Florida, she'd been at college. He hadn't come here to see Jennifer Mitchell. Beauing Jennifer about was camouflage.

Florida. How long had the Kings been south? A couple of months, something like that. Had it been evident, then, that the Kings were to have an heir? How much in love can a man be with a woman who was having another man's child? That wouldn't be his dish, he thought; but Tod Burton seemed a remarkably uninhibited type.

Larrabee had said that Veronica was tremendously in love with King, but that could be all over. Or it could be that Burton meant no more to her than someone to go places with, to play off against a husband that other women found too charming.

He fitted alternate pieces together, getting first one picture, then another, of the Kings' love life, then he said, "To hell with conjecture!" What did it matter whether she had loved Burton or not? She had been in pain and sniffed chloroform. . . .

"The lieutenant wants to see you. Just for the record."

Petorsky was in the doorway, looking about the room. He stared up admiringly at the canvas of the girl in blue. "That's a pretty picture of the young lady now."

"It's Mrs. King. Done a few years ago, I imagine."

"I thought it was the other. My wife's very fond of painting," said Petorsky, eyeing the portrait. "She wants me to take it up. In a small way like. She thinks everyone ought to have a hobby. Something out of his way of life, you know."

"It's an idea."

"Beautiful house. I see all kinds," he said in a satisfied voice. Then, with a confidential drop in tone, as Nick strode by him, "You'd be surprised at the houses that things happen in." At the head of the stairs he led the way to a door. "They're in here."

The room, from its impersonality, was a guest room. Wayland's big figure was crowding the springs of a soft, rose-beige chair, the others grouped about him. Nick's glance caught the gravity of Abbey's round face, the set immobility of King's, but his eyes were all for Jennifer Mitchell, sitting on the edge of her chair, her bare shoulders incongruously gay above her dancing dress, her bright hair falling forward as she leaned toward the policeman. Her profile was tense and hostile, her voice hotly indignant.

She was saying, "Don't you dare suggest that! My sister never committed suicide—never!"

Nolan was flushed but dogged. "I'm only saying it is one of the possibilities—"

"It is *not* a possibility!"

"Possibilities we must consider." There was a Scotch-Irish burr in Nolan's voice and a Scotch-Irish stubbornness.

The girl said angrily, "You're only trying to make a sensation for the papers. My sister did a foolish thing, a tragically foolish thing, and she died of it, but she never intended to die. She had everything to live for. Everything!"

"I'm only asking if she was depressed at all. Worrying about anything."

"Worrying?" It seemed to Nick that she tried to give the word back scornfully but that something made her hesitate. For the fraction of a second her eyes slid toward her brother-in-law, then came quickly back to the policeman. She said flatly, "She had nothing to worry about."

Nick thought, *She's lying.* There had been fright in her face.

"I think that's pretty evident, Nolan," said Wayland easily. "And this family's been through quite an ordeal. . . . Oh, Mr. Parr!" He turned to him, welcomingly. He wasn't, Nick thought, buying any of Nolan's suspicions. "We'll take your report now."

Nicholas gave it briefly. At the end Wayland asked, "You a friend of the family?"

"I've met Mr. King a few times. I've only seen Mrs. King once."

"When was that?"

"This week. Wednesday. She was in the office on a matter of business."

He didn't miss King's quick look toward him, as quickly averted. So King had not known she had been in. She had said she didn't want him to know. *Although it might save my life.*

Damn it, it didn't make sense. King was too decent. You couldn't make yourself believe, not all at once, that this shocked, stunned-looking young man had been holding chloroform against his wife's face. . . .

"Would you say she was in good spirits?" Nolan shot in.

In good spirits? That bitter voice. *I don't want him to have a cent.* Nick said slowly, "I'd say she was in very vigorous spirits. Alert. Decisive. That was my impression."

Plenty of time later to throw King to the dogs. This needed thinking about.

"There seems no question but what this was an accident, a very tragic accident, as Miss Mitchell puts it," said Wayland, "and there's no occasion to prolong the ordeal. I feel there's no need to examine Mrs. King's private possessions. This isn't a case of any suicide note."

He hoisted his big body out of the soft chair and said, "We won't trouble you any more tonight, Mr. King," and King said, in a controlled voice, "I appreciate your courtesy, Lieutenant." He shepherded them to the hall like a host again in charge of his own house.

But the authority was short-lived. A police ambulance summoned by the radio on Wayland's car had arrived for Veronica's body. King, startled and frankly angered, opposed the removal. Nick heard his sharp protests and Wayland's placating "Routine, Mr. King. We transfer to the mortician—" and he moved away, uncomfortably, out of earshot.

He had expected to drive Abbey back, but Abbey climbed into the ambulance. At that moment a press car came in, spilling out a reporter and a photographer who shot hurriedly at the stretcher being lifted into the ambulance, and the maids, two pretty Irish girls, arrived and began to cry hysterically on the fringes of the group.

Nick drove off before he could be questioned by the press. He was halfway home before he remembered about the girl upstairs. Had she come down while he was away or was she still up there, sitting nervously in her room, her dark eyes on the door, waiting to be discovered?

He felt profoundly curious about that girl.

Chapter Three

The Sunday headlines screamed, *Tragic Death of Young Socialite. Died of Self-Given Chloroform.* The picture of the stretcher was entitled *Leaving Home for the Last Time.* There was a picture of Veronica as a bride when she married King and a picture of her as a bride when she married McKenzie and a piece about the parties she had given and the charming hostess she had been, both as Mrs. McKenzie and Mrs. King.

The details had been gleaned from the police. His name was there but there was no mention of Nina Barrett. Veronica King, said the papers, had been alone in the house. So Nina Barrett had walked herself out of the house. A fool stunt, he thought angrily. If she was found out—

He called up Abbey, but Mrs. Siddons said the doctor was already out. "And not in until after three," she said, disapprovingly. Nick wondered at that.

His phone rang and Sally Waters, the red-headed girl who had written the piece about Veronica as a hostess, said joyfully, "Oh, Nick, I want to see you but *fast!* I want all the juicy details."

"You're loathsome, sweetheart," he said and hung up. He didn't answer the phone again. It rang incessantly. He had the house to himself, because his parents were away,

41

and for a time he prowled it restively, then telephoned
Larrabee.

"I've been trying to get you," said Larrabee. "Can you
come directly to the office?"

The Sunday elevator man looked at him interestedly.
"Terrible thing, wasn't it, Mr. Parr?"

"Terrible."

"I've seen her many a time. Used to run an elevator in
one of old Mac's buildings and she'd come to the office
there. I've seen her many a time."

Nick thought savagely, You won't see her again. He was
angry because he was in a very bad spot, two bad spots,
and he didn't know what to do about either of them.

Larrabee listened gravely to his account. He said that
he had not met Burton and he did not seem to take seriously Nick's conviction that he was in love with Veronica.
"Oh, it's possible," he admitted. "Veronica liked admiration. She—" He broke off. "But scarcely possible she
was—involved."

"Why not? She might have fallen for him. And King
suspected and threatened divorce—or worse. So she hurried to change her will. Hang it all," Nick said worriedly,
"I've got to testify at that inquest tomorrow. What do I
say?"

"Answer what is asked. That's all you have to do."

"Keep my mouth shut about the new will?"

"They'll learn about it in due time."

"And about what Veronica said? She certainly sounded
as if she believed King was going to kill her."

"She didn't believe it. She was being dramatic. . . . I've
had women in this office accuse their husbands of every
crime in the calendar, then break down and admit it was
all false. . . . My guess is that King had grown tired of her
highhandedness and was letting her know it. It would be

a shocking thing to create a *false* suspicion of King." He shot out suddenly, "And you *do* believe it false, don't you?"

"You've got me there," said Nick, uncomfortably. "Either I believe it false or I believe that King chloroformed her before he came for Abbey and that's a hard one to believe."

"You saw him when he found her. Didn't his shock seem real?"

"Yes, it did. He acted as if— Oh, hell, how do I know how a man would act?"

"It's a serious responsibility."

"Don't I know it?"

"In your place I should do nothing—definite—until you talk with Jennifer. She will know what has been going on. She was devoted to her sister."

"She at the house now?"

"Yes, her aunt's staying with her. I telephoned but she doesn't want to see anyone now. Time enough, after the inquest. An inquest isn't final, you know."

No, an inquest wasn't final. King's involvement could come later, if he *was* involved. . . .

Then Nick tossed out, "What about his secretary?"

"What about her?"

"I understand she's a spectacular girl."

"Oh, Miss Barrett," said Larrabee easily. "She's worked for him since he came here, about six years ago. I remember there was some comment at first, because she'd worked for him in the East—King was in the New York branch of the company before he became president and moved here to the main office—but that talk soon died out. She's an efficient girl and King likes efficiency. He never saw her outside the office."

"You mean they were never seen."

"People are always seen."

Nick let it go. He said nothing about the fact that
Nina Barrett had been at the house while Veronica King
was dying. If he was going to protect King's reputation, he
thought grimly, he'd protect the girl's, too. But he resolved
to have it out with Nina Barrett. Not today, for there was
no Nina Barrett in the phone book, but tomorrow.

Next morning, he marched into the office of King's company, where the hush-hush excitement was perceptible,
and was directed to a door marked President. As he opened
the door, he saw that it led into a small outer office, across
which, through another open door, he could see the larger
office beyond. Nina Barrett was there at a filing cabinet.

She looked up quickly, her hands motionless. Her eyes
were even bigger and darker than he remembered and they
fixed on him with wary intentness.

"Good morning." He closed the door behind him.
"What happened to our beautiful agreement?"

"What agreement?" She made her voice light.

"I was to keep still about you and you were to come
down and explain yourself."

She shut the drawer of the cabinet. In the same light
voice she said, "That was your agreement. I didn't promise
anything."

"Oh, come," he said brusquely, "don't try weasel words.
You know I thought it was a deal."

She gave up lightness. She said, her voice low but
charged with feeling, "Why should I have to come down?
What good would it have done?"

"To keep the record straight. To save explanations."

"This way saved explanations."

"Look, I don't blame you for wanting out. Newspapers
and all that. But it's bound to come out."

"You haven't said anything?" she asked quickly.

"Not I. I thought we had an agreement."

"Then it's all right!" She looked so relieved that she was actually radiant. "Everything's all right," she insisted. "I telephoned Mr. King yesterday and said I was sorry I wasn't there, that I'd left right after dinner, and he'd forgotten I was to stay. So it's all right."

"And the maids?"

"They don't know when I left."

"Suppose you have to testify? On oath?"

"Why should I have to testify? Mr. King will have told them I left early and they'll believe it."

Nick thought, *Women*. Larrabee said he'd never believe a woman witness on a stack of Bibles. Women had their own laws, their own ideas of justice.

He said ironically, "Simple as that, eh? Do you mind telling me how you got home?"

She looked at him hesitantly. "You took me."

"What?"

"I was in the back of your car. I ran down the back stairs and got into your car. I lay on the floor and put my coat over me."

He stared. He thought of her huddled on the floor of his car under her coat—fantastic. He shook his head. "Crazy! When did you get out? When I opened the garage?"

"No." Instantly she looked as if she wished she had said yes. She murmured, "When you got out to telephone. At the Lelands'."

"You were in the car the *first* time I went out? You must have cut down those back stairs fast."

She was silent.

"You meant to do that when you left me. You certainly moved fast to get down to my car before I did."

"All right—what if I did?" she flared. "I *had* to get away!"

"But how did you get home from the Lelands'?"

"I asked a couple of guests to take me into the city. They thought I was someone from the house, some secretary or something, helping with the dinner."

She had probably told them so, he thought. He asked, "Didn't they get a good look at you? Wouldn't they know you again?"

"No. I had a scarf over my head and I sat in back. They were having a scrap over a canasta game." At his continued scrutiny she repeated nervously, "I *had* to get away."

His look grew more intent. He said bluntly, "Can you give me one good reason why you had to bolt out of the house like that? Didn't you think how it would look to the police?"

"The police?" The very word seemed to terrify her. Then she stiffened and said in a defiant voice, "Yes, I can give you one good reason. That's it. The police. They'd give things out. And if it got in the papers—"

"That isn't a good reason."

"You don't understand. I happen to be engaged," she said, very coldly and distantly. "My fiancé is a sick man. At Saranac. When you're sick you get—peculiar. He imagines things. Once a paper spoke of me as 'Mr. King's beautiful secretary'—that was when we were at a convention— and he was very upset. I don't want that to happen again. Now do you see?"

It went so palpably against the grain for her to tell him this that Nick's anger ebbed. "That's tough luck," he told her. His curiosity made him add, "You been engaged long?"

"Oh, years and years." She sounded bitter.

He tried to lighten it. "You must have started early."

"Schoolmates," she said briefly.

He wondered if she was tired of it, holding on through loyalty. She had an unhappy air. He wondered what sort of fellow would hang onto a girl through all these years, getting "upset" at any talk about her beauty. He asked, "What's his name?"

"His name? Does it matter?"

"Not if it's any secret."

"Of course not. . . . Jerome Onslow," she said hastily.

"I was just trying to make it seem real," said Nick. "That you were an engaged gal and all that. You're a New Yorker, aren't you?"

"Not New York City. I came from upstate. A little place called Sharon." Her eyes were anxiously intent on him. "You see what I mean, don't you? Why I had to get away?"

"Yes, I see. Why you thought you had to," he said lightly. "Now we'll forget about your being there. Right?"

For a moment more her eyes kept their searching look, then the mistrust went out of them and she smiled radiantly. Nick said impulsively, "How's for having dinner sometime? Talking about something else, of course."

If he'd been blackmailing her she couldn't have looked more terrified. The radiance dropped from her like a toy from frightened fingers. She said, in a constrained way, "That would be very nice."

"Think nothing of it," he said hastily. "Merely one of my less well-considered suggestions."

Now she looked embarrassed. She apologized, "It's just that I don't go out much." Then, with placating eagerness, "But I'd love to go with you."

"Fine. I'll give you a ring."

The girl was a weathercock. And dinner had been a poor idea. Cheering a sick man's sweetheart. That showed what dark eyes could do to you.

As he left, she hurried after him. "Mr. Parr," she said, in a soft conspirator's voice, "if Mr. King asks why you came, what shall I say?"

Nick grinned. "Tell him I came for a date with you."

"No, but really?"

"Oh, say I wanted to see him."

King wouldn't be wondering why he had come. King had the inquest to worry about and after that the will. Once the will had been read King wouldn't be wondering about anything else.

Chapter Four

"Certainly I am going, ducky," said Hazel Taggart. "And so are you. You were one of Veronica's closest friends, weren't you? I mean, we were. And if we could go and drink her cocktails we can certainly go to her inquest, and find out if she died of the baby or killed herself for love of that young man you were so jealous of."

"I never cared a damn—"

"Of course not, sweetie. And you never cared when she married handsome Roger King. You thought it was lovely she was so happy. You only went on a three-day drunk because I had the dining room done over in chartreuse."

Taggart said thickly, "Sometimes I wonder—"

"Why you ever married me? Of course you do, a lusty lad like you and me an aging crone." The woman, ten years older than Chet, laughed cynically. "But on the first of the month you don't wonder. All those beautiful checks going out to pay the bills."

He was silent. He was a big, dark man in his early forties, with a square, dogged face. His eyes were deep-set, his forehead bulging, and there was a curious horizontal line about it, especially when he frowned, as if a cord had been tied about it and left its mark.

"We are going," said his wife, "because we were Veronica's friends and Roger and Jennifer will appreciate our

interest. And you are not going to drink another whisky
before we go."

"You'd better stay sober, too."

"I am exceedingly sober. I wouldn't miss a minute of
it." She laughed edgily. "After what you two have put me
through, you with your slavish adoration all these years,
I'm on the crest today."

Taggart turned to her. "Call it quits. Divorce me."

The woman faced him; her haggard face, heavily made
up, in which the ghost of a former girlishness haunted the
outlines, was full of mocking determination. "Divorce?
Why should I divorce you? Veronica never let you do more
than hold her hand, did she? Or help her on her horse.
And you can't divorce me. . . . And you'd better not try it,"
she said, slowly spacing the words.

Then she added, light and artificial again, "Poor old
Chet! Growling like a police dog. You wouldn't hurt a fly,
really. You never lifted a finger, did you, to pay her back for
brushing you off? Just sat there glooming, looking on . . .
Come along now. The inquest is at one-thirty."

"I'm not going."

"Oh, yes, you are. We were there at cocktails the day
she died and we owe it to the family to be there today.
Old family friends. Remember? First Mac and then Roge.
Come along now. The show's got to go on."

Heavily he got up. His baited eyes turned slowly about
the room, a room so richly English that it looked, as it
had been, lifted bodily from an old manor, then he moved
toward the hall. As he brushed past his wife, she suddenly
caught up his hand and brought it to her lips in a gesture of wild and despairing passion. "Oh, damn you, Chet,
damn you!" she said desperately. "Why do I love you so?"

The inquest was at the funeral home where Veronica
King's body was lying. When she saw the crowd and the
reporters and the cameras, Mrs. Taggart pressed closer to

her husband. "People are such ghouls, Chet. . . . Look, there's Roger."

Roger King was walking through the crowd, his head erect, with Jennifer Mitchell clinging to his arm. Her aunt, black-veiled, was on Jennifer's other side. Hazel Taggart murmured, "I wonder why Jenny isn't in black. I suppose it's the younger generation. That blue-gray suit—I remember when Veronica had a suit like that. When we first met her. Remember?"

"Will you shut up?" said her husband under his breath.

The witnesses were parked in a small side room. The Taggarts sat down by the door. "Look at those pictures—so funereal," Mrs. Taggart whispered. "But of course, it's a funeral home. There's Mr. Larrabee. Who's that with him, that young man? I've seen him—"

Her husband stared stonily ahead. In a moment more she whispered, "What's that walking about? In the other room? Oh, I know," she said brightly, "I've read about it. They have to view the deceased."

Taggart said, in a hard monotone, "If you want me to see this thing through—"

"But you'd look *too* conspicuous, bolting out! Overcome by emotion. If Roger can take it, surely you can. He looks as if he were carved out of wood. The very best wood, of course. But he's so damned correct—I'll bet that's what bored Veronica." She stopped her whispering a moment, then said, "Come on, they're going in. Can all those reporters go, too?"

"An inquest is open to the public."

Inside she took quick possession of two chairs. "Sit here. Where we can see. Is that the coroner?"

"Yes, Hatcher."

Hatcher was a big, bald man with a serious, exact manner. There were three women on the jury and Mrs. Taggart nudged her husband. "That's Miss Chalmers. We were in

the same Sunday School class." Catching Miss Chalmers'
attention, she smiled and got back a prim little smile in
return as if Miss Chalmers was not sure whether her duties
permitted her to recognize anyone or not. The coroner began the proceedings. Roger King was called and sworn in.

King gave his testimony in a low, steady voice. At the
end he said, very carefully, that his wife had used chloroform before to dull a toothache. He said, "I can only believe that she was in such pain that she did not realize the
danger."

"You have no reason to believe—" Hatcher hesitated,
then said firmly, "that she did it with premeditation?"

"No reason at all."

Hazel Taggart murmured, "Any fool knows that Veronica would never—"

Her murmur died away. Hatcher was taking up the
matter of the telephone. It appeared that the telephone in
the library was a plug-in phone and that the wire had been
pulled out. It could have been done that morning, King
said, when the room was being cleaned. That was the only
phone he had tried. It had never occurred to him that it
was unplugged—such a thing had never happened before.

"They do it with the vacuum cleaner," Hazel Taggart
said under her breath. "Who's that talking now?"

"Petorsky. A doctor."

"But where's Dr. Abbey? I thought he—"

Taggart's look warned her to silence. Petorsky gave a
short report Wayland testified briefly, then Lewis. The
prints on the chloroform bottle were those of Mr. King
who had stated he had picked it up and handled it. Any
other prints that might have been there were obscured.
Hazel Taggart breathed, "What good would Veronica's
prints do? They wouldn't prove whether she—"

Nicholas Parr was next. His statements were short and
concise. He had smelled the chloroform, he had opened

the window, he had seen the cotton when Dr. Abbey held it out.

Hatcher was looking at a paper before him. "Will you tell the jury when you last saw the deceased?"

"On last Wednesday."

"She was consulting you on a business matter?"

"That's right."

"You said—" Hatcher consulted the paper again—"you said that she was vigorous in spirit, alert and decided. That was your impression?"

"It was."

"Nothing to suggest that she—ah—contemplated making an end to herself?"

The young man was silent a moment as if searching his mind. "Nothing to suggest that," he said.

"That's all. Thank you, Mr. Parr."

A small, smartly dressed woman was next. Hazel Taggart breathed, "That's Fran! I didn't see her before." She leaned forward attentively while the young woman told, with studied quiet, that she had called for Mrs. King that Saturday, driven her to a luncheon, then a matinee, and driven her home. "I live just beyond her," she explained.

"Will you tell the jury, Mrs. Gaynor, your impression of her—of her mood?"

"Quite as usual. We had a luncheon date for next week."

The two Irish maids were sworn in together. Delia Walsh was the cook, Annie Kelly the second maid. There was another maid, they said, Agnes Clancy, who came by the day but not on Saturdays. Annie Kelly did most of the talking.

Indeed, she said, Mrs. King had seemed in very good spirits during cocktails and dinner. If she hadn't, neither she nor Delia would have dreamed of going out and leaving her, in her condition, that they wouldn't, dance or no dance.

"Mr. Coroner, may I ask a question?" Nolan had come forward and at Hatcher's nod he turned to the two girls. "Have you noticed any signs of depression in Mrs. King recently?"

"Depression?" said Annie uncertainly. "Why, she was always talking about another of those coming—"

"Not that kind," said Nolan, unsmiling. "I mean was she depressed in her manner?"

"Indeed, she was laughing hard, the way Mr. Burton was acting up as butler, pretending like—"

"Mr. Burton?"

"The young gentleman having cocktails with them. The one going out with Miss Jenny."

"Oh. But I didn't mean just that evening. Had she been at all—sad-acting—before that?"

The girls consulted each other with their eyes. Delia Walsh took over. "She was sort of up and down," she said, "but that was only natural. No, you could never call her sad-acting. If things didn't go to suit her, she let you know soon enough. Not but that she was a lovely young lady to work for," she said quickly, "and the mister, too," she threw in, with a warm look toward King.

Jennifer Mitchell was next. She was very pale, her face tautly composed, and she spoke quietly in a low but clear voice. Her sister was very happy, she said. She was expecting a baby. She had everything to live for.

"'Everything' is right," breathed Hazel Taggart "Husband, baby, sweetie—"

Taggart's hand gripped her arm. She went on swiftly, "There's that sweetie, Dr. Abbey. I do like him even if he said I'd be a dipso if I didn't swear off. . . . You're hurting me."

"Keep quiet."

Taggart took his hand away and cupped his chin in it, leaning forward as the doctor gave his evidence. Hazel

Taggart fidgeted, twisting her pearls in her fingers. The evidence was very factual, very detached-sounding. The position of the body. The chloroform. The time of death. As to that, Abbey said, he could not be exact, but death had occurred between one and two hours before he had examined the body. That had been at ten-fifteen.

"Ten-fifteen," breathed Hazel Taggart to her husband's ear. "We were just going to bed. Remember? We went early."

Taggart showed no sign of having heard her. The coroner was saying, "Now as to the cause of death. Would you say the amount of chloroform inhaled was sufficient to cause that?"

Abbey said slowly, "It could have caused death." Even more slowly he added, "But an examination of the organs—"

Sharply, angrily, Roger King broke in. "You mean—you subjected my wife—my wife's body—to an examination?"

Abbey looked about at him. "I did."

"But you had no right—no permission. I understood she was going to the undertakers—"

"It was necessary to discover the cause of death."

"You knew the cause."

"No," said Abbey in his mild, unshaken way. "I was in the dark. There was no reason, as far as I could determine, for the pain she had experienced. Labor had not commenced."

King leaned back abruptly. His handsome face had a sickened look. Abbey went on speaking. He had, he said, sought an explanation by looking for disturbances in the digestive tract. Then he said, "I have, only a few minutes ago, completed the examination. A toxicological examination has revealed in the body the presence of arsenic."

He said it so quietly that at first the word was like any other word. He waited, like a teacher waiting for a class to catch up with his meaning. Chairs creaked as bodies leaned forward. Hazel Taggart shot a quick, queer look at her husband. He had not moved. His eyes were on the stocky little man in blue serge.

"A large amount of arsenic," said Abbey. "Exceeding a lethal dose."

No one spoke. No one moved. Not for a long moment. Then a light bulb flashed as a cameraman got a picture. King's face, taut and rigid; Jennifer Mitchell, blankly staring.

Abbey was speaking again, with careful detail. He explained to the jury how the arsenic was known and how they could know it was not taken in solid form, as Paris green or white arsenic, but in the form of a liquid or solution. He said there was practically only one solution of liquid form in use in the United States and that was known as Fowler's Solution. A diluted potassium arsenite slightly flavored with tincture of cinnamon and oil of lavender.

He said, "There is no suspicious taste to it."

The jurors exchanged covert glances. One sharp-nosed young man, his voice charged with mounting excitement, asked, "You say, doctor, there's more than a lethal amount of arsenic in the stomach?"

"What was in the stomach is of no significance. I mean, calculations must be based on the weight of arsenic absorbed by the internal organs. In this case a quantitative examination showed that considerably more than a lethal amount had been absorbed."

"Then it was arsenic that killed her?"

"I cannot say with certainty. The arsenic would have caused death ultimately, but in her distress Mrs. King had inhaled chloroform. She took in an amount that was sufficient to cause death. The condition of the lungs—"

Jennifer Mitchell gasped and buried her face in her hands. King put his hand upon her arm and in a moment she straightened, staring out fixedly. The aunt had a hand-kerchief before her mouth as if to hide its trembling. Over it, her eyes, horrified and accusing, stared at Dr. Abbey as at a snake.

Then King spoke out, his voice strained. "Dr. Abbey, is it not true that each of us, in his body, has some trace of arsenic? I seem to have read—"

"Oh, yes," said Abbey. "Especially after eating lobster."

Someone tittered. Hatcher frowned a warning. Abbey said gravely, "That is a scientific fact. Arsenic is also found in the hair in amounts that increase with age. But not in lethal quantities. What was in Mrs. King was in excess of the lethal quantity."

Then he asked King, as matter of fact as if this were any sickroom consultation, "Did she complain of burning at the stomach?"

"Yes. Yes, she did."

"And was she weak?"

"Yes. I thought it was the pain—"

"Did she complain of thirst?"

King was silent, as if thinking back. "Yes, she asked for water. When we were having coffee. I got her a glass—the maids had left the kitchen. And I left water by her with the aspirin." Then he said, his voice stiffly defensive, "I did not realize there was anything significant—"

Wayland was bending over Hatcher, whispering. Hatcher asked, "Was there any Fowler's Solution in your house, Mr. King?"

"Not to my knowledge. My wife never permitted arsenic to be used. Not even for rats in the stable. She thought it cruel."

Hatcher turned to the doctor. "How long, doctor, would it take for arsenic to act? I mean, for the pain to be felt?"

"Depends on the amount. In this case about an hour. A little more, a little less."

"What time did you have dinner, Mr. King?"

"About six-thirty."

"And what did you have?"

"Last Saturday?" King looked helplessly toward the maids. "You'd better ask the cook."

Delia Walsh said indignantly, "Indeed there was nothing but the best used in my kitchen! If poor Mrs. King came to harm from anything she ate it wasn't from my kitchen!"

"Now, now, just tell us what you had," Wayland soothed, and, item by item, he extracted the menu: lamb roast, green peas, mashed potatoes, a tossed salad, a soufflé. Everything passed. He asked, "No soup?"

"No soup at all."

There was an uncertain pause, then Hatcher said, "The cocktails, then. What kind were they?"

King seemed to be thinking back. "Martinis."

"Now who mixed them?"

"I did."

"Did you both have the same kind?"

"Our guests took Martinis. So did I. Mrs. King had a Bourbon and water."

"A Bourbon and water." Hatcher's mouth seemed to clamp over this, his eyes had a now-we're-getting-somewhere expression. "Who prepared that?"

"I must have. . . . Yes, I remember pouring it out before I started on the Martinis."

"Where were you doing all this? Do you have a bar?"

"No bar. I was in the butler's pantry."

"All by yourself?"

"By myself? Why—most of the time. Annie brought in ice and things. I left the tray for her to bring in."

Annie spoke up quickly. "It was Mr. Burton carried it in, Mr. King. I never touched that tray. He got to it before I did. I was zipping up Miss Jenny in the kitchen. Don't you remember he was taking off an English butler making us laugh ever so?"

"Yes. Yes, Burton went after it."

"And before that Mr. Taggart came into the pantry—to say that his wife had dropped in and you'd better make one more. Delia had let her in while I was busy."

"And I was in the pantry, Mr. Hatcher." That was Jennifer Mitchell, her voice cold and steady. "I came down the back way to the kitchen to get Annie to help me with a fastening and she was in the pantry and I went in after her. I stayed quite a few minutes talking to my brother-in-law."

Hatcher gave her an embarrassed look. Wayland whispered to him again and he said, relief in his voice, "Mrs. King was out that afternoon. Mrs. Gaynor, perhaps you can tell us if you stopped anywhere, after the matinee, for something to drink?"

Mrs. Gaynor said precisely, "No, we drove directly back."

"After she was in the house then? Could she have had something before the cocktails?"

"I drove in just after she did," said Jennifer. She spoke slowly and consideringly. "We went upstairs together and I went into her room and we talked while she changed. Then Mr. Burton came, early—no, I was late. My sister went down to talk to him while I dressed."

"Could she have taken anything with him before you got down?"

Jennifer looked toward the maids. Annie Kelly spoke up. "There was nothing brought her. There's Scotch in the library but she never touched Scotch. Never. And there was no glasses used then. We picked up the room during dinner."

"I—see," said Hatcher, looking solemn and baffled. He asked, "When did you get home, Mr. King?"

"I? I wasn't out. It was Saturday. I had some work to do at home." King broke off, abruptly. Then he said, "I was in my study. Later I went to our room. My wife was then downstairs. I went down. Mr. Burton was there and Taggart. I think Taggart had just come."

"That was about six when you went down?"

"About six. Oh, a little before. Just in time to mix the cocktails."

Hatcher looked about the jury. No one spoke. He said slowly, "Well, I guess that's all that can be ascertained."

Carefully he instructed the jury. Slowly, self-consciously, they filed out. Chairs scraped back as reporters got up and made their way to the door, ready to rush to the nearest telephones. Undertones rose in louder and louder murmuring, then hushed, as slowly and self-consciously the jury filed back. A reporter, eyes on his wrist watch, jotted down the time out. The foreman read the verdict. Veronica King had died from arsenic poisoning or chloroform inhalation or a combination of arsenic poisoning and chloroform inhalation at the hands of person or persons unknown.

"How too, too bright of them!" That low-voiced mockery was the first sound to come from Hazel Taggart since the doctor had testified. Then, even lower-voiced, the mock flippancy edged with significance, she murmured, "But we don't want them to get any brighter, do we, Chet?"

Her husband looked about at her, at first blankly, like an awakened sleepwalker, then with smoldering animosity. He said harshly, "I don't know what you mean."

"Don't you? Don't you ever think of others? Of your good friend Roger?"

His hand on her arm urged her forward. He said thickly, "Come on. Get out of here."

Chapter Five

A tray of cocktail glasses, a shaker of Martinis, and a glass of Bourbon and water. Five people, Nicholas Parr estimated, had access to that highball in the pantry. The husband. The sister. The maid. Tod Burton. Chet Taggart.

Chet Taggart was X. Nick had seen him about; all he knew of him was that he was a member of the horsey set and was reported to have married for money. His wife was much older, played bridge incessantly at the club, and appeared to drink a lot. She had a loud laugh and incredibly bright hair. Larrabee said they lived across from the Kings so that was the house to which he had first driven, Saturday night, the house that had been dark.

One of the five, no four—rule out the maid—had put arsenic in the Bourbon. The husband had every chance. Any of the others would have had to dash into the pantry prepared with the stuff in a small bottle. Fantastic but not impossible.

His mind sorted this out as he sat in the small circle Wayland had drawn about himself in the rear of the emptied room. Wayland had shepherded King and Jennifer Mitchell to that corner and Larrabee, with Nick, had quickly moved in with a suave, "As counsel for the family—?"

Wayland's smile had been forced but he was keeping it smooth and friendly. He said, "This may be a matter for Hendrickson"—Hendrickson was prosecuting attorney—"but we don't want to lose any time, and I'd like the family to help us with the matter of motive." Wayland knew the value of immediacy, of taking advantage of the first confusion.

"Nonsense to talk of motive," said Larrabee, easily. "To my mind, this tragedy has all the aspects of accident."

They looked at him with various expressions. The most obvious, Nick thought, was Jennifer's. Her quick glance held a startled hope.

"Aspects of accident," repeated Larrabee. "That Fowler's Solution, Mr. King, could have been in your house without your knowing it. I expect the household did not share your wife's tender feeling toward rodents. It is quite likely they used the stuff and kept it, for disguise, in an old Bourbon bottle. And in some way that we may never know that bottle found its way into the butler's pantry."

He waited to let that thought take hold. Then he said, "One of the maids might have come on it and thought the chauffeur was appropriating your whisky. So she put it where she thought it belonged."

He looked as satisfied as if he had settled the matter. He knew better, the old fox, Nick surmised, but he was giving the police something to think about. Wayland was cautious on thin ice.

Wayland said thoughtfully, "It wouldn't taste like whisky."

"No, but King might have poured whisky already into the glass and needed a little more. Taken another bottle. Most natural thing in the world."

"Was it like that, Mr. King?"

"I couldn't say," said King slowly. "I don't remember."

"But you remember pouring out the Bourbon before you mixed the Martinis?"

"Yes, I remember that."

Nolan, his notebook open, said skeptically, "That's pretty far-fetched, Mr. Larrabee."

"Not at all. Things like that happen every day. Few employees would sympathize with a prejudice against rat poison. You, yourself, would use arsenic on rats, I think, Sergeant."

Nolan reddened. "What I do to rats isn't any part of this."

"Ah, but I think it is. The feeling toward them. The lack of scruple toward their pangs. I think my theory is the only possible one. But the careless girl who put it there will never own up. That is why I said, 'In some way that we may never know.'"

"We'll know, all right," said Wayland. "I'll be talking to them. And Gleason's out there right now and his men are going through that pantry with a fine-tooth comb. And every other place."

Nick could see King's eyes wince. Searchers in his home. Fingering private papers. But there was no outburst as there had been when King heard that Veronica's body had been examined. King was beginning to realize. . . . He must be almighty sorry he had gone on record against the possibility of suicide. That was one of the things that made Nicholas feel that King could be innocent. On the other hand, he could have been simple enough to believe that nothing but the chloroform would be discovered, and chloroform was better as an accident than as suicide. Believing it accident, the police would not start digging into their private lives.

Larrabee said, regretfully, "I'm afraid it's too late. The maids will have thrown out any suspicious bottle."

"No chance. They only heard about the arsenic at the inquest."

"Ah, but they'll have been worrying about those pains."

"Not with a baby coming, they wouldn't worry. And they'll own up, if they've got anything to own up to, when they see how serious it is."

His pause was calculated. Then he said briskly, "But we can't waste time on that now. We've got to look into the possibility—that Mrs. King was given poison with intention."

A nice way of putting it, Nick appreciated. Skirting the word murder. Poison with intention.

"Had she any enemies, Mr. King?"

"None." King was abrupt.

"No one with a grudge against her?"

Jennifer Mitchell burst out, "No one had a grudge against her! Can't you be satisfied with an accident, a dreadful accident?"

"Not until it's proved an accident, Miss Mitchell," said Wayland very seriously. "I don't say it wasn't accident. I don't say she didn't drink it herself, just before she went downstairs, though it doesn't look like stuff she'd take. And you don't think she'd take it, either, do you? You said, at the inquest, under oath—"

"N-no," said Jennifer waveringly. She pushed the hair off her forehead, and the little blue-gray cap rode back with it. She looked bewildered and uncertain. She said faintly, "It was some accident."

"Our job is to look into all the angles. Now your sister died of poison. Who would poison her?" He moved a fat hand in what he felt a gesture of pure logic. "If someone hated her, that's a motive. If someone would profit by her death, that's a motive."

"Profit?" said the girl hesitantly.

"He means money," said Roger King in a constrained voice. 'The answer is that I would. Our wills left everything to each other."

Nick thought, *He's done it now. He's laid himself wide open.* Larrabee cleared his throat. "You are forgetting the more recent will, Mr. King."

King stared. Then his guard went up, but not quickly enough. Wayland's face was like a small boy's biting into a piece of pie. "A more recent will?"

King was silent. Then he said stiffly, "I know nothing about it."

"It was *very* recent," said Larrabee. "I daresay, in the rush of things—" It was the best he could do for a man who had so glaringly failed to grasp his cues.

"Now what was in that will, Mr. Larrabee?"

"I didn't make it. I was away and the instrument was drawn by my junior partner here. He could regard its contents as a privileged communication."

Wayland looked hard at Nicholas, affability a thin mask now. "We could get hold of that will. But that will delay things, and we wouldn't feel so good to be held up. Mr. King, you don't want to put any obstacles in the way, do you?"

"No," said King automatically. Then, very distantly, "It makes no difference to me what disposition she made."

"Miss Mitchell?"

She was frightened, Nick thought. She knew what was coming. But she managed a cool "No. If you think it important."

"Now go ahead and tell us, Mr. Parr."

Nicholas tried to make his voice impersonal and detached. "Mrs. King left half her estate to a sister, half to her child, if a child her survived. In the event there was no child her surviving the estate went to her sister."

King looked at Jennifer. She was staring into her lap, her fair hair falling across her cheeks. Wayland asked, "You know about this, Miss Mitchell?"

She hesitated. Then she said quickly, "No. No, I didn't."

Nick thought, *She's lying.* That too-nervous denial. The girl gave a quick, upward glance at King and said, almost inaudibly, "I'm sorry."

"It's all right, Jenny," he said stiffly. "She knew I had enough of my own."

"That's it." She sounded eager and appeasing. "She knew you had plenty and she was afraid I'd be left without anything. That's it."

"No other bequests?"

"None."

Wayland rubbed the back of his neck thoughtfully. "How did it happen, Mr. King, that she didn't discuss this will with you?"

King was silent a moment. Then he said, carefully, "She knew it made no difference to me. I never wanted the McKenzie money." Even his nice voice could not make that ring true. He had been living well on the McKenzie money.

"H'm. . . . Had there been any difference between you, recently? Of course you needn't answer if you don't wish," said Wayland quickly before Larrabee could interpose, "but I'm sure you see no reason not to be frank with us."

"There were no differences between us." King sounded as if he could not make himself believe that these answers were required of him.

"About that phone." Wayland made a quick shift. "It didn't occur to you to try one of the other phones?"

"No. Naturally not."

"You didn't try to phone on the way in?"

"No. I thought the whole line was gone. And when I got into town it was as quick to go straight to the doctor's."

It sounded lame, but that's the way you felt, Nick thought. You hate to lose time by stopping and parking and climbing out to telephone and finding, maybe, that the line was busy.

Nolan leaned forward. "What about the two other men in the party?"

King's mouth tightened a little. "Taggart's an old neighbor. He and his wife are always in and out. Burton—we met him in Florida. He and—"

"He and I had become great friends," said Jennifer quickly.

Nolan asked, "Anything more than friends?"

She didn't flash back, as Nick expected. She didn't turn aloof and snub him. She said, almost archly, "Well, let's say *very* good friends."

He wanted, very much, to talk to Jennifer Mitchell. But when the group broke up, her aunt was waiting for her. He would see her later, he promised himself. Wayland was not through with Roger King; he asked him to come down to headquarters to make a statement there, and Larrabee went with them. Nicholas went back to his office, where Miss Miller was listening to a girl from next door who had heard the news over the radio. He shut his door and marched up and down, his mind sorting impressions and trying out one idea after another.

He wanted to see Jennifer Mitchell. And then the intercom sounded and Miss Miller, trying to keep excitement out of her voice, said, "Miss Mitchell to see you," and next moment she was showing her in, closing the door softly on her own exit as she had closed it five days before, and Jennifer was outlined against it, as her sister had been outlined, looking toward Nicholas Parr with the same air of hesitancy, then saying abruptly, as her sister had said, "I want to make my will."

She came forward and asked, "You can do it now, can't you? I know I haven't anything yet, but since I have—expectations—" she brought that out in a forced, breathless way—"I thought I ought to make a will. The sooner the better."

"Always a good idea." He pulled forward the big chair and she sat down. Unlike her sister she reached instantly in her bag for a cigarette and he lighted it for her. She drew deeply on it as if in great need of its comfort. He looked down on her compassionately. "No use saying anything, is there?"

She shook her head, her lips tensing about the cigarette. Nick said, "So we'll talk about the will. What disposition do you want made?"

"I want to leave everything to my brother-in-law."

She raised her eyes quickly to his; her young, upturned face seemed ready to challenge anything that might be in his. She flung out, "My sister never should have left me so much. It was sweet of her but—but I want to see that it gets back to him."

"It will be a long time on its way." He smiled involuntarily. "Why don't you just give it to him, give him part of it?"

"Do you think he'd take it? You don't know his pride. . . . I know this is only a gesture but I'll feel better if I make it."

"Then you make it."

He called in Miss Miller. It was a short will and it took little time to have it typed and signed and witnessed. After Miss Miller had gone out with it, Jennifer Mitchell turned quickly to him. "Oh, there's one thing more, Mr. Parr. Please don't let anyone know that I have made this will. I particularly don't want my brother-in-law to know I've made it. . . He might feel it—well, sort of patronizing. I don't want him to know anything about it."

It was meant to sound offhand, but to him it sounded rehearsed. He moved between her and the door and said gravely, "You're not, by any chance, thinking of telling him yourself?"

"Of course not. Why would I?" Her voice was startled and artificial. "No one is to know."

"And you'll tell him that no one knows. That no one knows that he knows. . . . Is that what you've been thinking up for a trap?"

Now her eyes blazed at him as they had blazed when he had stopped her from running upstairs. "I don't know what you mean."

"Oh, yes, you do." He was curt when he did not want to be curt, but his intensity could not help it. "Let's not waste time. I've been wanting to talk to you."

"There isn't anything to talk about."

"There's plenty. You see, your sister said some things to me, here, last Wednesday. If I'd taken her seriously she might be alive. *She might.* . . . I'm not making that mistake again."

Her eyes searched his warily. She said, as if picking her way through pitfalls, "What sort of things?"

"She said she wasn't going to live to have a child. That was when I was talking of a trust fund. I thought she might have a bad heart, something like that, which she knew about."

"She was nervous—had morbid ideas—"

"She said she didn't want her husband to know she'd made that will. Then she said, 'Although it might save my life. If I don't manage to. But I've got to prove—'" He waited a moment. "That was when she was going. And like a fool, I let her go. I thought she was hysterical—"

"She was—she was—"

"Was she?" he said grimly. "Larrabee said so, said she didn't mean a thing. I thought he ought to know—he knew her. He was going to check on Sunday. *Sunday.* . . ." He hurried away from that. "At first I thought King was hard hit—thought it was probably accident, since she'd used chloroform before. But that arsenic. That wasn't accident."

"But Mr. Larrabee—"

"Eyewash. You didn't believe him. You wanted to, but you knew better. You think King's guilty and you want proof. So you had this idea of trapping him. You think if he knows he's to get your money and thinks no one else knows that he knows, he'll make some move against you before you change your mind."

"But I don't think he's guilty!" she burst out. She stopped and looked up at Nick in desperation. The subterfuge went out of her. She said, despairingly, "I don't know what to think!"

He shook his head slowly. "I was counting on you. You know him."

"But I don't *know* him, really! I haven't seen very much of him, I've been away at college. But I've always liked him. That's what makes it so terrible. To be with someone you like and not know—not know if he's real or a—a monster."

Her voice was trembling. Nick said, "Sit down. You need a drink." He got out a bottle and glasses from the washroom and a box of crackers. "Nibble on these," he said, sitting down on the arm of the chair before her.

"I guess I do need something," she owned. Then she looked at the glass he had put in her hand and he knew what she was thinking and he said quickly, "Just what do you feel about him?"

"I've always liked him," she repeated. "I don't think I'd have dreamed of suspecting him if Veronica—you see, she said some of those things to me, too. And I didn't believe her."

Once the barrier was down she poured it out. "It was the day she came here to make that will. But before that, ever since I came home this spring, there was something funny between them—something not right. A sort of stiffness. She began throwing out things to me, bitter things about Roge. That he wasn't as wonderful as I thought he was. That she could tell me things that would surprise me."

She stared down into her glass. "I felt she was on edge about something. She'd been playing too hard down south. She did everything too hard. And when she didn't like people she could always make herself believe anything against them. So I didn't pay any attention."

He prompted, "But that day?"

"That was the Wednesday we were shopping. And she said something and I stuck up for Roge and that set her off. She poured out a lot of stuff. She said he was tired of her and wanted to get rid of her, and get her money. I honestly thought she was out of her head and I told her so."

"What things did she tell you? Specific things?"

"Oh, there was something that happened down south about sleeping pills. She was taking them regularly and she said one night when Roge was angry about something he'd given her an overdose and she'd nearly died. She said he pretended that she had taken the pills twice, forgetfully, and taken an extra dose each time, and she'd let him think she believed that but she knew better. And I said he was right. She *was* forgetful. It was unbelievable that he—"

"She didn't let him know what she suspected?"

"No. And then something else happened, something to her car. The brakes didn't work and she thought he'd tampered with them. She almost had a wreck. And there was something else about a fish cocktail that made her sick. I thought she'd built up a crazy complex—"

"But what made her—what made her turn against him?"

"I—I don't know."

"Did Burton get her to believe all that?"

"So you've guessed about him," said the girl bitterly.

"I saw him when he heard she was dead. . . . Was she planning to divorce King and marry him?"

"Oh, no! Veronica hated divorce. I told her, if she felt like that about Roge she ought to divorce him and she said she never would, that she liked her life the way it was. I'm sure she wasn't serious about Tod Burton. It was just the excitement."

"So you became 'very good friends' with him for camouflage?"

"It was something I could do for her," said Jennifer. "She didn't know I guessed. . . . I hoped she'd get tired. She wasn't serious about him," she insisted again. "She was only playing."

"Could be. But King could be afraid he'd be tossed out. And that's motive, Jennifer. So you and I are going to the police."

"Oh, no! If it's false, if it's something Veronica dreamed up, to make herself feel better about playing with Burton, I'd never forgive myself. I've got to be sure. . . . Oh, it's horrible," said the girl passionately, "to be with someone you've always liked and trusted and not know whether he's real or not. At first, when it seemed only the chloroform, I couldn't believe—"

She broke off, staring desolately ahead of her. "But anyone can poison. It's so easy."

"Yes," said Nick grimly. "Nice people poison."

"Yes. . . . But it doesn't have to be Roge."

"Who else? Not Burton?" he said derisively.

She shook her head and he told her, "Taggart's the other chance. Where does he come in?"

"Not Taggart. He's adored Veronica for years. Just worshipped her—the Old Dog Tray department. It really was like that. Veronica never cared for him. He was someone to ride with. Somebody younger than Mac. Mac was sweet but too old."

"That leaves Mrs. Taggart. She wasn't in the pantry."

"It doesn't have to be in the pantry. Tod put the tray on a table. He took a Martini and we dashed off and the tray was sitting there where anybody could have got to it."

"Maybe you've got something," said Nicholas, his eyes intent. "Not easy, though. . . . But why Mrs. Taggart?"

"She's awful," said Jennifer. "Don't you know her?"

"Seen her around the club . . . They were at the inquest today." He thought of her rouged face, her incandescent hair. "Older than her husband, isn't she?"

"Years older. He married her for her money—or maybe he liked her then. I wouldn't know. But she's mad about him. She always pretended to be great friends with Veronica, but she must have hated her. Veronica could ride with Chet and she couldn't, not after she hurt her back. And she drinks a lot. Oh, it's more like her than like Roge!"

"But why now? After all these years?"

"It got to the boiling point. She's unpredictable. . . . A lush with a mind gone to seed."

"She came in after Taggart did?"

"Yes. They live across the way and she must have been at the gate waiting for him. A jealous woman would do that. Lie in wait and spy. Then she came running over. I remember she laughed so loudly at the way Tod was clowning that I thought she was high already. She might have been getting up her nerve, saying to herself that if Chet stopped in one more time—"

"But to get the stuff in a glass—in front of everybody—"

"Nobody'd be watching."

Nick thought about it, excitement kindling. "But it would take some proving."

"Couldn't you get the proof?" The girl looked at him in naive trust. "You're a lawyer. You know what to do—

hire detectives and all that." She burst out, "I can't go to the police with all this. About Chet Taggart's being crazy about Veronica and Tod Burton's being crazy about her. It would make a scandal. . . . If you find out it's Hazel Taggart they'll never have to know about Tod. And if it is Roge, then they'll never have to hear about Hazel and her jealousy. Please take it on for me!"

He argued against it, against his own eagerness, warning her that the police had the authority, that he might have to work with them and tell them what he must. He warned, "It might not come out Hazel Taggart. It might be Roger King."

Her young face hardened. "I want the *truth.*"

"All right. Tell me about Nina Barrett, then. Was there anything between her and King?"

"Nina?" Jennifer looked astonished. "Goodness, no. Oh, she was the office wife, awfully on the job, but she was boring him to tears. I mean I thought so. Calling up to remind him of this and that. And she's engaged—though that's no reason. . . . What makes you ask?"

"Because she's so good-looking."

"But she hasn't much personality," said Jennifer. "She's too, too self-effacing. . . . At least that's been my impression when I've dropped into the office. And she's been with him for years and years."

A belated passion wasn't very logical. Jealousy of Tod Burton was more probable. Then he said, "You're dismissing Taggart too easily. He could be jealous, too."

"Jealous, yes. But as long as Veronica let him hang around he'd take it," said Jennifer, too confidently, Nick thought. "He wouldn't hurt anyone, Veronica least of all. He's the kindest man. Big and shy. When I was a kid he used to do tricks for me. And he'd let me ride his big horse—"

"What I'd like," said Nick earnestly, "is to get that scene re-enacted. It would be gruesome, but it would be enlightening. The goings and comings around the table. One of them has done it. One of them knows that he has done it, knows that everybody is watching everybody else. Under that strain someone might make a revealing move, give something away."

She said tensely, "It would be horrible." After a moment she said, "But it might work. . . . Hazel gets haywire when she's drinking. When she's cold sober she's shrewd and smart. . . . Yes, it might be a way. . . ."

When she left she said shyly, "I'm glad I've got you, Mr. Parr—"

"Nicholas."

"Nicholas"—she smiled fleetly—"to help me."

He held her hands tightly. "God knows what I can do. But I'll do my damnedest. And—I warn you—it looks like King."

"Then prove it is!"

"I'll try. . . . I don't like your going back to that house. I don't think King's fool enough to fall for a trap like that, not now he won't, but I just don't like it."

"I'll be all right," she said. "I can take care of myself."

A plucky girl. She had taken the shock like a soldier, never breaking down, setting her mind to work at once on the dreadful problem. She looked delicate but there was steel in her. She had spirit, this Jennifer Mitchell.

Suddenly he remembered to release her hands. "You do that," he said, speaking lightly. "You take care of yourself."

Chapter Six

There was no risk, no immediate risk, he told himself, as the door closed after her. King—supposing it were King—was not fool enough to make a revealing move at once. He stood still, hands deep in his pockets, his mind racing from one alternative to the other, then, abruptly deciding, he hurried into his coat.

The intercom sounded and Miss Miller, breathing plaintive patience, asked, "Can I go now? Or does someone else want to make a will?"

"'*May* I go,'" said Nick reprovingly. He felt gay with the heady elation a call to action always sounded in him. "Go with God. Better yet, go with me. You live out toward the Country Club, don't you?"

"Yes, but I've got a date."

So she had a date. "Oh, well," he said cheerfully, "better luck next time. I mean for you. *Adiós.*"

"There's a girl called and left a number. Said she was staying down and would you call back? She didn't leave a name but the number is Mr. King's office."

"I'll call her from the club."

"And Sally Waters called. Twice. Wants you to call her at the paper."

"No dice. *Muchas gracias.*"

He left a note on Larrabee's desk saying the firm had
been retained to investigate Veronica King's death. That
would scotch any hankering the old boy might have for a
spectacular defense of King. He must be having a long ses-
sion with King now. Nick went down to his car and drove
out to the club, rehearsing various approaches and attacks
on the way. The police had been ahead of him, he saw, for
there was Nolan's stiff, uniformed figure moving toward a
police car. Nick jumped out and hurried toward him.

There was a jut to Nolan's chin proclaiming exasperation and Nick said, "How you doing? Burton not cooper-
ating?"

"Burton?"

"Sure. Why else would you be here? You'd want his
story. He was seeing them in Florida."

Nolan said cautiously, "What do you know about this
Burton?"

"Never saw him before last Saturday night. All I know
is, he met the Kings down south and stopped over to see
them here."

"He got here as soon as they got back. He says he stayed
over to play around with the sister."

"Not surprising."

"A lot of people will want to play with her—when they
find out what she's got," said Nolan cynically. "Do you
know what he does for a living?"

"No idea."

"He's unemployed, he says. Asked if there was an opening on the Force. Quite a kidder," said Nolan disgustedly.
"Says his only permanent address is a club in New York
City." Nolan named it saying, "That would be a high-class
place, wouldn't it?"

"Right out of the top drawer."

"I thought so. Unemployed!"

"I take it you two didn't hit it off."

"There's something phony about him," said Nolan thoughtfully. "I may be only a dumb cop but I can tell when a man's covering up."

Covering up his feeling for Veronica King, Nick thought He said slowly, "I don't see how he matters. He's only important for what he can tell you."

Nolan merely looked at him cagily.

"And I gather he didn't tell you anything."

Nolan countered, "I take it your firm will be defending King if it comes to trial?"

"I don't know. We're counsel for Miss Mitchell. And Miss Mitchell," said Nick, in sudden frankness, "has just retained us as special investigators. Not that she doesn't have complete confidence in the police but she wants to feel she is doing something, too. She wants the guilty one punished, no matter who it is."

"And who does she think it is?"

Nick grinned. "I don't mind telling you. She doesn't know. She's completely in a fog. That's why she came to us. It gave her the feeling of doing something." Before Nolan could voice the sarcasm that Nick saw coming, Nick said quickly, "I'd like to work with you, if I could. I'm not after any credit. Our firm doesn't usually do such work. But I have a very special interest in this case. I was there that night, and I'd damn well like to get the one who gave her that arsenic."

"Killing is a monstrous thing," said Nolan. "And arsenic is a nasty thing." He gave Nicholas Parr a long, measuring look. "You could help," he admitted. "You could find out a few things for me, if you wanted to. You're on the inside. I take it, you're a member of this Country Club?"

At Nick's nod he went on. "Now Burton and Miss Mitchell were going out together. Were they going steady, do you know?"

Nick said carefully, "They'd only known each other two weeks."

"You heard what she said, '*Very* good friends.' I'd like you to find out just how good friends they are."

Nick put it together. He looked, in some amazement, at the sergeant. "But he didn't know about the new will."

"What makes you think he didn't? If she's sweet on him she'd have let it out to him. Told him how her sister had quarreled with her husband and was leaving the money to her. She'd tell him, all right—not thinking what ideas it might give him. She said she hadn't known about the will but she was covering up for him. She was worried sick, that girl was. I saw it in her face."

Nick turned over the fantastic thought. "But why in heck would he do it right away?"

"I'm not saying he did," said Nolan. "I'm saying it's a possibility. And as for doing it right away, he'd be afraid that the Kings would make up, see? And it would look better for him, now, before he was married or engaged to the girl. That guy is very sure of himself, and he'd be sure he could get the girl. She'd fallen for him right off. And the money is a lot of money."

Nolan added, "I'm trusting you, because you're a bright young man and don't want to get in wrong, not to pass this on to your client."

"My client would turn against Burton in a split second if she thought he was the one."

Nolan said, noncommittally, "She's in an unhappy position, that girl." That much was true, Nick thought. Then Nolan said, "She tells you she doesn't know and she hires you to investigate. But she didn't say anything about investigating Burton, did she?"

"No."

"She's hoping you won't uncover anything. She must be sorry she was so against suicide."

"She spoke of Mrs. Taggart," said Nick. "She might have something there. Mrs. T. had some cockeyed jealousy of Veronica King, and she drinks too much for her own good."

"Jealous, was she?"

"Wholly without reason, Jennifer Mitchell says. Veronica King had no particular interest in Taggart but I gather he's had one of those hopeless devotions for her ever since the early McKenzie days."

He could see that Nolan was filing that carefully for reference. "Mrs. Taggart is a possibility," he admitted. "And, to my mind, this Burton is a possibility. And Roger King sticks out like a sore thumb." He burst out bitterly, "Proof, we need! A lot of people playing ring-around-a-rosy round a tray! Not watching what anybody else was doing!"

Nick said slowly, "I've an idea if we could reconstruct that scene. . . get them to act it out again . . . we'd see something very revealing." He fed that thought to Nolan, then said, "Burton's circumstances might be an indication. What did you find out?"

"His father's a big bug in Pittsburgh and his mother's in Europe, married to someone else."

"Sounds affluent. A rich playboy."

"Maybe not so rich. Maybe he isn't getting on with his folks and they give him only chicken feed."

"Maybe you've got something."

He thought, *You keep on suspecting him. Keep him here as a material witness. I'm going to need him, if I get a case against King.* Aloud he said, "How about accident?"

Nolan's eyes glinted. "I don't mind telling you, because King has been informed, that no suspicious bottle was found in the pantry or on the premises. The garbage collector doesn't come till Wednesday and everything has been examined. And the three maids and the chauffeur and

the laundress, also the gardener by the day, all swear by all
that's holy they never laid eyes on any such bottle. That
came in just as I left headquarters."

"Quick work."

"Quick and thorough. I don't know your opinion of the
Force but there are competent men on it."

"I believe that," said Nick grinning. "It keeps me in
bounds."

He ran into the clubhouse, and called Burton on the
house phone. "This is Nicholas Parr. May I come up?"

Burton's voice was sharp and mocking. "Another policeman?"

"No, a friend of the Kings. The one there Saturday
night." There was a moment's silence. Then, "Why not?
Come up."

Burton opened the door. He was in shirt sleeves, his
collar unfastened. The shirt was an expensive one and
his tweeds were expensive and Nick thought, *Some chick-
en feed.* He had a fine, hard-muscled body, slim and nar-
row-hipped, and with a scarlet sash and a cape he would
have made a dashing toreador. The scar on his cheek
seemed just right for him.

There were scattered clothes on his bed and an opened
suitcase. He waved a hand at them. "Now I've got to undo
all that. No can go yet. Pending investigation. Did you
ever hear such rot?"

His offhand manner wasn't quite good enough. His eyes
looked hard and angry. "Have a drink? I could do with one
after that cop's questions. What will you have, Scotch or
Bourbon?"

"Rye on rocks, thank you."

Burton gave the order into the phone, saying, "Make
one double."

The things on the bed were neatly folded except for a
crimson silk dressing gown that was spread out. The edge

of an envelope was sticking out from it. Nick was carefully not looking at the bed when Burton turned.

"Sit down. Nice of you to drop in." His tone had a slightly insolent ring. "What can I do for you?"

"I wondered if you'd have dinner with me."

"Thanks, no. Frankly, I'm fed up with people. And I don't want to eat for hours yet. What did you want to lead up to?"

"The Kings," said Nick promptly. "I'm in the firm that handles their affairs, and we are trying to get a few facts together." It sounded thinner than when he had rehearsed it, but he went on, noting the quick wariness in the light gray eyes, "You saw them in Florida?"

"In Florida."

"Was there anything that made you think there was trouble between them?"

"You sound like that flatfoot."

"Sorry. But we want to be prepared."

"I don't know a damned thing about the Kings' private life. Period. King's your client. Ask him."

"Naturally he says things were all right."

"Then they were all right. Doesn't a client tell the truth to his lawyer?"

"Not always. King's reticent. We'd like to be prepared in case somebody turns up with a story that they were fighting."

"I didn't see any fights."

"The idea was," said Nick, stubbornly playing it out, "that King might have been getting something on the side and she found it out."

Burton looked at him without a flicker of expression. "That's an idea. What are you trying to do, pin it on him? You sound more like the prosecution than King's faithful retainers."

"Actually we are Miss Mitchell's retainers. She'd like to believe in accident—I mean, she hopes for proof that it was an accident—"

"That's what the afternoon papers said. Accident."

"But the police take a dim view of that. They'd like a sensational case. Our notion is they are going to jump on King, if they think they can make a case, and we'd like to beat them to the facts. You can see the spot we're in."

"I don't give a bloody damn what spot you're in. The thing's done and it can't be undone," said Burton violently. "It's up to you to find the answers. If King needs a defense he can pay those maids to own up." He gave Nicholas an oblique look as he said that.

There was a knock. The waiter was there with the drinks and Burton signed for them. Nick lifted a fold of the robe on the bed and dropped it fast. Beneath was a scattering of letters and the address on the envelopes was in a bold, slanted hand. Veronica's signature had been bold and slanted.

He was lighting a cigarette when Burton turned and he kept his hands busy with the lighter. "Looks like he made both double," he said. "Could I have some water in mine? Out of the tap is okay."

Burton stepped into the bathroom and Nick moved quickly. He had his hand out of his pocket when Burton came back. "Thanks," he said, and raised his glass. "Cheerio."

"To hell with everything." Burton tilted back his head and took his rye fast.

"We've done this before."

Burton shot him a quick look. The pupils of his eyes dilated. That, Nick thought, is a reflex you can't control. You read about the pupils contracting with emotion, but they don't, they dilate, Doc Abbey had once told him.

He said conversationally, "How come King didn't mix that highball in the library? With the whisky there?"

"That is very special Scotch. She didn't like Scotch—I believe," Burton said distantly. "Unlike little sister."

Nick took the cue. "Oh, is she fond—?"

"Not particularly. Not a drinking gal. Only that I"— he gave the words with a deliberate smile—"am more acquainted with little sister's likes and dislikes. Little sister is quite a girl."

"But you—where was it you met the Kings?"

"In Florida."

"So little sister didn't come into your life until you were here?"

The gray eyes moved a little. "As a matter of fact—not that it's any of your bloody business—I was lured here by her photograph."

"But you saw quite a lot of the Kings in Florida. You knew what went on. So tell me this—how did Veronica get it into her head that King had tampered with her car?"

"Her car?" The voice was unshaken, amused. The light gray eyes, motionless now, were amused. "I never heard of his tinkering with her car."

"She said 'tampering.' She told me something the day she was in my office. I had the idea that you agreed with her."

"I always agree with lovely ladies." The indifferent air was a shade too offhand for the watchful eyes. "But I never pay any attention to their talk. I don't remember anything about a car."

"It sounded like some trouble. Like something the police might turn up. That we ought to know about."

"Never heard about it."

After a moment, Nick got up. "Well—thanks anyway."

"Must you go?" The sarcasm was savage. "Don't let me keep you from your detecting." Then he said bitterly, "As if it matters a damn, now it's done. 'Can you pour back the spilled drops, old Priest? Return motion to the quiet limbs—?'" He laughed harshly. "End of quote. I mean, it's all so futile. Peering into their affairs. Chasing a bottle of rat poison. What difference does it make now? She's dead. Done. Gone. Close the book. . . ." He turned and lit a cigarette. He threw over his shoulder, "If King wants to get off the front page he'd better see those maids."

He did not look at the letter until he was a long way from the club; then he drew up along the street and pulled it out. The date on the envelope was November, all right, November of the preceding year. The Kings had gone south in January. It had been addressed to the club in New York. The letter was unsigned, without beginning, direct and terse.

"I can't manage the Thanksgiving thing but I'll work something out—fast. I must see you as soon as possible. We are both quite mad but I can't talk it out on paper. Wait till we meet and for God's sake be careful. *More than ever.*"

That was underscored. More than ever his? Or more than ever be careful?

Burton was not a man to be careful. He might have put things on paper. Jennifer had said, before she left, that Veronica was not likely to keep things, but she might have. If she had, King would have it now. But it was not important, what King had discovered after her death. What was important was what he had known before.

Nick drove to the office and put the letter in the vault. Burton might not miss one from many but you couldn't be sure of that. Nick wasn't risking being slugged and ransacked. Burton had eyes like cold knives. . . . A mistake, not to have taken more letters, but the paper had been thick and one had seemed all his pocket could hold without detection.

Now what? He wanted the rest of them but he had the feeling they were down the drain by now. Burton had been looking through them for the last time, not packing them. He was going to get rid of them. Veronica was dead. *Dead. Done. Gone. Close the book.* Burton was a man who cut his losses. He would want nothing left to show his connection with her.

What was Burton's own theory about her death? Not accident—his words about King's paying the maids to turn up a possible bottle showed he didn't believe in any accident. Burton must believe that King had killed her—or Taggart. Taggart's infatuation could not have been lost upon him. He must believe it might be Taggart or he would not have thrown out that hint on King's behalf. But he had said nothing to indicate Taggart. Nick thought that over. He had expected to find Burton keen for revenge but it seemed he wanted, more than revenge, to be undiscovered as Veronica's lover. He was hard hit by her death, but now he was thinking of scandal and publicity and he was putting on an act about Jennifer for cover. *It's done and it can't be undone.*

Nick picked up the telephone and reached Nolan. "I've been talking to your friend at the club. He seems a little too frank in admitting a warm interest in little sister."

Nolan could be counted on to be combative. "He'd judge that to be smart. Besides, she's admitted it. What did he say?"

"Just that. And that he was lured here by her photograph."

Nolan said thoughtfully, "He could have seen the Kings weren't getting on and had some idea—"

An imaginative cop, Nolan. And persistent. He'd keep Burton here, all right. And then, when Nick had enough on him, they could question him and make him admit

his intimacy with Veronica, which would show motive for
King. That motive was taking shape, and it apparently
wasn't inspired by emotion for that startled-deer secretary.

An affair between Burton and Veronica was plenty of
motive. But a man could have motive, all the motives in
the world—jealousy, hate, and self-interest—and not kill
because of them. You had to remember that. Also a man
could have position and breeding and charm and be secretly ruthless and unscrupulous. You had to remember that.

A note on his desk from Larrabee said they must discuss
the Mitchell matter the first thing in the morning. Also, a
young lady had phoned, asked for Nick and rung off, leaving no name. Nick looked at his watch. Seven-twenty. He
phoned King's office and Nina Barrett answered.

"Oh, Mr. Parr! I hoped you'd come in!" She was breathless and went on, in a rush of words, "You said something
about dinner, sometime, and I thought—would tonight—?
If you are free. I've been working rather late—"

She'd been staying down trying to get hold of him,
worrying for fear that, after the arsenic disclosure, he'd
change his mind about keeping silent about her presence
at the house that night. She wanted something out of him,
and that was all right with him, he thought tolerantly. He
wanted a few things from her. She would be worried about
King and warily defensive—the loyal secretary—but she
might give something away about Burton and she might
know something about the Taggarts. And—no denying
it—he was curious about that girl. He could see what Jennifer meant by calling her self-effacing, but Jennifer was
all wrong about no personality. It was wrapped in queer,
contradictory layers, but there was a lot of it. Something
had hurt that girl, made her afraid of life. Maybe that man
in Saranac . . .

He said, "Tonight is fine. In half an hour?"

"Some quiet place. I wouldn't want to be seen out, to-night, having a wonderful time."

"I know quite a few quiet sin spots," he assured her. "I'll meet you in front of your office in half an hour."

He located Dr. Abbey at the hospital. When Abbey said, "What's on your mind?" Nick felt surprised that there could be anything on a man's mind today except the King case. He told him, "Jennifer Mitchell has retained us to investigate. Wants the truth, at all cost. I want you to do something for me. Find out when Veronica was away last fall, and where. And when she first consulted you, about her condition. That will be on your books, won't it?"

"Consultations will. No idea about the times she was away."

"Okay. But dig up that date, won't you?"

He called another number and said, "Society, please. Miss Sally Waters."

After a minute a voice told him, "She's on another line. If you will wait—"

He waited. Finally her voice came, excited when she heard his name. "Nick, you louse! I thought you'd given me the brush-off. Now when—"

"Listen, Career Girl. I want something from you. You write about comings and goings. See when Veronica King was away this fall and where and let me know."

"That's easy," said Sally Waters. "I've been looking through the files. Is it a trade?"

"You couldn't do a purely kind deed, could you?"

"The way you've treated me these last two days I could pickle you in brine," said Sally, feelingly. "Here I've been frantic for some inside stuff—"

"Look, Sally, I'll give you something as soon as I can. This is important. We've been engaged to investigate—"

"Can I use that?"

"I'd say so. But check with Larrabee. He'll be at his home now."

"The papers tonight had it accident. We were being very discreet."

"Haven't seen them yet. What I want to know is where she went and when."

"Okay, here goes. And don't forget I gave it to you. They were in Chicago, both of them, the last of September. Attended a very *chi-chi* wedding in Lake Forest and some other doings. She stayed on by herself after that—she gets most of her clothes there—and got back just in time for the Altman party October eighteenth. No, sixteenth. She wore a stunning green strapless—'green glitter' it was called. Had a new emerald ring."

"Was she away any other time after that?"

"I know of one time. Just before Christmas. She'd bought a plane ticket to Chicago and I called up to ask what parties she was going to—usually she loved to give about that. But she was very upstage. Just going for a fitting, she said. Now what's all this about?"

"You'll be the first to know. Love undying."

"Never mind the love stuff. Orchids, no less."

He was laughing when he hung up. He telephoned again. Mosely was a safe man the firm had used before on confidential stuff. It was past his dinner hour but luckily he was in and Nick told him quickly what he wanted. "You have a man in Chicago you can reach tonight? Have him find out from the hotels—all of them—if Mrs. Roger King was registered the last of September or the first part of October. And any other time after that—especially just before Christmas. Also if Tod Burton was registered at the same times. . . . No, I don't know any other name than Tod. Just Burton will do. Dates and room numbers. The usual dope. Start him going right away and let me know as soon as you can."

Nina Barrett was at the appointed corner ahead of him. She was in black, a short black broadtail coat over the dark dress, but her hat was a small, off-white affair, that fitted her smooth dark hair like a silver cap. Each time he saw Nina Barrett he had the same surprised feeling about those eyes of hers. She would be wonderful, he thought, in a Spanish mantilla, like one of those gorgeous girls in Mexico City who drive around the ring before a bullfight with gay shawls over the car.

Almost instantly she asked where they were going. He said he'd heard the Wayfarers was good, a new place that specialized on foreign dishes, like rice *tafel* and curries. That sounded marvelous, she said. She was constrained and nervous and trying not to show it. She said, "That was terrible about Mrs. King, wasn't it?"

"Terrible," he said gravely.

"To do that to herself! But, of course, she counted on the chloroform."

He flicked her a curious glance. "You think she did it?"

"Of course! What else can one think?"

She was overacting, putting on a show on King's behalf. He said casually, "The family went on record against suicide."

"They couldn't know. She was terribly erratic. And she'd been very odd, lately. I know, from little things at the office."

So it was going to be like that. Protecting King. That was natural. He said vaguely, "Larrabee thought accident—"

"Oh, no, I don't think so. I think they'll find out she'd been very temperamental. Quite out of her head."

And that, Nick thought, would be a help to King if he tried to break the will. His mind made no judgment. It merely registered one impression after the other. He conceded, "The police were interested in suicide from the first. At least Nolan was."

"Oh, the police came to see me this afternoon." She said that lightly but with a quick turn of her head to him.

"They did."

"Two of them. Quite nice, really. The maids had told them I was at the house that afternoon and they wanted to know if I could tell them anything, but of course I couldn't. I was not downstairs at all."

"And you told them you'd left right after dinner. And now you're worrying for fear I'll give you away."

There was humor in Nick's voice but she didn't respond to the humor. "Not worrying," she said, carefully exact. "Because you wouldn't, of course—the arsenic doesn't make any difference. I was up there in my room. I wasn't downstairs at all."

"I know."

"And if I said anything different now it would look queer." She added pointedly, "For both of us."

"Sure," he said. "We're both in a spot." He didn't like her trying to bring that home to him but when you're scared, he thought, you turn on all the pressure. She didn't know that what really moved him was the thought of her hiding in his car under her coat. He felt such exasperated pity for her panic that he said brusquely, "You shouldn't have bolted like that. Like a scared bobby soxer."

She stared straight ahead of her. "Yes, I'm too old for that, aren't I?"

"I didn't mean that." They had stopped for a red light and a glance showed him her profile was tense and hurt. "But it was a crazy thing."

She said nothing to that.

After a time she asked, in a low voice, "What do the police *really* think?"

"I'm not in their confidence. The only one I've had a chance to talk with is Nolan, Sergeant Nolan, and he said

it couldn't be accident." He told her why. "He was out at
the club," he added, "trying to find out from Tod Burton
how the Kings had been getting on down in Florida. He
thought Burton was a queer cookie. What do you know
about him?"

"I don't know him at all. I don't," she said coldly, "know
anything about the Kings' social life."

"Then you're a darned poor secretary." Another red
light held them and he gave her a teasing look. "And Larrabee said you were an almighty efficient one."

Her smile was a mere tensing of the lips. There was
something very still, very withheld in that beautiful face
of hers. Humor did not reach her. She was deep in her own
world. . . . Well, naturally. She was worried for fear her
boss would be suspected of murdering his wife. She was
worried for fear she'd be known to have been at the house
after dinner.

He wasn't the only one who had heard that the Wayfarers was good, for every table was filled and couples were
waiting. He wasn't sorry, for the tables were too close together and the music too loud, synthetic Hawaiian, so he
said cheerfully, "Think nothing of it. I know a really quiet
place near here. Nothing fancy but elegant food."

They drove a few blocks and parked and he helped
her out and said, "Just around the corner." When she saw
Pierre's, she stopped short. She said, uncertainly, "Is this
a nice place?"

He looked up at the narrow house with its fresh painted window boxes of spring greenery and prim iron railings
and wondered what made her ask. She was actually hanging back. She must have taken his speech about "sin spots"
too literally. "Safe as a church," he said. "Come on, I'm
famished."

She was quite the most glamorous girl he had taken
there and he saw Pierre's face light up and then he saw the

recognition in it and heard it in the welcoming, "Good evening, madame."

Nina Barrett said, "Good evening," in a hurried way.

Pierre led them to a table and Nick ordered drinks. Pierre handed Nina a menu and said, "We have madame's favorite tonight. The *volaille*—"

"Thank you," said Nina, coldly and distantly.

Immediately impersonal, Pierre went on, "But perhaps madame prefers—" He indicated another choice and went away.

Nick looked at her and laughed. "Evidently madame has been here before."

He was taken aback by the blaze of fury in her eyes. She said, in a low, scornful voice, "I suppose you think this is clever!"

"Clever?" He didn't get it for a moment, then, "Oh, why shouldn't you have been here before? What's it to me?"

They stared hard at each other. Then she looked down at her plate. "That was silly of me," she said stiffly. "But I hate to be laughed at. And I thought—" Then in one of her rushes of words, "Yes, I've been here before. That was why I asked if it was a nice place. The night I was here there were terribly loud people at the next table."

Nick glanced through the long room, three old-fashioned rooms made into one, filled with quiet couples, mostly middle-aged, and murmured, "All under control tonight."

Talk was not easy after that. Nina Barrett seemed to be thinking ahead before she answered the most casual question, and she could not manage to hide an air of secret mortification at her outburst. The only time she was at ease with him was when the talk touched on music. She really knew music, he discovered.

She told him about concerts—she didn't seem to have missed one—and the records she collected, mostly folk

songs, some of them really unusual ones from South Afri-
ca. He said, "I'd like to hear them," and that ended music.
She shot him a startled-fawn look and fled, instantly, into
the shrubbery.

A peculiar girl, he thought. A beautiful girl, a sensitive
plant, a hasty bar. He didn't believe in the loud people at
the next table the other night she had been there. She must
have come quite frequently to have Pierre know her favorite
dishes. But what of it? Unless she had been with King.

So now he was back to his old suspicion, and he didn't
like it. It complicated his feeling for her, made him uneasy
for her. A sick fiancé in Saranac did not keep you from
being human. . . .

He dragged the Taggarts into the desultory talk. He
said, "I'm curious about those two. You know they were
there last Saturday?"

"I saw it in tonight's paper. I didn't know they were,
before. I was upstairs all the time."

"But have you ever met them? What are they like?"

"I don't think I've ever seen him. She came in once
when I was at the house doing invitations for Mrs. King.
All I remember it that she was the horsey type."

"She and Mrs. King were friendly?"

"They seemed so. I couldn't say."

"How did Mrs. King seem on Saturday? Upset over anything?"

"I didn't see Mrs. King. I didn't come to the house until after she had left."

*Mrs. King asked me to stay all night. . . . But she was all
right—*

Larrabee had a quotation he attributed to Montaigne:
". . . he who has not a good memory should never take
upon him the trade of lying."

Nick reached for a toasted cracker. "Sure you won't try
this cheese? It's the real thing."

"Nothing more, thank you."

When he was paying the bill she went to the powder room and he headed for Pierre, a piece of folding money in his hand. "Tell me," he said confidentially, "the name of my rival. I want to know how much I'm up against."

Pierre looked politely blank. Nick besought, "Have a heart. Remember I fought for *la patrie*. Is he rich? Is he young and good-looking or fat and bald?"

Pierre suddenly twinkled. His voice, under its sympathy, was tinged with amused malice. "He has the air of prosperity. Entirely of the best. Young, not as young as monsieur, I think, but of an attractiveness remarkable."

"Oh, the devil! And his name?"

"I seem to remember—" Pierre hesitated and Nick's hand moved out and Pierre pronounced, "Jenkins. Mr. Jenkins."

They drove back without much speech. She lived in an odd place, a converted garage back of a garden that belonged to a big corner house. The garage opened on a side street and one wall of it ran back along the alley. Nick asked, "Is this all yours?"

"Oh, I like living alone," she said quickly. "And it's nice to have a convenient place for my car." There was a big door for the car and a small one, green-painted, for her, into which she fitted her key.

"Thank you so much," she said formally. "It's been lovely."

"We must do it again sometime."

Thoughtfully he watched the door close upon her, heard the bolts inside it go across. Very out of the way. The perfect love nest. As he got into his car he saw the lights had gone on in the wide windows upstairs, then the curtains were drawn. A lonesome place for a young woman. What did she do with herself when she wasn't going to dinner with Mr. Jenkins or to concerts? Sit up there alone and play records of love songs?

He felt sorry for her. That, he felt, was her dangerous quality for him, not her beauty. Beauty he could cope with. But a girl who made you sorry for her, because she'd made a hash of her life, and was a plain damn fool with her lies—

I didn't see Mrs. King. . . . But she was all right— Another sentence came out of his memory. When he had asked if King had known she was staying all night she had said, *Of course . . . He heard Mrs. King ask me.*

Chapter Seven

It was all very well to say to Nicholas Parr that you were all right, that you could take care of yourself, but words did not fight off that desolately alone feeling or the terrible uncertainty. It was dreadful to be going back to a person you had always liked and trusted and not know whether he was the man he seemed, suffering as you were suffering at this awful death, tortured by the mystery of it, or whether he was a cold and evil killer masquerading behind his good looks and good manners.

Aunt Emma did not help the loneliness. Aunt Emma, though she would have indignantly denied it, was reveling in the terrible excitement. When she called for her aunt, the house was full of friends and the telephone kept ringing, and all the way out to the Ridge Aunt Emma was babbling about poor dear Veronica and poor dear Roger and what people would say.

"You'll find it's something the chauffeur brought in," Aunt Emma kept repeating. "Something like that."

Jennifer felt with cold certainty that no accidental bottle had found its way to the pantry. Things did not happen like that. She would ask Delia and Annie, of course, and Agnes Clancy—and the police had already been asking them—but it couldn't have happened like that Larrabee's theory of Roge's taking a little more from a second bottle was too, too plausible. She couldn't believe it. Yet how desperately she wanted to believe it!

Under the porte-cochere she let her aunt out. She looked at the white flowers on the door and a shudder started at the back of her neck and her stomach tightened into a hard knot. She said abruptly, "I think I'll run across to the Taggarts'."

"But, Jenny—"

"Be right back." She started the car.

She had to be doing something. The answer to the hideous question might be Hazel Taggart and to find out things about Hazel Taggart you had to be with her. She drove across to the big stone house and rang the bell. The butler, a plump little old man, looked at her in startled sympathy. "They're in the trophy room," he said, and she walked down the hall to it.

The Taggarts were having cocktails as she had known they would be. Husband and wife were sitting, in silence, apart from each other, each nursing a glass. The trophy room had been done for Chet; his silver cups were there in lighted cabinets, and on the walls were bold arrangements of framed ribbons and pictures of his horses and of famous Derby winners. Chet was supposed to collect those old racing prints but Hazel had a man in London on the lookout for them.

"I came for a spot of cheer," said Jennifer from the doorway. She made herself smile into Hazel Taggart's big eyes. Like marbles they were, the spotted green and brown agates she had played with as a child. "And to get away from Aunt Emma."

Hazel half-rose, then sank back. "Come right in," she invited. "Sit you down."

Taggart came quickly forward and placed a chair for her. He was surprisingly light on his feet for so large a man, just as his big hands were surprisingly light on a horse's mouth. He was a wonderful rider and Veronica had always said he was a good dancer. He gave Jennifer an embarrassed, pitying smile.

"I saw you there today," said Jennifer directly. "It was swell of you to stand by."

"Yes, wasn't it?" Hazel Taggart gave her abrupt, irrelevant laugh. "I was afraid it might look morbid but Chet wouldn't hear of anything else—would you, Chet?"

She was a little high already, Jennifer thought coldly. And she thought, *Maybe another drink will lead to something.* The butler came in with a glass and Taggart filled it from the shaker on the table.

"Don't be afraid of it," said his wife. "We're all drinking the same."

Taggart said, "Hazel!" in a warning growl.

The woman said airily, "Oh, I always take that precaution with Chet. It's no secret he's sick of me. And we've simply tons of that stuff about."

A forced smile contorted Taggart's heavy face. "She's upset. So she talks like that."

"I know," said Jennifer. She sipped at her glass, leaning back in her chair. "It's a shock. . . . Are you having one with me, Mrs. Taggart? Or may I call you Hazel? You and Veronica were such friends."

"Of course. Call me Hazel. . . . Yes, I'm going to miss your sister. She was a good deal more in my life than anybody knows." She had another sudden laugh at that, a laugh that sounded slyly pleased at her choice of words. "But maybe you'll take her place," she threw out, and looked, with what she seemed to feel was secret significance, at her husband who was standing, as if protectively, behind Jennifer. Hastily he moved away.

Jennifer felt that she was taking part in some outrageous play. "Thank you," she said mechanically. Now what should she say next? What would provoke some revelation?

If only she were clever, she thought. She felt inept. She was silent, looking down at her glass.

"Yes, I'll have another." Hazel Taggart held out her empty glass. "Oh, fill it up," she insisted, when her husband stopped pouring. "I need a pickup. So do you. You know," she said, turning to Jennifer, "I think Chet ought to go over and see his old friend, Roge. Nice how Roge took Mac's place, isn't it? I suppose he's home now?"

"I suppose so. I wouldn't know. I left Aunt Emma at the door. I haven't seen Roge since—since—" She did not finish. She said, "He went off with Mr. Larrabee and that Lieutenant Wayland."

"Oh, yes. Discreet questions." Hazel Taggart took a long drink of her cocktail, then said lightly, "I thought your Annie was too, too marvelous today! So anxious to defend 'the mister'—to let them know that Chet had been in the pantry, too."

Her big eyes roved in open banter to her husband, then back to Jennifer. "You know, I feel quite left out, not to have been in that pantry."

Jennifer thought, *I can't take any more of this.* And then she told herself, *You can take anything you have to.* This disorder was what she had been counting on. Aloud she said evenly, "I don't think the pantry is the only suspicious place. The tray was sitting out, when I left, where anyone could have got at it."

There was a silence. "Why, so it was!" said Hazel Taggart, very brightly. "Now let's think. Who went up to it, Chet? Didn't you give Veronica her drink?"

The man turned his haggard face toward her. "I took a glass. And then you did."

"Did I? How noticing you were! I remember Roge's saying he'd made her a highball, that gin wasn't good for her. Was it you or Roge who handed her that highball?"

"Stop talking about it." His face was livid. Then he said, forcing the harshness from his voice, "Jennifer came in for a spot of cheer."

"Cheer," said the woman. She looked down into her glass. "We could do with some of that, couldn't we? . . . But it seems so silly to pretend that nothing's happened. And I wish to God it hadn't!" she said in a violent, unsteady voice. "I never thought I'd hear myself say that. But I didn't know—"

Taggart looked at Jennifer. "She's tight," he said in a low voice. "You'd better go."

Hazel Taggart was saying, "Did I give her that glass? What did I do—?"

Jennifer got up. "Thanks for the drink. Good-by."

"Don't listen to him," said Hazel. "He's afraid I'll give him away. That's a joke, isn't it, Chet? Don't go. It doesn't matter who gave her the glass. . . . It doesn't matter she's dead. It doesn't change anything."

She wanted to stay, to listen. But Chet Taggart was shepherding her out. Slowly she moved down the hall.

"Oh, Jenny!" Hazel was calling after her. "If you find any of Chet's threatening letters about the house give them back, won't you? He never meant anything, you know."

Jennifer's knees were shaking as she got in her car. She thought, *She did it. Or he did and she knows it.* Violently she rejected that last idea. *She did and he knows it,* she substituted. They were like a pair tied together in damnation. Then her heart began to beat in wild relief. It was not Roge. Roge was innocent.

Inside her gate she stopped the car to think about it. Roge was innocent. You couldn't prove it, not yet, but you could let yourself believe it now. Now she knew. She had been right. That dreadful woman . . . She ought to telephone Nicholas Parr. But perhaps the police were listening in on their phone. They did, in stories. She could say it, anyway. What if they did hear?

She drove into the garage. Anson, the chauffeur, was just leaving. He was a nice young married man who lived somewhere across the tracks. He looked at her in an embarrassed way, his face growing red. Then he made himself speak. "I just want to say, Miss Jenny, I never found any bottle—"

"I know." She was surprised how quiet her voice was, how adult and soothing. "I know. That was just an idea, Anson."

She walked across the drive to the kitchen door. Annie and Delia were bustling about in belated preparation. "Them police and their questions!" said Delia bitterly but importantly.

"Poking into everything!" cried Annie, snatching the center of the stage from her. "Asking about everything that went on in this house. And about those bottles. In the first place we never found any, and, if we had, we'd no more put them in the pantry, without a by-your-leave, the way the mister's so particular about his drinks, than we'd—" Comparison failed her, but she finished dramatically, "And I couldn't say different if it was my life depended on it."

But it wasn't her life that might have depended on it, Jennifer thought. She said, mechanically, "No one wants you to say anything that isn't true."

Delia declared, "It was something she took at that luncheon."

"Or maybe it was something she got for a painkiller," said Annie. "The poor soul dreading pain the way she did and the baby coming and all and the store sold her something wrong."

"Now don't go on talking about it," scolded Delia. "Miss Jenny's got a queer look to her. It's been a dreadful day, Miss Jenny, dear. You let me make you a nice hot cup of tea."

"No tea," said Jennifer. "I'll just stretch out till dinner. Give me a ring, won't you?"

She went up the back stairs to her room and flung herself on the chaise longue, feeling suddenly at the end of her strength. A day of nightmare. First she had had to steel herself to go through with the inquest. She had told herself that once that was over. . . . And then—that arsenic. She could hardly take it in, at first. All she could think of, when Dr. Abbey was saying those dreadful things, was that Veronica's body had not been lying quietly at the mortician's, that they had been doing hateful things to her. . . . Queer, that it mattered at a time like this, but it had mattered; the horror of it had gripped her, had faced her with images of laboratories and men in white—perhaps her mind had clung to that horror to save itself a moment more from confronting the stark truth.

She had felt in a pillory, sitting there beside Roge with all those people staring at them. She had been so stunned and shocked that it had not been too hard to be quiet and unrevealing. Then reason had begun to move in her, implacably questioning. The doubt and fear had grown till she felt choking; till she was terrified that Roge would sense the tumult in her, would read what was in her mind.

Oh, poor Roge! Now she could let herself feel truly sorry for him. She wondered if he had divined any of the unease, the uncertainty that she had been in since Veronica's death. She had told herself then that it was outrageous to suspect Roge, that Veronica had been utterly wrong in her crazy accusations, but the suspicion had been there, kept hidden, looked at askance.

No, she thought, Roge couldn't have suspected what she felt, those first days, for he was so dazed himself. They

had been like two numb creatures, saying only the necessary things. Then this afternoon—? She had been all right
with him, she thought. She had been on guard not to betray herself.

Now she must tell him about the Taggarts. He would
hate to have Hazel Taggart's jealousy made public but he
must see that it was necessary. And now she could explain
the will to him. She could say frankly, well, semi-frank-
ly, that Veronica had thought he had cooled toward her
and was being dramatic and resentful. They would both,
tacitly, leave Burton out of it. Tod Burton had made all
the trouble, she thought bitterly. He had been mad about
Veronica. And Veronica had loved that. She had played
with him. As she had played with Chet Taggart. Veronica—but Veronica was dead. You must not blame the dead.

And you must stop thinking and get a little rest before
it was time to face people again. Now you could relax, or
whatever you called it when you didn't have to be afraid
your sister had been murdered by her husband but only by
a neighbor.

Sitting through the dinner was dreadful to her. Roger
King was silent and remote, his face shuttered against betrayal of feeling. Her aunt, excited and emotional, made
little spurts of distressed talk. Annie seemed to tiptoe
about the table. Toward the end of the meal King was
called to the phone. When he came back he stood a moment by his place as if he could hardly bring himself to
say what he had to say, then he forced out, "The police
have informed me that they are 'releasing the body' to me
tomorrow noon."

His voice put quotes about the ghastly phrase. He went
on, "We will have the burial in the afternoon. Private.
Utterly private."

"In the afternoon? Tomorrow afternoon?" Mrs. Taylor
stared at him, protesting. "Why, there won't be time—"

"That is time enough. And it was Lieutenant Wayland's suggestion."

Jennifer's tension grew tighter and tighter. They were advising Roge to bury his wife at once. Giving him a breathing space for that—while they made their investigations. . . .

"But why?" Mrs. Taylor gave that up. She said, "We must telephone Dr. Mobray at once. . . . It must be quiet, of course, but we can't shut out all our old friends—"

"No friends," said King. "I'll telephone Mobray." He turned and went out.

"Jennifer, you mustn't let him—after all, I am her aunt," said Mrs. Taylor, excitedly, "and I don't want it to look *furtive*—as if there was anything we were *ashamed* about. And old friends are a consolation. Why, there'd be only we three and my Susie and her husband—I don't believe Emily could get here. It would be—"

"Aunt, don't you see he can't bear to have people about? And if you ask any friends at all you have to have a lot. I don't want anybody, either," said Jennifer desperately.

"Well, that isn't the way Veronica would want it! And where does he plan—? I suppose that little chapel at the cemetery. That will be so *forlorn.*"

"What does it matter! Please don't argue. It's his wife. It ought to be as he wants it. Aunt Emma, don't you realize—" She stopped short as Annie brought in the dessert. "I can't eat any dessert," she said. "Let's go into the library and have coffee."

They went into the library. Would she ever drink coffee again, she wondered, without remembering that Veronica had been drinking coffee when she felt those cramps? She thrust the memory away. "I'm sorry if I was rude, Aunt Emma. I'm on edge, I know."

"I feel just as badly as you do, Jenny. Or almost," she qualified more gently. "Veronica was my sister's child and to have her die in this way. . . ." The self-protective excitement had gone out of Mrs. Taylor and for the first time she looked at her niece with something like bewilderment and question in her eyes. Then she pulled herself together. "But conventions have to be carried out, and I don't think Roger is in any state to see to them. I'll talk to Dr. Mobray myself."

She called the clergyman and Jennifer slipped upstairs.

She found her brother-in-law in the study on the third floor. It was a room that Mac had used, and it had never been done over, only added to. There was a typewriter and stand by the window and books on the shelves of the cabinets where Mac had kept old records and samples of ore. There had been a bag of nuggets there, Jennifer remembered. It had been a childish thrill when Mac had poured them into her hands. She hadn't thought of that for a long time. What had become of them? Jewelry for Veronica, she imagined.

Roger King was looking through the files of a cabinet with the helpless air of a man who has always had a secretary to hand him the right papers. "I can't find those papers," he told Jennifer. "About the lot. Larrabee must have them. I'll have to phone him."

The lot would be the McKenzie lot. There was no other. She wondered if Roge would put Veronica beside McKenzie, but she could not ask. She said, "He'll take care of it. There's time enough."

"They must be in his office."

"You can phone him later. I want to talk to you, Roge."

"Yes?"

She said determinedly, "First I want to tell you how sorry I am about that will."

She could feel the stiffening in him. She said quickly, "She shouldn't have done it. She was just being impulsive.

So I made a will, this afternoon, leaving it all back to you. So if I got run over tomorrow Aunt Emma wouldn't get it." She waited a moment, then ran on, "I'm not going to tell anyone yet—we don't want any more talk—and I told that Mr. Parr I wasn't going to tell even you. But, somehow, I wanted you to know."

Why was she saying this? Why was she going on with this thing now, when she did not suspect—? Or wasn't suspicion quite dead, was it a snake that lived on, as she had been told as a child that snakes lived, long after the head was cut off?

He was looking at her very oddly, she thought, but then, that was natural, she was saying odd things. He said, "You made a will?"

"Yes, but that isn't important. Roge," she said abruptly, "I know who did it—who killed Veronica."

She was utterly taken aback by the way he looked at her. There was sheer horror in his eyes. "You're wrong," he said violently. "You can't know. Don't say such things."

But she had said nothing yet. "I *will* say it," she insisted, bewildered. "It's Hazel Taggart. That's who it is."

The expression went out of his face, at least any expression that she could interpret. He got up and moved away, his back toward her. Very slowly he took a cigarette from a box on the table. "What makes you think so?" he said, over his shoulder.

"Because she was jealous of Veronica—let's face it, Roge." He did not answer and she went on, "She drinks. She'd do anything when she's worked up. And she's got the stuff about—she told me so." She told him how she had gone in for cocktails with the Taggarts and of Hazel's baiting her husband, and he listened carefully, turned toward her now. She finished, "She sounded as if she were putting it on Chet—when she said that about 'threatening letters.' I don't know what letters she could mean, do you?"

She waited a moment, then said, lamely, "But I expect Chet used to sound off when Veronica got bored with him." She hurried on, "But it wasn't Chet. It was Hazel. She almost owned it, the things she said. That she was sorry, that she hadn't known that she'd ever feel like that. That she 'didn't know.' She did it, Roge. And if she's questioned she'll break down."

He looked at her sternly, almost threateningly. "Don't say this, Jenny! Not to anyone. You don't know."

"But it's reasonable, Roge—"

"You know nothing. Keep out of it. Let the police do their own dirty work."

"It isn't 'dirty work' to find out. Someone did it." And he was the obvious someone. It was time he realized that, came out from that stiff barrier against reality. She insisted, her voice sharp with her determination, "Someone killed her."

"She killed herself."

She could only stare at him in disbelief.

He said, his voice less hard but with an inflexible quality, "I know. I thought she didn't. But it's quite evident that she did. Her—condition—had deranged her. She felt she was never going to live through her pregnancy and she was afraid of the pain and took this way out. We have to accept it."

After a moment she fought back. "But I don't accept it. I don't think it was like that at all. She's my sister and I want the truth—"

"Keep out of this, Jenny!" The sternness was strange in him. "If I feel she could kill herself you will have to accept it. That is my conclusion. I have told Wayland it was the only possible one—after thinking it over. . . . It would be criminal of you to drag in the Taggarts. I don't want any talk about them. Or about anybody else. . . . But I can't discuss this any more. She killed herself."

She came out of the room feeling dazed. All she could see was that Roge preferred the story of suicide to any scandal about Veronica. He must know he was running a risk himself but he didn't realize how great a risk it was. He seemed to think that if he told the police the conclusion he had come to they would accept that conclusion. He felt too immune. It showed he was innocent—surely a guilty man would have been evil enough to have jumped at a scapegoat—but it was a stupid innocence. The police wouldn't be put off like that.

She was in an agony of revolt and angry frustration. And then—she could hardly have told when she began to think of it but the memory wormed into her consciousness like one of those snakes to which she had been likening suspicion—then she thought of the way he had looked at her when she had said she knew who had killed Veronica. She saw his face, startled, aghast. What had he thought that she was going to say? His face had held a fearful suspense. Or was it so terrible to him that anyone had killed Veronica?

Aunt Emma was just turning away from the telephone. "I've got Louis Roberts for the organ. Roge never arranged about the music," she said, with a shade of triumph. "I thought 'Rock of Ages' and 'Lead, Kindly Light.' But if you have any choice, my dear—"

Jennifer shook her head mutely. *Lead, Kindly Light.* She could see herself and Roge and her aunt and her married cousin and her husband sitting stiffly. . . .

"I'm not any good at planning," she said. "I think, if you'll excuse me, I'll go up."

"Susan said she'd drive out tonight, if you wanted her. I told her I'd let her know if you did—that perhaps Roge would rather be alone."

"He would—I would."

"And tomorrow night would be better, anyway. There's always the letdown—"

Aunt Emma knew all about funerals. She knew all about what happened to people's feelings, afterwards. But she did not seem to realize what might happen to Roger King, if the police decided to make a sensation of it. *Something the chauffeur brought in.* Aunt Emma was a fool.

"If you'll excuse me," Jennifer said again, and went upstairs.

She could not sleep. She tried to put Roger King out of her mind and think, logically and practically, about the Taggarts. She was glad she had told Nicholas Parr about them. Not even Roge could stop him.

What had Hazel meant about "Chet's threatening letters"? She remembered that Veronica had once said amusedly that Chet Taggart, ordinarily so inarticulate, could spread himself on paper. Had Chet been angry about Burton? If there had been something from Chet in Veronica's desk Roge would have it. That she knew, because on Saturday night, when she had lain wakeful like this, she had suddenly thought of what the police had said about looking through Veronica's things and how awful it would be if they changed their minds, and she had got up and gone to Veronica's room. Roge had said he would sleep in the guest room.

But he had been at Veronica's desk. She had told him she came for a sleeping pill and had gone out.

If there had been any letter Roge had it. But Veronica was never one for keeping things.

Perhaps Chet Taggart had not always been such a tame bear. She remembered seeing Veronica and Taggart riding off together, in the old days, and Taggart had seemed another may on a horse, sure and confident. Mac sometimes cautioned, "Take good care of my little girl." Veronica, tall and beautiful, had hated to be called a little girl.

Another memory. Hazel Taggart, sliding an arm through Mac's, saying, "We old folks have to keep each other company." Turning the knife in her heart.

Veronica and Taggart. Veronica and Burton. It was Tod Burton who had changed her, Roge must hate him, yet Roge had never given a sign except once, in the cold tones of his voice, saying, "Is it absolutely necessary for you to—?" Then he had stopped, realizing she was within earshot.

Veronica never feared danger. Yet Veronica had been worried, those last days. Not about Roge—Roge was innocent. Those fantastic accusations were merely something Veronica had thought up to justify herself. . . . Had she been afraid of something ugly flaring up between Chet and Burton?

Suddenly Jennifer sat up in bed. That letter! The one Veronica had received on Saturday morning. The mail had come just as she and Veronica were driving out to the cleaner's for a dress of Veronica's, and Veronica had glanced through it, taken out one letter, and handed the rest back for the mailman to take up to the house. That letter she had looked at quickly and as quickly thrust it back into its envelope and pushed it into the glove compartment in the car.

When they had returned with the dress they had gone directly into the house and Veronica had not used her car that afternoon.

Jennifer got up. It was nearly midnight She put on slippers and a coat, moving quietly in the dark, then opened her door and stole out. The house was dark and quiet. Softly she went downstairs. On the lower floor she hesitated. Suppose the police were outside, watching, for fear Roge might make a getaway? It did not seem possible, but you never knew. The cellar door was the safest exit. It was in a corner, away from the service door, and the police probably didn't know about it.

She wished she had not thought of it, for now she had to make herself go that way and she hated going down into the black cellar. It was not much blacker than the kitchen, but was stranger to her and there was a dungeon feeling to it. It would be ironic to fall and break her neck and have Nicholas Parr think Roge had done it!

Carefully she went down the stairs and groped past wine closet and preserve closet and laundry room to the outer door, drawing back the bolts with difficulty. She wedged it open for her return, waited a moment to accustom her eyes to the night, then moved slowly across the back drive to the garage.

The door, sliding back, sounded loud in her ears and she stood still, listening, but all she heard now was the pounding of her heart, the thumping of blood in her ears, and she quieted and stepped inside. Veronica's car was at the right. The darkness was absolute after the pallor of the starlit night and she groped her way cautiously.

She opened the car door and the light that went on showed her blue leather and bright chromium. She opened the glove compartment, took out a flashlight and sent its beam into the interior, pushing aside gloves and cigarettes, and saw the crumpled envelope of stiff white paper. There had been something about the way Veronica had thrust that letter away, without a comment. . . . Breathing quickly, she drew it out and shut the compartment.

Why she slipped out of the car to read it she did not know—perhaps it was the feeling of Veronica's presence on that front seat, reading it herself. She felt ashamed to read it. It was an assertion that the dead had no rights, but she had to read it. She closed the car door softly and stood beside it in the dark, focusing the flashlight on the page she unfolded.

The sheet held only a few lines. Printed clearly. Unsigned. Her eyes took them in, then moved slowly over them again, as if refusing what they saw. Her mind refused it.

I will have not only you but my child. Either you tell him or I will tell him myself. My love, make up your mind without delay.

Her hands folded the words out of sight, thrust the paper into her coat pocket where she had stuffed the envelope. There was nothing now, she thought, that you could be sure of. She was not sure, even, whether it was Taggart or Burton who had sent Veronica that letter. No—not Taggart. How could Taggart claim "his child"? Taggart was married.

Absorbed, she had not been aware of any sound of footsteps. It was a nearer sound that brought her head up sharply, sent her gaze toward the open door of the garage. A brilliant beam from a stronger flashlight than her own struck into her eyes, blinding her.

"What have you got there? Hand it over."

That sharp, low voice she scarcely recognized. She said, "Roge—?" uncertainly.

The light played over her figure, freeing her vision and she made out a dark shape, instantly lost in the darkness of the garage as it came toward her. It was Roge and he was saying in that almost unrecognizable voice, "Give me that letter."

"It's my letter." Astonishing how steady the words were when her body was trembling. The one instinctive thought in her was that he must never see that letter. She said, "It's something I forgot—"

"Give it here!"

She edged back along the car. She said, "It's mine—" still retreating, hardly able to believe that this was Roge, demanding so fiercely. The light shot into her face again, blinding her, and then he made a lunge and gripped her arms, and both flashlights went clattering. Frantically she twisted back, terror pounding in her—he was not after the letter, he was after her. Oh, fool, fool that she had been!

She felt herself going down before his onslaught and the last wild thought in her was that she had left no revealing letter with Nicholas Parr, that no one would ever know what had really happened to her.

Somewhere water was running. It was over her face, flowing down her neck, filling her nose and mouth. She made a strangling, sneezing sound and struggled to move.

"Are you all right? Jenny, are you all right?"

There was a light bulb hanging from the ceiling, in the bright circle of a reflector. She stared up at it. Then she saw Roge's face over hers. He was kneeling by her, dabbing at her with a sopping towel. She said faintly, "Take—that—away."

"Are you all right?"

Now she could see the light again. She saw the walls of a room she recognized as the toolroom of the garage. She seemed to be lying on the floor, why, she could not think for a bewildered moment.

"I thought I'd killed you."

Abruptly, it came to her. The lunge. The fall. The terror of thinking he was killing her. But why? She said, confusedly, "What happened?"

"I slipped. I had hold of you and we went over. Oh, Jenny, I thought I'd killed you!"

Now it all came back. The letter. He had been struggling for the letter. He had not meant to kill her. The letter. She groped, found her pocket, fumbled in it. The letter was gone.

He was feeling her head. "Does it hurt? It isn't cut. I think you hit it after we went down. . . . Oh, God, Jenny—"

"It doesn't hurt." She sat up and he put an arm quickly around her.

"Take it easy."

"I'm not dizzy at all."

"That's the shock. I'll get Abbey—"

"Don't be silly. It's only a bump. It didn't put me out. I think I fainted."

"Fainted?"

She couldn't say, *I thought you were going to kill me.* She said, "I was all in. . . . Roge, did you read it?"

He got up and moved away, wringing out the towel in the toolroom sink, hanging it methodically upon a rack. His movements were slow and deliberate, prolonging every gesture as if he never wanted to turn to face her.

He had read it. Somewhere, even in his fright for her, perhaps before he realized what he had done, his eyes had skimmed those lines. She could see the dreadful words, big and black, carefully formed on that stiff white page.

I will have not only you but my child. Either you tell him or I will tell him myself. My love, make up your mind without delay.

She felt sick with shame. Veronica was her sister and Veronica had done this to him. She hunched up her knees, putting her arms around them, hiding her face in her arms. She said indistinctly, "I'm so sorry—so sorry—"

"I'm sorry you read it, Jenny. It wasn't yours."

"I thought of it in the night." She was crying wildly now. "I knew there was something funny about it when it came and I began to worry—"

"Don't, Jenny! Don't cry." He was kneeling beside her again, talking, unsteadily himself, to the top of her bent head. "It's all over now. It doesn't matter. . . . I knew she was hiding something. I didn't know how much. . . . I hoped it would all blow over. But it doesn't matter now. Don't ever speak of it."

She put out a hand blindly and he clasped it and held it. She choked out again, "I'm so sorry—so sorry—"

"I'm sorry I was so rough. I don't know what got into me. I saw you were after something she had hidden and I had to get it. I *had* to know. A man can stand just so much of this living in the dark."

She squeezed his hand. Confusedly she wondered what had happened to the bright, beautiful feeling there had been between them, between him and Veronica when they had married. . . . But it was all useless to wonder.

He was asking, "Are you really all right?"

"I'm cold." She was shuddering. 'This floor's cold and you soaked me." Her voice held the sudden humor that is the reaction from emotion. "Let's go in."

He helped her up. He said, "I'd better get the flashlights," and came back with both of them. "Mine's all right," he said, as if that mattered, and turned it on, switching off the lights, closing the door after them with careful softness.

She murmured, "How did you happen—?"

"I was up in the study. I couldn't sleep. And then I heard something in the garage. . . . Do you hurt anywhere?"

"Just bumps. . . . I left the cellar door open."

"I'll close it later. Now you must get to bed."

At her door she caught hold of his arm. "Roge, let me say one thing."

"Not a thing. . . . You get those wet clothes off."

The barriers were up again now. He was walling himself in with all the unhappy things, wanting no intrusions. She said desperately, "Roge, I *must!* Veronica never killed herself. Hazel—"

"Stop it! You know *nothing!* I won't have her brought into it!" Then the anger was gone and he said, wearily, "You'll have to accept it, Jenny. It was suicide. Don't make it harder for me. Good night."

Perhaps, she thought, Veronica had made him so unhappy that he could understand how Hazel Taggart could
poison her. Perhaps he could—not forgive her—but refuse
to punish her, to have the scandal aired. *But I am not like
that*, thought Jennifer passionately. *And I am not going to
let Roge live under suspicion. Even if he is not arrested he
will always be suspected. I can try to clear him. I can do that
much for him.*

Chapter Eight

After Nick left Nina Barrett he drove absently, with mechanical precision, his mind searching the things she had said. *I didn't see Mrs. King. . . . Mrs. King asked me. . . .* A hasty liar. A forgetful one. A frightened girl. The only times she rang true was when she was bitter or angry. The most revealing moment was the flare of anger when she suspected he had brought her to Pierre's to see if she was known there.

She had been there with King, of course. Jenkins was a smart name for King to use; the names were enough alike so if anyone spoke to him it could be passed off. Jenkins. J. R. King. Nevertheless; he would investigate any possible Jenkinses. He would take nothing more for granted.

At the nearest telephone station, armed with silver, he put in a call for Sharon, New York. He said, "Sorry, Dark Eyes," to the scrawled-over wall of the booth. In a little place like Sharon—and it seemed there was a Sharon—the operator might know how to reach the high-school principal. The operator did. "Mr. Lettich?" said a woman's voice. "All righty—I'll ring his house."

Mr. Lettich was home. Nicholas Parr said his firm was anxious to locate a Jerome Onslow who had graduated eight or nine or ten years ago. "Onslow—?" said Mr. Lettich. "I've only been here two years. But I've heard the name—"

"He's thought to be at Saranac now. One of your doctors might know. We'll be glad to reimburse you for your time if you can help us locate him. Could you phone us, charges reversed, tomorrow?"

There was a light in Abbey's house, and he stopped and Abbey handed him a paper. "Here's the date you asked for. The first time Veronica came in." The date was the fourteenth of November, two days before the date on the envelope to Burton. The evening papers were spread on the table. *Socialite Death Due to Arsenic* was one headline and *Arsenic Death Called Accident* was another. That was what Sally Waters called being discreet. There were pictures of Jennifer and Roger King snapped the instant after the revelation. *Hears Arsenic Caused Death.*

"You certainly made a production of it," said Nick wryly.

"Sorry for it," said Abbey. "Unavoidable. . . . Want to finish that chess?"

Nick shook his head. "Want to talk. In confidence. Hippocratic oath or what have you. I need help, Doc. I need an angle on Hazel Taggart."

He told of Jennifer's visit to him, of the will she had made, of her suspicion of Mrs. Taggart.

Abbey's blue eyes rested on him soberly. "I've been thinking of her," he admitted. "Of all of them. It has to be one of them. That's what makes it so difficult. People you know."

"Seventy-five per cent of murder is done by nice people, Doc. Not by the regular criminal class. Passion, love, revenge, self-interest—they happen on all echelons."

"Doesn't make it any easier when you know the nice people. . . . Any evidence against her?"

"Hell's bell!" said Nick explosively. "The case isn't a day old yet! I'm just reaching into the wide blue yonder."

"I thought I had something," said Abbey. "Remember the dishes in the sink? I happened to notice there weren't any cocktail glasses there—"

"You sure of that?"

"Oh, yes, I'm a noticing chap. I thought that might be significant. If the maids hadn't washed them, that meant that King—or X, the poisoner—had. But the maids had washed them. During dinner."

There was one glass they had not washed, Nick reflected. The cocktail glass on Nina Barrett's tray. That had not been downstairs during dinner.

Suddenly he stiffened. He felt as if a cold, a very cold finger was traveling down his spine. He said abruptly, "You know those maids, Doc?"

"Oh, yes. I've treated Annie—"

"I've got to talk to them. They'll be question shy, now, but if you'll take me over, vouch for me—"

Abbey reflected. "I could take you tomorrow afternoon. The family will be at the funeral. Veronica is being buried tomorrow. Wayland," said Abbey, "advised King to hold the service tomorrow. Hendrickson's idea."

"In a hurry, is he?" said Nick thoughtfully. "That looks bad for King. Hendrickson needs a conviction. All these racketeers that have got off—that hasn't done him any good. Nor smashing slot machines. But if he can get a nice, sensational, society conviction, his stock will go up. And King looks guilty as Judas. And I'll believe him guilty if I can prove he knew that Burton was Veronica's lover."

"Burton?" said Abbey, in his unsurprised way.

Nick told him about Burton. He told of Jennifer's admissions and the letter he had stolen from Burton's room. He told of Nolan's fantastic notion about Burton and his intentions toward Jennifer. Abbey looked very grave. He said soberly, "I hope Jennifer isn't—involved."

"*Involved?*"

"I mean, emotionally. With Burton."

"Lord, no! She was trying to camouflage—"

"He's attractive. I've seen him about."

"Preposterous," said Nick shortly. Then, hastily, "Here's another thing you can help me with, Doc. The whole thing is confused. The comings and goings about the tray and into the pantry. I've a cockeyed notion that if we could make them act it out again, go through all the motions, saying what they remembered saying . . ."

Abbey murmured, "Ordeal for the unstable? Of course the innocent generally appear guilty. But the guilty seldom manage innocence."

"That's it. One of them did it. He's thinking about it all the time. He's worried. The others were not watching him at the time, but now they'll all be watching. There might be some word, some movement, that was overlooked or forgotten that would come to light. Back me up in this, will you, Doc? Your word goes a long way at headquarters."

Abbey looked half-quizzical, half-skeptical. "I doubt if the mere performance—but the psychological strain . . . You're thinking of Hazel Taggart, aren't you?"

Nick nodded. "And of King. He might crack and give himself away. He blew up, remember, when you took Veronica's body away. And at the inquest when he found there'd been a post-mortem."

"That puzzles me, Nick. His astonishment at the inquest. A guilty man would have worried about a post-mortem, would have steeled himself for a revelation. King's outburst had the romantic touch. The horror of having his wife's body mutilated. We meet that, constantly, you know."

Abbey added, "And a guilty man would not have been so decided against suicide. . . . Unless he was being subtle."

They talked it back and forth. Nick put it all on the table, all except Nina Barrett. Abbey said gravely, "You are holding out too much from the police, Nick."

"I'll give it to them when I've got a case."

"But you can't withhold evidence—"

"I don't know that it's evidence," said Nick stubbornly. "It looks like evidence, but—"

"You're running a risk."

"Look! If I fill my hand I give it to them. If I don't fill it why should I expose King? That isn't justice. Maybe Veronica and Burton didn't have an affair, just a beautiful friendship. Maybe it was an affair but King didn't know about it. Maybe he knew but didn't kill her for it."

"That's for the law to decide."

"Would you let Wayland—or Hendrickson—make a diagnosis for you?"

"Medicine is not their field."

"I know. I know. But there is something in me that has got to be sure before I wreck a man. If I come a cropper, Larrabee can throw me out. But I've got to play it my way. Fish—and fish fast—in the troubled waters. I want to see those maids. I want to see the Taggarts. And I want to put over that cocktail-party scene. I've got a hunch—"

The morning papers were less discreet. *King Case Baffles Police. Highball Alleged Fatal.* Roger King was handled with kid gloves, but the suspicious items against him were all mentioned though not labeled suspicious. Just mentioned. The accident to the telephone in the library. The accident to the car on the way for help. The accident that Mrs. King was alone. A reference was made to Mrs. King's fortune, the assumption being that King would inherit. It was mentioned that he had mixed the "fatal highball."

The police had not given out about Veronica's will. When that hit the press King would be convicted in the public mind, Nick thought, reading the accounts as he ate a hasty breakfast. On the woman's page was a picture of Veronica dressed as a gypsy in black lace and curls, telling fortunes at a benefit last Christmas. The story beside it described how she had read her own fortune and flung the cards on the floor, crying out, "I don't believe it!"

Sally Waters had written that, and, knowing Sally, Nick did not believe it, either—it had the Carmen touch—but somehow it brought Veronica sharply alive again. He could see her in his office, tense and determined, tearing up the will. He could hear the brittle voice. *I don't want him to have a cent.*

He went early to the office and called an agency in New York that the firm had used before for confidential work. Worrell wasn't any ball of fire, but he was dependable and had good operatives. Nick asked for information about the relation between Roger King, when he'd been manager of the company in New York, and Nina Barrett, secretary.

He said, "Be as hush-hush as you can and see it doesn't get back to King. Keep our names out of it. If you get crowded to the wall remember that the investigation was started by Mrs. King some weeks ago. Mrs. King has died recently, but the firm is carrying on for the estate."

"Then Mrs. King does not want a divorce?"

"Mrs. King cannot use a divorce. Mrs. King is dead. But the evidence should be the same kind—gossip, rumor, facts if you can get them. The trail is six years old but if those two were playing round, some old gal in the company will remember, all right. And work fast. We need it now."

He put the instrument down. Sounds in the outer office indicated Miss Miller's arrival and he went in and presented her with the telephone book. There were columns of Jenkinses and he set her to sorting out the butchers and bakers and listing addresses possible for a prosperous-seeming young man.

She gave him a baffled look. "Is he supposed to have done it?"

"Done what?"

"Put arsenic in Mrs. King's highball?"

"Could be." Then he had a better idea about Jenkins. "Forget it," he told her. "Look up planes for Saranac."

"Saranac?" She gave him another look. "Don't you mean Arizona?"

Arizona was where Loomis was, with his breakdown. "Not yet I don't," said Nick. "Yours not to question why. But don't get on the phone for a few minutes."

He went into his office. Sally Waters would not be down yet but Ned Roper would and Roper had been in Basic with him. Nick got him on the wire and told him what he wanted and Roper said he'd get it for him. Then Nick called Mosley. "Your Chicago man reported yet?"

"Not yet."

"One night was enough to get that dope. He's stringing it out for the expense account. Call him up and call me back. I've got to move fast."

By the time Larrabee came in he had the report. But he did not begin with it; he began by telling Larrabee of Jennifer Mitchell's visit to the office and what Veronica had said to her and how she had discounted it and of her divided suspicions now. When he spoke of the will that Jennifer had made Larrabee showed alarm.

"That mustn't go on," he said sharply. "It's a patently open trick but there's no safe margin for a murderer. Not, mind you, that I believe in King's guilt. I believe nothing yet. I require evidence. But I would take no chances."

In his eyes was an uncomfortable admission of the chances he had taken in refusing to credit Veronica's wild words, and Nick looked back at him with the same uneasiness. "Right," he said. "I believe in King's guilt a lot more than I did yesterday. There was an affair between

Burton and Veronica. King could have guessed it—could have thought that the child was not his—"

He told of his descent upon Burton and the letter he had taken. He brushed off Larrabee's "Nicholas, I do not approve—" and produced the letter. Then he turned to the dates he had taken down from Mosley at the telephone. "She and King stayed in Lake Forest for the wedding, then came to Chicago and spent three nights at a hotel. King checked out and went home but she stayed on, presumably to shop. Burton was at the same hotel, had been there for ten days. She might have met him by chance. Certainly King didn't know about the meeting. Two nights after King left Burton changed his room to the one next to hers. They were there for ten days, to the middle of October."

He pointed to the last dates. "She was in Chicago again, early in December. You notice her letter said she couldn't make 'the Thanksgiving thing.' She went to this other hotel and Burton had registered there a few days earlier. His room was on the same floor. They were there for four days."

Larrabee looked at the list of dates Nick laid before him with an expression of profound distaste. "Astonishing folly," he said. "Difficult to understand. She and King were so obviously in love."

"Time marches on."

"That is undeniably her writing." He peered through his pince-nez at the letter again, then leaned back. "At least," he said drily, "she preserved appearances. No love nest."

Nick thought of a converted garage with a green-painted door and the lights in the upper windows going on over the lonely shadows of the garden and street. Veronica might have suspected, might have been in the mood to avenge her herself. Burton was dynamic. For his money,

Burton would be a better lover than King. Especially if King's heart was in a converted garage.

A long-distance call came for Nicholas. He listened, his face intent. He said, "Thank you—you're sure there are no expenses?" and hung up. He picked up the intercom and told Miss Miller, "Never mind about that plane to Saranac."

"Saranac?" said Larrabee.

"I thought of weekending there. A spot of quiet."

He had, he found, no intention of telling Larrabee at the moment what he had just learned. His instinct was to consider it. There was a Jerome Onslow, the principal of Sharon High School had reported, who had graduated nine years before. His mother still lived in Sharon. Jerome had gone to Kansas City after graduation and was there now. He was married and had two children. He had never been in Saranac.

"All that this indicates," said Larrabee, looking down at the letter and the paper of dates, "is that Veronica and Burton knew each other, intimately, before the alleged meeting in Florida. The next step is to discover what went on there, whether King showed resentment of Burton."

Nick was thinking of Jerome Onslow. A fiancé in Saranac had been a carefully thought-out device that would account for Nina's not marrying, not going out with the men her beauty attracted. He doubted if the name of the man had been thought out. Probably no one had asked—at least, not recently. The engagement was an accepted thing, a shadow in the background, something she did not talk about. But he had crowded her, taken her by surprise, and she had given the first name that had come into her head. Since she had just said the man was an old schoolmate, she had tossed out the name of a schoolmate.

A hasty liar. His verdict repeated itself. Part of his mind listened to Larrabee's report of Wayland's questions and

King's statements, another part focused on Nina Barrett. A hasty liar. But the bitterness, the bitterness with which she had said, "Oh, years and years!" was a real bitterness. She had hated the device, hated the years of surreptitiousness. When she had first told him that she was engaged her voice had hated what it was saying.

She had been King's girl. He felt as sure of it as if he already had a report from New York. It was highly probable that King was keeping her now. A secretary's salary would not furnish that little house, pay the rent, support a car. A quiet lovely in the background. One more incentive for King to free himself from a marriage that had become a liability.

Was she in this with King? They had been together in the house that afternoon and she might have urged him to free himself before Veronica did. No, King had already planned it, for he had the poison ready. But she might have known his intention or suspected it.

Why hadn't she left the house? Before King did. That would have been the sensible thing to do. But she wasn't a sensible girl. Perhaps she had told King she would go, then found herself unable to leave, held by fascinated terror, by the burning desire to know—there had been something strange, Nick's memory insisted, in the slow, hesitant, almost fearful way she had come down those stairs.

She had shrunk back in horror when he had said Veronica was dead. . . . That might have been the instinctive momentary horror of a sensitive criminal, an amateur, at the realization of the irrevocable fact.

"It is the matter of motive that is holding the police back," Larrabee was saying. "I am afraid—I am very much afraid—that you have unearthed the motive. And I feel you should give this information about Veronica and Burton to the prosecuting attorney at once."

"Not till I've talked to Jennifer."

"Hendrickson will be after you at any moment. He will want to know about that will. Once he starts asking questions—"

The telephone rang as he spoke. Nick jumped up and thrust his head out the door. "I'm not here," he told Miss Miller. "I haven't come in."

"It's Miss Mitchell."

"That's different. I'll take it out here."

Jennifer's voice sounded urgent and excited. "I'm so glad you're in. I overslept and I wanted to reach you the first thing. Maybe there's someone listening on the line but I don't care! They can all hear. *He* didn't do it."

"Huh?"

"I'm sure. Utterly sure now."

"Well—that's fine," said Nick, blankly. "How do you know?"

"I can't tell you over the phone."

"When can I see you? I'll come out—"

"Oh, no. I have to get ready—the—the funeral is today. . . ."

"I see. . . . I'm sorry. . . . What time is the funeral?"

"Two-thirty."

"At the cemetery?"

"Yes. Just for the family."

"May I see you afterward? Alone? I'll park outside your gate and you come out as soon as you can."

There was a moment's silence. "Yes, I guess it would be better that way," she said a little hesitantly. "The important thing is—not to lose time." She said significantly, "*They* have the stuff in their house. *She* told me so last night. I was over there."

"You be careful," he said, not lightly now.

She gave a faint laugh. "Being careful wouldn't have got me anything!" Then she told him, "The only thing I don't understand—"

"Yes—?"

"*He*—oh, Roge, I mean—seems to think it's suicide. He *wants* to think it's suicide. But I don't. So you go right ahead."

Nicholas went back to Larrabee and told him, "That was Jennifer Mitchell. She wanted me to know she was absolutely sure now that King didn't do it. She couldn't tell me why over the phone. But she urged me not to waste time. Meaning to concentrate on the Taggarts. She said that *they* had the stuff in the house, that *she* had told her so last evening. She was over at their house. She added that King believed, or wanted to believe, it was suicide but she did not. And I was to go right ahead."

He asked, ironically, "Now do you want me to walk over to the prosecuting attorney and tell them all about Veronica and her boy friend?"

Larrabee considered. "What proof can she possibly have?"

"I'm seeing her this afternoon, after the services. I'll know then."

"She is an important client," said Larrabee thoughtfully. "You'd better stay out of the office, Nicholas, until you've seen her."

"Right. I'll be going hither and yon. A fact here, a fact there. Pieces in a jigsaw puzzle. . . . But this word from Jennifer doesn't fit into the picture I was making."

"Suicide," mused Larrabee. "Suicide would be an excellent solution."

"The murderer would love it."

He drove to the paper and Roper had the prints ready. Two were blurred but one was clear and sharp, a group picture, taken two weeks before at the Country Club, labeled *Returning Socialites*. King was in golfing clothes, looking very handsome, and Veronica, beside him, was smiling into the camera. With them was a girl Nick did not know, her face turned toward Tod Burton.

He took it to Pierre. Pierre was busy, bustling about a women's club luncheon, but Nick drew him aside. He held out the print. "Is that Mr. Jenkins? My rival?"

Pierre studied the picture carefully. He said slowly, "Yes, that is Mr. Jenkins." He put his finger on the picture of Tod Burton.

Nick stared blankly at the print. He had the sensation of being suddenly unhorsed in mid-gallop. He heard himself saying, with honest chagrin, "Oh, Lord. . . . I've got competition, all right. . . . Well, thanks a lot."

"It is nothing," said Pierre. He hurried away.

They could, Nick reflected, over his own luncheon, have met in King's office. They must have met soon after Burton came, for they had been in the restaurant more than once to have Pierre greet her with such recognition. Of course she was a girl you didn't forget. . . . Had it been a piece of surreptitious fun, kept secret for fear of Veronica's jealousy or King's jealousy? It could have been, on Burton's part. He remembered his own quick impulse to take out that dark-eyed girl. Or could it be that Burton was curious about her, wanting to get something on King? And she could have been curious about Burton, wanting to get something on Veronica.

At any rate, his pretty theory about Jenkins as a nom de plume for King was down the drain. Worrying, to have been so wrong. He might be wrong about her having been King's girl. She had invented a sick fiancé—yes. She had lied about Jerome Onslow's being the fiancé. She had lied about seeing or not seeing Mrs. King. That might have been simply not to get involved. She lived better than the average secretary, but she might have something of her own, or be a darned good manager. He set up the alternatives, then brushed them aside. He'd know what to think when the report came from New York.

The day was bright and warm. The leaves on the oaks along the side wall were still tight-furled buds but the grass was a brilliant green in the spring sun, the bright emerald of new pasture grass. A colored boy was uprooting early dandelions with a plunging stick and a colt that was following him on teetery legs sheered off skittishly at each plunge of the gadget.

Nicholas Parr and Chet Taggart were at the stable door. When Nick had appeared at the house the butler had told him that Mrs. Taggart was resting but Mr. Taggart was at the stables, so Nick had gone there and introduced himself. Taggart had been about to go for a ride. This was the hour that Veronica was being buried and a ride, Nick thought, was as good a way as any to make yourself forget for a moment what was happening.

Taggart had seemed to welcome Nick's advent. He had promptly shown him through the stable, quite the most beautiful Nick had seen, with rounded corners of walnut and brass, cement gutters, box stalls bedded with sweet straw, wide windows carefully screened, and an electric trap for flies at the door. Some early winged thing ventured in while Nick was there and a shrill "ping" marked its demise.

"*That* will never both my beauties," Taggart had commented with satisfaction, fondling a satin smooth head that was reaching over a stall door.

Nick had tried to study him, this big, sturdy man, in riding clothes that gave out an aroma of horse and leather; he had scrutinized the square, heavy face that seemed to him an infinitely sad face, and the dark, deep-set, uneasy eyes. But how, Nick thought, can you judge a man when you see him at his best with the animals he loves? Taggart's hands were gentle on the horses, his voice soft to them, often silly-sounding in its fondness.

Now at the door, Nick said, "I shouldn't have taken up so much of your time but—"

"Nothing else to do."

"What I dropped in about was that chap Burton."

Taggart looked at him impassively and waited.

"You were intimate with the Kings so I can put the cards on the table." Briefly, with what he hoped was an air of frankness, Nick explained his position. He said, "If there was any trouble between King and Burton, we, as counsel for Miss Mitchell, would like to know it before the police stumble on it. It's hard to get anything out of King even for his own protection."

"Protection?" Taggart's heavy voice seemed examining the word curiously.

"He's in a very difficult position."

Taggart looked off. "I don't see that."

"I'm afraid the police do."

"Don't they have to prove possession of the stuff?"

So Taggart had been giving some thought to it. Nick told him, "It could have been obtained while he was out. I mean, that's what the police would say. Or he might have had access to some of yours."

Taggart said nothing to that. He merely asked, after a short pause, "What's Burton got to do with it?"

"Wasn't he what they delicately call 'attentive' to Mrs. King?"

Taggart's expression did not change. "In a social way, perhaps," he said carefully. "Naturally. He was interested in Jenny, you know. Her sister. He was taking Jenny out."

"How did he and King get on?"

Taggart's silence seemed considering that. "Fine," he pronounced. His voice had a firm heartiness. "King liked him fine. He was a little old for Jenny," he said carefully, and Nick had the feeling that every word had been thought out, was being set down by a hard effort of the will, "but that was up to Jenny." His eyes moved to Nick, then stared doggedly ahead. "That's the way things were."

Another silence stretched between them. The mare Taggart had been about to ride was pawing restively and the colored boy who held her made soothing noises. Nick said finally, "Would you say the Kings were happy together? I have to look into this, to have the answers ready when the police start asking."

"Nothing to ask about."

"Afraid there is. Mrs. King died of arsenic, you know."

Taggart's face registered no reaction that he could see. His deep voice said, as if reciting by rote, "She took it for her own reasons."

"You think she killed herself?"

"Nothing else to think."

"There's no evidence of intention. And it seems the last thing on earth that she would take to kill herself."

The last thing on earth.

Taggart muttered, still staring off into space, "She must have done it. People do queer things. You can't explain them." Then he said painfully, "She was a sick woman. Having that baby. She wasn't herself."

So Taggart wanted it believed suicide. And King was saying it was suicide. Nobody but Jennifer wanted to know the truth.

A stableboy had edged out the door behind them, waiting his chance to approach, and Taggart spun round as if glad to end the talk and exploded, "What the devil are you hanging about for?"

The outburst did not bother the boy. He grinned and asked, "Boss, kin you change this folding money so's I kin have four bits?"

"Four bits?" Taggart sent his hand into his pocket and it came out with silver. "Let's see this folding money of yours," he said, suddenly jocular. "Sure it's all right?"

The boy's grin widened, as he handed over the bill. "You gave it me. Las' Sat'day."

"Okay." Taggart examined his silver. "Four bits and half a dollar. How's that?"

"That's fine, suh."

"Here's the four bits." Taggart dropped them in the outstretched palm. "And here's the half."

He held it out. Then it was gone and there was nothing in the boy's palm and nothing in Taggart's big fingers that were outspread above it. "You must have dropped it," Taggart said, and the boy stooped and looked about, then glanced up, half-grinning, half-bewildered. "You didn't give it, boss—"

"Why, so I didn't! What do you know about that?"

The half dollar was shining between Taggart's fingers; he made a gesture of tossing it and it disappeared. The boy stared. Taggart burst out laughing and tossed again and the coin lay bright in the pink-brown palm that closed tightly over it. Both of them laughed. The boy ducked back into the stable and Taggart turned to Nick, smiling a little sheepishly.

"It always gets them. Kid stuff."

"You're good," said Nick. His voice was carefully casual. *He used to do tricks for me.* Jennifer had said that. "Well, I'll be getting along. Got to talk to the maids over there," and he nodded in the direction of the King house.

The momentary boyishness vanished from Taggart as memory repossessed him. He stared out toward the King house, at the stretch of roof between high trees, all that was visible at this distance, and his face had a terrible sadness. Then what Nick had said seemed to reach in to him. He turned and looked at Nick, with slow, careful attention.

"Don't stir things up," he said, in a low, harsh voice. "Keep out of it." He looked at Nick a full moment more, as if to be sure he understood, then raised his hand in a half salute of farewell and moved to his horse. He swung himself lightly up and trotted off along the bridle path beneath the oaks toward the woods. Nick watched him, then moved slowly toward his car on the drive. That harsh, low voice. . . . There had been something of warning in it, something of apprehension. . . . Before his eyes, like an image retained on the retina, lay the picture of the coin in the pale brown palm. . . .

He was so absorbed that he would have got into his car without noticing the woman if she had not waved to him. She was ahead of him on the drive, a woman in a gray flannel skirt, and a flamingo pink sweater vehemently at odds with the bright hair. He moved toward her. "Mrs. Taggart! I'm Nicholas Parr."

"I know." Her big eyes, flecked with brown and green, examined him. "That fool butler should have called me. I was reading a detective book and said not to be disturbed, but he should have known—a young man like you—when we're so short of dinner men, these days. . . ." She gave her sudden, disconcerting laugh. "What's Chet been doing? Entertaining you in the stable?"

"It's a beautiful stable."

"And you're Veronica's lawyer. Or Jenny's, I should say. What were you trying to make Chet tell you?"

No fool, this woman. Not when she attended to anything. Nicholas Parr's nerves tightened as a man's hand might tighten on a wheel he was guiding. He said, "It was really you I came to see."

"That's flattering," she said mockingly.

"You were an intimate of Mrs. King's."

The face, freshly and brightly made up, smiled at him. "Yes?"

Nicholas had an uncomfortable feeling of being transparent. He abandoned any attempt at a subtle approach.

He said bluntly, "King now thinks that she committed suicide. Do you? Had you noticed any little signs—?"

"You sound like the police. They were here this morning, asking all sorts of things."

Taggart had not mentioned that. "Did your husband see them, too?"

"Of course he saw them. But he could not tell them about any little signs, could he? He's *Roge's* friend, you know. Only saw Veronica in a crowd. So, naturally, all he could say was how happy Roge was with Veronica. That ought to clear things up, don't you think?"

"It's a help," said Nick.

"Of course it would be more helpful if Roge and I got together on a nice little story—that's what you want, isn't it?"

"It's not like that. We represent Jennifer Mitchell and Jennifer wants nothing but the truth."

"Jennifer!" she said violently. Her fingers twisted in the strand of pearls about her neck. "Barging in like a—" She checked herself. "She's a rash child," she said lightly. 'Truth's a big order. And what difference does it make? It can't bring Veronica back. . . . There was an accident. Or Veronica had a mad moment and decided to end it all. Everyone has those moments."

"But did you know she had them? Did she ever—I mean, you have some of that Fowler's Solution on your place. You might know if she had access to it?"

Hazel Taggart surveyed him with cool amusement. "What am I supposed to do? Show consternation because we have the stuff? No, Mr. Parr, charming and naive as you seem, I am not buying that one. Of course we have it. I told that fat policeman and his little notetaker that we had it. Of course she could have got at it—it's in the greenhouse. Of course Roger King could have got at it. But I know nothing about it. I am baffled and grieved. I am *desolate*," the jeering voice insisted while the shrewd eyes smiled, "that I can tell you nothing, Mr. Parr. But I'll gladly remember you when I am in a dinner-giving mood."

Nicholas smiled at her. "You and your husband should get together."

The painted face was very still. "What do you mean?"

"You aren't sure it was suicide. He seems very sure."

"Chet's very logical," she said lightly. Whatever it was that had tensed her for a moment had passed. "He's right, of course. Since it wasn't one of us, it has to be suicide, doesn't it? Accident is really implausible. So of course she killed herself. Only she never hinted to me that she was going to do it, so I can't help you out there, even for Roger King." She added airily, "Just a bystander."

Abbey was waiting in his car inside the King gates. "I'm leaving a letter for Jennifer," he said, as they stood before the door, waiting for it to be opened. "I'm sorry about yesterday. But she must realize I had no choice. Now about these girls," he said quickly. "I'll start you off with them, then I'll have to leave. They're nice girls, both of them, but I gather the talk of a wrong bottle in the pantry has got them defensive. I'd go easy on that."

"I'm not asking about that. And not trying for anything about the Kings' personal life. I'm checking the sequence of the cocktail party." He added, "I've just been over at the Taggarts'. Gathering impressions."

"Any useful ones?"

"That woman knows something," said Nick. "Or thinks she does. . . . Or wants you to think she does."

"She's a sick woman," said Abbey. "Mentally, she—" He broke off as the door opened and said cheerfully, "Good afternoon, Annie. Glad you're here."

Sitting in the King kitchen reminded Nick of Saturday night, when he and Abbey had sat there, drinking coffee, with Veronica dead upstairs. Now the kitchen had a different air, no dishes stacked in the sink, everything bright, the sun shining in the windows, but it was hard to get away from the feeling of what had happened in this house. Hard not to think of that bedroom, and the bright hair on the pillow, and the sickish smell of chloroform. Now he sat in the dining corner of the big kitchen with Annie Kelly and Delia Walsh and explained, in the pleasant, easy way that was his, what it was he wanted.

"I'm trying to get it straight in my mind. I know the police have bothered you with questions but I'm not after any gossip about Mr. and Mrs. King. I just want you to go over the cocktail part of it once more."

"It's the way I said," said Annie. "The mister came out in the pantry—"

Once started, she ran on, and Nick listened, his eyes narrowed, seeing picture after picture dropped in place before him like a sequence of slides. King mixing the highball, then starting on the Martinis. Annie coming in and out, bringing ice cubes and lemons and plates of canapés, olives, and nuts and toasted crackers with cheese.

"Nothing fancy. We hadn't expected the Taggarts," Delia interposed.

There was a picture of Taggart coming to the pantry to say his wife had dropped in and to make drinks for one more. "She'd take plenty," said Annie.

Nick asked, "Did he stay long?" and Annie reflected a moment. "Oh, not so long. He said that about his wife and the mister said, 'The more the merrier,' in a nice way. Mr. Taggart, he was sort of grumpy like. He asked how long Mr. Burton was going to stay in town and Mr. King said he didn't know. Mr. Taggart acted as if he was going to say something more but he didn't—he just hung around a moment looking glum, then he went out."

There was a picture of Jennifer coming in to say her zipper was stuck and would Annie help her. "It was a new dress," said Annie, "one of those short dancing dresses." Nick remembered the dress as a rustling of silk and a laciness very off the shoulders. He could see her in its incongruous gaiety, confronting Nolan and Wayland.

Annie went out then into the kitchen but Jennifer had not followed so Annie had stepped back into the pantry, thinking Jennifer might want the dress fixed there. But Jennifer went into the kitchen with her. The zipper was stuck, a thread in it, and by the time she had it working and hurried back to the pantry Burton was leaving it with the tray of drinks, and would not give it up, so she had followed with the canapés, and Jennifer had come after her.

That was when Burton had been "comical like" as Annie said, with his parody of a stiff British butler. "I couldn't keep my face straight," she said. "And Miss Jenny was laughing, ever so. He made everybody laugh. I didn't know he had that much fun in him." She seized on the drama of it. "To think how we was laughing, the missus as hard as anybody, and the death already in her. . . . She'd took some pain killer," she said pointedly to Nicholas.

He smiled at her. "You have a very clear memory."

"I can see a thing that happened like it was in the movies," she acknowledged.

Delia remarked, her rosy face looking a little miffed, "I've got my mind so set on my work I don't pay so much attention to what goes on around."

"It was you," said Nick to her, "who let Mrs. Taggart in, wasn't it?"

"I did. Annie was acting that busy—"

"How did she seem? I mean, was she in a bad temper, or anything?"

"That one!" said Annie, snatching back the role of reporter. "You never know what she's like the queer way she acts."

"She's no worse than a lot of others I could name," said Delia, warmly. "I know what you think of her, but I know Margaret Murphy who's cooked for her for ten years and there couldn't be a nicer lady to work for, never fussing about the bills, never buying anything but the best, nothing but butter served in that house, and when Margaret's sister had the accident and no money saved it was Mrs. Taggart paid her bills and no call at all but her good heart. So I say, there's something to be said on her side, and a long time it's gone on."

Annie tossed her head. "You can stick up for her all you like, but I say she's a queer one." She turned to Nicholas with a quick smile of apology. "Delia and I can fight about the Taggarts any day," she said, her cheek dimpling. "But that isn't what you came to hear, is it? Is there anything else you'd like to be asking?"

"Well, I really did want to know if she was in a bad temper. It looked a little like it, her running in like that, after her husband. And you say he was—grumpy like."

He thought a quick caution came into both girls. "She sounded all right," said Delia carefully. "She went ahead to the library calling out to them in a joking way. Something about was her 'darling husband' there. Making light of it."

"Where did she leave her coat?"

"Why, she wore it in on her. She went that fast."

"I was just wondering about her. I can't make her out myself," he said conversationally. Then, idly, "With all you were doing how did you ever find time to run up with that cocktail for the secretary?"

The girls looked at each other as if surprised at this new tangent. "We didn't take it up," said Annie. "She comes down for her tray, whenever she stays for a meal. Not to give trouble," she added with satisfaction.

"And you'd saved her a cocktail. That was pretty nice. You always do that for her?" Nick was smiling.

Annie smiled back. "We do not. She asked for it, herself, or rather, the mister asked her would she like one and she said she would."

Nick's face did not change. His voice kept it light, kept it easy. "How did he happen to ask her?"

"Oh, he could do no less, him coming into the kitchen asking for the ice cubes and finding her there—she'd come down early for her tray and the roast wasn't done. She said she'd like a drink," said Annie, the urge of total recall sweeping her on, "and she went into the pantry with him to get it."

The picture stayed motionless in Nick's mind, like a slide stuck in the projector. Nina Barrett and Roger King together in the pantry.

"And then she went straight upstairs with it," Delia supplied. "I thought that was a funny thing to do—as if we'd expect her to share it. She came down again for her tray while we were serving dinner."

That was another picture. Nina Barrett slipping up the backstairs with a cocktail glass. But the picture did not give him what was in her face. . . .

"How did she happen to be staying for dinner? Who asked her?"

"Oh, it was raining cats and dogs and the chauffeur not on duty. She didn't come in her car—she came out from the office on the electric. It wasn't raining so much just after lunch. . . . The mister must have asked her. She said something about staying the night and I'm surprised she didn't. The little bedroom off the study is always ready."

He had been a fool. He had been a fool every step of the way. He had found her out in one lie after another and yet he had not believed that she had been lying about not being downstairs. He had checked up on it, yes, but he had hoped—he knew now how very much he had hoped—that her passionately reiterated statement had been truth.

There was no truth in her. And it wasn't going to be easy explaining to the prosecuting attorney that he had concealed her presence in the house last Saturday evening. He was on thinner ice than he had known.

Aloud he said pleasantly, "Thanks so much. . . . Please tell Miss Mitchell you've been a great help, getting it all straight in my mind."

Outside by his car he stood thinking, his hand motionless on the door handle, while his mind roved over the implications of the revelation. King *could* have concealed Nina's presence in the pantry out of decency, a refusal to involve a girl he believed—or knew—to be innocent. A girl for whom he felt responsibility, one who had invented for him a Jerome Onslow. But the picture was of two furtive, whispering conspirators. . . .

A car was coming up the drive. A low-hung convertible, the top down. It stopped behind his car and Tod Burton slid out from behind the wheel and, after a glance ahead, walked toward him. Nick noticed again his erect litheness, his distinctive grace of carriage that reminded him of a bullfighter advancing into the arena.

Burton said, with his air of mockery, "Look who's here! You waiting for Jennifer, too?"

So he was carrying on the game of being Jennifer's intimate. It couldn't be easy for him. It couldn't be easy to come to this house again.

"Just leaving," said Nick.

"Snooping around in absentia, eh?" Burton laughed, a hard, humorless sound. "How's the detecting business?"

"Fine," said Nick. "Never a dull moment. But there are snags."

"That's too bad."

"There's one you could clear up."

"Yes?"

There was that matter of dining out with Nina Barrett. Nick could not resist getting a rise out of him.

"How come you like to dine with brunettes?"

Twice before he had seen Burton's face change violently. He had expected no such reaction now, nothing but a flash of resentment at being caught out, but Burton turned actually livid, the white scar on his cheek standing out like mother of pearl. The pupils of his suddenly intent eyes dilated so that the gray iris made a thin circle about the black. He took a step nearer Nick and said softly, but with an edge to his voice as thin as a knife edge, "What gave you that—idea?"

"Other people go to restaurants."

"To whom have you mentioned this?"

"I haven't mentioned it."

Some of the astonishment he felt was in his voice. Burton continued to eye him as if probing his sincerity, then, abruptly, his manner changed and the flippant lightness was back.

"It's not important," he said. "Just a gag. A stunt. Think nothing of it."

Chapter Nine

It was horrible to have a photographer on the next lot, pretending to be a mourner putting flowers on a grave, then pulling a camera from the flowers, but anger can stiffen you against grief, Jennifer Mitchell discovered, and she stood straight and proud-looking between her aunt and brother-in-law, holding so hard to her indignation that the clergyman's words did not seem real to her and it did not seem real that it was Veronica, the shell of lovely, unpredictable Veronica that they left lying beneath the flowers.

The photographer was something to talk about on the way home. Roger King did not talk; he sat in front beside the chauffeur, but Aunt Emma and her daughter, Susan, and Will Tenning, Susan's husband, were voluble about the outrage.

"I don't see how a decent editor would permit it."

"They love it," said Susan. "The public loves it."

Susan did not really care, Jennifer thought, staring out the window. She only thought she did. Susan was getting a terrific kick out of the sensation and the scandal for the high and mighty Kings. Aunt Emma had loved Veronica, in a way, as her sister's child, but Susan had not loved her—she had been secretly proud to be related to Mrs.

Roger King but she had envied her and been affronted not
to be included in her gay parties.

"Oh, well, it's all over now," said Will Tenning philo-
sophically. "There will be a picture tonight but tomorrow
it will all be forgotten."

Jennifer thought, *Oh, no, it won't.* This was no ordinary
death. This was murder. The prosecuting attorney had
suggested this hurried funeral. He was merely waiting—

It might be a good thing to go to see the prosecuting
attorney. She'd talk to Nicholas Parr first and tell him
about last night and then she, or the two of them, would
confront that mysterious thing, "the law." It would not be
so hard to talk about Hazel Taggart's jealousy as it would
have been to talk about Roge and Tod Burton. She could
say, "Irrational jealousy," and "unbalanced through drink."
Roge would not like it, but there was no sense, Jennifer
thought decisively, in sitting tight and waiting to see what
happened. Being arrested was what would happen to Roge.
The police would not swallow any suicide theory now.

Nicholas Parr had said he'd park outside the gates and
she had intended to slip out, later, and join him; she had
not expected to see him standing by the gates, halting
the limousine. He looked embarrassed, but he explained,
half to her, half to them all, that he was anxious to see
her alone and that Tod Burton was waiting for her at the
house.

She felt dismay. She looked quickly toward her brother-
in-law, who turned away, staring ahead. She said hastily,
"Aunt Emma, will you and Susan take care of Tod? Roge
ought not to be bothered with people."

"But, Jenny, you're not getting out? Your head—"

"It's all right," she said impatiently. "It doesn't ache. . . .
Tell Tod I had an appointment," she said, stepping down
beside Nicholas.

She looked after the car as it went up the drive. "I wish Tod would stay away," she said under her breath.

"The show must go on." Then, more seriously, Nicholas Parr said, "It can't be fun for him, either."

She hadn't thought of that. She hadn't thought of Tod Burton's feelings at all. And she didn't intend to, she told herself; she had quite enough to cope with besides Tod Burton's illicit grief. She walked with Nicholas to his car and sat on the front seat with him and he lighted cigarettes for them both. She drew on hers gratefully. Then she began to talk.

She started with her visit to the Taggarts', trying to remember every word. "She did it," said Jennifer firmly, "and he knows it. And I think she knows he knows. That's why she's bedeviling him so, like a cat with a mouse. Knowing he'll never give her away. Throwing out those queer things about 'Chet's threatening letters.' They sit there like two condemned creatures waiting for the tumbrils. There's an awful feeling about them, something hopeless and help-less—"

"I saw her this afternoon," Nicholas said. "There was nothing hopeless or helpless about her then. She struck me as exceedingly shrewd and competent."

"That's when she's on her toes. But when she's down—or high—you can see into her. . . . I'm terribly sorry for poor Chet."

"He's got his horses." She thought Nicholas Parr was rather dry about Chet Taggart. He demanded, "What next?"

She told him, hurrying through the talk in the study to get to the scene in the garage. She explained, "It was what Hazel Taggart had said about threatening letters that made me think this letter Veronica had left in her car might be something. So I went down—"

It made quite a story, she thought, that lonely-feeling excursion through the dark basement to the garage. Nicholas Parr interrupted once. "Is that what you call being careful?" She owned, "I wasn't very bright, was I? But it's a good thing I did it," and she went on to the moments in the garage, when she had taken out the letter Veronica had left in the glove compartment of her car, and the panic she had been in when Roger King had come out of the dark and demanded it.

"I wouldn't give it to him," she said, "and he went for it. And I thought, I was so worked up that I thought he was going for me—that my corny little plot had worked. You see, I'd told him about my will up in the study. It was all in a flash—he grabbed me so hard we both slipped and went over and I fainted. And the next thing I knew he was drowning me with a wet towel and so worried about me— he thought I was out because I'd bumped my head."

She stopped to catch her breath and looked at Nicholas Parr. "He wasn't pretending," she said earnestly. "He was being himself. Human and sorry and worried. I was so ashamed of what I'd been thinking—"

And ashamed for Veronica. But she wasn't going to tell Nicholas Parr about that. She thought of herself on the floor of the toolroom, her head on her knees and Roger King's painful voice, *I'm sorry you read it, Jenny.* She could see that hateful letter with its bold, printed words.

She was puzzled by the way Nicholas Parr looked at her. By the way he said, "Is that all?"

"Isn't it enough?" she said. "It made me sure of him. You wanted to know how I felt about him—you said yesterday you'd counted on knowing that. Now I'm sure."

"And that's all that convinced you? That he knocked you down and was sorry for it?"

"Why, don't you see? If he'd wanted to kill me it would have been the perfect chance. He could have put me in the car with the engine running and everyone would have thought I'd come down in a fit of despondency over Veronica. I'd already told him about my will. It was the perfect chance for him."

"They'd have found the knock on your head and known you'd been hit and shoved into the car."

"He could have put me so it would look as if the fall had hurt my head."

"He could. But all that this shows is that he did not want to hurt you now. It doesn't offer a shred of proof that he did not kill your sister."

"But it does! The way he acted proved it to me. I know he was sincere. He's what I always felt he was, kind and good."

"That's fine!" She felt the resentful warmth coming into her face, then Nicholas said quickly, "No, I'm not being sarcastic. I respect convictions. But what the law demands is evidence. Being kind and good after he'd knocked you down to get a letter away from you isn't evidence that he didn't kill your sister for her money. And from jealousy."

"But he wasn't jealous! I mean, he didn't know how serious it was until—" She stopped, angry at her inadvertence. Nicholas said instantly, "That letter? What was in it?"

"I can't tell you that."

"Was it from Tod Burton?"

"I think it was. Yes, I'm sure it was."

"What did it say?"

"I can't tell you. It was Veronica's letter."

"God give me patience with you," said Nicholas. "You ask me to solve a case and hide the evidence."

She said stubbornly, "The letter had nothing to do with Veronica's death. Hazel Taggart killed Veronica. Why do you have to pry—"

"Listen!" he said. "I already have a letter of your sister's to Burton. After you left the office yesterday I went to see him and there were a lot of letters in your sister's writing on his bed under a dressing gown—he'd been going through them when Nolan arrived. I stole one. It was written to him in November. *November.*"

The implication went home but it wasn't any news to her now. She demanded, "What did it say?"

"That she wanted to see him, that she would make some plan. But that's not all. I set a Chicago dick to work and I have the dates when they were registered at hotels in Chicago—not together, but on the same floor. In October, when I think she first met him, and again in December. They didn't meet in Florida."

"What of it? Where they met isn't important now."

"It's important to her husband. He may or may not have suspected it. But he must have suspected what was going on in Florida. That gives him motive. What happened last night proves nothing except that he isn't putting himself in jeopardy now about *you.*"

After a moment, "All right!" she said shortly. "I see what you mean. But it does prove more than that—because Roge didn't know there was anything really serious between Veronica and Burton until he read that letter. He'd suspected but he didn't *know*. He'd hoped everything would blow over. He said that to me. But his imaginings, all bottled up, were driving him crazy. After Veronica died it must have been worse—not knowing what to think about her. That's why he was so frantic to get that letter. Something from her car that I had stolen out in the night to get. . . . If you'd seen the way that letter hit him—"

"What was in it?"

"You don't have to know the *words!*"

"Let's guess the worst," he said easily. "The child was Burton's."

After a moment she said bitterly, "All right. The letter said he was going to have both her and his child. If she didn't tell Roge he'd tell him. She was to make up her mind without delay."

"When did she get that letter?"

"Saturday morning."

"And that was what they were talking about. Before cocktails. . . . And then Chet Taggart barged in. . . . But not for some time. What was Burton like when he went off with you? What sort of mood?"

"Gay. Very, very gay. I felt some of it was put on—but he was really up in the air."

"You don't think he'd persuaded her?"

"Persuaded Veronica?" She laughed briefly. "Of course not. But she'd got it fixed up. She was keeping him on and making him like it."

She thought, *I sound hateful.* But it was the things she had to say that were hateful. She made herself say quietly, "Anyway, you know now why I believe in Roge. He didn't know there was an affair. He hoped the thing would blow over. He never dreamed of killing Veronica. Tod Burton put those ideas in her head, to turn her against Roge, to make her leave him."

Nicholas Parr said slowly, "Would a jury credit his denial of knowledge? Wouldn't a jury believe he guessed that letter was incriminating and wanted it so he could destroy it—thus destroying evidence that there was an affair? You have to look at it from all angles. You have personal conviction but no proof. . . . To prove him innocent we've got to prove somebody else is guilty. . . . You say he insists now it was suicide?"

"That's the strangest thing!" she burst out. "You'd think he'd be afraid—but he seems more afraid of a scandal about the Taggarts. When I told him I knew who'd done it, who'd killed Veronica, he looked absolutely terrified."

"Terrified?" She could feel he was turning the word over in his mind. He said, "Tell me, as exactly as you can, what he said and what you said."

"I can't give it exactly. I know he said, 'Don't say this, Jenny!' and I said I would say it, that it was Hazel Taggart. I know he walked away from me then and I kept talking at him, and then he turned and said again I mustn't say it, that I didn't know anything, that Veronica had killed herself and we had to accept it. But I *don't* accept it—"

She broke off. Her voice had grown unsteady. She heard Nicholas Parr saying, softly, "No, she did not kill herself. . . . He's in one hell of a spot."

There was something very queer in his voice. Then, abruptly, he started the car. He told her, "I must take you back. You're tired. And I've got things to do."

Back at his office he found that the prosecuting attorney had called twice, leaving word for him to come to head-quarters. "I'm not here," he told Miss Miller. "I haven't called in for messages."

He picked up the telephone and called the New York agency. Donovan, the operator put on the case, had just come in, and gave his report in high spirits. Nick, leaning against his desk, with the instrument making noises in his ear, felt no surprise. This was something that he had known a long time. This was like sitting through a familiar movie.

"I played in luck, all right!" Donovan had a pleasant, humorous, confidence-winning voice. Nick saw him as youngish, well-turned out, a little hearty. "I went to the office with a tale about getting the Barrett dame's address on account of some money left her—that's a story that always makes them curious. And one of the secretaries had been there ten years and knew Barrett all right. Boy, was she burned up about her coming into any money! She wanted to know all about it and I 'lowed as how I didn't know the amount but it was from some old beau, I thought, and she made a crack. Something about maybe

Barrett thought she'd get another chance now, since the boss' wife had died—she'd read in the papers that Mrs. K. had died of chloroform in some accidental way. I kidded her and took her out to lunch—I'd timed it for that. And, boy, did she give!"

He chuckled. "The boss and the Barrett girl had been crazy about each other from the day the girl started to work. They used to go out all the time, all very open—everybody in the office thought they'd be married for sure. They didn't get married but they kept on going out. Then Mr. K. got to be president and moved to your city and it looked like Barrett was left flat. That was about—"

He stopped as if to consult notes and Nick, staring down at his boots, said, "Six years ago."

"Yeah. About that. I didn't pin her down to dates, didn't seem too interested. I was just listening to a good yarn, you know. The money story had got her started. Then, a couple months after Mr. K. left, the Barrett girl goes west. All she said was she was going on working for the company, but some of them did think she'd hooked the boss at last and the others went along with it as a gag. Anyway, they gave her a bridal shower for a good-by party. My gal said Nina Barrett hit the roof at first, then tried to carry it off. She just loved telling me about it."

He said, "Dames!" with cheerful cynicism. Then he said, "That's about all she knew. Barrett didn't have any particular friends, so nobody heard from her. The salesmen reported she was working for the boss, all right, but they weren't going out now, not according to the grapevine. My gal said she didn't believe that at first but finally she did. After the boss got married, I guess. She said, 'Nina just didn't make the grade—even with her looks. Maybe she thinks she's got another chance now but she hasn't been getting any younger.' Dames!" said Donovan again.

Then he said, "I tried to get down to cases but she
wasn't saying that the president of the company had ever
had an affair. She thought it, all right, but she wasn't
saying so. And she didn't really know it, either, that's my
guess. Now do you want me to try for some evidence, Mr.
Parr? The trail's pretty cold now, but—"

"Not yet. I'll let you know."

"This is what you wanted, isn't it?"

"You did fine, Donovan. It's what I asked for."

He called the office of the prosecuting attorney. When
he gave his name, Hendrickson himself came on the wire.
"Parr? I've been trying to reach you all day. I want you—"

"I want to see you, Mr. Hendrickson. May I have an
appointment tomorrow morning?"

"Tomorrow? What's the matter with right now?"

Hendrickson was going to rush this through, Nick felt.
He had come to office on a wave of reform and started
out briskly breaking up slot machines, but he had been
dropped into the thick of strikes and gangster killings
where he couldn't get indictments or convictions, so the
King case was a godsend to him, to distract the public. He
wouldn't let that go unsolved.

"Tomorrow," said Nick, "I may have something you
want. I'd like to give it to you then."

"If you have anything we could use we ought to have
it now. Are you trying to solve this case yourself? I heard
something like that."

"Certainly not," said Nick. "Miss Mitchell retained us
to investigate but she understands we hope to work with
you. We're merely trying to be helpful. For instance, Sergeant Nolan asked me to find out some things for him.
From the inside, he put it. There are several angles—"

"Nolan!" The prosecuting attorney cut himself short.
"The sergeant has imagination," he said more temperately,

"but I happen to be in charge. And I am not chasing rainbows, I believe in facts, Parr. And I would like some from you. You made that will of Mrs. King's."

"She gave me no reason for her change of will."

"The fact she made it speaks for itself. I want your statement."

"It's complicated," said Nicholas. "The relationships. By tomorrow morning I think I'll have something you want."

There was a moment's silence. Then, "Okay, okay," said Hendrickson irritably. "Nine o'clock sharp."

"Right." Nick put the phone down quickly. He thought, *Why do I do it this way?* He did not relish what he had set himself to do. There was a very nasty feeling in the pit of his stomach. He glanced at his wrist watch. Five-fifty. A bit too soon. He fell to pacing his office, hands deep in his pockets, his mind adding up the two and two that made the irrevocable four.

The small house looked isolated and alone between the alley and the garden. The windows were dark except for one vertical streak of light between curtains not drawn quite together. He could hear faint music coming from the curtained room above, and somehow the music intensified the lonely feeling. He thought about what Nina Barrett had told him of her love for music, and of her records, and he thought it was about the only truth which she had told him.

He rang the bell beside the narrow, green-painted door and the music stopped. In a moment there came the sound of steps descending wooden stairs. Then Nina's voice, on the other side of the door, raised to carry through it. "Who is it?"

"Nicholas Parr."

The door opened on a chain and Nina's face showed. "Oh!" she said. "I had to make sure—" The door closed and opened again, this time wide.

"May I come in?" he said formally, and walked in. Nina
was in a long red robe and her hair, which he had only seen
drawn back, smooth as satin, hung loose to her shoulders
in a dark cloud. It was beautiful hair, but wearing it loose
did not make her look younger but gave her, he thought,
a witchlike air. Perhaps this was because her face was so
instantly sharpened with inquiry. "What is it? Did you
want to see me?" she asked. And then, "Won't you come
up?"

The garage was a vague darkness behind her in which
he could make out the outlines of a car. Against the wall
by the small door a narrow flight of stairs led to a good-
sized room across the front of the little building. There
were windows on three sides, covered now with drawn curtains of a rich red like her robe; the walls were pale and
so was the rug, which reached almost to the walls. A big
chair with loose cushions was beside a record player. There
were another big chair and some smaller ones and several
tables and cabinets.

"What is it?" she was saying in an alarmed voice.

He turned to her and said bluntly, "Nothing you'll
like."

"You haven't told?"

"Not yet. I want to ask you something first. Let's sit
down, shall we?"

Moving slowly, she sat down in the big chair by the
record player and he drew a smaller one opposite. Her
eyes never left him; they were wide with apprehension. He
asked, "When did you last see Veronica King?"

She continued to look at him steadily. "I don't think I
remember."

"When did you see her—on that Saturday?"

"Saturday? But I didn't see her then. I—"

"You said that Mrs. King had asked you to stay to dinner. You said so to me that night."

"Did I?" Her voice grew light and artificial. "I don't remember, but if you say so—I must have meant that she had sent me the message."

"Who gave it to you?"

She took time to think before she answered. "It was Mr. King. He said she wanted me to stay. He said that when he came back to sign some letters I'd been typing."

"What you said to me was that he had heard Mrs. King ask you."

"Did I?" She looked confused, then she stared down at her lap. Her fingers were pleating a fold of the red robe and instantly they quieted and stayed very still. "But of course he heard her ask—she gave him the message. He heard her say she wanted me to stay. That's what I meant."

"King didn't see his wife after she came in, until he went down to the library."

"But he did! He—" She checked herself. Then she said, evidently thinking very carefully, "I wouldn't want to contradict any of his statements, but he does forget—"

"King said, 'I was in my study. Later I went to our room. My wife was then downstairs. I went down. Mr. Burton was there and then Taggart came.' That's his statement to the police."

She pondered that and then said, very brightly, "But, of course! That's the way it was. But *before* he went down to his room, *before* Mrs. King went down to the library, she came up, part way up, to the study. She called, 'Are you there? Are you finished?' Something like that. And he went out to see her. When he came back—to sign those letters—he told me she wanted me to stay all night. That's what I meant by saying he'd heard her ask. I should have said she'd told him. It's just a mix-up in words."

"I think," said Nick, "that she came *into* the study and asked you. And King did not mention that to the police because if they knew you had seen Mrs. King they might have asked for some statement from you and King did not want you involved."

She spoke with a rush of artificial-sounding lightness. "But how silly—which one asked me! What difference does it make? But I didn't see her. I just heard her call. I didn't see her at all."

"When I told you she was dead you said, 'But she was all right—'"

"Did I? I don't remember. . . . I must have meant she was all right that day or she wouldn't have gone out. That's what I meant."

"And you said, 'I wasn't downstairs at all.' But you *were* downstairs. You were in the pantry where her drink was waiting."

The color drained out of her face. It had been milk white, a luminous white, and now it was like chalk, a chalk triangle between the blackness of her hair and the red of her robe. She stammered, "What a horrible thing to say! Who says so?"

"The maids."

Her startled look betrayed she had grown to count on their forgetfulness. She said, 'They never said so!" And then, "It isn't—"

He interrupted, "It's no good to deny it Both of them remember it."

"I wouldn't think of denying it! I was going to say it isn't important. I'd simply forgotten it myself. Because it was so unimportant. I mean whether he gave me my cocktail in the kitchen or in the pantry. What difference does it make?"

"I think it made a lot of difference to Veronica King."

She shrank back, staring at him. "What are you saying?" And then, on a louder note, "What do you think you know about me?"

"I'll tell you. Here's how I see it. A girl from Sharon came to New York. She went to work for a man who was young and handsome and they fell in love. She expected he would marry her but he wasn't the marrying kind."

Her eyes on his were following every word with the intentness of a lip reader. He plowed on, doggedly, "That was hard for her to believe. She must have kept on hoping because they kept on going out together. I don't know what terms they were on—"

Her face did not tell him. It did not change and she did not move except to lean a little more to him in that absorbed intentness.

"But I can guess. Then he got to be president and moved away. He was still in love because he sent for her and she went on working for him, but he didn't take her out openly any more. He was in the social set now and he had ambitions. They saw each other secretly, very secretly. And she invented a sick fiancé to explain her solitary life, and the lack of men in it."

Something flickered then in her eyes, something bitter and furious, but she said nothing. She waited for him to go on.

"They were very careful, for King was careful now of his reputation. He was a popular young man, moving in the best circles, and what he was doing, I'd say, was eating his cake and having it, too. But I expect that all the time she hoped he'd marry her. Then he married a young widow, a very rich young widow."

He couldn't keep on looking at her. The painful attentiveness of that still face was hard to meet. He kept his eyes on the tip of the cigarette he had lighted.

"I'm not sure about this part," he said. "I'm not sure whether he was really in love with Veronica or whether he deluded himself or was just pretending. Anyway, it didn't

work out as well as he'd expected. He kept on seeing the
girl. Perhaps she was hoping his marriage would end in a
divorce."

He made himself look at her now. She was still intent,
but something in her was working to the surface. Her eyes
were smoldering and her lips were pressed tightly together.

"Then the wife was going to have a baby. The girl knew
that would be the end of her hopes. King would settle
down to wife and family. He was like that. She grew frantic. From wishing his wife dead was a short step to dream-
ing of how she could bring about the death and then to
planning it. Poison. Women usually think of poison. It
wasn't hard to get. She waited for the right chance. She
knew the Kings always had drinks before dinner. So, Saturday, she slipped down for her tray, too early for it, but
when he would be mixing drinks, and she got to the tray
and, by what seemed to her a lucky chance, there was a
special drink for the wife. It wasn't hard to divert King's
attention, to get between him and the tray, and empty that
container she had been carrying about with her. . . . That
is the way I see it."

Nina Barrett laughed. It was a ghastly-sounding laugh.
"Oh, you fool!" she flung at him. "You think *I* did it? So
he would marry me. . . . That's the last thing he would
do!"

She straightened, and pushed back her hair, and put
a hand to her throat as if to choke down the hysteria in
her. "That's the last thing he would do," she repeated, in
a hard, bitter voice. "The last thing."

Her lips twisted in the mockery of a smile. "The first
part is true enough. We were in love. I thought he'd marry
me, but he didn't. That's funny, isn't it, because I'd thought
I could get anyone I wanted. Men were always after me.
. . . But I wasn't enough for Roger King."

Nick thought she was going to laugh again but she choked it back. "It's true I hoped," she said. "I never stopped hoping. I thought that if I held him. . . . I did everything to hold him. I pretended to be happy—I *was* happy—no, I was *never* happy!" she contradicted fiercely. "I wanted *him*. I wanted to be sure. And I never was sure."

She was looking past him now as if talking to herself. "But I held him!" she said. "After he'd left New York I made him send for me. He was still fond of me but he was afraid, too. Afraid of scandal. I knew he wanted to break away but I didn't let him. I did everything to please him. If I could have only a little bit of his life I'd take that and be thankful. I was with him in the office—oh, I was the perfect secretary. And here I could cook his meals and pretend—"

She was tearing herself to pieces. There was something dreadful in that nakedness of feeling. "Let's not," said Nick. "I'm sorry. I'm sorry for the girl from Sharon." That had a stilted, sentimental ring and he hurried on, "But I'm not sorry for the woman who gave poison to Veronica King."

"And you think *I* did it?"

"Who else? That's what King thinks. The chloroform he believed accident. But when the arsenic was discovered he woke up. He's in one sweet hell of a spot. He's suspected and he knows he's suspected, but he isn't giving you away."

"He doesn't suspect me." She wasn't looking at Nick now, but staring ahead, her eyes fixed. Then she began to smile, a thin acrid smile of lips pressed tightly together. "I hadn't a chance. And he knows I knew it. What do you think I'd have to gain? Now, of all times!"

She went on, in a dry, bitter voice, "When he married Veronica he wanted to break with me. He wanted everything sweet and clean in his new life. He offered me money to go east. I begged him to let me stay. As a friend, I said. Friendship was all I wanted, I told him. And I begged to stay in the business. I said that was my life, all the life I had left."

She seemed looking back. "He was too soft-hearted to be unkind to me. So he let me stay. He kept on giving me this place, and he gave me—friendship." She said it with a terrible bitterness, a terrible self-derision.

"He never liked to come here after that. To be reminded. He would take me out to dinner every so often, but he was always uneasy, afraid. It was only in the office that he was comfortable with me. He was used to me there. Sometimes, I think, he actually forgot that I'd ever meant more to him. I suppose men do forget—?"

She paused as if considering. Then the bitter recital went on. "Anyway, he did. But it was something to have him depend on me there. To see him every day. It was everything I had. That and a few dinners in a restaurant."

"You went to Pierre's?"

"Sometimes. I thought you knew it that night. I thought it was a trap. *Was* it?" she asked, quickly, turning her eyes to his.

"No. I'd no idea of that. . . . I had had some thoughts about you and King but I'd dismissed them. Did you call him 'Mr. Jenkins' in front of Pierre?"

She hesitated. Then she said, as if it did not matter now, "Oh, yes."

"But Burton? Why did you go out with Burton?"

"Burton? I never went out with him. I never met him."

But Pierre had pointed to Tod Burton in the picture as "Mr. Jenkins." Of course! As Pierre would say, "But naturally!" Mr. Jenkins was a good customer and Pierre was discreet. He was not going to get a customer into difficulties. So he had pointed to a face he did not know.

Then why, Nick's curiosity wanted urgently to know, had Burton been so furious at the reference to brunettes? Had he been fishing in other forbidden waters?

Nick thrust that question out of his mind. Nina Barrett was saying, "So you see I had no hope. I did not want him free. If he were free—"

"That's all very plausible," said Nick. He lighted a cigarette, giving himself time to think. "But you were seeing him. He was giving you money. You knew Burton was in their life, even if you hadn't met him, and you must have known the marriage was going a little sour. Yet Veronica was to have a baby and that meant they'd probably make a go of it. So this was your last chance. . . . That's the way I see it. And I'm telling you this," he said, with slow distinctness, "because tomorrow morning I see the prosecuting attorney."

She stared at him out of those great eyes of hers with a look of shock. "You'd tell him?"

"I'd rather you told him. That's why I stalled him off till tomorrow. It will be a lot better for you to come in, voluntarily, and tell your story than to have me do it. . . . You'll get off easily," he said, a hard irony in the back of his voice. "Get a good attorney and he'll work the angles. Innocence betrayed. Temporary insanity. Unfortunately there was premeditation for you'd brought the stuff with you but he'll get around that. And there's no death penalty here. Veronica is dead and buried," he said harshly, "burned out with poison, but you'll stay alive."

Her eyes were blazing now. There was terror in them and fear and a mounting fury. "So that's what you want?" she flung back. "A confession? You want to scare me into a confession. . . . You're a *fool!*" she said violently. "I've got nothing to confess to. Roger King knows that. He *couldn't* suspect me, because—"

She stopped herself, thinking ahead. Something wary
and calculating moved in the wildness of her eyes. "Because he knows, he *must* know, who it is," she said. "Of
course he doesn't want to tell! And I hadn't meant to tell.
. . . I thought it could be passed off as suicide. . . . But if
you mean to drag me into it—"

She jumped up and began to walk up and down the
room. She flung out her words jerkily. "You're fooled, like
all the rest. . . . You see only the blue eyes and the blond
hair. . . ." Her voice was savage. "You think she's a dear,
sweet girl—"

"What are you talking about?"

She whirled and faced him. "Jennifer!" she said loudly.
"Your precious Jennifer. She's the one!"

Chapter Ten

Nick said, "That's nonsense." His nerves had jumped but his voice was unstirred.

She walked up to him. "Let me tell you a few things," she said in a low-pitched, metallic tone. "Jennifer met him before Veronica did. She brought him to the McKenzies'. She thought he was hers. Perhaps he would have been but she went back to college and Veronica was older and smarter than little sister."

There was cruel vindictiveness in the measured voice, hammering out these words, and in the white, witchlike face staring down at him. The scene had a nightmarish quality.

"McKenzie died and as soon as she could Veronica married him. Jennifer didn't like that. She pretended it was because it was too soon and she was so fond of Mac but she wanted Roger herself. But Jennifer had to put up with it. She had to play the dear little sister. He really was dazzled by Veronica then."

Nina drew a deep, shuddering breath. "That was when he wanted to break with me. I told you that. . . . You think I kept on hoping. It was Jennifer who kept on. She spent her vacations with them. And Jennifer was young and gay and let him see she found him wonderful. Veronica was hard to live with but Jennifer was all sweetness and light.

She used to run into the office and sit on his desk and chatter to him. Oh, I saw it all!"

She had tortured herself with jealousy, the secretary that Jennifer had said was "too, too self-effacing." Nick could see her, looking at the two of them in the office.

"I saw it all," she repeated. "Every time she came I could see what she was after. She was hoping for a divorce. But the baby upset that. That was the end, as you said. But not for me—for Jennifer. She knew he'd never break away. But he would be hers for the taking, if only he were free. Maybe he didn't know it but she did. There's little these young girls don't know. It was now or never for her and she did it. She chose a time when there were guests about, and she could hurry off—"

His cigarette was burning his fingers. He looked hastily about, reached toward a Chinese bowl, and dropped it in. He thought, *She really believes that Jennifer was out for him.* That had the authentic ring of jealousy. And in her hate and fear and defensiveness she had snatched up this accusation as her weapon.

"Oh, come," he said, almost lightly to cut the tension, "you know you can't make me believe that."

"Oh, you can't believe it of her!" she mocked. "But you can believe it of me!" Her voice took on a bitter irony. "I, who had everything to lose if he was free! I, who was hanging on so desperately to the little I had!"

The words had a desolate sincerity. For the second time that day Nicholas Parr felt himself jarred, abruptly, out of a conception of the case. He looked at her intently. If he were wrong about her—and this instant had made him feel that he was wrong—

Then she said, the low, metallic voice again, harder than before, "But it does not matter what you believe. The police will believe me. And if you drag me into this, if you say anything about me to the police, I will tell them about Jennifer. I'll tell the papers—I'll tell them all!"

"I wouldn't, if I were you."

"You think I can't prove it?"

"I know you can't. It just isn't so."

She looked at him strangely. He thought she would flare up again or burst into wild weeping but instead her face stilled and firmed and something sly and dangerous came into it. "Suppose I saw her? Saw her put it in the glass?"

"You saw nothing of the sort."

"Suppose I did?"

She waited a moment, then, not looking at him now, staring ahead, she said with slow precision, "I came back for my tray. Only Delia was in the kitchen. She did not see me, had her back turned. I could hear Jennifer talking with Roger in the pantry. I was curious, jealous, if you like; I pushed open the door. Annie was holding a lemon and he was cutting the rind off it. He was intent on it, to cut only the yellow, not into the white. Neither of them was looking at Jennifer. . . . She was talking to them but she was doing something. . . . Pouring something into that highball. I didn't think anything about it, then. I thought it was water. But after—after the inquest—"

Her eyes came back to him again, meeting his with menacing defiance. He said nothing. Then she looked beyond him, as if staring at the scene she had conjured up, and her voice went on, slowly, carefully.

"I closed the door. I did not want to intrude. I could see that my tray was not ready so I went upstairs. . . . I did not realize then—but I must have realized when I heard she was dead. Because I was so worried and so anxious to get out of the house. Not to be questioned. And after—after the inquest—of course I *knew*."

It was nine-thirty when he left the house. Nothing more of moment had been said. He had told her, "I had begun to believe you. That you did not kill her. But now, this thing about Jennifer! Unsay that, and help me get at the truth." But she would not unsay it. She would say nothing now. She merely looked at him in tight-lipped antagonism.

Slowly he drove back. He was profoundly troubled. He had underestimated her, he thought wryly. A hasty liar, yes, but a clever one, on occasion. He wondered if she had prepared that defense, that accusation, knowing she might be suspected or if it had sprung, full-clad, Minerva-like, from the frenzy of retaliation. He had hoped for two things, that night, for a confirmation from her, and for a decision to give herself up—he had acted in what he felt to be part shrewdness and part kindness, and he had blundered badly. And—to make it worse—his conception of her guilt was undermined.

I, who had everything to lose if he was free! I, who was hanging on so desperately to the little I had!

No, he concluded, mulling it over, that did not make it worse. It was better he did not suspect her, for if he had to denounce her she would accuse Jennifer. And that would be hideous. Unbearable. Coldness went up and down his spine at the thoughts that came. He had told her that he would say nothing about her to the police, but he wondered if she had believed him. He would see her tomorrow, when she was saner, and convince her. He ought to telephone her early, for she knew he was seeing the prosecuting attorney at nine o'clock. No, he could not telephone her at her house for she was not in the book. He'd have to drive out. . . . She might not wait to be accused. . . .

The lights were on in Abbey's house but the doctor was out. "There are too many sick people calling at all hours," said Mrs. Siddons disapprovingly. "Some doctors refuse to make home calls, but not my doctor."

She disapproved of the demanding sick, but she was proud of her doctor. "Won't you come in?" she asked Nicholas. "He ought to be back soon."

"Thank you, but I'll go on home. Ask him, please, to ring me up as soon as he gets in."

"Are you coming down with something?"

"Oh, no, I'm all right."

"You don't look all right. You come in, Mr. Parr, and I'll make you some hot tea. With some of the doctor's brandy in it."

Nick smiled at her. "It's a temptation. But I've got some work to do." He tapped his head. "Just ask him to ring me up. Never mind how late it is."

His home was only a few blocks away. Slowly he took out his keys and unlocked the garage door. Then he started to get into the car to drive in. A crack across the back of his head sent him lurching forward against the wheel. Pinpoints of light crackled before his eyes. Astonishment and pain dazed him. Then he had the sickening awareness that there would be another blow. He felt off in space, looking down at himself sprawled across the steering wheel, above him the impending blow, descending, descending, in a suspense of slow motion. He would hear his skull crack, he thought.

He heard no crack. He felt a hard impact. Then he blacked out.

His first consciousness was of a roaring in his ears, loud as a waterfall, then it died down to a hum of machinery. He had the freakish impression of being carried along on a converter belt in an assembly line and made a spasmodic effort to fling himself off it but he could not move. He grew aware, then, that he was on the floor of his car and that the engine was running. He lay in darkness, finding it hard to breathe. He felt like a lump, a slug.

Carbon monoxide. The words got through to him, and he struggled to overcome the deadening lethargy. He got one hand up in a clawing gesture that brushed the inner circle of the wheel, and the horn sounded faintly, and, to his helplessness, ironically. His arm fell back and he sensed that he was passing out again, and that there was nothing he could do about it.

"I can't believe it!" Someone was saying that and Nick wished he'd stop for it made his head ache. Then he realized it was his own voice, not loud at all but thick and groggy. He opened his eyes to a glare of light. He moved a hand and felt cement, then grass.

"Easy now."

He said, "That's Doc," and felt very bright to know that it was Abbey's voice. Abbey was kneeling astride him, hands on his chest. He said, "Breathe deep," and Nick said, "I'm sick," and rolled over drawing in deep breaths of air. He lay still and the nausea passed. He felt Abbey's fingers on his head. "What's this?" the doctor said.

"Hit. Getting in car. Knocked me out."

"That knocked you out?" Abbey sounded pleased. He told him, "That's better than monoxide. I was afraid you were in a coma from that. But you were breathing fairly normally. Knew you'd come to. . . . Skin's a little broken. Not serious. . . . Who did it?"

"No idea."

Nick was trying to sit up and Abbey said, "Easy, now," and put his arms about him. "How do you feel? Dizzy?"

Experimentally Nick moved his head. "No. It aches. And I feel sort of lousy."

"CO's bad stuff. I was afraid you had passed out from it. That would mean," he said, worriedly, "that 50 per cent of your hemoglobin had been put out of commission. As an oxygen carrier, that is. But if you passed out from the knock—that's better. You can't have taken in so much if you've no dizziness."

"Hit twice," said Nick. "I remember that. And I remember coming to and trying to get up and sounding the horn. Then I passed out again. I thought it was curtains." He asked suddenly, "Doc, how come you're here?"

The doctor told him that he had come home just after Nick had driven off and that Mrs. Siddons had said Nick had wanted to see him and wasn't looking well. "So I came over," he said. "House was dark in front so I walked around to the back to see if there was any light—that's how I happened to hear the horn."

"God bless," said Nick. "God bless the horn and God bless you and God bless Mrs. Siddons."

"She likes you," said Abbey. He cleared his throat. "She'd have missed you, you know. . . . Now how did this happen?"

"I was getting into my car. About here. After opening the garage. Never saw a thing."

"He didn't take your watch," said Abbey. "Your money?"

Nick put a hand to his pocket. "My wallet's here."

"H'm . . . not robbery." The doctor got up and walked about the edges of the drive, flicking his flashlight about. "Someone was standing here," he said. "Behind this bush. . . . No print, I'm afraid. . . . On the grass. Trampled. . . . Waiting for you. Then ran the car into the garage and shut the doors. H'm."

"Funny," said Nick. This was what Jennifer had said could have happened to her, if King had wanted to kill her. He could have thrust her into the car and left the engine running. "Funny—coincidence," he said. "Come in pairs."

He got to his feet and Abbey came quickly back to him. "Easy does it, boy. . . . Nick, have you no idea?"

Nick stood leaning against the doctor's car. The head-lights of the car, parked on the driveway, sent a bright swatch of light ahead. The bushes at the side were blacked out, the darkness, in contrast to the light, black as a cavern. . . . Nina could have come here ahead of him. He had driven slowly. And stopped, those few moments, at Abbey's. Nina had been furious enough for anything. There had been pure hate in her eyes.

"Whoever did it was an amateur," he said slowly. "Hit me twice. Could have smashed me the first time."

"Maybe he was being careful. Wanting to make it seem the CO. You were on your back when I found you. Unnatural way to fall, to slip beneath the wheel like that. That was to account for the head injuries. . . . You must know who's got it in for you, Nick."

There had been hate in Burton's eyes, too. The Taggarts? Chet Taggart had shown no hatred, but there had been menace in his last words. *Keep out of it.* Hazel Taggart? She had not seemed in the least afraid of him. . . .

"It could be any of them," he said. "I must have come close to something. God, I wish I knew what it was!" Involuntarily, he started to rub his head and flinched. "Ouch! The man says, 'Skin's a little broken. Not serious.' It's sore as a boil. . . . Doc, call up Wayland or the prosecuting attorney and tell them to keep this under their hats but to find out, quick, where the Taggarts are just now. Where they've been. Also—"

Nina would have had time to get home. But someone, on the other side of the street, might have noticed her car going in or out. He gave the number of her house. "Don't have them go there. That's important. But see if the neighbors noticed a car going in or out. And they might check on King. Also—not to leave anybody out—on Tod Burton."

"I'll do that. I was going to get you to the hospital—"

"No hospital. I'm okay."

"We'll get oxygen to the house, instead. Do you no harm. And I'll stay the night."

"No need—"

"He might come back. So I'll have the house watched. I'm a cautious man," said Abbey, "and I like my sleep. . . . Also I want that grass examined by an expert. So come along."

"It's a joke," said Nick bitterly, "to be slugged for something I'm too damned dumb to know I know! Doc, I want you to see the prosecuting attorney tomorrow morning with me. At nine. I'm up against it. A stone wall, every way I turn. . . . My only chance, now, is to blow the lid off with that cocktail scene. The re-enactment. If someone is jittery enough to slug me, tonight, there's a chance he'll crack up."

"Not easy to get away from the hospital by nine."

"Oh, come, Doc! If I'd passed out just now you'd have been busy with my cadaver tomorrow morning, determining what per cent of extinction was due to monoxide and what to the crack on my head. . . . I need your backing. The scientific touch."

He was very glad of the doctor's presence when he presented his scheme in the prosecuting attorney's office the next morning. There was such an air of good sense and dependability in Abbey that when he said he thought such a procedure feasible his words carried weight. Hendrickson was dubious, as Nicholas Parr had known he would be. He said, unenthusiastically, "This is a very sensational suggestion, Mr. Parr."

"This is a very sensational case."

"You know," said Wayland, a sly smile crinkling his fat face, "I thought you'd be bringing in the suspicious bottle you happened to find in the garden." Then he glanced at the prosecuting attorney and his face re-formed into a reflection of his dubiety. He said, "This is like something in a book."

"It's been done in a book, so Abbey tells me," said Nick. "But I didn't know that. I got it out of my head. It seemed a chance to solve this thing."

He looked about the circle of faces. "I got hit last night because I was close to something. Any one of them could have done it. Your checkup shows they were all out. King was driving home from his office about that time and Mrs. Taggart coming back from an early movie with friends—coming back alone—and Taggart had broken away early from a sportsman's dinner. And Nolan's friend, Tod Burton, had dined alone in the city and wasn't back at the club until after ten-thirty. Any one of them had the chance for a crack at me."

"That private garage you had us check?" asked Hendrickson. "What's the connection there?"

"That's King's secretary. There's a car there."

No one on the street had noticed whether Nina's car had gone in or out. It would have told him something, Nick reflected, if he had had the police go in to see whether the engine was warm or not, but he had not dared risk a contact between her and the police. He was uneasy now because he had not been able to reach her by telephone. She might have calmed down and decided to wait on events. Or she might have worked herself up to the boiling-over point—she had certainly been close to it when he left her—and decided to forestall any accusations.

He went on quickly, "The point is, it was a jittery piece of work. Someone's nerves were badly strained. Someone is worried. Now if that someone had to go through the ordeal of re-enacting the cocktail scene—"

"But why the attack on you?" said Hendrickson.

"I've been asking questions of all these people—except King. I must have come close to something. Someone thinks I know too much. I do know that each of them has something to hide. And one of them has a murder to hide.

I don't know which one it is but Jennifer Mitchell believes it to be Mrs. Taggart. As I told you. Now a woman like Mrs. Taggart might break if she had to go through that scene again. The doctor, here, will tell you so."

"Is there any evidence against Mrs. Taggart?" asked Hendrickson. "Wayland, you took her statement. You didn't find anything in it that was suspicious, did you?"

Wayland shifted, in discomfort. "She has the stuff in her possession. On her premises. She came right out with that. She's a smart one, all right. But a queer one—very flip-acting. I wouldn't know what to make of her. But Dr. Abbey, now, he knows her—"

The doctor, twice appealed to, said slowly, "I've known her a long time. I've always liked her, oddly enough—not many do. She's unstable and she's unhappy. She's drinking too much. I couldn't venture to say what she would *not* do," he said carefully.

"You wouldn't say that she'd do it, but you wouldn't say that she wouldn't," Hendrickson interpreted. "But we haven't got anything on her except the Mitchell girl tells Mr. Parr she was jealous of Mrs. King."

"That's motive," said Nick.

"How do you get any evidence of it?"

"If I might say so, Mr. Attorney,"—that was Sergeant Nolan, looking like a combative terrier straining on a leash—"Miss Mitchell is *wanting* to believe it is Mrs. Taggart. She's worried about that fellow of hers, Burton—"

"No, she really believes it," said Nick.

"I'm asking about evidence," said Hendrickson wearily. "All the evidence we have is against King. Motive—plenty. They'd had a fight or she wouldn't have changed her will. And he didn't know she'd changed it. He picks a night when the sister will be out and the maids go off early and the chauffeur isn't on duty. He hadn't counted on the others being around, Burton or the Taggarts, who would know that Mrs. King had a separate drink, but he didn't let that stop him. I guess the maids would know that, anyway. He put the telephone out of commission so there wouldn't be help—"

Nick shot in, "That could have been a vacuum-cleaner accident. Or any of the others could have done it, when they went in. It isn't hard to pull a plug out. If they put their coats near that place—and a small sofa by it is an obvious place for coats—"

"You're working hard to protect King, aren't you?"

"No, Mr. Attorney, I'm not. I only want to protect him if he's innocent. Miss Mitchell is convinced that he is. She'd be a strong witness for the defense. So I think it would be smart to examine every other suspect as quickly and closely as possible, before committing the prosecution to a case against King that might backfire. It would do no harm," Nick argued, "and it might turn up something you would find significant. I wouldn't have had that crack on my head last night if someone wasn't worried."

It was the crack on his head, he thought afterward, that put the scheme over, that and Dr. Abbey's quiet, professional voice saying, "I feel it an expedient worth attempting. It might be—revealing." It was Abbey who had insisted on the autopsy, Abbey who had created the actual case, and Nick could see the attorney considering that, reflecting on Abbey's reputation of not making mistakes.

"Okay, okay," Hendrickson said finally. "I'll go along with it. Keep it out of the papers, that's all. They'd make a monkey of me. Don't let any of the people know what they're in for until they are in the house. Just tell them to be there, that we want to take more statements. We'll pull it off this afternoon. At four."

He looked at Nicholas and said combatively, "Then if nobody breaks down and cries in his beer we'll work on what we have. There's no man so prominent that I'm afraid to try him for murder."

Larrabee listened attentively to Nick's account. He took off his pince-nez and polished it reflectively then settled it firmly on his high-bridged nose. "I shall be there," he said. "This is going to be very interesting—in a gruesome way. But it is your case, Nicholas. You undertook it, and I am leaving it to you. . . . You recall that I urged you to give your findings, re Mrs. King and Burton, to the police at once?"

"You did," said Nick. "And you supposed I had. That's your story and you stick to it." He grinned at his senior partner. He slid off the corner of the desk he had been sitting on and began a restless pacing of the room. "I'm scared stiff," he flung out, "that they will stumble over that affair. It would give them their case against King."

"Yet, in spite of it, you think he's innocent?"

"He didn't kill Veronica," said Nick. "But he thinks he knows who killed her. . . . He thinks it was his dark-eyed secretary."

"Indeed?" was all Larrabee said.

"Indeed and indeed." Nick came back to the desk. "Here's the story," he said. He told it tersely. At the end Larrabee asked, "Did Veronica suspect this?"

"I don't think she had the remotest idea of it. Jennifer hasn't. And I haven't enlightened her."

"Astonishing," said Larrabee. It was what he had said of Veronica and Burton, Nick recalled. This time he enlarged on it. "Astonishing what you find in people's lives—"

"When you go into the bedrooms," said Nick flippantly. Then, morosely, "The devil of it is the police may hit on that story. I don't see how they can help it, once they really start in on King. . . . And if they do—"

He wondered if he ought to tell Larrabee about Nina's threat of accusation against Jennifer. No, he didn't want to put that into words. He repeated vaguely, "If they do . . ." and let his voice trail off again. Then he said briskly, "I wish I had a black mustache."

"Why that?"

"Disguise. So my assailant of last night won't know I'm surviving. I've had Miss Miller say I'm not down yet. There have been two nameless calls. A woman and a man. I'm hoping for a look of discomfiture on one of the faces of our little group this afternoon."

He clapped on his hat and winced. "Meanwhile I'm going into hiding. . . . At Doc Abbey's, if you want me. Mrs. Siddons will stay me with flagons of hot tea and comfort me with apple compote. . . . And I shall brood over every possible combination of circumstances. . . . See you at the Kings' at four."

It was going to be hard to live through the hours until four.

Chapter Eleven

He would have liked to see Jennifer first but Hendrickson had said, "I'll handle it," so he drove out with Abbey behind the two police cars. "I've kept in hiding all day," said Nick. "That well-wisher who left me on the floor of the car last night must have reason to hope I'm still there. Or there *still*. And if I can catch a look of startled surprise at my appearance—"

"I'll be watching," said Abbey. "Whoever did it was afraid of you. Of what he thought you knew about Veronica's death."

"Unless—" Nick hesitated, then went on, "unless it was Nina Barrett. If she slugged me she did it out of rage and fear. And that proves nothing about who killed Veronica."

"You're convinced she didn't kill her?"

"Ninety-nine per cent convinced."

"It couldn't be her eyes?"

"Not her eyes. Her voice. Her despair. Her fear of losing King utterly if he were free. . . . That's my conviction." He went on thoughtfully, "Somehow I don't think Nina slugged me. She was mad enough to, but it seems more a man's act—or the act of a husky like Hazel Taggart. . . . But how about Hazel's back? I understood she hurt it some years ago and gave up riding."

"Riding, yes." Then Abbey owned, sounding reluctant about it, "But she could push. She could have pushed you onto the floor of the car."

"Someone did," said Nick. "And if I could just catch a startled *What-are-you-doing-alive?* look, I'd know something. . . . And then how do I prove it?" He said tensely, "I've staked everything on this show. I don't know *why* I was slugged. All I know is who *didn't* kill Veronica. And that's Nina. And—I think—King. But that's Jennifer's conviction. . . . I'm on edge, Doc. This show today is my one hope. Someone has *got* to break!"

Larrabee drove in as they arrived. They made quite a formidable procession coming down the hall, the six men, two of them in uniform, and it was no wonder, Nick thought, that Annie's eyes rounded, as she held open the door into the drawing room.

It was a long drawing room and Roger King and Jennifer Mitchell were sitting at one end of it, Jennifer with some letters in her hands. She was trying, Nick felt, to make it seem a normal family scene instead of two scared people waiting for the police and a possible arrest. He could see the fear in her, the nervous way she glanced from the police to her brother-in-law, then he stepped out in clear sight and concentrated on King's expression.

There was surprise in it, yes. But no more, he thought, than was natural, for King had expected only the officials. He couldn't tell. He glanced at Abbey and got a negative look. Then he moved toward Jennifer but Abbey was ahead of him, and he saw Jennifer put out her hands to the doctor and say, impulsively, "I'm sorry, doctor—" so Nick stood aside.

Hendrickson took over now. He explained to King and Jennifer the purpose of the gathering. "I appreciate that it will be painful to re-enact the tragedy," he said, "but our hope is that it will be revealing. I'm sure Miss Mitchell, with her suspicions, will understand."

"Oh, I do!" said Jennifer. She sounded excited, relieved that it was not an arrest of Roger King. "Yes, I think—I think it might be revealing."

King said nothing. Nick could not see his face, but he could imagine the distaste in him, the aversion, the sense of the utter futility of the performance, for he was believing in Nina's guilt, and the hard forcing of acquiescence to the demand. He had a wry, masculine sympathy for King now. After last evening he didn't blame any man for backing away from marriage with Nina Barrett.

Whatever King had done, whether he had ducked out of the marriage from personal ambition or from sound sense, whether he had kept on with her through weakness or fondness or fear of her or a mingling of all three, he had had no bed of roses. And these last months of his had been plain hell. His wife had been infatuated with Burton. She had been killed and he believed that Nina had killed her. He knew he was suspected of the murder and he could only clear himself by incriminating Nina, which he wasn't doing.

But there was one thing King didn't know. He didn't know that if he was arrested and Nina became involved she would accuse Jennifer. That was one thing King didn't have to worry about. He, Nicholas Parr, was doing enough worrying about it for two. Every time he looked at Jennifer, so innocent of any danger threatening except the danger to King, Nicholas felt taut with apprehension.

He was by the door when the Taggarts came in. Taggart's face showed nothing—nothing that he could read. It was set in lines of grim endurance. Hazel Taggart looked surprised. She said immediately, loudly, "Why, a party!" and her eyes roved from Nicholas to Larrabee, to Abbey, to

Hendrickson, Wayland, and Nolan. She called out, "Sorry to keep barging in like this, Roge, but this is by request. I don't know why we have to go on making statements, or why we have to make them here—"

"If you'll sit down, Mrs. Taggart," said Hendrickson, "I'll explain why we asked you and your husband to come here."

She sat down, shrugging back a short fur cape. She wore a russet brown tweed suit, flecked with green like her eyes. Restively she glanced about again, then said, "Yes, Mr. Hendrickson?"

"As soon as we are all here. No, don't take off your coat, Mr. Taggart. I'd like you to take that to the other room."

Taggart stared at him but said nothing, merely moved to stand behind his wife's chair. Seeing him like this, hatless, not in riding clothes, Nick felt he looked older and harder.

Burton arrived. He sauntered forward with an air of assumed negligence but his light gray eyes had to Nick the look of a wary hunter approaching dangerous game. Their expression did not change when he encountered Nick's searching look. He glanced past him toward King, raised one hand in an informal salute, and went straight to Jennifer. "Ah, Jenny, my dear." Then he turned to the officials. "Present as requested," he said lightly.

Hendrickson cleared his throat. "What we want—" he said, and proceeded to tell them carefully what was wanted. "The idea is," he summed up, "to reconstruct as much as possible the movements of each one at the cocktail party. In that way we can get some idea of the sequence of events."

There was a moment of constrained silence broken by Hazel Taggart's laugh. "How too, too marvelous! You mean, so you can get an idea which of the suspects had the greatest chance?"

"Now, now"—Wayland was so hearty he was almost waggish—"we're not saying that. It's just for the record, you could say. If you'll be so kind as to go through with it."

"Command performance!" said Tod Burton in his mocking way.

It was a ghastly business but Nick had known it would be a ghastly business and he was in a fever to have them get on with it. Nolan, at a nod from Wayland, shepherded them out into the hall and to the library. "Will the visitors please bring their coats? I mean, if they had them the other day. You, Mr. Burton, you were shown in to this room the first. Will you stand at the door? The others—" Nolan looked around the room critically and directed, "just fit yourselves in where you won't be in the way. Against the walls."

"I feel," said Larrabee under his breath to Nicholas, "as if I were impersonating the invisible man in a Japanese play."

He had the *sang-froid* of the invisible man, Nick thought as he watched him select a small chair in the corner and sit down and survey the room. King deliberately walked the length of the room and turned his back and stared out a window. The Taggarts stepped inside and stood close together. The three officials stood at one side. Jennifer stepped hesitantly to one side of the door. Nick and Abbey came in and pressed back against the wall. Nick looked an inquiry at the doctor and Abbey shook his head. So that hope had failed, Nick thought, and immediately brushed the thought of it out of his mind and concentrated on the scene ahead. Burton was standing alone in the doorway.

"Now, Mr. Burton," said Nolan, "you were shown in here, is that right?"

"Right."

"Where did you sit down?"

"I haven't the faintest idea."

"You had your coat on?"

"I had it on. I expected to be going right out." His look deliberately sought Jennifer. "But Miss Mitchell wasn't ready."

"So Mrs. King came down," said Nolan.

Burton said nothing. In the silence Nick grew painfully aware of that big portrait of Veronica in gauzy blue smiling down from the wall ahead of Burton. He had the feeling that everyone else—except Nolan—was uncomfortably aware of that picture.

"You sat and talked," Nolan was continuing. "Didn't you take your coat off then?"

"I took it off. And I put it—" Burton glanced about— "I rather think I put it here." He indicated a small sofa by the door, next to the cabinet on which stood the telephone. "And I think," he said, his eyes glinting amusement at Nolan, "that I put my top hat *on* the cabinet. *And* my white scarf. I was all dressed up. Stepping out that evening, you know."

"I know," said the sergeant.

Nicholas Parr could feel the tension building up in Nolan. Tod Burton was his suspect. He was Jennifer's boy friend, a reckless playboy, capable, in Nolan's opinion, of being willing to kill for a chance at millions. Nick could feel the effort the sergeant was making to keep excitement out of his bearing.

"Will you be kind enough, Mr. Burton, to put your coat where you said? And sit down where you sat? Maybe you remember where you and Mrs. King sat."

Burton hesitated. Then he stepped into the room, tossed his coat to the corner of the sofa, and sat down in one of the chairs. Opposite him was a big, empty chair with a small table beside it, the table, Nick remembered, on which had stood a cup of coffee when he had first seen it last Saturday night. Veronica's chair.

Nolan did not leave it to inference. "Mrs. King sat here?"

"She sat there."

"And you two were talking. . . . Now was it about your attentions to Miss Mitchell?"

"My attentions to Miss Mitchell?" The mockery in the voice put the words in comic quotes. "It might have been."

"Mrs. King was objecting to them, I take it."

"Not at all," said Burton coolly. "On the contrary."

Nolan studied that a moment. "Now what did you talk about?"

"Just talked," said Burton carelessly. "Filling in till Miss Mitchell came down."

"Now the record," said Nolan, looking about at the silent spectators to make sure they were attending, "shows that no drinks were served from the kitchen. But it appears there is whisky kept in a cabinet in this room. Can you tell me, Mr. Burton, what bottle you used?"

This was his surprise, Nick thought. This is what he hoped would jar Tod Burton. And Tod Burton did look at him curiously. "We did not use any. There is only Scotch here, some special Scotch that King keeps for occasions. Mrs. King happened not to like Scotch. We had no drinks."

He said it slowly and precisely as if drilling it into the head of a not very bright child, but Nick seemed to feel a quickened attentiveness beneath his assured manner, as if he were straining to catch the implications of the question. It must puzzle him, Nick thought. It would fill him with bitter irony if he knew what was in the sergeant's mind.

Nolan was eyeing him searchingly. "You say you and Mrs. King talked about your attentions to her sister?"

"I didn't say it. I said she approved my attentions. . . . I haven't the least notion what we talked about just then."

*I will have both you and my child. Either you tell him or
I will tell him, myself. My love, make up your mind without
delay.*

The words filled Nick's mind. His imagination pic-
tured the low-toned colloquy, the clash of wills. What was
it that Jennifer had said? That he was very, very gay, afterward. "She was keeping him on. She'd got it all fixed up."
Of course the gaiety could have been pretense. It did not
matter now. Veronica was gone. *She's dead. Done. Gone.*
Burton's harsh words replaced Jennifer's.

Hendrickson, in the background, was losing patience
with Nolan. He prompted, "When did Mr. Taggart come in?"

"That's your cue, Chet," said Hazel Taggart. "Now you
go over to the door and rush in."

Slowly, stoically, Taggart moved away from her and
went to the doorway. Nolan said, "You had your coat on,
Mr. Taggart? Now where did you put it?"

"I don't know. Just anywhere."

His wife spoke up again. "It was on the sofa, Chet.
Next to Tod Burton's. Following in his footsteps, as it
were." She gave one of her abrupt laughs. "I know, because
I put mine on it."

"Then, Mr. Taggart, will you put your coat there? And
take the chair you took?"

Taggart, with a tortured look, turned and dropped his
coat beside Burton's coat. He looked about at the chairs
and sat down in the nearest one. Burton turned and grinned
at him. Taggart did not look at Burton; he did not look
at anything, least of all, Nick noted, at the empty chair
where Veronica had sat.

"Then what happened?"

Burton said, "We had a nice, three-cornered conversation."

King turned abruptly from the window. "I came in," he
said. "I came in, then went out to mix the drinks."

"You went out which door?"

"That one." King nodded to it, a door at the other end of the room. "I crossed the hall into the pantry."

"We'll call the front of the door the pantry," said Nolan. "Will you come and stand there, Mr. King? And Miss Mitchell"—it was almost, Nick thought, as if he had a prompt book in his hands—"will you ask your maid in? Annie Kelly. We'd like her in the so-called pantry here."

Jennifer moved quickly toward the door. She looked back appealingly toward King, a look that said, *Let's see this through. Maybe something will come of it,* and King slowly crossed the room. King, Nick felt, was not sustained by Jennifer's wild hope.

"And now you came, didn't you, Mrs. Taggart?"

"Oh, is this where I came in?" Hazel Taggart came forward, with a chaffing smile at the sergeant that made him flush self-consciously. He said doggedly, "That's for you to tell us. Did you come right after your husband did?"

"Not *right* after. He was in his car and could get up the drive quickly. I was at our gates, waiting for him—we're like that, you see—and I saw him turn in. After a minute I crossed over and came, too. And I went down the hall to the library where I heard voices—I mean, Veronica's voice. The men," she said, with a glance of open raillery at the two men, "did not seem to be talking. A communion of souls, perhaps. Two souls with but a single thought."

Nick saw Tod Burton look at her. A level-lidded deadly look.

"I was wearing this suit," she went on, with an air of mock exactness, "and this cape, and I tossed the cape on the sofa here, over the men's coats. Like so."

She flung her cape down on the sofa. "This is right by the telephone, isn't it?" she said, with her bright air of grasping the nettle openly. "So any one of us, if we'd stooped over our wraps, could have pulled out that telephone plug. By accident, of course." She smiled maliciously at the prosecuting attorney. "I expect you've thought of that."

She looked utterly assured, and yet, Nick felt, the assurance was a thin glaze. Her eyes were not the cool, shrewd eyes that had mocked him the day before; they had a restless glitter, a quick, questing uneasiness as her look shifted from one to the other.

"Then I sat down here by Chet." She took a chair beside her husband. "I know I smoked because I asked Veronica if she hadn't given in yet. She'd sworn off, some time ago. I said, 'Haven't you given in yet, darling?'"

The flippancy was intolerable in that tense room. She was like a callous child, showing off. Nick saw Taggart's face and it shocked him. The man was sweating, his skin pallid, the drops of moisture running down unheeded. He was looking at his wife in what seemed an agony of warning.

"And then?" said Nolan.

"Then my husband went to tell our host I'd come, to be sure there were drinks enough." Her laugh erupted on the stillness. "Of course the cook—she let me in—could have told him but Chet wanted to be with Roge, I suppose. That's what he came for, of course. . . . Shouldn't you go and act it out, ducky?"

Taggart made a negative, grunting sound. Mercifully no one insisted. Hendrickson merely said, "You went to the pantry, Mr. Taggart?"

"Yes. To the door."

"Didn't you go in?"

Taggart hesitated. "I don't know. I think I talked from the door. I don't know."

"Why, yes, Mr. Taggart, you came in," said Annie Kelly. She had come into the room with Jennifer and was standing in the space the police had designated as the pantry. Her voice was the only one in the room that had sounded

without self-consciousness; she spoke with her natural
eagerness for detail. "First you put your head in, and then
you came in. Don't you remember? You said to me, 'Hello,
Annie, we keep you pretty busy, don't we?' And then you
talked to the mister. I was mopping up some juice that got
spilled when I opened the olives."

"Isn't she marvelous?" said Hazel Taggart clearly. "But
you didn't stay long, Chet. She'll have to say that for you."

Nolan asked, "You came back here? And sat down?"

"I guess so. I mean I came back."

"But you didn't sit down," said his wife. "You prowled
about the room. The way you do. And then Roger came
in from the pantry. I remember I said to him, 'You didn't
know you were giving a party, did you?' And he said something pleasant—he's so *dependably* pleasant. And then he
sat down by me where Chet had been sitting." She turned
toward her husband. "Chet, you ought to get up and give
Roger that chair."

Chet Taggart got up. Roger King came forward and sat
down. It was true, some part of Nick's mind noted, that
he was dependably pleasant. His good manners were so
bred in the bone that it seemed impossible for him to do
anything ungraciously. He gave to his compliance now the
dignity of those good manners. He was like a man walking
courteously through a nightmare.

"And Veronica said—" Hazel Taggart broke off, then,
her voice rising, "It's so awful—that empty chair! We can't
act it out without Veronica. . . . I'll tell you—I'll take her
part after I've done mine. . . . Veronica said something
about you must have made a lot of drinks, Roge, you'd
taken so much time at it."

Her husband was standing behind her chair, in that
suggestively protective position, and she twisted her neck
to look up at him. "You didn't stand there, Chet. You
didn't come near me." Taggart moved away hastily, and

she directed, "Just poke around. The way you do. And you ought to keep staring at the chair. Veronica's supposed to be in it. It won't look the same, of course, when I'm in it!"

She shot a sudden look at Burton. "Maybe you'd rather I didn't play at being Veronica?"

She was either a madwoman, Nick thought, or she was diabolically clever. No one was asking her anything about her reasons for coming, her feelings toward Veronica. She had taken over and her dominance swept the scene along. Now she turned to her husband again. "I'll tell you what you said. You asked when all those drinks were coming. Very thirsty-sounding, I thought. And Roge said they'd be along, that he'd left the tray for Annie, and Annie was in the kitchen but she'd be along."

She lifted her eyes to where Hendrickson stood in the background with Wayland. "Don't you think I'm a good witness, Mr. Prosecuting Attorney? I am the only one who seems to remember *anything!* I don't think the rest of them know their lines at all."

"But you've given so much thought to it," said Burton, his voice soft yet tight as a slip knot. "I'd say you were letter perfect."

Taggart turned to him with a sudden movement that seemed truculent. Hazel Taggart shot her husband a glance, then said to Burton, "Well, you carry on, then. It's your turn now. I remember you said, 'Well, what are we waiting for?' and jumped up and went to the pantry and brought out the tray yourself. Pretending to be a pompous butler. It was quite an act. Why don't you go and come in like that now? Make that entrance. . . . Why, there *is* a tray!" she cried, her eyes widening.

On a table in the area designated as the pantry a tray had appeared. There was a cocktail shaker on it, glasses of Martinis, and a filled highball glass. It was a macabre touch that Nicholas Parr had not envisaged. Nolan's excited eyes showed him who had thought it up. Wayland spoke up apologetically. "We took the liberty, Mr. King, of asking your cook—"

"It's very important," said Nolan earnestly, his *rr*'s rolling with his Scotch-Irish burr, "to carry out the idea exactly. Mr. Burton, it was you, was it not, who brought in the tray?"

"Don't ask me to repeat my butler act. I'm not up to it again."

"But will you bring it in?"

"Why not?" said Burton lightly. He got up, moved leisurely to the tray, and contemplated it a moment. "They've got this wrong. No lemon peel in the Martinis." The lightness fell flat

Then, with a swift gesture, he picked up the tray and carried it across to the low table before the fireplace. Behind him Annie, unprompted, advanced, her hands outstretched as if carrying a plate of canapés. "You come after me, Miss Jenny," she said in a reminding voice. Jennifer did not move.

"Enter laughing, should be the cue," said Hazel Taggart. "Mr. Burton was deliriously funny. This isn't the same at all."

"This is where I bow out," said Tod Burton. He was very pale. The scar on his cheek scarcely showed at all. "I left then with Jennifer."

"Oh, not right away!" Hazel Taggart told him. "You stood at the table first and had a drink. A quickie. Then you took Jennifer and ran her out. It was almost," she said, her loud voice half-indifferent, half-amused, "as if you didn't want to see what was going to happen."

There was a profound silence. Nolan's eyes lit up like jack-o'-lanterns.

"But, of course, you didn't do it. We know that. You weren't the underdog. But if we're going to have this exact

we have to show things the way they were. It's only fair to
say how you behaved. You see, Jennifer was at great pains
to point out that it needn't have happened in the pantry,
the poisoning, I mean, which means that I had a chance at
the tray—and Chet, too. And then Chet was in the pantry.
Annie insists on that. And Chet's so clever with his hands.
There's no use trying to hide that, is there? So if we're
going to be implicated you might as well be, too."

"That's very sweet of you," said Tod Burton suavely.
"If you think my manner was suspicious I'll act it out for
you."

He stooped over the table, took up a Martini and drank
it down. His back was toward the room and Nick noted
that anyone in his place would hide the table from the
others. Then Burton went to the sofa, caught up his coat,
gestured toward an imaginary hat and scarf, took Jennifer
by the arm and spun her about to the door.

"Here we go. . . . Be seeing you," he threw over his
shoulder, then whirled about, turning Jennifer with him
like a puppet, to face the room again. "Does that give the
idea?"

"It does, Mr. Burton." Hendrickson sounded almost
apologetic.

Burton held his pose a moment more, the picture of a
carefree young man going out with a pretty girl, and only
the set, embarrassed face of the pretty girl was not in keeping with the gay picture. Then Burton released her, drew
up a chair for her, and sat down on the arm of it. Jennifer
sat stiffly, her cheeks flushed, looking suddenly utterly
sick of the whole miserable, futile, harrowing business.

Wayland took up the questioning. "Who took a drink
next?"

Mrs. Taggart said, "You did, didn't you, Chet? You
picked up a Martini next."

"Yes, I think I did." Taggart's voice was suddenly careful and precise, the voice in which he had said to Nicholas Parr that Veronica had killed herself. "I went to the table and picked one up." He looked toward the table but did not move to it.

"You were going to take it to Veronica," his wife reminded. 'Then Roge said he'd made his wife a highball—that gin wasn't so good for her. Now, did you give her the highball, then? No, you didn't," she decided. "You had started to her with the Martini and when Roge kept reminding her what the doctor had said you stood still and drank it."

She pointed to a spot near the empty chair. "You stood there. I remember because I went to the table then. No one brought me a drink and I went to get one. Like so."

She got up, stepped to the table, took up a Martini and drank half of it down. She turned about to look at Nicholas Parr. "You couldn't see if I did anything to the highball, could you?"

Nick shook his head mutely.

She commanded, "Roge, you come here, too. You jumped up when you saw me getting a drink and said 'Sorry.' And then—then I think that Chet was coming back for Veronica's highball but you reached for it—I can't remember whether you took it to her or not."

"Does it matter?" said Taggart hoarsely. "For God's sake, keep still about it."

She looked at him with a smile that contorted her face. "Of course it matters. Mr. Hendrickson wants this very exact. And we've nothing to hide, have we?" She drank down the rest of her Martini and said, "Now I'll be Veronica." She went to the empty chair and flung herself into it, staring out at them.

"This gives me a very spooky feeling," she said loudly. "But it brings things back. I remember now. I was looking at her and thinking how marvelous it would be to be young and beautiful and lean back against cushions and have men rush to hand you things—especially your own husband. I have to pay people to hand me things. . . . I thought that because I saw you giving it to her, Roge. The highball. Aren't you going to give it to me now?"

King carried it to her. He carried it with a curious, meticulous care as if every faculty he possessed was concentrated on doing it. He did not look at her as he gave it to her, the big, flamboyant woman who sat where his wife had sat. He moved back to the table and with the same slow care he picked up a Martini.

Hazel Taggart sat there, holding the highball, looking about the room. "Well," she said vaguely, "this is it. That's the way it was."

No one seemed to know what to say.

"Well," said the woman again, in a strained voice, "what do I do now? . . . If I'm Veronica, I'd better drink this." She lifted the glass. She drank and broke off in a paroxysm of coughing.

Taggart started forward. He caught the glass as it fell from her hands. Her hands tore at her throat as the coughing changed to choking. She fell forward and Taggart's arms received her and eased her back into the chair. She lay limply, the bright, too-bright, head lolling. The face, what could be seen of it, was contorted, the eyes staring.

Chapter Twelve

For a moment, a stunned moment, Nicholas Parr stared
at the unbelievable scene, the slack, grotesque figure with
no dignity of death about it, the russet suit rumpled, the
too-tight skirt pulled up about the legs. The face of the
husband, the big, pallid, deep-lined face, was turned now
toward the room. On it was not so much surprise as sadness, a dreadful sadness, as if some wretched, irrevocable
thing that he had long expected had happened.

Nick was not aware of any sound or movement about
him until Dr. Abbey got up and crossed to where Mrs.
Taggart lay. There was something so matter-of-fact, so
competent about the short, stocky, blue-clad figure that
it gave a sense of normality again, a grateful feeling of
sanity going about its business. Everything about Abbey,
thought Nicholas, said that he was a doctor, that he knew
what to do.

He bent over Hazel Taggart, he felt her heart, he lifted
an eyelid, he stooped closer and smelled her lips, then the
glass that Taggart had caught as it fell from her hands and
set down. Nick tried urgently to remember what poison it
was that could be detected on the lips. He saw Abbey lift
first one of her hands and then the other and sniff each
finger in turn. Very gently he replaced the lax hands.

His action had broken the shocked stillness, Nick heard Larrabee murmuring, "Good God!" to no one in particular, heard Annie Kelly starting a scream which Jennifer's voice hushed. Wayland and Hendrickson were beside Abbey now, and Abbey said, "Cyanide." There was a quick, low-toned exchange of words, then all three men began looking hastily through the folds of the woman's clothes, into the chair, and on the floor about it. Nolan hurried to join them, going down on his hands and knees, feeling the carpet.

The container. Of course. Nick went swiftly to the low table where the tray stood. The shaker and the glass which Taggart had not touched were on it. He peered into the shaker, seeing nothing but a little clear liquid, and ran his fingers about the table, then inspected the floor. Here by the table or by the chair were the only places where she could have dropped it.

What was it? A bottle? A capsule? There had been that moment when her back was toward them, when she could have put it in the glass. *You couldn't see if I did anything to the highball, could you?*

Nothing on the floor. He straightened. Taggart had moved back from the group about his wife, looking on with an air of helplessness. King was standing with his Martini glass still half-raised, staring fixedly. He did not seem aware of Nick's presence, then he said, not looking away from the group, "What are they after?"

"The container."

Hendrickson snapped, "No moving about. No leaving the room. Everyone stay where he is."

Nolan was hurrying to search the table. Nick's glance swept about, saw Burton stepping back again to where Jennifer stood, her hand gripping Annie Kelly's arm. There was shock in her young face, shock and horror, but as Nick watched he saw her turn and look toward King as if she were trying to say, *I told you!*

To Jennifer it was as simple as that. Hazel Taggart had found it intolerable to live with her sin and had taken the way out.

The hurried search for the container went on. Abbey said, "Stuff's volatile," and turned suddenly to King. "Have to do this, you know," he said in his detached, professional way. "Just put that down," he pointed to the Martini glass and lifted each hand and smelt the fingers. He turned to Taggart next. Taggart growled, "What's this for?" as Abbey reached for his hands, then he said hastily, "I caught the glass, you know." Abbey nodded, smelling very carefully. Without comment he released the hands. Hurriedly he brushed his face along the fingers Nick extended.

Nick heard Jennifer's bewildered-sounding voice. "What's he doing?" and Burton's ironic, "Smelling out a suspect."

"A suspect?"

"Sit down," said Tod Burton in a different, suddenly gentle voice. "I'll get you a drink."

"No, I—"

But he went quickly to the tray and caught up the Martini that Taggart had not taken and brought it to her. "I expect it's safe," he said with a return of his flippancy. "We've all been drinking it."

Jennifer, sitting down again, sipped at it. Her face was pale. She was hard hit, Nick saw, by the realization that Hazel Taggart might not have died by her own hand. But he had no time to think about Jennifer's feelings. His mind was racing.

Abbey was in front of Burton now. "This is all poppycock," said Burton. Smiling at the poppycock, he spread out his fingers. "The container could roll."

"Oh, it could!" said Jennifer eagerly. As she held out her hands to the doctor she burst out, "She *must* have killed herself, Dr. Abbey."

He gave her a quick, pitying glance, sniffed her fingers, then Annie Kelly's hands, then made for Larrabee who waited with an ironic smile.

The circuit had taken only a few instants. Now there was an uneasy pause, a low-toned colloquy between the doctor and Hendrickson and Wayland. Nolan was still peering about, going down on his hands and knees again. Then Hendrickson stepped forward.

"Ladies and gentlemen." He sounded, Nick thought, as if on a platform. "I am sorry to inconvenience you but there will be a search, of the room and of your persons. Please cooperate as pleasantly as possible. We must do our duty. . . . The poison that killed Mrs. Taggart was cyanide of potassium. That came into this room in a container and the container is in this room. We'll look about the room, first. Everyone is to stay exactly where he is. . . . Nolan, will you phone for a woman searcher for the ladies—"

"Here it is!" cried Nolan excitedly. He had gone back to the low table again and lifted the silver tray. He stood gripping it, his eyes glinting with triumph. "Under the tray. Under the edge of it."

On the table on the piece of Chinese brocade that lay on it was a tiny vial. A small, cylindrical thing, one end broken. Abbey approached it, bent cautiously over it, lowering his head by degrees. Finally he straightened and nodded decisively to Hendrickson. "That's it."

"Right under the edge!" Wayland glared at his sergeant. "And you reported nothing there."

"I'd have sworn there wasn't. I got down and looked all around that edge. It must have been far in. It wasn't till I lifted the tray—"

"And a good thing you thought of it!"

"A very good thing," said Hendrickson, putting an end to that. He walked over and looked down at the tiny vial. "Well, there's no need for searching now. That's a relief. Sergeant, will you phone for Lewis? Get him here quick. There must be prints—"

"I've got my kit," said Nolan. "I always carry it. I can do the job as well as Lewis and save you time."

"That he can," said Wayland, making amends for irritation at him. "He's done it many a time."

The next minutes seemed interminable to Nicholas Parr. This was it, he thought. This was the revelation. It was hard to wait for it, not because he did not know it, but because he did, and if it was hard for him to wait, if his nerves were tight, his throat dry, what was it like, he thought, for the one whose fingers had been on that vial? How could the face keep its stolidity, its quietness, its air of unconcern? And yet stolidity, quietness, and unconcern were all that he could see on any of the faces.

Then his heart sank. He knew, from the way that Nolan looked up, what he was going to say. The sergeant's face was; flushed and frustrated. "No prints at all," he reported. "The thing's wiped clean."

"No prints? But on the edge? We can reconstruct, from an infinitesimal—"

"There's not a print. It's had a good wipe, that's what it's had. On the brocade, I'd say."

"That's just too bad," said Hendrickson grimly. He thought a moment, breathing deeply. "Well, this narrows it, anyway," he said. "There were only three of them who came near that tray. Mr. Burton, for his quickie, the lady herself, and Mr. King. Yes, that narrows it," he repeated portentously.

"Not Mrs. Taggart," said Abbey. "There was no smell of it on her fingers. Only on her mouth."

"You said the stuff was volatile."

"Not *that* volatile. I got to her quickly. I'd have detected it, if she had used it."

"You'd testify to that?"

"Yes. I'm positive. . . . I did detect a faint odor still on the fingers that Taggart had put inside the glass when he caught it. So my nose can be trusted. . . . Taggart wasn't near the tray, you know," he reminded.

He looked toward the figure in the chair, that distressing figure which their eyes, thought Nick, were all carefully avoiding, and said quietly, "You can leave the lady out of it."

There was a strained, indecisive silence, broken abruptly by Tod Burton's ironic voice. "Oh, let's not leave *Mr.* Taggart out of it! Let's not be too exclusive."

Faces turned to him. He glanced about at them, gathering in the startled attention. "Taggart didn't take his drink, no. He made rather a point of that, didn't he? Of not going to it. But he was roaming near the table before then. I happened to notice him when I was at the door with Jenny. When you were all looking at *us.* He was very brief about it. But with those sleight of hand tricks of his—"

He stopped and waited. Then he said, "And he was very, very tired of Mrs. Taggart. Perceptible even to the eye of a stranger in your midst like myself. And his roaming near the tray was *after* Mrs. Taggart had said she'd play Veronica. Anyone who knew her would know she'd drink that highball."

The deliberate satiric voice sharpened. "He was very afraid of Mrs. Taggart. He had been very, very enamored of Mrs. King. Very resentful that she did not reciprocate his emotion. He had, in fact, made a howling nuisance of himself. So Mrs. King had brushed him off. He was furious about that. . . . So let's not leave Mr. Taggart out of it."

Taggart stood staring at him. A baited bull, Nick thought. And Burton, eyeing him relentlessly, his light gray eyes cold and purposeful and deadly, his whole bearing the same under its air of light audacity, needed only the scarlet cape to be in character.

Hendrickson said slowly, "Dr. Abbey, did you say you detected the odor of cyanide on Mr. Taggart's fingers?"

"It was almost imperceptible. On those fingers which had caught the rim of the glass."

"Or those fingers which had broken the vial," said Burton.

"You did not detect it on any others in the room?"

"No. No cyanide."

Nolan, Nick saw, was whipping out his notebook.

"That is—significant," said Hendrickson solemnly. He seemed to take counsel with himself, then addressed Taggart. "Mr. Taggart—you need not answer if you feel it inadvisable but it is always better to be frank—Mr. Taggart, is it not a fact that you and your wife—that there were differences between you?"

Taggart did not look at him. He shifted his gaze to a point just beyond the prosecuting attorney. "I don't know what you call differences," he said. "Everybody has some differences."

"Your wife was much older."

"Oh, that. Yes."

"You did not have the same interests."

Taggart said defensively, "We went out together."

Hendrickson glanced briefly at Roger King, with a shade of embarrassment, then made his voice firm and impersonal. "This devotion of yours to Mrs. King that Mr. Burton mentioned—we have already had reports about that. Reports well substantiated. It is known that you were devoted to her even when she was Mrs. McKenzie. You don't deny it?"

Taggart said slowly, "No, I don't deny it."

"Your wife had reason to be jealous and disturbed. It would not have appeared surprising if she decided to take her own life. But she did not take her own life. She did not put that cyanide in her highball. It was put there for her."

He frowned, marshaling his thoughts. "Put there, it would seem, after she had said that she would act the part of Mrs. King. You were near the tray then. You had opportunity. . . . And you had motive. As Mr. Burton said, you were afraid of her. She knew too much. She knew of your feelings for Mrs. King. You don't deny that, do you?"

"Oh, she knew, all right," said Taggart somberly.

"And she knew that Mrs. King had tired of—had lost patience with you. Mrs. King liked younger people, people her own age. Your feeling for her was an embarrassment. She wanted no more of it and made it clear to you. You were furious. You wrote her threatening letters."

Taggart shot him a sharp look then. He appeared surprised. "I didn't mean anything," he muttered. Then he said angrily, "What do you know about my letters?"

"Your wife knew. She talked about those letters—after Mrs. King had died. She must have had her ideas about how—and why—Mrs. King had died and you must have known she had those ideas. You knew you could not trust her to keep a secret. She was not discreet. She drank too much. You never knew, from one minute to another, what she would say next. Not that she meant, I think, to give you away, but she was secretly bitter at you and liked to torment you. She had you, in fact, over a barrel."

Surprisingly Taggart nodded. "Yes," he said broodingly. "Yes, she did."

Hendrickson took a step nearer him. "You were afraid of her."

"I was afraid of what she'd say," said Taggart. "I was afraid I'd have to own up if she got suspected."

"To own up! To confess you killed Mrs. King?"

Taggart stared. "I didn't kill Mrs. King. I wouldn't have hurt a hair of her head. . . . But I was afraid—well, I can say it now. It won't hurt her now. She did. My wife. I have to believe it. It was driving me crazy."

"Are you trying to put that over? That your wife was guilty and killed herself in remorse?"

"Well, that's the way it was," said Taggart doggedly. "It has to be that way."

"How could she do it? Kill herself with no smell on her fingers? No prints on the container?"

"She could have used a handkerchief."

"There was no handkerchief on her person. There was nothing on her that smelled of cyanide. Except her mouth."

"I don't know," said Taggart confusedly. "But it has to be that way."

"To save you, you mean. . . . But the facts are against it. The very fact that the prints were wiped off. A desperate woman, resolved on ending her life—and ending it in public does not wipe off her prints. Why should she?"

"Just to make it a mystery. She liked stirring things up."

"Nonsense," Hendrickson said curtly. "If she had, there would have been the smell on her. On her fingers. And there was none. *There was none.* That is conclusive evidence, Mr. Taggart, that your wife did not kill herself."

Sweat was starting on Taggart's face. Drops ran down into his eyes and he got out a handkerchief and slowly dabbed at them. "I don't know," he muttered. "I can't see into it then. I can't see who'd—"

"Murderers," said Hendrickson grimly, "use a familiar pattern. Poisoners stick to poison. Apparently you had your choice of poisons. We know the arsenic was available to you. Where you obtained the cyanide we do not know. But you had it in readiness. You did not use it for Mrs.

King because you needed something more slow in action. But the cyanide was just the thing, you thought, for your wife. The thing a suicide would use. A thing you could—manipulate. You did not know just what chance would offer when you came, but you had the stuff with you, in expectation of some chance. And with your legerdemain ability—"

Taggart was staring at him, looking as if, for the first time, he comprehended the reality of the accusations. He seemed confused and oddly astonished. He said urgently, "That's not the way it was."

"No, that's not the way it was."

For so long there had been only the two voices in the room that there was a startled turning when Nicholas Parr spoke. He stepped forward a little, straightening his lean shoulders, and took his hands out of his pockets. He met Hendrickson's combative look with as easy a smile as his inner tensity could muster.

"Were forgetting one thing," he said. "One thing that lets Mr. Taggart out. You're assuming that he poisoned his wife because she knew that he poisoned Mrs. King. But he didn't poison Mrs. King. . . . He didn't poison her drink because, you see, at any chance he had to poison it, he did not know it was her drink."

Nick looked about at them, letting the words take on meaning. "We all took it for granted that it was her highball, that she'd wanted a highball. It wasn't until just now, when the scene was being re-enacted, that the facts came out. It was King who decided that his wife should have a highball. The doctor had recommended less gin. I gather that Mrs. King did not take the advice seriously but King thought she should. As soon as he went to the pantry he decided to make her a highball."

He waited a moment, then said slowly, "No one in the library, not Mrs. King, not Burton, not the Taggarts, knew it was being made for her. . . . You remember that Mrs. Taggart said that King, after the tray had been brought in, reminded his wife of what the doctor had said. There appears to have been a moment or two of argument about it."

In the silence the rustling of Nolan's notes and Wayland's heavy breathing were the only sounds. Then Hendrickson said consideringly, "Yes, she did say that. But that doesn't let Taggart out. Taggart went to the pantry. He'd have seen the highball on the tray and asked about it."

Assurance, momentarily dissipated, was back in him. "So he knew, all right," he said triumphantly.

"But he didn't ask. Annie Kelly was in the pantry while he was there and heard all that was said. She told me that Taggart said his wife had come so King had better shake up a few more and King said the more the merrier. I gather that Taggart was a bit bothered by her arrival or by something else for Annie mentioned he was 'grumpy like.' He asked King how long Burton was staying in the city and King said he didn't know. That's all the conversation that Annie reported and Annie has a total recall memory."

"You wouldn't be prompting her, would you?" said Wayland. He jumped up and went over to the girl, waving Jennifer away from her, and began a low-toned interrogation.

Hendrickson turned to King. "What is your memory of the conversation, Mr. King? Was the highball mentioned?"

Roger King looked back at him in what seemed a desperate groping for recollection. "I couldn't say," he said finally. "I mean, I simply don't remember."

"You mean you were the only one who knew the highball was for Mrs. King?"

Larrabee jumped up, shedding his fine air of disinterested spectator. "Mr. King, you are not obliged—"

King rejected the warning. He said stiffly, "I mean I do not remember."

Wayland announced, "Miss Kelly, here, says that's all there was to the talk. What Parr said. She says they didn't speak of the highball at all because she, herself, never knew who it was for."

Nick went on quickly, "And remember this. Mrs. Taggart said specifically that her husband picked up a Martini to take to Mrs. King. He was away from the table, on his way to her, before King said she was to have the highball. King spoke of the doctor's advice and while that was going on, Taggart stood there"—Nick pointed—"then he drank the Martini himself. He started back for the highball but King had already picked it up. Obviously Taggart couldn't have put anything in the highball then. And that was the first time he'd known it was for Mrs. King."

Hendrickson took time to think this over. He wasn't going to love him for this, Nick felt; he had palpably relished the thought of Taggart as a suspect and warmed to the marshaling of the case against him, but Hendrickson was a realist. Facts were facts. What he was making of them showed in his next words.

"Then King was the only one who knew the highball was for Mrs. King?"

"That's right."

Wayland said hastily, "But that doesn't let Taggart out of his wife's death. He knew *she* was going to drink the second highball."

"What about his motive? . . . Look at the picture. The only thing he had to be afraid about was that she'd give herself away."

Wayland's eyes were slits of calculation. "No, he could be afraid she'd incriminate *him*. She was spiteful and maybe he thought she was spiteful enough for that. He felt it was safer to have her out of the way—"

"Not he! You heard what he said. He was going to be noble and take the rap himself if she got involved. He was pretty sick about it but he was holding hard to the hope that Veronica King's death might still be considered suicide. . . . Believing his wife guilty, he never grasped the fact that she believed *him* guilty. I think she believed it."

Taggart blurted, "Why, she couldn't—"

"I think she did," Nick repeated. "She never stopped to think he didn't know the highball was for Mrs. King. And *he* never realized, either, that *she* hadn't known it was for Mrs. King."

"You're wrong there," said Taggart hoarsely. "When I thought back I knew just when it was we knew about that highball. And Hazel was the only one at the table right after that. King came after. King couldn't have killed a cat. And he hadn't any reason. . . . So that's why I thought it was my wife. There was nothing else to think."

Nick spoke across him to Hendrickson. "Taggart had no chance to poison Mrs. King's highball, *after* he knew it was for her. We can't get away from that. . . . And he didn't kill his wife. He's been trying to protect her. That's the way it was."

"You seem to have come to a great many conclusions, Mr. Parr," said Hendrickson acidly. "You seem very sure who did not do it. Now can you tell us who did put in the poison?"

"I can tell you."

"That's fine." Hendrickson's sarcasm was heavy. But his eyes were seriously attentive. He said, "Let's take the first case. Mr. King appears to be the only one who knew that Mrs. King was to drink the highball."

"That's right."

A faint, quickly smothered sound came from Jennifer Mitchell. In spite of himself Nick glanced toward her, then quickly away.

He said slowly, distinctly, "King was the only one who knew. Anyone else, looking at the tray, would have assumed the highball was for King."

Hendrickson took that in. His eyes flickered. Nick went on, "King liked them more than his wife did. He kept a special Scotch for himself in this room. The poison in the highball was for King."

Very slowly the prosecuting attorney turned that over. His voice was expressionless as he asked, "In your opinion who put it there for King?"

Nick looked about. "This man here. Tod Burton."

After an instant's silence Tod Burton laughed. It was an easy laugh, amused and contemptuous. "This tears it. The wonder detective. . . . And why, Sherlock Holmes," he asked mockingly, "did I put poison in Roge King's highball?"

"You wanted to marry his wife."

"Aren't you a bit confused? *This* is the young lady I want to marry." He looked at Jennifer with a smile.

"Camouflage," said Nick. "You were in love, very desperately in love, with Veronica King. You had met her in Chicago about the first of last October. She stayed on there after her husband returned. He had not met you. You moved to a room next to hers in the hotel. In December you were both for some days at another Chicago hotel, not together, but on the same floor."

"So were fifty other people! Were they all desperately in love with her, too?" Burton eyed Nick scoffingly. "This is funny." Then his voice sharpened. "But your accusations aren't funny. They're a pack of lies."

"Not lies. I have a letter of hers written to you in November. November of last year. In it she said she could not manage 'the Thanksgiving thing' but would arrange something later. The meeting in December was evidently the something later. In Florida you pretended to meet for the first time."

Hendrickson asked, "You can prove this, Mr. Parr?"

"Dates and places."

"So what?" said Burton coolly. He took a step forward, eyeing Nick with the same fixed mockery. "What's the difference when I met her? *If* I met her before. She was charming. Her husband was charming. I had fun with them. Then I fell for her sister. What could be simpler?"

"You didn't fall for her sister. She went out with you to keep people from talking about you and Veronica. You wanted Veronica to divorce King. You made her believe that King was tired of her. That's why she changed her will. But she wouldn't divorce him. She didn't like divorce and she liked her life with King. She also liked having you adore her but she wasn't going to break up her life for you. But you were confident that if King were out of the way she would marry you. And so—"

"Damn it!" said Burton. "I hate to seem indelicate—but why would I want to marry a woman who was about to become a mother?"

"You felt the child was yours."

"Marvelous!" said Burton with level scorn. "A soap opera."

"That is substantiated by a letter of yours to Mrs. King. She received it last Saturday morning. You said you would have both her and your child. That she was to make up her mind without delay."

For just a moment Burton did not speak. He must have thought Veronica had destroyed that letter. He said, "I sent no such letter. . . . Better ask friend Taggart about that."

"It was your letter. And in your talk with her, before cocktails, you were trying to persuade her to divorce and she refused. You were desperate. So you carried out your other plan. You had the arsenic with you, and when you saw the highball, when you went to the pantry for the tray, that seemed to you the perfect chance. So you came out, carrying the tray, going into a butler act, making an impression of gaiety—"

Burton said mockingly, "Enter death, laughing!"

"Right," said Nick harshly. "But even your nerves did not want to see Roger King drink that highball. So you snatched your quickie—you needed that drink—and got yourself and Jennifer out fast. And there was your mistake. Veronica drank it."

Not a muscle of Burton's face changed. His gaze did not shift. His jeering voice had a thin, cutting edge. "And you thought this all up by your little self—?"

"I should have known before," said Nick. "When I told you Veronica was dead. When you said, 'Everyone else all right?'"

"Trying hard to save Taggart—or King—aren't you? But it won't work." Deliberately Burton looked about, his lips putting on a thin smile. "This would be funny if it weren't so devilish. I happen to be interested in Veronica's sister."

"Let's not go into that routine," said Nick. "Though it might interest you to know that Sergeant Nolan, here, suspected you from the first because of that. His basis was wrong—he didn't have the facts I had—but his intuition about you was dead right."

"Wonderful!" said Burton. "So this is your bright idea of getting your friends out of a fix. . . . Am I also supposed to have killed Mrs. Taggart? And why, for God's sake? Did I get her with child, too?"

"You killed her. You had the cyanide and you brought it here—you didn't know what to expect from this questioning. . . . Or you were keeping it safe, in case your room was ransacked."

"And then I just decided to use it on Mrs. Taggart? Just like that? Because I didn't like her hair or something?"

"Because you were damn well afraid of her. She knew too much about you and Veronica. She talked too much. This afternoon she said you left as if you didn't want to see what was going to happen. It was after that, when you took your drink, that you put the stuff in for her."

"I suppose you saw me?"

"You had the chance."

Burton taunted, "The chance! What does that prove? Everyone had the chance. . . . And how was I supposed to know she was going to drink it?"

"It wasn't much of a gamble. She'd said she'd play Veronica. You said, yourself, when you were deviling Taggart, that anyone who knew her would know she'd drink that highball."

"Oh, the hell with it!" said Burton. "I'm not going to take any more such crap. If the police know their business they'll give you a swift kick in the tail. You *don't* know I had any cyanide, you *didn't* see me use it, but you *do* think I'd stick my neck out by killing a harmless old gal so she wouldn't chatter about me. . . . After first killing my lovely hostess. . . . I'm not a local character so you want to pin the dirty work on me. But it won't work. You need a little thing like evidence."

"Oh, there's evidence," said Nick. "That container was not on the table just after Mrs. Taggart died. I looked before the sergeant did. I ran my finger about the tray, under the edge. The container was not there. You had it on you, then. You'd meant to rush up to Mrs. Taggart and drop it near her but you hadn't a chance. I got to the table first and then Hendrickson kept us back. Kept us in place. You had a bad moment then. But you thought of a drink for Jennifer. When you got the Martini you tucked the tube under the tray. You were the only one at the table after I had searched it and the sergeant had searched it, until the sergeant came back and looked again."

"What about my hands?" said Burton derisively. "What about that smell of cyanide? You forgot that, didn't you? You forgot that little item. My hands were pure."

"You put them in the Martini," said Nick.

Burton gave a bark of laughter. "Bright boy! Go to the head of the class. Something else you thought up all your little self. That you didn't see."

"And you sloshed the Martini on your hand as you carried it back. *That* I saw."

"Oh, that you saw! Who doesn't spill, carrying a full glass? And the rest you just imagined. Your imagination—"

"I didn't imagine the crack on my head."

Burton's stare was exaggerated. "So you were hit on the head! I thought you'd better have it examined. . . . What's that to do with this?"

"I was hit," said Nick, "because I mentioned your taste for brunettes."

Slowly Burton looked about as if calling them all to witness this last inanity. "I don't happen to have a taste for brunettes."

"So I know. Yet you'd been out with one. I had the wrong one in mind—an authentic brunette. I tossed that out to you, for no particular reason except to razz you, and you looked murder at me. That night I was slugged. Getting into my car. Then left in the car, the engine running. Dr. Abbey, here, knows all about it. He fished me out. I didn't know who'd done it. The police checks show that everyone connected with the case could have done it—each one out alone and unaccounted for. I knew I'd come close to something. Someone was worried. Worried enough to kill. But what was the reason?"

"I'll bite," said Burton contemptuously. "What was it?"

"There was a picture of Veronica in the papers. Dressed as a gypsy, at some benefit. She had on dark curls. . . ." He stopped a moment, seeing the picture again, seeing the lovely face he had seen in his office, with the smile of a wicked child. *Dead. Done. Gone.* Burton had said that,

Burton who had killed her, not meaning to, but because it had seemed a good idea to kill her husband.

Nick's voice was hard when he went on. "When I saw—just now—that you had killed Veronica, I knew it must have been you who had slugged me. But why? And then suddenly it clicked. That picture . . . It wasn't easy for you to see her alone in this city and not have people talk. You might be seen, even in any out of the way place. But with dark hair . . . She put on the curls after she went out. And you thought I'd found out, that I was hot on the trail of your intimacy. If that came out you figured you were in jeopardy. At any moment it might come out that the highball had seemed to be for King. And if it were known you had any animus against King—"

Burton stared at him a long moment before speaking. "I'd like to bump you off," he said, no mockery in his voice now. "It would be a pleasure. I don't like you."

"I don't like you," said Nick.

"I wish whoever slugged you had put more power into it!" Then his voice grew light again and confident. "But you can't pin that on me. What you think is one thing and what you can prove is another. If you've been trying to make a reputation for yourself in the eyes of these gentlemen, you've made an ass out of yourself."

He turned with all the assurance in the world. He caught up his coat and flung it over his arm. And Hendrickson stood there, unmoving, incertitude in every dumb line of him, Nick thought furiously. Hendrickson could not see, when the glasses were held to his eyes—Hendrickson was not going to act—

"Oh, I don't think there'll be trouble proving the attack," said a mild voice from among the bystanders.

Burton spun about. Abbey came forward a little, his round head cocked on one side, his blue eyes fixed thoughtfully on Burton. He said, "About the fingers—they were wet with liquor, you know. . . . No cyanide odor. . . . But about the attack. You stood quite a time behind those bushes. We had the prints photographed next morning."

Nothing but trampled grass, Nick knew. No prints at all. He stared at Abbey in perplexity.

"And rosebushes have a way of snagging clothes."

Abbey's right hand reached into a pocket and brought out a folded paper. Carefully he opened it and picked out the contents.

He said, in an instructive, factual tone, as if addressing a class, "These threads—these few threads—" he looked reflectively at them, then held them up. "An examination of your wardrobe—"

Burton lunged and wrested the threads from Abbey's hands. He thrust them into his mouth and swallowed them. Then he was out the door like a shot, banging it shut after him.

Nick led the stampede to the door and down the hall. The outer door slammed and before he got to it the scream of a police siren wailed down the drive. The car was out of sight before he ran from under the porte-cochere. It was Hendrickson's car that had been parked at the head of the others and the policeman who had been sitting in it was scrambling to his feet holding his hands to a slugged jaw. The siren sounded now from the highway, speeding toward the city.

"Clearing the way for himself!" Wayland panted. "But we'll get him! Come on, sergeant. Into my car." The policemen piled in, then piled out. A tire had been slashed.

"The man's quick." Abbey was at Nick's elbow, surveying the confusion—Nolan running futilely down the drive, Wayland barking at the slugged policeman, King hurrying to the garage, shouting for the chauffeur. "Glad he didn't use that knife on you last night."

"Get your radio going!" Hendrickson snapped at Wayland. "Alert all cars. I'll get on the phone." As he passed Abbey he demanded, "Any chance of getting back those threads?"

"More chance of his destroying the garment."

"He won't have time. I'll phone the club."

He hurried into the house, all briskness and business now, and Abbey looked after him. "He's all right, once he's started. And started on the right track."

"God bless," said Nick. "God bless you and God bless the rosebushes and God bless the threads."

"Ah, yes, the threads," said Abbey.

"'On such frail strands do weighty things depend.'" Larrabee was twinkling at them through his pince-nez. "Very dramatic, doctor. . . . And excellent reasoning, Nicholas." He lowered his voice. "For a moment, there, it looked awkward. The point that King was the only one with pre-knowledge. But 'All's well that ends well.'"

"Not ended yet," Abbey muttered.

Back in the library Hendrickson was at the phone giving orders to the Country Club. "Deny admittance. . . . I'll get a man there. . . ." He called his office and looked up to say, "Nice work, Parr. Nothing like being on the inside. . . . Hendrickson speaking. I want Tully. . . . Our stage business helped you out, didn't it?"

"That did it, Mr. Hendrickson."

"Sorry it did for the poor lady."

He jerked his head toward the chair. Someone, Nick saw thankfully, had spread a coat over the dead woman. Taggart, undoubtedly, for Taggart was sitting by her, with an air of somber waiting. His hands were gripping the arms of the chair and his eyes stared ahead, ignoring the turmoil in the room. There must be unconscious relief in him, Nick thought, pitying. It was the end of a nightmare.

Of several nightmares. For her, too. And then he thought, *Easy rationalization. She did not want to die.*

"Yep. Call me here." Hendrickson finished his orders and started to swing about, forgetting he was not in his office chair. "If the clothes are in his room we'll have them," he said. "Too bad you let him get away with those threads, doctor."

"He's a very sudden young man," said Abbey.

"And you don't know those fellows the way we do. We'd never have given him the chance. . . . But he gave himself away. Yes, sir, he gave himself away." The prosecuting attorney was pleasurably excited. He rose and went over to Taggart. "No hard feelings, Mr. Taggart?"

Taggart said, "No hard feelings." He let his hand be grasped.

"We have to do our duty, you know. That's what you elect us for. We have to follow every possible angle."

Taggart nodded.

"And we'll get that son of a gun! This is one case where we'll get a conviction!" The harassment in the man slipped out but he hurried away from it. "Now we'll take care of your lady." But before he could phone again Wayland and Nolan and King hurried in and he demanded, "Got the cars on it, lieutenant?"

"Yes, sir. They'll catch up with him any minute now."

"Any minute," Hendrickson repeated.

And it seemed to Nick no more than a minute or two before the call came. Burton had overplayed the police right-of-way and crashed into a truck at an intersection. He had lived long enough to say to the bystander who reached him, "Better than doing time!"

Hendrickson said heartily, "Now we can wrap it up nicely, Mr. King. Nothing about—about anything personal, you know. He killed Mrs. King because she refused his attentions. And Mrs. Taggart—well, he was afraid she knew it. We'll do the best we can to wrap it up, Mr. King."

"I'd appreciate it," said King.

He'd appreciate it with campaign contributions, Nick thought ironically. Jennifer would give him back half that money—she'd make him take it now. King had been through hell. Now he could get rid of that dark-eyed secretary even as a "friend." And a good thing for her, too. She was young enough and stunning enough to make herself a new life—and Heaven help the man she made it with!

"I am infinitely relieved," Abbey was saying to him. The doctor had got out one of his good cigars and was smoking it with evident satisfaction. "I did not relish," he said, confidentially, "the prospect of a trial. Very awkward, explaining I didn't get those threads off the rosebushes."

His blue eyes twinkled at Nick's stare. "Just some ravelings of my own," he murmured. "I got them ready midway in your eloquence. You had convinced me—that container was convincing—but I had the feeling you'd need some reinforcement."

"Doc," said Nick, "I want you always on my side."

"It was *your* side," said Abbey. "As the late Mr. Burton remarked, you thought it up all your little self. . . . Coming for that chess soon?"

"Soon." Nick smiled at him.

Then, restively, he looked about the room. Jennifer Mitchell had vanished. Suddenly he remembered something and went quickly out the door and into the pantry. There was a telephone there and he got on it, before Hendrickson got on the line again, and as he dialed he looked about curiously. This was where it had begun. Where Burton had poured in that arsenic. How does a man feel who puts poison in a cocktail? The first time must be the hardest.

He said, "Society please. Miss Sally Waters." Her voice came and he spoke quickly. "Sally? I promised you a break. Here it is."

"Nick, darling!"

"Listen. The King case is solved. Tod Burton killed her. Reason—Mrs. King turned down his attentions. He also killed Hazel Taggart at the King house within the hour. Cyanide in her highball. Because she knew too much. He broke under questioning, stole a police car to make his getaway, crashed into a truck, and died almost instantly. Last words, 'Better than doing time.'"

"Nick, you—you're not making this up—?"

"Word of honor. Get going. Oh—Sergeant Nolan suspected him from the first. But masterly work was done by Hendrickson and Wayland in forcing the showdown. Now beat the police reporters to it."

"Oh, *thanks!*"

She had hung up.

He grinned and pushed open the swing door into the kitchen. Annie would find her for him. He would like to see her when she wasn't tense with grief and worry, when she wasn't being brave and gallant and proud. Anyway, he would like to see her. Period.

And there she was. She was sitting at the table with Annie, where he had sat yesterday with the girls, and they were drinking tea and talking and crying and Delia was standing over them with a teapot in her hand.

He said, "Don't I rate any tea?"

Jennifer jumped up. Her eyes were bright with tears, tears of excitement, relief, reaction, and her cheeks were flushed. She was lovely. Through the tears her eyes smiled warmly at him.

"Tea would you like?"

Annie started for a cup, then paused to demand, dramatically, "Oh, wasn't he the grand one, Miss Jenny, standing there, outfacing them all!"

"Wasn't he!" said Nick, laughing. "And wasn't it your grand memory that helped!" The thought brushed him, *And Hazel Taggart's grand memory.*

"Take him up to the study, Miss Jenny, dear," said Delia quickly. "Annie'll bring you a tray. Maybe it's coffee you'd rather be having and some fresh bread and baked ham. You take her away, sir, out of this trouble. Where you can talk things over quiet like."

"My very thought," said Nick. His eyes had never left Jennifer's. "Will you come?"

She tucked her arm through his.

MURDER IN
ROOM 700

Chapter One
Six Hours

She stood trembling in the middle of the room, staring at the figure that lay sprawled upon the floor.

Philip—was that Philip? That black, still figure, lying so limply. . . . Then it was all true.

Desperately she fought back the horror that was shaking her. There were things she must do, if she did not want to be caught like a rat in a trap. She stared about the room.

It was a hotel living room but with signs of more than a transient's occupancy. A wide, flat-topped desk was littered with untidy papers. A bookcase was crowded with books. By the windows, with drawn shades, a small baby grand piano bore a mound of sheet music on the Chinese robe that draped it. . . . Nothing there that she must take away. . . . Then she saw the suitcase, dropped beside a low couch.

She stepped forward, then stood hesitating. She could not have Philip lying there. It was too horrible. If she threw a coverlet over him that would attract the attention of the chambermaid when she opened the door next morning. Every hour was needed for escape.

Fearfully she brushed past the body and opened the door into an inner room. It was a bedroom, untouched, with not a personal thing in sight. She must get Phil onto the bed.

Cold with fright she stooped above him and tried to lift the heavy weight. She did not want to see his face but she did—Phil's face frozen in that furious surprise. Only the dark, tousled hair was like the Phil she knew. . . . And it had been so little time since he had been smiling disarmingly at her, those lips making their easy promises.

What was it he had said? *Safe as a saint, Jinny dear!*

Faint with terror she forced herself to self-control and swift action. Crouching, she shouldered the burden on her back and staggered toward the bed. She thought her strength would break with the effort. He was so heavy. . . .

He was on the bed now. She straightened the limbs, already chilling, and buttoned the tweed coat to hide that blood-stained hole in the shirt beneath. Then she covered him with the blanket on the foot *of* the bed and drew it high above the shoulders.

Let the maid look in! She would think him sleeping and withdraw. Every hour gained was vital.

She must get away as soon as she could. It was almost one o'clock. The clerk downstairs would think it queer for her to be leaving alone at such an hour. She must hurry. No time to yield to terror or compassion.

Closing the door behind her she turned back into the living room and went swiftly to the case on the couch, a small, brown leather overnight case, lettered in gold. She caught it up, then put it down, hesitating. If she went out, carrying the case—surely that would awaken suspicion. She must make her going seem natural. And yet she must not leave a trace.

She opened the bag and eyed the contents anxiously. The silver fittings were monogrammed—well, she could tuck some of them in her handbag and stow the rest, with the other things, about her person. Lucky for her that she was fairly tall, with a slim, almost meager body! And lucky that the evening frock was a gossamer chiffon and

the night robe a wisp of silk! The silver slippers and the
mules were a harder problem but frantically she packed
them about her, winding the frock tightly, and tucking in
handkerchiefs, fittings, every telltale personal thing.

Then, the bag emptied, she searched the room with
desperate eyes. There was a tiny handkerchief on the table
beside the unopened bottle of ginger ale and a glove on
the couch. Oh, fool, fool, to scatter her things so reck-
lessly! But who could have foreseen what this night was to
bring, what desperate madness and danger. . . .

Safe as a saint, Jinny dear!

And all the time he had been planning, been contriv-
ing. . . . Planning anything but *this*.

Keenly now she looked about the room, telling herself
to make sure, very sure, that nothing was left that might
betray identity. This was her only chance. Everything
depended on it. . . . She had looked everywhere, searched
every corner. For a last moment she stood, staring about her.

She was a slim creature, a woman who might be anywhere in the early thirties, but who now, in her stark terror, looked the eight and thirty that her beauty would
have denied. Her dark hair banded the pallor of her tense
face; she had a nun's brow, wide and low, over dark, stormy
eyes, and a mouth whose delicate, ironic curves derided
both the calm brow and the mutinous eyes.

Frantically now those eyes were searching. . . . Ah, the
overnight bag itself! A chill sweat broke out on her at that
oversight. The case was monogrammed.

Furiously she set to work with manicure scissors, scrap-
ing at the three small letters, *V. A. C.,* till the leather was
shredded. Then she went through the case again, to make
sure it was utterly empty.

Of course, she was leaving fingerprints. That could not
be helped. But unless something unforeseen dragged her
into this her fingers would never be examined.

Now she must go. She slipped on the black coat she had discarded when she packed the things about her, and drew the beige fox collar high. She pulled low the black casque of hat. In the glass her white face and burning eyes stared so starkly at her that she brushed on rouge with shaking fingers. It stood out like a bull's-eye but it might deceive the clerk. She must steel herself to seem casual when she addressed that clerk.

One more look about the room, one more look into that inner room, her eyes seeking, in awful pity and farewell, that still figure on the bed. Oh, Phil—poor, poor Phil! But she must not let herself think of him now. She must keep her head, act coolly.

Had she got the key to the suite? Yes. Now turn out the light. Queer how that sudden darkness made her hammering heart lurch again. Now out the door.

She gave a swift look up and down the hall as she turned the key in the door—it was not self-locking—then slipped the key with its huge disk into her handbag already bulging with silver. She pressed the button for the elevator.

It seemed eternities before it came. She thought of the stairs, but that might look evasive. She was on the seventh floor—too much chance of meeting some one. She must seem natural, above all. It was natural to wait for elevators.

The night service was slow. This was a second-rate hotel, of course, where people went for secrecy from their own kind.

The elevator at last. The colored boy was staring at her—did she look strange? He spoke to her, a forth-putting boy, she thought, as boys probably were at these hotels.

"Late, ain't it, lady? Anything I can get you?"

"Oh, no." Her voice was quiet enough, though brittle to her own ears. "No. Just an errand I have to do myself at the drug store."

He looked as though he were going to speak again, then stopped. Probably he did a little bootlegging himself.

Downstairs the elevators opened on a hall that was just off the main lobby. The building had been made over into a hotel and was full of makeshifts. Beyond the elevators was a side entrance that led out to Sixth Avenue—a little lane of an entrance between the Smart Clothes Shoppe on the corner and the florist's tiny cubby-hole.

As she glanced down it the boy, who had come out from the elevator cage, said casually, "That door's locked now, lady. After twelve." She flung a fluttery "thank you" over her shoulder as she turned into the main lobby.

The place was empty. The ornate red velvet, pseudo-something-or-other chairs were vacant by the little stands still littered with the cigar butts and ashes of the evening's occupants. Over them hung silly looking palms from jars of brilliant reds and blues.

She felt the eyes of the night clerk. She went straight to the desk and he leaned toward her, over the registry book, a small, bald, spare-fleshed man, with pouches under his sharp eyes. She thought those eyes were immediately questioning—clerks in such places must be nurtured on suspicion.

Her own glance stole to the open book. She wished she knew under what name Phil was known there—what he had written there that evening. Suppose the clerk asked her her name? All she knew was the room number. Seven hundred.

"Is there a good drug store near?" she asked the man.

Her voice was too tense; he mustn't think her anxious. She summoned a slight smile. "It's nothing but indigestion, but I must get a prescription put up."

"One right across the street," said the clerk. He had a manner better than the hotel; he must have come down in the world, and he peered at her as if recognizing her own unsuitability to the place.

"I'll send the boy for you," he added.

"Oh, no—I want several things. I shall have to see what they have."

She walked away, across the lobby, and out the door that a lounging colored man sprang to open for her, then crossed the street to the drug store. She felt sure they were watching. She went in and ordered aspirin, then asked for Catosen—a made-up name.

"Never heard of it," said the clerk. "Something new? What per cent is that?"

She murmured something and started down the street.

It seemed empty for New York, even at that hour. Few people were in sight. . . . She was walking too fast; she must slacken to the definite-seeming pace of a woman out at night, alone but unobtrusive. She felt as if she were being followed.

So she forced herself to stop at another drug store and asked for Catosen there. Then she hurried toward Broadway and its lights.

There were always throngs on Broadway—even at one-thirty. And she must not look back over her shoulder like that, as if she were being followed. Suppose that clerk grew suspicious when she did not return and had the door opened?

All they would see would be that quiet figure in the bed. Surely they would not disturb it. But if they spoke, to explain the intrusion, and had no answer—

At any moment they might be after her.

She could not go home, not at this hour. She had said she was going for the night, to be back early. She must live up to it, do nothing to focus the servants' attention. She must stay away till a reasonable hour in the morning.

Two young men who had passed turned and strolled by her again, their eyes bold and inquiring. They had dark, foreign faces. At her flash of contempt they laughed loudly. She hurried on.

There were other lone women in sight. But not quite like herself. She could not walk like this much later. Where did people go to hide?

The subway! A tired woman, coming home alone, would not be strange there. She saw a station and went down into it. It had been years since she had been in the subway; she expected to buy a ticket and had to be directed how to drop a coin into the mechanism that released the turnstile she must pass through.

Into the first train that came. There were others there, some rowdy youths, a well-dressed man, a couple with a sleeping child, a young pair snuggled close together. The air was close, the roar deafening. She sat still and watched the white-tiled walls slide by with amazing speed, her eyes mechanically noting the advertisements at the stations.

"Change for Brooklyn Bridge."

Brooklyn—that was the place. It must take a long time to get there. . . . She kept looking at her watch, forgetting what it had been the last time.

In Brooklyn she got out and turned vaguely into the darkness of unfamiliar streets. When a policeman looked at her her heart stopped. She walked till she found another station and rode back to Manhattan.

She felt that she was in a never-ending nightmare. Her only consciousness was of roaring, hurtling speed tearing through white-tiled tunnels. Noise and bad air and peanut shells.

She sat still till she was alone in the car. She did not know how far the train went. She was surprised when it ceased to run underground and became an elevated train.

At last she got out and found herself in shadowy streets, among tall, dark-windowed apartments. A taxi veered toward her and she walked rapidly away. She angled about two squares, then followed the elevated back to another station.

To Brooklyn again. She lay back and pretended to be asleep.

It was after three now. It was after four when she got to Brooklyn, about five when she returned to New York. At five one could walk about the streets, she thought.

Gray, queer streets, with queer people on them. Peddlers pushing their carts. Workmen plodding along. Taxis finishing the night's prowling. Strange people that she had never seen before, people with bags of black oilskin, who were poking in the garbage cans set out at the curbs. She saw a woman salvage an old corset, a remnant of bread, some rinds of melon.

She turned toward the Avenue. She was near the park. Men were hosing down the sidewalks. Servants were out airing the dogs. A housemaid in uniform with a Pekinese on a leash was murmuring something intimate to a footman with a police dog. A bored-looking English maid passed with an equally bored Scotty.

She felt more conspicuous here and hurried over to Sixth.

The newsboys were crying the papers. "Murder—all about the hotel murder. Murder!"

So soon! They must have found out at once!

She bought a paper and went into a restaurant, where she sat down at a white-topped table and ordered breakfast.

Her heart was hammering horribly as she unfolded the paper. Her wrists were weak; for a moment she thought she was going to faint. That was ridiculous—here, after all she had gone through. She called on the sternest stuff in her to bear her up. It was real; she must face it. She had grown to feel that it was a nightmare from which she might waken. But no wakening for her. . . . Or for Phil.

The type danced. She read it in snatches.

PROMINENT PLAYWRIGHT MURDERED
FOUND DEAD IN HOTEL ROOM
WOMAN COMPANION FLED

One of the most startling mysteries of years confronted the police at three o'clock this morning at Room 700 of the Highgate Hotel, when the well-known playwright and clubman, Philip Darrow, was found lying on the bed, fully dressed, shot through the heart.

The dead man was known to the management of the hotel as "Mr. Deering," under which name, on the private registry of the hotel, he had kept a suite of rooms in which he worked from time to time, evidently to escape the interruptions of his usual life. His real name and identity was discovered from papers found in his pockets. [Oh, why hadn't she taken those—that might have delayed things!]

As "Mr. Deering" he had come into the hotel at ten o'clock accompanied by a woman whom the clerk described as of youthful appearance, attractive, and fashionably dressed. He stated that she was his sister, and might spend the night there. In case she did he would require no other rooms, he said, as there was a day bed in the living room.

There was nothing in the woman's appearance to arouse suspicion, and she was bringing luggage with her, a case found later, empty of contents, with the initials cut away.

The first evidence that the management had of anything wrong was when the woman appeared in the hotel lobby, alone, shortly after one o'clock. She told the clerk that she wanted a prescription put up for a stomach disorder and inquired the nearest drug store. She was directed to the one across the street and, later, was seen by the hotel doorman to leave it and walk down the street, but the doorman thought nothing of it then, as he imagined she had not found what she wanted and was looking further.

When time passed and she did not return, the hotel clerk, Mr. Dakin, became uneasy and communicated with the manager, who finally went to Room 700. Receiving no response to knocks upon the door, he finally unlocked it and proceeded to the bedroom.

The occupant was found, fully dressed, lying on the bed, apparently asleep. But he was stone dead with a bullet wound over his heart. An odd feature was that the coat was buttoned over the wound, although there was no bullet hole in the coat. The vest within was not buttoned in place, but the bullet had penetrated the vest while it had been buttoned, and the bullet had been fired at short range, for the woolen goods showed the scorching of powder marks. Evidently his companion had unbuttoned the vest to examine the wound, then drawn the coat above it.

There were no signs of blood on the bed, though a rug in the living room showed bloodstains. There were no marks of struggle in the room. Darrow had evidently been taken unawares.

The assassin undoubtedly used a silencer as the occupants of the next room, who were playing

cards till midnight, heard no noise, nor did any
one at the hotel. The shooting took place some
time before midnight, according to Medical Examiner Corrigan, who examined the body. He set the
time as about eleven o'clock. The woman did not
leave until after one.

When the management discovered the body
they immediately called in the police. Identification of the body instantly followed, from papers
in the clothes of the deceased, and friends, who
were summoned, completed the identification. No
one could give any clew as to the identity of the
woman.

The management of the hotel stated that Darrow as "Mr. Deering," visited the hotel erratically,
ordinarily coming in for several hours at a time
during some days. He received no mail there and
entertained no visitors. He used his rooms as an
office to which he could retire for seclusion.

The theory of suicide is not held tenable by the
police, as the gun was missing, and the woman
would hardly have removed evidence which might
have protected her. Also, the shot was fired slightly from the left, a position impossible for the victim's own right hand.

Mr. Darrow was a well-known figure in metropolitan life and a playwright of distinction. Two
successes of his have had phenomenal runs, "The
Turning Point," and "Her Move." He was socially
prominent, a member of the following clubs [her
eye raced past the familiar names] and a member of
the polo team that successfully defended the Whe-
don Cup. He was thirty-eight years old.

His domestic life was known to be unhappy,
as his wife had been pronounced insane ten years

ago, and has been in a sanitarium ever since. From
time to time his name has been connected with
various members of his companies, but no possible clew for murder could be given by his friends.
They profess themselves utterly in the dark as to
the identity of the unknown woman.

When last seen by the clerk she was wearing a dark, fashionably cut coat with light-col-
ored fur about the throat, a small black hat,
brimless, black shoes and tan silk stock-
ings. [Sharp eyes, that clerk!] A complete description of her was obtained by the police who are
confident of running her down.

Over and over she read it, as she forced herself to eat the
breakfast brought; each mouthful choked her, but eat it
she must under the eyes of the waitress. She felt stunned
by the swiftness of the police. She had counted on its not
being discovered till nine or ten in the morning.

If only she had known what Phil had told the clerk—
that his "sister" might not spend the night! Then she could
have left naturally and not given that excuse which aroused
their suspicions.

And so he had not been so sure of himself after all!

She wondered what friends had been summoned—how
long before her phone would ring.

She could not sit there at the table any longer. Out
in the street again. Almost six now. She could be at the
apartment by seven. She took a taxi to the Grand Central, then, in a panic, remembered the station would be
watched, gave another direction and soon got out.

There was little money left in her purse; she could only
afford one more taxi, so she walked until time for it. Then
she gave the man her address, one in the east Nineties.

It was a building of quiet and well-ordered correctness;
the day man was at the door, with his ready smile, tinged
now with frank surprise.

"You're early, Mrs. Channing!"

"Terribly early." She smiled as he opened the door and
said a bright "good morning" to the lanky foreign youth
in the elevator who slammed the gratings and pressed the
buttons.

"Ten," she reminded him. She had nearly said, "Seven."
Seven. Seven. Seven hundred.

She stepped into the little hall, turned to a door on the
left and rang the bell. Her heart was hammering in cease-
less panic as the door opened. What did she expect—to see
uniforms lined up to receive her, detectives questioning
the maid, Nina in hysterics—?

Chapter Two
Questions

There was her accustomed hall, green-paneled, quiet, filled only with the accustomed things—yellow roses in a Chinese bowl given back by the mirror behind them, Ellen in her trim gray and white, holding open the door. It was like reaching sanctuary. The sense of peace, of safety, was almost nerve-shattering in its seeming security.

Her smile quivered as she faced the maid. "Oh, I'm so tired," she said with a confessing sigh. "Those terrible morning trains."

Oh, why had she said that? She must remember that she had said trains. She did not know yet what alibi she was going to give for the night's absence. All she had explained was that she had been called to *a* sick friend. Now she must remember that she took a train to that friend's house.

She was yielding her handbag when she remembered its contents and gripped it again.

"Never mind, Ellen. . . . Miss Nina awake?"

"No, ma'am. She came home after you left—headache, but nothing bad, she said. She didn't go to the house party. She was moving about, packing, late into the night."

"I hope she hasn't undone that good packing of yours," said Mrs. Channing. "Well, there's no hurry about waking her—her boat doesn't sail till noon."

"I'll have breakfast soon for you, ma'am—"

"I had breakfast on the train."

Oh, did they have diners on those early trains? Why hadn't she said in the station? She added, "Don't bother about anything till Miss Nina is ready."

There was no one else to plan for. She had been a widow for ten years.

She went down the green-paneled hall and opened the door into her room. She realized she was still holding the paper in her hand. Had Ellen noticed it? Had Ellen read the story in the one delivered at the apartment—or was it only in the later edition sold on the streets?

If Ellen had read it she would think it strange her mistress came in so smilingly, with no word of it. . . . She stood still a moment and shut her eyes. Well, she could explain. She could say she had not looked at the paper till she came in.

First she must rid herself of those things. Hurriedly she reached under her frock and divested herself of the swathings—the chiffon frock, the peach night robe, with the slippers bound in its folds. . . .

The silver she laid casually out. Then she stood with the key in her hand, considering. A big, red disk was attached to it, with the number seven hundred.

No hiding place occurred to her. None that would baffle a shrewd search. New York apartments are not prolific of cubby-holes. For the present it was safe in her handbag. She always carried a bag.

Then, holding the paper, she went through her bathroom and opened a door into the room beyond. Silently she looked in. Nina lay there asleep; her mop of dark hair—she was letting it grow—outspread on the pillow about her made her seem younger, more helpless, than she seemed awake.

Nina—her little Nina. Flushed with sleep, long lashes dark on the smooth cheeks. Her little face with its poignant, almost heart-breaking beauty, was turned toward her mother, and one bare arm lay across the pillows. Little Nina, so vulnerable, so young, looking so much younger than the sixteen she had but lately ceased to be.

It seemed to Virginia Channing that she could rather die, there, on her tired feet, than go in and wake her child, and speak the words that must be spoken. But she must not show the white feather now. Time was flying.

She stepped toward the bed, the paper in her hand.

"Nina, Nina darling," she said softly. "Nina—it's morning."

Half an hour later she came out of the room and sought the maid.

"A terrible thing has happened, Ellen," she said quickly. "It was in the paper I brought home with me. Did you see it? About Mr. Darrow?"

The girl turned a blank face toward her.

"He was killed last night—shot at some hotel," said Mrs. Channing. "He went there late with some woman. No one would have believed it of him, would they? . . . The woman made her escape—no one knows who she is. . . . I've just been telling Miss Nina. You can imagine how this hurts her—hurts us both."

"God in His Mercy!" said Ellen, wide-eyed.

"It's pretty bad, Ellen," said Mrs. Channing, unevenly. It was a comfort not to try to hide her agitation—it was natural enough. "There will be a terrible scandal. And since there is this—this other woman in his life—I think it would be best if you did not tell any one he was here at all last evening. We don't want to be dragged into it. I suppose the reporters will be busy asking questions. And we don't want to be dragged into it," she insisted. "To have him coming here—and then going to a hotel—with some woman—"

"Who'd 'a' thought it?" said Ellen, her blue eyes scared. "Oh, never a word out of me, Mrs. Channing. . . . Can I see the paper?"

"Miss Nina's reading it. Perhaps it's in this one."

Virginia went to the one folded beside her plate in the dining room, glanced at it, and held it out. "Here it is. We must be very careful, Ellen, not to get talked about. I know I can rely on you."

"You can that," said Ellen fervently.

Ellen was loyal—loyal and unsuspecting. But she was young and feminine and there would be those in her circles that she would think she could trust— However, it had to be risked.

Back into her room. A cold shower and a fresh frock— was there a dull stain on the back of the one she took off? She hid that beneath a ball gown in her closet and pulled on a black skirt and a blouse of Chinese red with gay gold and black embroidery.

No feeling of sanctuary now in her home. Her mind had begun to rush out to meet the dangers. What about letters? She should have looked through Phil's pockets— he might have kept some reckless lines that would point suspicion.

There might be anything in his desk at home. He was so careless. And Dervish, his man, might have overheard various telephonings, even the arrangements for the evening. She'd have to chance that. Now she must plan an alibi that would be question-proof.

A sick friend, she had said. What sick friend? Whom could she trust to stand by her? Searchingly she began to turn over, one by one, the possibilities of her friendships. A friend at a little distance, since she had said trains.

Lita? Lita was loyal—but Lita had a husband and a household. The Whedons? They had too large a place—too many servants. Aunt Helen? There was her housekeeper, with her austere conscience, to reckon with.

Virginia's mind raced hither and thither. What friend was there for such a need? What friend anywhere?

The bell. It was only eight o'clock. Who was coming at this hour. Some reporter?

She was standing, rigid, in the hall, when the maid brought her a card.

"He says it's important, Mrs. Channing, or he wouldn't trouble you so early."

Mrs. Channing looked down at the card. Stephen Ryder. . . . Stephen Ryder. . . . That name ought to mean something to her. Fear was numbing her faculties.

"Just a moment, tell him," her voice was saying automatically to Ellen, and she stepped back into her room. Red on her lips—that was better. Not too much—just warmth and life. A smoothing touch to those dark bands of hair gathered in a knot on her neck. A brush of powder over her white skin. Now she could face him. She caught up her handbag and walked lightly into the drawing room.

A man was standing there, in a gray tweed overcoat, holding his hat in his hand. A big man, lean but large framed, with broad, straight shoulders, and blunt features, square-angled, and clear hard gray eyes. A man, very definitely, to be reckoned with.

"Mrs. Channing?"

"Yes—?"

"I'm Stephen Ryder. Phil Darrow's friend."

Of course. Her mind must have been paralyzed. That she had not reacted to the name told her what fixity of fear was numbing her. But there was more to it than that: some association which was escaping her.

"Indeed I know your name," she was telling him. "Won't you sit down—and take off your coat, Mr. Ryder?"

She was proud of her voice. It was low and troubled but no more than it ought to be.

"You've seen the papers?" he said abruptly.

"Yes. . . . A great shock." She was sitting on the edge of her chair, her eyes alertly on his face.

Something very like fury burned through the cold guard of his eyes. "It's damnable," he said abruptly. He added, "I came at once to you to help us out, Mrs. Channing. You were so close to Phil that you must know a number of things that would help us."

"Us?" she echoed.

"Our office. I'm Assistant District Attorney."

That was it! That was the lurking association which had eluded her. She stammered, "Of course. I ought to have remembered, Phil talked of you so—I was too upset to think."

"He used to guy me for going in for it," said Ryder. "Solemn citizen stuff—*you* know him."

His eyes smiled a little. That was a good sign. Or was he trying to reassure her—take her unawares? He looked somehow too big, too honorable for that, yet an Assistant District Attorney must be shrewd. Phil had spoken of him as a marvel.

"They got in touch with me at once this morning when they learned who it was. Swaney went through his clothes. There was a letter from me there. I went right over. And I've been busy ever since. They have put the case in my charge. As Phil's friend—"

"Naturally," she said in that breathless-sounding voice of hers. Her eyes, intent, anticipating, never left him.

"Curious you and I have never met before," he told her. "He spoke to me often of having us meet."

"I don't think Phil liked to share his friends," she answered slowly. "Except verbally."

He thought that over. "Perhaps," he dismissed it, disliking, she thought, the implied criticism of his dead friend.

"At any rate I've come straight to you," he went on, "for I believe you nearest of any one to Darrow. Fond as I was of Phil I didn't know much of his inner life or his comings and goings. Ours was a man's friendship. But you—"

"He was an old friend," she said quickly. "You know the sadness of that marriage, of course—his wife insane so many years. Our home was a—a refuge sometimes."

"Yes, I know," he said quietly. "And I thought that perhaps you, from your intimacy, could give me some lead—that you would have some knowledge—some clew to—"

"Yes—?" she said again breathlessly.

"To the woman who was with him."

She met his intent regard. She gave him her eyes with steady frankness.

"I couldn't give you an idea."

"You mean you haven't one yourself?"

"Not the least in the world."

She added. "That would be the last thing Phil would tell me. . . . Haven't *you* any guess? A man would know better that side of his life—?"

He shook his head. "It puzzles me in Phil," he said slowly. "I would have thought him the last man in the world to go lightly to a hotel—with a light woman—under the circumstances."

His last words were significant. He knew something, that man! It would have seemed unnatural to avoid them.

"What circumstances?" she forced herself to ask. "I know that Phil was in love with some one—that he wanted a divorce in order to marry her. He could not get a divorce in this state and if he got one elsewhere and came back

into this state—remarried—his brother-in-law threatened
he would have him and his new wife indicted for adultery.
. . . He had Phil, you see. . . . Phil had to be here. His
work, his friends, everything was here."

She held her voice desperately quiet. It seemed to her
that the blood was draining from her heart.

"Did he tell you whom he wanted to marry?"

"Never. Never a name." He seemed to be looking at her
very significantly. "And I can understand—after the scandal of the hotel—that she would want to conceal it. But
between us, Mrs. Channing, there ought to be no conceal-
ment. You see, I drew his will."

"His will?"

"Are you going to tell me that you are ignorant of the
conditions of his will?"

"I am completely ignorant."

"He left you everything of which he died possessed—
barring an annuity set aside for his wife's maintenance."

"I—I can't believe it," said Mrs. Channing faintly.

Either her astonishment was genuine, or she was a con-
summate actress, he thought.

"Why should you be so surprised? To whom did you
think he would leave it?"

"I—I didn't think. I mean, I thought it was all settled
long ago on his wife—in trust, of course."

"It had been, for years. But he made a new will yesterday—the day he died. I drew it for him in my office that
afternoon." He paused. "That will left everything to you.
I don't know exactly how much it is, but it will run well
up to a million."

"A million." Her voice sounded aghast. "No wonder
you thought—I can only tell you again that it comes as a
complete surprise."

She added with energy, "And an unpleasant one. I don't
want the notoriety that this will bring. It was a sweet and
friendly thought—but I wish he had not."

Either she was telling the truth or no woman ever did, Ryder thought. He believed her, and she saw that he believed her. If she could only make him her friend—

But, oh, to get him out of the house now! For some time she had heard Nina moving about. The phone had been ringing. There were things she must say to people.

He sat motionless, turning this over. "Apparently, then, the girl he wanted to marry didn't need it and he thought of you, as his best friend. . . . He was in a towering rage when he made that will. He had just that moment come from a final interview with that brother-in-law. He was resolved, in revenge, to place every cent he had beyond the possibility of that man's ever touching it."

The telephone again. She had told Ellen to say she could not be called. But she was needed. If only he would go now.

"Perhaps his going off like that was another result of his fury of frustration," he was saying slowly. "Phil was like that. Only he was always so completely loyal to an idea, or a woman who possessed him, that I could not at first believe—"

"What *did* you believe, Mr. Ryder?"

She dared the question, her eyes friendly, inviting.

He gave a short, embarrassed laugh.

"I believed—I hoped to find—that you were the woman he was to marry and you would know of his entanglements. And that," he continued deliberately, "that in his bitterness and fury you, yourself, had gone with him— and you would know what happened. Some other woman might have followed you—"

"Some woman *may* have had a hold over him," she said thoughtfully, "and may have tried to threaten him, and then gone further. Philip was capable both of folly—and defiance."

"Yes, this looks like it. And you have no idea—honestly, Mrs. Channing—who that woman might be?"

"None."

"When did you see him last?"

She seemed to reflect. "Four or five days ago, I think. He was here in the afternoon. But he hasn't telephoned since. He helped me about steamers. My little daughter, my only child, is sailing for Europe this noon as it happens."

"You have been kind to give me so much time."

As if she could have helped it!

Still he made no move. "You are not going with her?"

"No."

"It is really necessary for you to be here. I am sure ideas may occur to you. . . . But now—can you tell me the woman who was closest to him, whom he was planning to marry?"

She shook her head. "I am sorry to fail you so—but he didn't take me into his confidence about that, either." She added, a little ruefully, "I am afraid I talked mostly about my affairs to him."

"I see. But think it over. A little later perhaps—"

He rose. He was actually going. Her heart raced in triumph, like a hare's that has escaped the hounds. . . . His eyes were cordial, even pleasant. He believed her. About money. About everything. He had found nothing to suspect—save that she was the woman Phil wanted to marry.

The palms of her hands had been wet with fear. As she rose with him she opened her bag and pulled out a handkerchief. A key came with it and clattered on the floor. A large key with a disk fastened to it. A disk with three numbers on it.

Chapter Three
The Key

As the key clattered between them both glanced down and stooped. The man's reach began in courtesy, then his gesture quickened. But she was swifter than he. Her hand closed over the big disk and she thrust disk and key back into her bag.

"May I see that key?" he asked instantly. She looked into a hard, boring gaze.

Danger steadied her. There was no more than surprise in her dark eyes.

"Why, certainly," she said politely, yet with an air of reserve at the oddness of the request, and started to open her bag.

Then she snapped it shut and a spirited anger flashed out at him.

"I think not, Mr. Ryder. That is too extraordinary."

"What key is it?"

"A hotel key, as you saw. A friend carried it away and at the station gave it to me to return to the hotel. I was intending to take it there to-day."

"What hotel?"

"The Biltmore."

Oh, why had she said that? What had prompted her? She knew—it was because Lucia Harley had been staying there. She was ready when he said, "What friend?"

"Mrs. Harley of San Francisco. . . . I don't understand. Is this a cross-examination?"

He met the proud resentment of her eyes with a level, considering steadiness.

"I am afraid that it is. And I am afraid that I must ask to see that key."

"I dislike being coerced. There is no reason why you should see it." And then she smiled, with a desperate courage that masked its terror. "You can come and see me give it back to the Biltmore."

She had the air of teasing him. He felt oddly at a loss. He remembered the affection and admiration that Philip Darrow had always expressed for this friend. But he could not afford to overlook a single circumstance.

"When did Mrs. Harley carry away the key?"

"Oh, weeks ago. I've been negligent. But what on earth makes you behave like this about it?"

"Your refusal to show it to me," he said soberly. He added, deliberately, "I do not believe that you appreciate the gravity of the situation for any of Philip's friends so closely associated with him."

She kept her look on his. "What has that to do with my key? . . . Do you mean to say, Mr. Ryder," and a faint ring of incredulity, of detached distaste, ran chillingly into her voice, "that you are involving—me—in your suspicions?"

He considered her gravely. An old friend of Phil's. A lady. A lady with quiet, irreproachable connections. . . . But he judged there was something out of the ordinary in her, an energy of spirit, a pride and resolution, that might well lead her into strange places.

"I would suspect Calvin Coolidge to solve this case," he told her, "and your refusal to show me that key is very strange."

She laughed. "I'm feminine, that's all. I refuse to be treated so ridiculously. The world is full of hotel keys. You can come with me and watch me return it. And then I shall never, never forgive you," she added lightly.

"For doing my duty? Remember I am here in a serious capacity. Phil's friend—yes—but a representative of the law that must avenge him. I shall have to ask you some questions."

"Can't you postpone them? I must see my daughter—"

"Answer one now. Where were you last night?"

"Between the hours of ten and one?" she returned mockingly. "I have a perfect alibi, Mr. Holmes. I was with a friend."

"What friend?"

"I will go into that later, if you please. It is a long story. But now—"

She moved, restively. He could not fathom her. She might be a capricious creature, resentful of his interference and taking a childish pleasure in baiting him. She looked too intelligent, but one never knew with women. . . . In any event she was a woman against whom a man would need armor. There was too much of the Circe in her dark eyes.

Why didn't he take the key by force? He realized that her proud and assured bearing was making him feel like a bungling policeman. It was difficult to associate furtiveness and guilt with her. With this knowledge of her background and Phil's friendship.

Yet she had evaded telling where she had been last night. She had a key she refused to show. But she might be telling the truth about that. One in every twenty-two guests carried away a hotel key.

The very inadvertence of the accident might be argued to prove its innocence, but Ryder was too experienced to argue in such fashion. Inadvertence—carelessness—was the undoing of the shrewdest of criminals and this woman was no experienced criminal. If the worst were suspected

about her she was the victim of some flare of passion or
cupidity.

Cupidity appeared untenable. But nothing in life was untenable—her astonishment and regret about the will might
be all a piece of her perfect acting. Or she might be sincere
in that—he was loathe not to credit her there—but have
given way to some wild fury of resentment and jealousy.

Then the fact that he was trying to excuse her from
the baser motive and fit her with a more forgivable anger
made him catch himself up sharply. He hesitated, in two
minds which way to make a fool of himself over the key.

If he wrested it by force, he might be abasedly finding
it the key of the Biltmore. If he let her keep it, he ran the
risk—if it were a key of guilt—of having her do away with
it. If she lost it, he thought, that would be a certainty, and
he would have her arrested.

Perhaps it was better to wait and let that guide him.

Behind them in the living room wall, the curtained
glass doors into the dining room opened suddenly.

"Mother?" said a young voice, with a touch of impatient urgency. They turned to see Nina Channing standing
there.

Her mother flashed on the man a look of warning
entreaty, as if beseeching him not to touch the fringe of
this young thing's consciousness with any unpleasantness.

"This is my daughter, Nina," she said swiftly. "Nina,
this is Mr. Ryder, Stephen Ryder, Mr. Darrow's friend, you
know. He has come to consult us in this—in this trouble."

The girl looked swiftly at Ryder. What a beauty, he
thought, involuntarily. Big, dark eyes, like the mother,
with the same lovely lift of eyebrow above them, like the
curve of a wild bird's wing. The same wide, low brow.
The same ivory of skin and darkness of hair—hair that
the girl wore in a loose wave, with a clustering of curls in
the nape of her neck, an endearingly childish arrangement

that warred with the sophistication of her fantastically scarlet mouth.

She was an exotic looking creature. Some foreshortening of her features, unlike the mother's, had given her an odd, pixie-like allure that was irresistible. Darrow had told him there was a Channing kid, Ryder reflected, but the girl had been growing up fast.

"I was sorry to let you breakfast alone, Nina," Mrs. Channing was saying swiftly, "but we had some things to talk over. However, I'm ready now"—she forced herself to turn and smile at Ryder—"if you'll excuse me?"

"I'll not keep you longer," he said pleasantly. "I'll wait and have the pleasure of taking you to the boat, if I may."

"That's very good of you," said Virginia instantly, and her heart sank.

Her jailer! He meant not to let her out of reach till he had satisfied himself about that key. And about her night.

Should she hide the key? Give it to Nina to throw overboard? No, she would not involve her child in this horror. . . . As she hurried away with the girl she felt breathless and giddy. She felt as if she were walking across a chasm on a swaying rope. And already she had bungled so hideously! But she dared not waste a second's emotion over her wretched carelessness in dropping it—time enough for that in the watches of the nights to come! Now she must plan. . . . The key. . . . The alibi. . . .

She could wrap the key in paper and hand it across the desk at the Biltmore with a casual word. But would that satisfy Ryder? Suppose she wrapped another and hid this? But where was the other? . . . And the alibi?

She might telephone Margery Jenkins.

There was a telephone connection in Nina's room and, sending Nina on a message to Ellen, she lifted the receiver. She heard a man's voice on the line saying, "A Mrs. Harley, did you say? I will see."

So Ryder was verifying the story. Well, that much was safe. Lucky for her she had given a real name! She must hide the key and brave it out with him. She'd telegraph to Lucia.

She tried the telephone again in a moment.

Margery Jenkins was out. Whom could she get? She tried to think clearly and quickly, but she felt as if she were going mad. There was confusion about her, the bags, the packing of last things, the bustle of departure. The telephone ringing with farewell messages from people who wanted to gasp over Philip Darrow's death. Nina's eyes on her. . . . The feeling of that quiet, determined man, waiting like a cat at a mouse hole.

"It's so queer, mother, his coming," Nina was murmuring.

"He thinks he's being helpful, to take us," she returned. "And he wants to ask me about money things—next of kin and all that. Don't bother, Nina. . . . Is Ellen bringing more flowers? Which ones are you going to wear? John's?"

"None of them," said Nina. "Oh, mother, how can I go—"

"Taxi's at the door," Ellen reported.

There Ryder was in the hall, waiting for them. Helping with the luggage. Going down in the elevator. Then in the taxi. Quite one of the family! Virginia wanted to laugh hysterically, as she sat there, her hand closed over her daughter's, trying to make normal sounding speeches about schools and addresses and things abroad.

He was looking at her clothes. She had on the black jacket of the ensemble—never would she wear the coat with the beige fur again!—but her black hat was the same. There was no help for that—but women's hats were so much alike anyway.

The Garlands, with whom Nina was traveling, were already at the pier, a distinguished looking couple with a daughter of Nina's age. They were surrounded by a vivacious group that was struck to sudden constraint as the Channings appeared.

Talking of the murder, Virginia knew. Of what it must mean to the Channings. Looking at them with that sly curiosity and avid zest for compassion. . . .

She chose to ignore the topic, greeting them with grave composure, saying the banal last things. Nina went through the motions; her beauty always made up for any lack of effort on her part. Ryder's presence merged in the group, but Virginia saw him taking them all in, quietly and keenly.

At the last she drew Nina a little apart. She had no more words, but the touch of her hand, on the girl's arm, was tense. But she was grateful beyond words that the girl was going. When the last call sounded she kissed her abruptly, then hurried down the gang plank, Ryder at her side.

The boat was moving. Nina's lovely face was only a speck among other specks. . . . She managed casual farewells to the others. She was in the taxi alone with Ryder. She leaned back, closing her eyes. Thinking. Thinking.

Back in the apartment the phone was ringing.

"Say I cannot come, Ellen. And bring some tea for us, please, in the drawing-room." To Ryder she murmured, "I had breakfast rather early."

In the green drawing-room, with its black Chinese lacquer furniture and ivory-colored porcelains, they took the tea almost wordlessly, a little lacquer table between them. Ryder saw that she was sipping her tea very slowly, apparently in deep thought.

Then she put down her cup and looked up at him.

"Now I will answer what you like, Mr. Ryder."

He smiled, in sincere ruefulness. "It is the same question, Mrs. Channing. After you have answered it you are going to laugh me out and end our acquaintance. But I must put it. . . . Where were you last night?"

She looked long at him. "If I tell you—if I trust you completely—will you promise me not to disclose the information until—until you are convinced that it is absolutely necessary? I really think you can promise that."

He reflected that the phrase "absolutely necessary" gave him wide latitude. "I can promise you that much."

"I rely on that. . . . I was at the hotel with Philip Darrow." Nothing changed in his face. He simply looked at her rather harder and waited.

"That was the key you saw," her breathless voice went on. "I am the woman who escaped. . . . But I did not kill Philip Darrow."

"Who did?" He shot the words at her.

She gave him a look of utter helplessness. "I haven't the least idea."

"Perhaps you had better explain."

"I will. You were quite right about me—Phil wanted to marry me. But I did *not* know about the will," she interpolated fiercely. "He had said nothing of that beforehand. . . . Well, you know how he felt about that divorce. He was so frustrate and so bitter that I agreed to spend the evening with him. I said at home that I was going to a theater— but we didn't. We had dinner and then went to the hotel where he had his secret studio—we wanted some place to be alone to talk."

She swallowed and added, "My daughter was to be at a house party at Long Island."

"And then—?"

"Then, at the hotel—he ordered some ginger ale. I went in the bedroom when the boy brought it up, as I did not want to be seen. He went to his desk to get out a flask and I went back in the bedroom for the handkerchief I had left there. I stopped to powder a moment—it wasn't more than a moment. I was just starting to open the door to come back when I heard a sort of groan and fall. I was frightened; I stood listening a moment but could hear nothing. I pushed open the door. The room was dark, except for the light from the bedroom just behind me. Phil was on the floor in front of me. He was dying—dead in an instant. He never spoke. The hall door was closed. . . . There was no gun anywhere. That is everything I know."

He said dryly, "You've been seeing 'The Trial of Mary Dugan.'"

"No. But I know the story—the man was killed while the girl was out of the apartment, wasn't he? By the wife's lover. But unfortunately for me, poor Ethel had no lovers in her sanitarium."

"Was the door of the room locked—I mean before you went into the bedroom?"

"Wasn't it a spring lock?" She looked confused, trying to recollect something. "No, it couldn't have been. I remember locking it from the outside when I went away. That's why I took the key. Phil must have left it unlocked."

"That seems curious, doesn't it?"

"He was so careless," she said faintly.

"You found it unlocked after he was shot?"

"Why—I suppose so. I don't remember."

"Didn't you open it—look out? Look for his assailant?"

She shook her head. He was staring at her between narrowing lids. His face did not betray an iota of feeling.

She added faintly, "I was afraid of being found."

"Didn't it occur to you to lock the door then?"

She looked curiously uncertain. "Yes, I believe I did. I seem to remember that."

"Do you remember where you found the key?"

"Inside the door, I think." She made an obvious effort. "You can imagine one forgets little things like that."

Still he stared, as if he would read into that mask of a
white face which had confronted him so steadily with her
earlier lies. . . . So this woman, this slender, aloof creature, had been the woman in the room with Phil. She and
Phil were lovers. . . .

That much, at least, he could believe.

"What time did this happen? The murder?" he said with
brutal definiteness.

"I don't know exactly. Not long after we got there."

"About ten-thirty, then—or a few minutes after. . . .
And you did not leave till after one? Why not earlier?"

Her eyes seemed to implore his for understanding. "I
was dazed at first. . . . It took time to control myself. Then
I had to—to pick things up."

"But a woman as capable as you—it was strange you did
not realize how vital it was for you to leave early."

Her smile was a quiver of spent irony. "I knew—too
late."

A surge of curious compassion went through him. If
this were true—what agony of spirit she had endured. Her
lover dead—herself a fugitive. . . . But was it true? Was it
all the truth? Was she shielding any one? Some one who
had fired that shot?

"Why did you tell me this?" he said slowly.

Her eyes were as rueful now as a child's. "I had to. Since
I dropped the key you were determined to find out where
I had been—and I hadn't any answer to give. I couldn't
think of any alibi—none that would be good enough. I
knew you would find out I had been out all night."

"What did you do after you left the hotel?"

She told him.

"But why didn't you come back at once?"

"I had telephoned my maid—earlier in the evening—
that I was going to be with a sick friend. That I probably
wouldn't be in till morning."

A slow, painful color crept into her white face. She could feel him saying to himself, "Then you meant to be out all night." And she could feel him reflecting that she had always intended it, since she had taken the bag. His next words corroborated this.

"But you had the bag with you when you went out— supposedly to the theater."

"Y-yes. Yes, of course. But that might have been anything. I took a dress to leave at the cleaner's. Only I forgot it. I had the dress in the bag."

Defiantly she forced herself to go on. "It was ridiculous of me to stay out the rest of the night—I could have come back and said my friend was better. But I thought I ought to keep to the plan—that it would be less strange to be seen coming home in the morning than before dawn. I suppose I was hardly sane—my mind wasn't working rationally. . . . You don't know what it is to feel so hunted—so numb and frightened. I expect I behaved foolishly. I knew I had when you asked for that alibi and I hadn't any to give you."

"But hadn't you some friend you could have named—?"

"Did you ever stop to consider, Mr. Ryder, how many friends you could trust utterly to lie for you—in bitter need—under suspicious circumstances? I've tried to think of one this morning—you may believe I have—and I haven't found one. If I could have thought of anything, *anything,* that would hold water I would never have confessed to you. . . . But you were on me too soon. Before I had time to prepare anything. If I'd only had a few hours—! But after that key—I could not see my way out. So I decided to tell you and ask you to help me."

"Surely you had arranged something," he said a little grimly, "when you phoned you were to be away for the night?"

"Nothing. I meant to give only a casual explanation."

"To your daughter?"

His voice was curiously harsh. Her own sank before it. "She was absorbed in her preparation. I could name almost any plausible name to her. I have gone to sick friends before—really gone," she cried out, and flushed again, hotly.

"Did no one see you go out together?"

She hesitated, her eyes evading him. "I went out alone."

"Carrying your bag and saying you were going to the theater? And, then telephoning later about the sick friend?"

"Yes. Yes. . . . What does it matter about all that—what I did or how I did it? That has nothing to do with who killed him! Don't you see that you can leave me out of it now? You know all I have to tell you. You know where to start from. Everybody else will be wasting time trying to find that woman at the hotel but you know she had nothing to do with it."

She leaned toward him in desperate entreaty, "Won't you help me to hide from them? Dragging me out will do no good! It will only do harm—it will waste precious time, for the police will stop looking anywhere else for Phil's murderer."

He said slowly, "Don't you think your story will be believed?"

She struck her hands together. "No! Of course not! You know that. They will think we quarreled—they will begin to look for motives—they will seize on that wretched business of the will. Everything will be against me. Especially that will."

Yes, that will rather did for her. Or, more truly, she had done for herself, going to the hotel. But it was a heavy penalty.

"Don't you see," she persisted feverishly, "that if they know about me it will waste their time and give the murderer his chance to escape? And what good will it do, dragging my story into the papers—you know everything there

is to know now. You can go on from there and not waste
time over the woman in the room."

"And what am I to go on?"

"You have Phil's life to go on! That's where we must
look. Find the people who hated him—the ones he might
have wronged. You know what Phil was—what he had
been—with women. There must have been men jealous of
him, jealous of his success, angry at something he did—
perhaps in a business way. Phil was high-handed. There
must be something somewhere, some clew that you can
find. I'll try to help—"

"Whom do *you* think—?"

"I tell you I don't know! If I only did!"

"Did you know any one who was jealous of him?"

"Not that I ever knew."

"Of you, then?"

"Of me—? You mean some man?" she stammered; her
thoughts seemed to dart off at some secret angle. Then,
violently, "Oh, no, no! There could be no one."

"Could any one have known you were going there?"

"No one—no one I know of."

"Could any one have followed you? Where did you
dine?"

"Where—? Oh, some little place, a speak-easy, you
know. In the fifties somewhere. I never looked. Phil just
took me."

"Had you ever been there before?"

"No."

"You took a taxi from there to the hotel?"

"Yes."

"Had you known of that room at the hotel before? That
secret working place?"

"No. No—I never had."

"When did you plan to go out with him? You said you
hadn't seen him for several days."

"Late that afternoon—he telephoned. He seemed very angry and unhappy."

"He did not speak of any enemies—any trouble with any one?"

"No, he said nothing about it."

"And that is everything you have to tell me? That is all the help you can give?"

Her look was pitiful. "It's nothing, isn't it? But there must be clews. If any one hated him enough to come and murder him—surely there must be clews to that! Some one got in that hotel and got out again. Some one either knew of that room or followed us. And there must be clews in Phil's life. This couldn't have come out of a clear sky— there has been a storm brewing. The guilty one is some- where near Phil—somewhere to be found. . . . Some one in the company may know something. Actors will talk. Or Dervish, his man. The murderer *exists*. He is real. He is somewhere to be found."

She was talking feverishly, her eyes racked with an agony of appeal.

"You can find him all the better without dragging my poor name into it! You know I had nothing to do with it— the ruin of my reputation would do you no good. And it would kill my child—"

She felt like a spent wave beating against a granite coast. His expression seemed to remind her that she was a little late in thinking about her child.

"You know what Phil would want you to do," she urged frantically.

"It isn't what Phil would want—or what I would want," he said painfully. "We are past that. I am here to serve the ends of justice."

"But you'll not be serving justice if you drag me into the limelight," she cried swiftly. "You know it will con- fuse the situation and give the guilty one time to escape!

You know every one will turn on me and stop searching for the real criminal. They'll overlook everything else—everything that ought to be helping you. Oh, Mr. Ryder, don't you see what it would *do—against* justice? Don't you see—?" Again she besought, "Oh, don't you *see—*?"

His remote face gave her no inkling of any feeling behind it.

Breathlessly she besought, "You would be *hindering justice* and you would be doing *injustice! You* believe me—you believe I am innocent of that murder—but those others will not believe in me. They'll try to convict me—they may even do it! You couldn't see me tried for what I'm innocent of, could you?"

Her eyes, like fires of despair, burned into his. "Even if I am saved, if the real murderer is found—and he's sure to be, if they don't waste time on me now—why, I shall be ruined! Nothing will be left of me, of my name, my position. I shall be a marked woman forever—and my child marked through me. . . . And I don't deserve that. Not just for—for going to a hotel with Phil. You aren't trying to find the woman he loved. You are trying to find who killed him. . . . Oh, you couldn't give me away now, when you know that it will do no good to the case—only harm to it—and brand me forever. You couldn't do that to me, could you? It would be against every feeling in you for justice."

"It would," he said brusquely. "And you are right—it wouldn't help the case! It would harm it. . . . But even so, I can't hope to shield you long."

But he was going to shield her *now!* That was what let her breathe again. She stood listening, her agony of relief and hope in her look on him.

"I shall have to say," he went on, thinking aloud, "that you have given an explanation of your evening which satisfies me. What shall it be? Theater with friends? The Garlands who have just sailed. What play?"

She could hardly speak for her emotion.

"'Journey's End'?" he offered.

"Not that." She found her voice with sudden energy. He wondered at the peremptoriness of her swift objection. "Anything else. Let's say—'Strictly Dishonorable.'"

The edged irony cleared the air. For a moment their eyes held each other. All the gratefulness she could find no words for flamed in her own; in his was a suddenly revealing and poignant pity, a deep compassion and a grim foreboding.

Then he rose abruptly.

"I haven't a moment to spare if I am to save you," he said soberly. "I have a wide field before me. You haven't given me much help, you know, except where not to look."

Chapter Four
The Conference

It was a wide field. In the taxi, on the way down to the Criminal Courts Building, he stared grimly at the problem. This was none of those convenient little house party murders where you can count the suspects and find the footprints in the snow. The field for suspicion was as unlimited as Darrow's contacts.

A man was killed. Somewhere in his life he had aroused the animosity that had killed him. Find the animosity.

He did not doubt Virginia Channing's story. He reflected a little on his certainty of her unsupported word, for she had lied like a trooper during their first interview, but believe her he did. Only—he was not sure but that she was keeping something back. That flicker in her eyes when he had suggested jealousy of herself as a possible motive. Was she shielding some man?

Darrow might not have been the only man in her life. Her husband had been dead these ten years. Other men must have wanted her—wanted to marry her. Darrow's ambiguous relation was explained by the impossibility of his marrying her, but there might well have been another, more legal aspirant, resenting, even to mad violence, Darrow's intrusion. . . . And women are fanatically loyal to men who love them, even when they do not return the love.

It would bear thinking of.

He made one stop on the way down town to his appointment. He stopped at the Highgate Hotel and wandered through the lobby to examine the entrance again, in the light of his new suspicions. He saw that the secondary entrance, at an angle from the main lobby, gave an approach to the elevators that might well be unseen by any one at the desk.

Also there were stairs. They were continuous to the third floor, he learned; then their place was shifted farther to the rear. After the seventh floor there was another shift in location to the fourteenth story, which was the last.

Some one who knew where Darrow's rooms were would have had no difficulty in gaining a stealthy entry to them.

At the desk, Ryder disclosed his identity to the clerk, a Mr. Viner, whom he had not seen in the very early hours of that morning. Viner was a young, good-looking chap, fulsomely hearty.

"I couldn't tell you a thing more than I did the other man from your office, Mr. Ryder. I couldn't identify her. Mr. Dakin, that's the night clerk, the fellow you saw early this morning, says he could all right. All I got was an impression of some one young looking and lots of style. The elevator hoy who took them up says he'd know her again—says she was a knock-out. Had class. I said, 'Class like Texas Guinan?' and he says, 'Hell, no—like Beatrice Lillie.'"

Ryder joined in the expected laugh.

"That's all right," he said. "We can identify her if we get her but what I want to know now is—did you have anybody coming in, after Darrow, that was a bit unusual? Who else took a room?"

"I can tell you that right off. No one but the Greelands, a couple from Newark who have been here before, and a drummer called Sloane. He's been here before, too."

"Did anybody ask to see the book?"

"No—and they wouldn't 'a' found this Deering—that's the name we knew him by—and the dame if they had. He was on the private register. He just wrote, 'and sister,' after his name that night."

"You didn't notice anybody hanging about?"

"Well, say—come to think of it there was a fellow at the door, asking about Deering, Jim says. Jim's on the afternoon and evening shift—hey, Jim!"

The colored man at the door, watching the colloquy at the desk, hurried importantly forward. "Yes, sir, Mr. Viner."

"Tell this gentleman about the fellow you said was asking about Deering last night."

"It was just after Mr. Deering went in, sir. A man kinda stepped up to me, outa breath like, and asked had Mr. Deering gone into the hotel and had he gone up yet? I looked in and he wasn't in the lobby and I said he'd gone up."

"Did he say anything about the lady?" Ryder wanted to know.

"Well, he might have. He might have said 'They' or something like that—I wasn't noticing. Anyway he said it was no matter—he just wanted to catch him but it wasn't important enough to go up with, or something like that, and went away."

"What sort of man was he?"

The doorman reflected. "Well, I couldn't say exactly—"

"Tall? Well dressed?"

"Not so tall, kinda little fella. And whiskery— yes, sir, he had hair on him," said Jim triumphantly. "Kinda like a preacher, if you know what I mean."

"Respectable, eh?"

"Respectable, yes, sir."

"And you say he had whiskers? A beard?"

"Yes, sir. I didn't look very careful. I just remember a kinda old fella."

"And this was right after Deering had gone in?"

"Yes, sir—he wanted to know had he gone up yet."

"What color were those whiskers?"

"Kinda old-looking whiskers," said Jim doubtfully. "No color."

"You mean they were gray?"

"Gray, that's it, sir."

"And you are sure he asked about Deering and not Darrow?"

"Yes, sir, I'm sure a that. I wouldn't 'a' known who Mr. Darrow was."

Ryder turned to the clerk. "Did you see him?"

"Never saw the fella."

"Then he couldn't have found out from you where Mr. Darrow's room was."

"Nope. Not from me."

"Could he have slipped around to the side entrance and got up in the elevator with them?"

"No, *sir*," the doorman intervened with his emphasis. "They was gone up in the el'vator when I looked in—they wasn't in sight, Mr. Deering and the lady. The old fella went away—down the street."

"Is the same elevator boy on duty now?"

"Sure—he comes on at twelve. Get him over, Jim."

The boy was produced, eager to repeat his testimony. But Ryder cut short his descriptions of the classy dame. He wanted to know if the old man had approached him, had asked for Mr. Deering's room.

Nothing like that had happened, the boy said.

Had he taken any old man up in the elevator?

The boy shook his bullet head. "Don't recollect any at all of that description, sir. Course I take a lot of strangers up—people coming and going all times. But nobody asked me nothing about Mr. Deering's room."

"Well, that's that." Ryder turned again to the clerk. "If something does come up—if anything occurs to you—let me know at once."

"Okay," said the clerk, with genial importance. "Say, Mr. Ryder, what do you think—"

But Ryder was back in his taxi, exhorting the man to make all speed to the Franklin Street entrance of the Criminal Courts Building.

Three men were in his office when he entered, Sergeant Devlin of the Homicide Bureau of the Detective Division of the New York Police Department, Detective Benson, one of his men, and Inspector Ascher, Chief of the Detective Division.

Devlin was a long, loose-jointed individual, with a casual-seeming eye, and the cynically jocose aspect of the old hand. A pendulous cigarette hung from his lips; his eyes were on the door as Ryder entered.

"Well, brother, got the murderess in your pocket?" was his greeting.

"Just what I haven't." Ryder dropped into a chair beside him.

"Too bad. Thought you were going to be a swell detective and save our department a lot of work." Beneath his joking was a strain of animosity. Ryder was a newcomer, an outsider, a "swell," in Devlin's classification, who had jumped from private practice into the political ranks and had yet to prove himself. Devlin was alert to resent any high-hat theories or manners.

"Let me know what you have found," said Ryder.

"Not a damn thing. Just as flat as we were this morning. All we know is that Darrow is as dead as a doornail from a bullet in his heart at the hands of person or persons unknown."

Ascher, who remembered Ryder's relation to the dead man, said evenly, in his quiet voice, "Corrigan's all through, Mr. Ryder. The bullet was a thirty-two. The remains are at Sill's mortuary. I understand you are making the arrangements for the funeral. We've locked the room at the hotel and left Walsh in charge."

"I've just been at the hotel—but not at the room. I've something to tell you later, but that can wait. Keever been over?"

"Here's the fingerprints." Devlin pushed a stock of papers to him, brilliant with black swirls of thumbs and fingers. "The place was lousy with them. Here's one with half a hand showing. Keever got that off the inside of the bedroom door."

Ryder stared down at the black whorls and shadings. His face was devoid of expression as he bent over the photograph, but he was seeing Virginia Channing standing there, in terror, gripping the knob as she listened to those sudden sounds. . . . Not the chance of a snowball in Hades for her if they ever got close enough to her to demand her fingerprints.

"Correspond to anything we got?" he asked easily.

"Not a thing. Been through all the files."

"We've been counting on you, Ryder," said Inspector Ascher, "to have some line on those lady friends of his."

"I'm too respectable," said Ryder. "I didn't know the gay ones. I know a lady who was a very good friend of his, a Mrs. Channing—and I've been seeing her now, trying to get a line from her, but she is in the dark, too. She says that is the last thing he would let her know."

He felt sure that Mrs. Channing's name was bound to crop out, sooner or later, and he wanted to present it as easily and naturally as possible.

"How good a friend was she?" Devlin wanted to know.

"Just friends," said Ryder. "She knew him for years—
before her husband died. He always admired her—but
there was never anything in it."

"Where was she last night?" said Devlin cynically.

"At the theater—'Strictly Dishonorable'—with friends,
the Garlands."

"They corroborate it?"

"I've just seen them." . . . By Jove, he thought, in grim
dismay, he was letting himself in deep on this! His own
career would smash with hers if anything were discovered.

"They sailed for Europe, this noon," he went on, "with
the little Channing girl, and I went to the boat. Mrs.
Channing," he added deliberately, "has known Darrow
almost as long as I have and I hoped very much that she
might know something, but she does not."

"Isn't holding out on you, is she?"

"Lord, no, why should she? She's as anxious as we are
to have Darrow's murderer found. But she doesn't know
a soul who hated him—except his brother-in-law. . . . Or
rather," said Ryder thoughtfully, "it was Darrow who hated
his brother-in-law. The man was blocking his divorce.
Darrow had a furious row with him only yesterday—just
before he came into my office."

"Swell!" said Devlin enthusiastically. "Can't we pin
something on the brother-in-law? Who is the bird?"

"He's Henry Bartlett."

Devlin gave a long whistle. "Laff that off!" he observed.
"But I'd sure like to pin something on Henry Bartlett!
What that snooper has cost me in bootleggers!"

For Bartlett was one of the men who feel themselves the
custodians of public morals, busy with all enforcements,
an untiring censor of plays and books, a bitter opponent
of the Birth Control League. He was a well-known citizen
of aggressive public spirit, always taking a stand in the

press, and making life uncomfortable for other-minded brethren.

"So Henry Bartlett is Phil Darrow's brother-in-law!" Devlin murmured. "Is he the brother of the crazy wife? . . . Well, I always knew he was a nut," he pronounced with satisfaction. He gave his cigarette a flip to the other side of the mouth where it hung, defying all laws of gravity. "But I don't just see him as shooting Darrow down."

"Hardly," said Inspector Ascher impatiently. "Bartlett might close one of Darrow's plays but he would hardly murder—even for a bedroom scene. I think he is out of the picture."

"But he might have something on Darrow," Devlin cogitated. "You say they had a row yesterday? What about?"

Ryder told them, briefly.

"Naturally he didn't want to lose Darrow from the family," was Devlin's comment. "He was too good a thing. . . . By the way," he interjected, "who gets his money? He hadn't any kids. The crazy wife?"

"She did—in trust—until yesterday afternoon. Then he was so mad at Bartlett he came into my office and made a new will."

"Now who gets it?"

"That will hasn't been opened. And I'd rather you didn't make this public yet. He left his estate—except an annuity for the wife's support—to Mrs. Channing. I feel there is nothing to be gained by dragging her into publicity."

He was conscious that Devlin was raking him with that slant-angled glance of his and Ascher was staring fixedly.

"Give the public something to chew on," Devlin urged. "Seen the noon papers yet? Hotel Murder Baffling Police. Mystery Woman Escapes the Law. . . . Oh the press is howling for action."

"We'll give them action," Ryder promised grimly. "They will have plenty without Darrow's will. . . . I ask you to regard that as a confidence."

In the derisive eye that Devlin cocked at him was a quick and ribald speculation, that he outstared and said calmly, "Not so good, this publicity, when you know the people."

"How long you known this widow?" Devlin inquired.

"I couldn't tell you the exact number of years."

"I don't see that publishing the will does us any good," Ascher agreed, pacifically. "It would distract attention— give the papers more headlines—but we are not here exactly to serve the press. We are after the woman."

"The murderer," Ryder amended.

"Same thing, isn't it? Don't you think so?"

"I think it looks like it," said Ryder cautiously. He leaned back, straightening his long legs under the table and lighting a cigarette. "But I hate snap conclusions. . . . I've been over *to* that hotel. There's a second entrance to the elevators practically invisible to the desk. Any one could have got to Darrow's room, who knew where it was. And just after he went in, with the lady, a man came and asked the doorman about Mr. Deering."

He related the details. "It may be anything or nothing," he concluded, "but we don't want to overlook it. Somebody may have got up there and shot him—perhaps out of jealousy. The woman may have beaten it in panic later."

"Why would she do that instead of giving information?"

"Her reputation," said Ryder promptly. "Even chorus girls have reputations, Ascher! Besides, it might have been her husband. Even chorus girls have husbands."

"But a preachery sort of guy with whiskers doesn't sound like the husband of a chorine," Ascher objected. "Maybe a father, avenging his daughter's loss of virtue—"

"Yeah—like the helpful old pa in 'Coquette,'" interjected Devlin. "But whether the man did it or the woman, the woman knows, and we want the woman. And if Darrow wanted to get married so bad that he rowed with his brother-in-law for standing him off a divorce then there's some woman he wanted to marry. Maybe this was the one. Maybe it was another and he was giving this one the air and she shot him. Anyway we got to find her. *Cherchez la Skirt,*" said Devlin positively.

"He's been seen out with women pretty frequently," Ascher supplied. "Benson here has the dope. Spill it, Benson."

Benson, who had literally not opened his mouth since the conference began, hitched his chair a little nearer the table. He was a quiet, noncommittal man, with mild, near-sighted blue eyes. His unobtrusiveness and a certain sympathetic air about him accounted for a good deal of his extreme success in disguise work. He was the sort of door-to-door salesman to whom women of a certain class instinctively confide their troubles and the doings of the family upstairs.

Talk, unending talk, had rippled into Benson's ears, and from its currents he usually managed to pick up some floating jetsam of seeming unimportance that fitted, like a piece of a jigsaw puzzle, into a vacant space.

"I went to the restaurants and night clubs, first off, as you suggested," he told Ryder now. "Some of them knew Darrow by name—some recognized his photograph. At Pierre's he'd been seen recently with two women, one very young, one older."

"That's the Channings," Ryder said casually. "Mother and daughter."

"What's the girl like?" Devlin shot in.

"Just a kid. Goes to school in Europe."

"Look like Darrow?"

"Look like—? Hell no," Ryder exploded. "He never knew the mother till long after she was born."

"Keep your shirt on. . . . I was just thinking about that will. Go on, Benson."

"At the Alsatian and the Circle he'd been seen with other women. Usually some actress."

"Same one?"

"No—sometimes with Miss Fane, the leading lady of his company, sometimes with a girl from the chorus. Tony, the headwaiter at the Alsatian, says the girl is Topsy Minn."

"Now we're hot," Devlin grunted. He spat out a burning cigarette and replaced it dexterously. "Give us a match, Inspector, darling. . . . I want fingerprints of those dames—I'll get them to-night, backstage. And, Benson, I've arranged a job for you as extra night watchman behind scenes—you listen to the chatter."

"I've met Florence Fane casually several times," said Ryder. "She's blond—a real one."

"She's an actress, ain't she? And I'll bet that mascara on her eyes and a tight black hat would make her brunette enough looking. Oh, I'll get her prints. Last night was Sunday and that girl wasn't playing—neither of them were, thanks to our friend, Henry Bartlett."

"I'll have a chat with both of them," said Ryder. He rose. "First I'll have a talk with Darrow's personal servant, Dervish. Anybody seen him yet?"

"Oh, I had a darling time with Dervish," Devlin reported. "Wait till you meet that bird! But I forgot—you've met him socially. But I was of the Po-lice. He looked as if he wanted to delouse me. God, how he despised me!"

"Wasn't he civil?"

"Civil as hell! Yes, sir, he'd been Mr. Darrow's man seven years. No, sir, he couldn't say as to Mr. Darrow's engagements. Not his place to notice, sir. Hardly in his province, you might say, sir." Devlin's voice was mincing sarcasm. "I told him he needn't sir me—I wasn't a knight—and he said, 'You'll excuse me, sir—I'm so accustomed to being with gentlemen, here and on the other side, that you've no idea how difficult it is to adjust oneself.' But for the laugh

I got out of him I'd have given him one swift kick in the pants. . . . I didn't know there was anything like him this side of the footlights."

Ryder grinned. "That's where he got most of it. He never was nearer the aristocracy on the other side than on shipboard. He was room steward on some liner when Darrow took a fancy to him."

"Well, you take him on," Sergeant Devlin advised. "Maybe you can get something but applesauce out of him. Me, I'm for locking him up till he babbles names and dates."

"I'll see him first off." Ryder picked up his coat and started to the door.

"What are we going to give the papers?" Ascher called after him.

"Oh, damn the papers," Ryder thrust an arm into his coat and struggled vigorously. "Tell them the usual stuff when we're up a tree. We are working on clews—leaving not a stone unturned—"

His irony mocked him as he made his way out of the building and into a taxi. This was his first big piece of work since he had taken office; it meant everything to his career and everything in the world to him personally, for Phil had been dear to him, and his resentment was hot at the coward who had shot him down—and what had he done about it?

He had withheld information from his colleagues; he had lied flatly; he had smashed every oath of his office. If this thing became known, he was done for.

As it was, he was not sure how well he had thrown those men off the track. They had stayed behind to talk him over. There had been speculation in Devlin's gaze—Devlin probably thought he wanted to marry the widow who was inheriting Darrow's money—and Ascher's bland face might veil a variety of conjectures.

Ascher was friendly—he had backed up the request to keep the will quiet—but it was a calculating, political friendliness that would never lead Ascher into jeopardy. Devlin might like him well enough as a man but Devlin had a streak of malice toward him on account of his position. Devlin would like to show him up. He had a feeling that they might work together quietly, and not take him into their confidence.

If he was to uncover the criminal he must lose no time, before they began questioning Mrs. Channing. . . . The responsibility he had taken bore heavily on him. . . . But he had done right, he insisted stubbornly to himself. It would have been the most flagrant miscarriage of true justice to have flung that helpless woman into the limelight, branding her forever. The thought of the publicity awaiting her revolted him beyond words.

She would undoubtedly be charged with the murder. She might—barring other suspects—even be tried. And even if she were freed she would be made infamous forever—life would have no more meaning for her. It would be a brutal and callous act to hand the woman Phil loved to that undeserved fate. . . .

And it would only delay the discovery of the real criminal. Tenaciously, in self-justification, he clung to that. Those men he had just left would never believe her. They would pounce on her like a pack of hounds and cease trying for other trails. . . . If only he could keep her under cover till he found something.

He was genuinely worried about his own ability. He had never had to run down a criminal before, but had based his prosecutions on data that had been given him. He had been keen at deductions; he had wrested certainties from nebulous confusions, but here he had nothing yet to study, nothing to deduce from.

It was all to do and he was to do it.

He had always believed tremendously in the virtues of clear, hard thinking. He would have been a fool—which he was not—if he had not known that his mind had a keen, razor edge. He had always trusted to it, and so far it had always cut through the difficult obstacles.

But it was going to be a hard job to gather in the data from which to think out a theory to fit this case. He was bitterly afraid that in his inexperience, or through some freak of chance, he might overlook something that would be an important clew. He was no superman—no wizard of detection. He'd just have to work like hell, he decided, turning over everything.

And if he failed, it was not only he himself that would go down to disaster; Virginia Channing, without a scrap of corroborative evidence to shield her, would be flung into pitiless publicity and into the jeopardy of her life.

Chapter Five
In Darrow's Rooms

Darrow's flat, in the east Forties, was the third story of a made-over building. Darrow had clung to it because of the unusual width of the building and the garden in the rear on which his dining-room windows opened. It was flanked on either side by narrower buildings. The lower floor of one announced itself as the Rose Tea Garden and the other bore on its window in gold: *"Louise. Toilettes. Chapeaux. Bijouteries."*

There was no doorman. In the outer hallway he pressed a button; from long association he was familiar with the loud click that announced the releasing of the door. In the inner hall he had the choice of mounting winding stairs or confiding himself to a cage-like elevator walled in, as an afterthought on the part of the remodelers, between the stairs and the hall.

The lift mounted slowly with him and at the third story he got out, clanging both doors shut. He rang a bell on the opposite door and heard the bang of chair legs coming down to the floor. The opening door gave him a view of a policeman's fat, somnolent face with an unlighted cigar in its mouth.

The face creased in smiles. "Afternoon, Chief."

All higher-ups were Chief to the diplomatic Ryan.

"Afternoon, Ryan," Ryder stepped into the hall. "Anything doing?"

"I'll say there is. A dame raising hell to get in. Says she's an actress. Wouldn't give her name. Says Mr. Darrow had her part or something she was to say and she needs it to-night and she wants to see his papers. I told her nothing doing till you gave the word. She's back every hour to find you."

"Anything else?"

"Telephoning and flowers. The fellow in there takes care of that." Ryan jerked his head toward the back regions. "That Mr. Bartlett—says he's a relative—came this morning, but just talked a little to the fellow."

"What's the woman like? Young? Pretty?"

"All the trimmings, Chief," said Ryan with a grin.

Ryder knew his way about that flat. He went down the long hall to the kitchen where he found Dervish, a small dark green apron over his creased trousers, polishing the silver. It was the day to shine silver and Dervish was doing it, like a well-conducted person. Ryder had a dryly appreciative feeling that Dervish was not devoid of quiet dramatics.

He was a lean little man with a narrow face, a bulging forehead, a long nose, a retreating chin, an acrimonious voice and a tremendous sense of dignity. The insignificance of his appearance seemed to have enraged a nature sensitive of its worth, and to have so inflamed his pride that sheer, invincible character had overcome the mishap of its outer clothing and imposed itself upon the World.

He had an eye that would make a weasel quail and Ryder could gather that even Devlin had not been unpierced by its cold, sharp remoteness.

He rose punctiliously to greet Ryder.

"I see you're carrying on, Dervish."

"Yes, sir. But what's to be done with all this now?" Dervish wanted accusingly to know. "It's not to be left to the other gentleman's use, I hope, sir?"

The other gentleman was an architect who had been sharing the apartment for the past year. Darrow had taken one of his impulsive likings to the man, a liking in which Dervish had no open share.

"No, take care of it for the present," Ryder told him, "It's safe with you. . . . There's a will, of course, and I'm executor under it, but it hasn't gone to probate yet."

He reflected, as he spoke, that Darrow had made no provision in that will for his servant and he had forgotten to remind him. Darrow had always talked of taking care of Dervish in remaking his will, but in the passion of the moment it had slipped his heated mind. . . . Well, he could probably get Mrs. Channing to do something about it. There was generous blood in her, he thought.

"Where's Mr. Renfew?" he asked. Renfew was the architect.

"Down at the office with a very bad cold." Dervish spoke without sympathy. "He came in with it unexpectedly yesterday morning from Springfield and was in bed all day. And this morning I brought in his tray with the paper folded beside it. I never glanced at it myself, sir—my first news was when he called me."

Ryder nodded. Under the cold accusation of the little man's eyes he felt like saying, "I should have called you, myself, Dervish," but he did not speak. He reflected, however, that perhaps to none of Darrow's friends did his passing mean more than to this daily servitor. He wondered what emotion there was under Dervish's chill imperviousness.

He asked, "Renfew here all the evening?"

"Yes, sir. In bed—asking for things."

"You were here, too, then I take it?"

"Yes, sir. It had been my intention to take the evening out—when about noon Mr. Renfew came in and that afternoon Mr. Darrow told me to stay and take care of him."

"Mr. Darrow was not expecting to be home then?"

"He said nothing of his plans, sir. He merely told me in the morning that I could be away and to have some pickup things for dinner in the ice box."

"When did he change his mind and tell you to stay in?"

"When he came in, sir, late in the afternoon, and found the other gentleman in bed."

Evidently Darrow had expected to have the flat to himself that evening for dinner and Renfew's sudden arrival had made him change his plans.

"Then he told me he'd dine out, and for me to take care of the other gentleman."

"Was he upset, do you think?"

"I didn't think he liked it, sir."

"Then he went to the phone?"

Dervish's voice grew remote. "He did go to the phone, now you mention it."

"Did you hear what he said?"

"I never overhear, sir."

"Rubbish, Dervish, every one overhears, at times, whether he wants to or not. I know how Darrow talks." The present tense smote Ryder hard, but he went on in the same casual voice, "Was there anything said over the phone that might tell where he was going?"

"Nothing, sir. He was just talking, in an earnest sort of way. It was all as usual, sir. I paid no attention."

Ryder wondered why Virginia Channing had not told him that at first she had planned to go to Darrow's flat for dinner. If Darrow had said something about a restaurant, when he phoned her the change of plan, that might have given the clew to any listener. But what listener could

have been on the wire? Who could have overheard but
Dervish or Renfew?

It disturbed him that she had not been completely frank
about these details. Indeed, she had given him to understand that she had made the engagement with Phil only
that afternoon by telephone, when Phil had been so angry
and unhappy. Well, perhaps the engagement had been only
tentative in her own mind, but Phil's insistence over the
telephone had decided her. Certainly it had decided her,
or she would never have packed that bag. To be sure, she
had still camouflaged her intentions, by putting in a frock
to be taken to the cleaners—a frock that had never been
delivered.

Still, she had taken the bag. She had gone prepared to
succumb to temptation. . . . Oh, damn it all, what did that
matter to him—he was not going to sit in judgment on
that frantic, harried woman! And he knew how appealing
Darrow could be, how irresistible in his impetuosity.

But he wished Mrs. Channing had been more explicit
about those plans.

"Did you know where Mr. Darrow was going, Dervish?"

"Naturally not, sir."

He wondered if Dervish noticed that he did not ask
him if he knew with whom Darrow was going. Undoubtedly he did. Undoubtedly the man understood that between
them, so closely bound to Darrow, existed a tacit con-
spiracy of silence in regard to the lady Darrow had cared
for. He wondered what Dervish was thinking about it all,
behind his remote barriers.

"Did you know of the existence of this suite of his at
the hotel?"

Dervish seemed to hesitate before he committed himself.

"Yes, I did, sir," he said at last. "I was in his confidence, I may say."

"Who else knew about it?"

"No one else, sir."

"Not Mr. Renfew?"

"No, sir. Indeed it was partly on Mr. Renfew's account that he needed a retreat for real work. That and the telephone here and the people after him. I could have taken care of him here, sir, but you know what he was—when he heard a bell ringing he'd take an interest. He had to have a place where no one could get at him."

"And you think you were the only one who knew about it?"

Dervish was not so ready this time. "As far as I know. He did make that statement."

"Did you know the number of his rooms? Were you ever there?"

"Never in the rooms. I did not know the number. When I sent important letters down to him there, I sent them to Mr. Deering, private register. Once or twice I brought something down he phoned for and delivered it at the desk. I never had occasion to know the rooms."

"Would the clerk there know you again?"

"He might—although I was never there but once or twice."

"And you think no one else knew of the place—some old doorman at the theater, for instance?"

"The theater would be the very last place where he would want it known."

"Did you ever know of his taking any ladies there?"

"Never, sir. He did his entertaining here."

"Did he sometimes use it as a place to sleep?"

"Only when he was working very late. He liked his own place and—if I may say so—myself about him."

"I'm sure of it. . . . How long had he had these rooms?"

"About a year," said Dervish, which corroborated what the hotel had told Ryder.

"Did he tell you he was going to be away that night?"

"No, sir, not in words. When he had finished dressing—he changed to another suit but not to dinner clothes—he said, 'Bye-bye, Dervish. See you to-morrow,' and was gone like that."

Dervish's voice altered a little on the last words. Ryder could conjure up the image of Phil at the door, cheery and blithe again, now he was sure of his tryst. Going so unknowingly to his death.

"Dervish, I want you to think back and tell me every circumstance that comes to your mind of Mr. Darrow's life—his secret life, you understand. People he was involved with—anything at all that may have some bearing on this case."

The man's face took on a curious obstinacy that made it look like a mule's. His small mouth pinched in.

"If you'll excuse me, sir, I never hold with giving away your gentlemen."

"It's not a case of giving him away. It's a case of helping us find the man who killed him. Every clew counts—every conversation—every phone call. And it isn't a matter of your choice," he added, and Ryder had a way of making his words count. "It's my job to find out, you know."

"I knew you were something official," said Dervish, as one who glances askance at the bar sinister.

"I am Assistant District Attorney. Of course, the office can take you down to Headquarters"—he saw the mulish obstinacy harden in the man's face—"but it is much simpler for me to find out directly from you, here. I know a good deal, of course. About the girls and the night clubs."

Dervish picked up a chamois and began his polishing again. "I daresay, sir, you know a great deal more than myself."

"What telephone calls did he have?"

Ryder was reflecting that if it was a jealous woman who had followed Darrow, she would have been likely to be telephoning constantly, clinging to the relationship.

"I could hardly say, sir. You see he had a way lately of going to the phone himself so I didn't hear the voice."

"But it must have rung when he was out? And sometimes you must have answered before he could get to it?"

"Well, sir, there were always ladies—"

"Miss Fane?"

"Oh, not often now, sir. Not for a long time. Well"—Dervish appeared to reflect—"every once in a while she'd call, several calls together like, till she got hold of him, but nothing like old times, if you know what I mean."

"Quite. And the others?"

"Just the usual friends, I would say. Of course, I knew there was some one in particular—but I paid no especial attention, sir. Hardly my province, you might say."

"And there isn't a thing that suggests itself as important?"

Dervish appeared to reflect. "Well now, sir, there was a man's voice—a foreign, common voice it was—calling up and never leaving a name. And only yesterday morning he was in when the voice called and I heard him flying into one of his rages at the phone. 'Don't try threatening me,' he said, and hung up."

"And you've no idea who this man was?"

"None in the world, sir."

"Nothing out of the usual has happened at the house?"

"No, sir. Nor of the usual, I might say. It's been a long time since he's had one of his parties—you know that for yourself, sir."

Not since he'd fallen in love with Mrs. Channing, Ryder reflected.

A bell peeled suddenly through the room.

"That might be the young person again," Dervish mentioned, stepping to the hall to press the release.

Ryder followed him and stood listening till he heard Ryan's large tones informing some one that the Chief was here now and she could wait.

Chapter Six
Enter Miss Minn

But Ryder did not go at once into the front hall. He walked slowly through the dining room, where he had shared so many jolly meals, and on into Philip's bedroom.

It was neat, as the hand of Dervish always kept it, remedying Phil's disorder. There was a magnificent Spanish bed, a deep lounging chair, an old chest of drawers with silver dressing things outspread. Ryder thought of that other bedroom, in the hotel, with its anonymous furnishings, on whose bed he had found his dead friend that morning.

Swaney, the lieutenant of the precinct, had found a note from him in Phil's pocket, and, cutting short the usual routine of notification, had phoned him at once to come and identify the body. The thing seemed still incredible to him. . . . It was incredible that Phil would never come back to this old room of his.

The walls were crowded with framed photographs, mostly of actresses, but only two pictures stood on the dresser, and Ryder walked over and picked them up. The big one, in a silver frame, was of a girl in a Spanish costume, a gorgeously beautiful little creature. For a moment he thought it was some footlight favorite, then the dark eyes, with their arching brows, and the odd, troubling mouth and the pointed chin took on identity. It was the little Channing girl, dressed for some fête. She looked infinitely older in her shawl and mantilla, yet it was a look of borrowed maturity, a haunting foreshadowing of the years to come.

The other picture was a snapshot vivid with life—three figures lounging on the sand, Darrow, Mrs. Channing and the daughter, looking very small and childish again. Quite a family group, Darrow had his arm about the little girl.

He remembered Devlin's jocose sharpness. But there could be nothing in that. He remembered when Phil had first spoken of the Channings. He had said there was a young couple and a child. Channing had been an invalid, he remembered vaguely.

He put down the pictures and went out into the front hall, where Ryan was standing, his broad back to the living room, his impassive-seeming eyes watching the young person as Dervish had named her.

She was a small, black-eyed girl, her red hat pulled low over plucked eyebrows, a red coat with black fur opened over a red frock. The vogue for longer skirts had not affected her daytime appearance; she had a most extensive pair of legs clad in sheerest chiffon, as lovely a pair, Ryder thought, as Ryan had ever been privileged to contemplate.

"Here's Mr. Ryder, the Chief," said Ryan. "Now you can be telling him."

The girl tilted toward Ryder a shrewd, sharp-featured little face with a vixen's mouth of a red exactly matching her costume. The big black eyes were belligerent for all the smile she flashed him.

"My name is Minn," she said in a sharp, shrill little voice. "I'm Topsy Minn, I'm in Mr. Darrow's play and he has some gags of mine—something he was rewriting in the part—I have to have them at once."

"Suppose we come in here." Ryder led the way into the darkness of the long drawing-room, where Dervish had decorously drawn the curtains. He clicked on the lights.

"They are in that desk," said Miss Minn with a sharp toss of her head toward the big armoire standing between two windows veiled now in velvet hangings. Apparently she was acquainted with the place.

"Now will you tell me exactly what I am to look for?"

She gave him a shrewd look. She was laboring under a good deal of excitement and it was evident she was telling herself she needed her wits about her. But she burst out impulsively, "You don't look like a policeman—you look like you had some sense. You could understand. I don't want to be mixed up with this case. I want to get my letters."

"I thought you said it was your part."

"Applesauce for the dumb-bell there." She jerked her expressive little head toward the hall. "I thought it might work. But you're a gentleman, Mr. Ryder. You don't want to see a girl's name dragged into a case like this when she had no more to do with it than—than Queen Marie."

"Tell me how you are likely to be dragged into it?"

Hip eyes, dark and distrustful, consulted him doubtfully.

"Well, it was like this: I used to be friendly, in a perfectly nice way, with Mr. Darrow. Nothing intimate, you understand?"

She waited till Ryder gave his nod of understanding to that special stress.

"He used to take me out and he promised to fix me up with a part—I'm in the chorus. He certainly promised a lot, and I'd never had no breaks at all, not so'd you notice it, and I certainly counted on him. The second soubrette was leaving and he said he'd get me the job—but, say, did he remember? I'll say he *did—not!*"

Vindictive emphasis shrilled through her. "When it happened he was off with some of his society Janes and I was just where I was before—leading the line. And I'd learned her part and worked up a dance and he hadn't said nothing to nobody about me. After he said he was going to fix it. And I was mad. Well, I had a damn good right to be."

Ryder said sincerely that he thought she had.

"And I called him good. I wrote him a letter—maybe I didn't have the right to put all the things I did in that letter, but I was mad, you understand—gee, I hit the ceiling. It was an awful mean letter. I told him I could cut his heart out and there'd be nothing but dirt in it. I told him I'd pay him back sure—and maybe the time would come sooner than he thought. I knew a thing or two."

"And what did he do?"

"Oh, say, he laughed and told me he was going to frame it for a real mash note. He had me laughing before he was done—you know how he could kid you out of your pants—boots. Told me he'd fix me up yet. Oh, I wasn't mad long."

"When was this?"

"A month ago—six weeks, I guess. I wrote him it on a Friday. Well, I never thought about it no more—I was pretty busy with some things myself—then when this busted open I went crazy, thinking the flatfeet might rake it up. So I want it back."

"You're sure he kept it?"

"Yeah, he kidded me about it only a few days ago he said it was burning up his desk with its passion. I know he's got it. Won't you let me look?"

"You think it might make you suspected—?"

She stood biting her scarlet mouth. She gave him another distrustful glance. "Well, they wouldn't take me for his best friend."

"But no one would think you got so mad over losing a part that you followed him to a hotel and shot him, would they?" said Ryder definitely.

Her laugh was shaky. "Not over a part—no, but this letter don't say nothing about a part—it just calls him for throwing me down. I didn't put in the particulars. It might mean anything—see?"

"And where were you last night?"

"Nobody's business," she flamed.

"That wouldn't sound well at Headquarters?"

"Well, I was with friends. I was with a particular friend," she said sullenly. "We went to a speak-easy—the Jigsaw, if you got to know, at nine-thirty, and stayed there till one. Then I went home to the girls I room with."

"Names and address?" Ryder's notebook was ready.

She gave the names of the girls and the hotel, a theatrical one in the west Forties.

"Who was the man with you?"

"My husband," said Miss Minn. "I got married three weeks ago, but we're keeping it dark because if his dancing partner finds out she'll crab his act. She's just nuts over him. He's in vodvil. As soon as their time runs out he's going to team up with me. But we have to keep it dark now, see? Accounta her jealousy. She wouldn't feed him his lines. She's terrible. . . . And now you see why I gotta get that letter back. If it ever got into print that boy would raise hell. You know what it looks like—like Darrow had throwed me down and I was squawking. I just gotta get it—"

"Who is your husband?"

"Raymond La Salle," she said proudly. "La Salle and Leser is the act at the Palace now. But we're to team up as soon as his contract's over."

"And La Salle was with you last night?"

"Sure."

"Till one o'clock?"

"I don't see what one o'clock has to do with it," she looked sulkily defiant. "If you want to know, he spent the night with me—we girls got two rooms. Ain't he got a right to?"

"What about keeping your marriage dark?"

"Well, we didn't have to tell the girls we were married or anything," said Miss Minn practically. "They ain't narrow-minded. I'd do as much for them."

She added: "You can check up on all of us if that's what's eating you. We got nothing to do with your business. And I want to keep out of it. I want that letter back before it busts up my life—"

An honest worry sharpened her little face. Or Ryder thought it so.

He told himself that so far his part had been a passive one for beseeching ladies to work upon. First Virginia Channing, then Topsy Minn. He went to the desk, took off the seals, opened it and looked within. Phil's usual confusion. Bills . . . letters . . . invitations . . . telegrams. . . .

"Mine was green." Topsy Minn was standing close beside him, her nose sharp as a pointer dog's. "That's it, behind there."

Ryder drew farther away from her to read it through.

She had certainly spit it out. It was a shrill scream of anger and vituperation, venomous as a snake. It bristled with dark threats.

Carefully Ryder put the large green sheets back into the envelope. "I have no power to return this," he was beginning when eighty-five pounds of Topsy Minn hurled themselves upon him and small, wild hands made their desperate clutch.

He staggered, struggled. It was like shaking off a tiger cat. She clung, grabbed, clawed.

His left hand was occupied with the letter, but his right took the young lady by the throat and, straightening his hand, he held her off in a sharply constricting clutch.

She collapsed, her hands at her throat, looking at him with the furious, raging eyes of a thwarted child.

"It was mine," she gasped.

"It was Darrow's—and it's evidence." Ryder put it in an inner pocket, his eyes still wary. "You damn well deserve to have me turn it over to the papers to-night."

"It would be a dirty trick. I'm innocent—and you'd get my husband all steamed up for nothing."

"Was he jealous of Darrow?"

She gave a gamin-like grin. "Say, he's jealous of every egg I eat! You'd think I fell twice a day. . . . Did I scratch your hand, Mr. Ryder? It's bleeding. . . . I'm sorry—but you know how it is when you're in trouble."

"Look here," said Stephen Ryder reasonably. "I can't give this back—it belongs to the case. But I don't want to make you trouble. I can hold it up a little while, hoping some real clew will break so we won't have to use this. Now what do you know that will help us? What was this thing you were telling Darrow you had on him?"

"Ah, mostly hooey. I didn't know so much as I made out. But Florence Fane's been getting money out of him right along—she showed us an emerald he gave her for her lovely work in the show. I bet it was for some lovely work somewhere else. The funny part is he ain't crazy about her. I can tell."

"How does she feel about him?"

"Ask me another," said the girl jeeringly.

"I'm asking you this one. Was she in love with him?"

"She's in love with Florence Fane—but at that she might have been serious about Darrow. She was jealous anyway," said Topsy with her gamin grin.

"Jealous enough to shoot?"

"Not that baby! She ain't mixing in no hotel murder! Poisoned candy's more her style."

"Who do you think did it?"

"How should I know? A boy like that is bound to get into trouble. The women were wild about him—not myself, you understand," said Miss Minn carefully. "He got a hot one this time, that's all. You find that girl," said the chorus lady viciously, "and leave me and my letter alone. I wish I'd never told you about it. Only I thought you'd run on to it."

"So I would, within the hour. Now I must go through the others if you will excuse me. Don't be alarmed if some one comes round to-night at the theater for your fingerprints. They are checking up on every woman that Darrow knew well. I'll keep your letter out of the papers for a while, but it's up to you to find some clew that will keep it out forever."

She gave him a long look under her beaded lashes.

"Well," she said a little comically, "I wish you was one of these susceptible big boys that would give the little girl her letter, but since there's nothing I can do for you—"

With which obliqueness she nodded farewell and her silken legs took her airily to the door.

As a detective, Ryder reflected, he was a good confidant! Two women now had thrust their secrets upon him. All he seemed to learn was who was innocent.

But he was not sure about this Topsy Minn. Swiftly he went to the phone and asked Headquarters to set a watch upon one Raymond La Salle now at the Palace and find out as much as possible about him. Had he *a* foreign-sounding voice, for instance?

If Topsy were lying—if she had not been with her husband and he suspected her of being with Darrow—if he had somehow followed Darrow to the hotel and, not seeing who was the woman with him, and shot him down—?

On second thoughts he went again to the phone and had Miss Minn also shadowed. The soubrette story might be all a lie and some brief affair might have flourished between Darrow and Topsy— Not very good hearing for Virginia Channing. But she must have known of what volatile forces Phil was made—or hadn't she?

He hated looking through his dead friend's letters, but it had to be done, and he did it in the quickest possible time. There was nothing to detain interest. The letter in green had been the only vital thing in the desk.

There was nothing from Mrs. Channing but a note asking him to dinner some weeks back. That he secretly destroyed. There were two from Florence Fane, one saying curtly she must see him soon, the other apologizing for having asked him for something—unspecified—again so soon, but declaring it was really necessary as she'd explain when she saw him.

He hoped for better luck from Miss Fane herself.

He did not telephone for an appointment. Preparedness on her part would be a handicap. He planned to be at her apartment at the early dinner hour which her profession necessitated.

Sealing the desk again he left Ryan to his guardianship of the place which he meant to examine more thoroughly the next day, and, after a word of farewell to Dervish, went down to the street.

He turned into the Rose Tea Garden for a hasty sandwich, suddenly realizing his tea with Mrs. Channing had been a meager luncheon, and there the proprietress, with whom he had often chatted at meals with Darrow, waited on him herself.

She was bright-eyed with curiosity. Her bosom—Miss Rose had never overcome an old-fashioned addiction to bosoms though she had managed to subdue hips—heaved with emotion.

"My, we never thought when we saw him last night—he was on his way, then, waiting for a taxi. He smiled at me and waved his hand. Who'd 'a' thought he was on his way to—"

"One is always on his way to something," said Ryder.

Miss Rose misunderstood. "I hope not, always," she said a little primly. And then, "Whatever can be said against him there was no kinder-hearted gentleman. When sister was sick and we were having a struggle here, saying not a word to any one, he seemed to know of himself and insisted on our taking a loan and you know there never was a word out of the way between us. My, my, who'd 'a' thought— Yes, I'll tell that girl to hurry with your sandwich."

Again at his side she resumed, "I remember I was surprised at his going out, for his man had been in that afternoon for some sandwiches and chicken salad and ices for dinner. Then I said to sister, 'They must have been for the other gentleman,' for I'd seen him coming home with his bags. I meant to ask the man about it, when I saw him that evening, but he never stopped."

"When did you see the man in the evening?" Ryder wanted very quietly to know.

"Oh, some time after Mr. Darrow went out—it was when I was waiting on a couple at the window table. I looked out and saw Mr. Dervish walking along and I thought, there can't be any company for he isn't serving—but perhaps he doesn't serve the other gentleman. I know he has given me the impression that he is not very much pleased at having him there."

Ryder's voice was casual: "What time would you say that was?"

"Perhaps about eight-thirty—it was after the rush. Yes, it must have been about eight-thirty—I remember I was clearing the cigarette ash and coffee cups from the other tables between seeing to the couple at this one. . . Some time about eight-thirty."

"You are quite sure it was Dervish you saw?"

"Oh, yes, indeed. Not that he spoke to me—he never looked up but walked very fast, but I saw him, plainly. My—what makes you ask—?"

"Only that Darrow made a point of Dervish's staying in last evening when Mr. Renfew had a cold," said Ryder easily. "The man seems a perfect servant, but I fancy he did as he pleased when Darrow was away."

"That's human nature, Mr. Ryder. You've no idea the worry I have with the girls here—girls you think would know better, who pretend they want to learn the business. Why, only last week—"

"Did you happen to notice the time Dervish got back?"

"I didn't see him come back. I wouldn't of, for sister and I had dinner at a back table. I'm sure he seems a very reliable man, honest in what he buys if you know what I mean—"

"He's a good chap, but independent. Did you see anything of Mr. Renfew?"

"Not last evening, but he stopped in on his way out this morning for some cigarettes. He said the police were up there, talking to the man. Think of the police at Mr. Darrow's! . . . He said they had no idea till they read the paper. . . . He was terribly upset."

"I didn't call Dervish—I meant to come straight up to see him, then I went somewhere else," explained Ryder absently.

So Dervish had been out! And he had said he had been in the flat all evening.

Quickly he turned back into the building. Dervish was still at his polishing and the sight of that lean, energetic little body and bent head affected Ryder curiously. The man inspired both trust and distrust.

"Dervish," he began abruptly, "why did you tell me you had been in all evening when you were seen on the street?"

The face that Dervish turned to him was like a ship with battened hatches—not a sign of life stirred.

"Seen? On the street?" he repeated mechanically.

"You certainly were. On this block."

The man's frozen features relaxed. "I beg your pardon, sir, I could not imagine what you meant. Certainly I went out to post a letter—but I should hardly call that going out, sir."

"What time was that?"

Dervish reflected. "I couldn't say exactly, sir. Some time after I had cleared away Mr. Renfew's supper tray. He seemed to be sleeping so I stepped out with the post."

"And you came right back?"

"I was in the house by nine, sir. The telephone rang then and I answered it and Mr. Renfew called out to know who it was. He was expecting a business message of importance, he said. . . . I noted the time, for I always put that on the notes I leave for Mr. Darrow."

"Who was it?"

"Mr. Bartlett, calling up to ask for Mr. Darrow. He wanted Mr. Darrow to call him at his house if he got in before midnight."

"Did you say he was away for the night?"

"I said I hardly expected him before midnight, but I would give him the message if he returned. Mr. Bartlett said that it was important. But I don't hold with explaining a gentleman's absences, sir, to his friends."

"I'm glad to get that straightened out," said Ryder. "I dislike puzzles. You ought to have mentioned it before."

"Yes, sir," said Dervish resentfully.

Ryder went out to the street again. This was something to think about—something or nothing. The man was back at nine. He could check that through Bartlett.

All that he could suspect about Dervish was that the man knew more than he told. Habitual caution, perhaps.

He had a sudden impulse to telephone Virginia Channing and tell her he had a possible clew in La Salle, but decided against it. That speculative look in Devlin's eyes! They might be having her wire tapped. . . . Devlin would like to get something on him.

Five o'clock. He'd see if Bartlett were at his office. He consulted a telephone book. Bartlett had a business—besides other people. Something in bonds and investments. The Colony States Realty and Investment Company with offices in Wall Street.

But Bartlett had left for home. Good, Ryder reflected, that was nearer. In the east Sixties. As rapidly as his taxi could dodge through the traffic he made his way there.

He had never seen Bartlett's house before and he acknowledged its suitability to the owner as he was being shown in—a solid old-fashioned brownstone, with carpeted halls and heavy dark paneling.

Word came back that Mr. Bartlett was in and would see Mr. Ryder immediately, so Ryder followed the maid—a settled, housekeeperish looking person—up the stairs and along the hall to a large room across the front of the house.

It was not the first time the two men had met. Stephen Ryder was familiar with Bartlett's large domineering presence, his authoritative oratorical voice. But he studied the man now with new interest.

He saw a very solid-looking citizen, a somewhat fleshy man who, he knew, was somewhere in the fifties, with silver-gray hair topping a ruddy face. The bulk and the ruddiness gave a certain air of geniality that the coldness of the eyes and the tightness of the mouth belied. He looked self-esteemed and uncompromising—a man sure of himself and his self-righteousness. . . . He had heard Phil on the subject of his brother-in-law uncounted times.

"You know what brings me here, Mr. Bartlett," said Stephen, abruptly. He disliked discussing Phil's death with this man who had been so antagonistic to him. "You were one of the last persons to see Phil alive. Have you any idea what enemies he had?"

Henry Bartlett gave his visitor a slow look, while gesturing him to a chair. "I was not in my brother-in-law's confidence," he said dryly.

"I know that relations between you were not wholly amicable."

"My attitude to Philip," said his brother-in-law, "was always friendly. I am sure I possessed his entire respect—if not his confidence. But I was obliged to oppose several of his mad desires—if that is what you mean, Mr. Ryder."

"I mean that you opposed his desire for a divorce," said Ryder specifically, "to such an extent that you threatened to indict him for adultery if he obtained one and remarried." His gorge always rose at Bartlett's pompous statements.

"I certainly opposed his desire to divorce my sister," said the other man. "Marriage is a sacrament, Mr. Ryder."

"Philip could hardly feel his marriage was a marriage at all. A wife who unfortunately has been in a sanitarium for ten years—who was unable to recognize him—"

The irises in Bartlett's eyes contracted and the gray about them seemed to expand and sparkle.

"Having driven my sister to a sanitarium," he stated, "I hardly felt it was his duty to abandon her."

"My understanding was that Mrs. Darrow lost her mind after childbirth—the birth of a dead child, fortunately—and that Philip then discovered that her aunt and her grandmother had met the same fate."

As he spoke Ryder was furious at himself for engaging in this controversy, but his loyalty to Philip, his hatred of

misstatement and injustice, had got the better of his sense
of discretion for the moment.

Bartlett looked grimly at him. "I do not find it necessary, Mr. Ryder, to maintain the integrity of my family
against these accusations. I did find it necessary to maintain the integrity of the marriage bond against a man who
met his death in a lewd hotel with a woman of the streets.
I do not see, however, of what interest this can be to you
now."

"It is of no interest, Mr. Bartlett. Our understanding
of the situation and our sympathies are naturally opposed.
. . . But our interests in discovering Phil's murderer must
be identical. So I came to you for whatever information
you could give to aid the search."

Bartlett, too, seemed to find it desirable to rein in his
animosities. He considered quietly for a moment. Then
he shook his head. "I am so totally unacquainted with the
details of my brother-in-law's life that I can offer no suggestion."

"Am I correct in saying you telephoned his flat last
evening?"

"At nine o'clock. I had had a discussion with him that
day and I wished to talk the matter over when he had had
a chance to reflect. I was here, at home," he added, "and
I left word for him to call me if he returned before midnight. I waited till midnight for that call."

"Who answered your telephone at his flat?"

"His man. Dervish, I think the name is."

"And this was at nine? How do you fix the time?"

"I can tell you that. I had been out to mail a letter and
on my return to this room I looked at my watch to make
sure I had been in time for the nine o'clock collection. I
had been. Then I telephoned to Philip."

"He never gave you any intimation that he had any
enemies—any one threatening him?"

"He gave me no confidences of any kind. But I can tell you, Mr. Ryder," said Bartlett steadily, "that I know the cause of Philip Darrow's death."

Chapter Seven
The Leading Lady

"You know the cause of his death?" Ryder echoed, astounded. Involuntarily he got to his feet.

"I do, sir." Bartlett, too, rose. There was a pontifical dignity about the man. "I do, indeed. It was sin, Mr. Ryder—his own sin. The wages of sin is death. And Philip was sinning greatly."

The reaction of Ryder, instead of anger, was a contemptuous desire to laugh. His scorn was at once too weary and too deep for words.

He merely said, "If anything definite occurs to you, we will be glad if you will let us know."

Well, that was over. Dervish's statement had been confirmed.

Courteously Bartlett followed him to the door. "It is a little early to speak of these matters, perhaps, but I assume that you were Philip's legal adviser. I believe that I am named executor under the will and—"

"Not under the new will, Mr. Bartlett."

The big man stiffened in his tracks. His rigidity reminded Ryder of men he had seen beside him in war in the shock of a sudden wound. The same look of numb incredulousness. . . .

Then the strong voice came with a rush of grating suspicion.

"The new will? What new will? I was not aware that he had made a new will!"

This was the voice of Bartlett the denouncer, harsh and implacable.

Ryder took a distinct pleasure in responding levelly, "He made one yesterday in my office."

"That is impossible, sir! At what time?"

"After his interview with you. About four o'clock."

"About four—? Why he—he told me he was on his way to a rehearsal that afternoon. He threatened that he would remake the will the *next* day! . . . He said he would get hold of you the *next* day—"

The reiteration trailed into silence. Bartlett stood staring ahead of him, then, apparently with an immense effort, he collected himself and turned to Ryder.

"What were the terms of that will?" he said peremptorily.

"They are not yet made public. He provided an annuity for his wife, I can assure you, however."

"An annuity? Do you mean his estate—the bulk of his estate—was diverted?"

"He left it elsewhere."

"That is madness, Mr. Ryder. Madness and insanity. The man was out of his head when he talked to me. His money belongs in the family. To my sister, when she recovers her health, as will undoubtedly be the case. . . . That will will never stand."

Neither silver hair nor florid skin could tinge Bartlett's aspect with geniality now. Gold fury looked out of him.

"I made it water tight," said Ryder quietly.

"You will regret this. It will never stand." And then Bartlett's self-control came to his aid.

"Naturally this is a shock, Mr. Ryder. And I consider it an unwarrantable outrage—a reflection upon my sister. But Philip was undoubtedly out of his head. Temporary

insanity. . . . You may discover that he shot himself in that
state of derangement—and that the woman merely fled.
. . . As my sister's custodian I shall naturally oppose that
will, when you bring it into probate, with all the earnest-
ness in my power. . . . I regret that you, his lawyer, did
not dissuade him from that step. . . . Unless you are that
friend?" he added suddenly, his eyes boring like augers
into Ryder's.

But Ryder had his own inscrutability. He merely smiled.
"You'll know in thirty days, Mr. Bartlett."

That interview with Bartlett had done him good, Stephen Ryder reflected, as his tall figure swung south along
the avenue. It had given him something tangible to punch
at for a moment.

Let the man contest and be damned! He might make
trouble—he might even have his sister declared sane, if
she were fit enough for an appearance—but Ryder had
confidence in his own legal powers. That will would stand.
Virginia Channing should have at least the comfort of the
money Phil had wanted to give her.

He turned into a drug store and called Headquarters.
He got Devlin on the wire.

"We've just had a report on your man," Devlin told
him. "Quick work. We found he had a room at the Highgate Hotel but he checked out of there this noon."

"Good!" Ryder's delight was explosive. La Salle at the
Highgate! La Salle at the very hotel with the man he was
jealous of! Significant, at the least.

Then Devlin went on. "What do you want done about
him? He isn't trying any get-away—was at the Palace this
afternoon and playing poker with some pals at the Algon-
quin now. Our man is watching downstairs."

"Keep him shadowed, that's all. We'll get his prints
to-night. Get some of Keever's stuff, will you, for taking
them?"

306   *Mary Hastings Bradley*

"Sure. Keever's going to Darrow's show to get the whole works there. All the dames. And I suggest he gets your Mrs. Channing's, too—just for the collection."

Ryder's heart missed a beat. But his voice was unstirred. It seemed cool and untroubled.

"You leave Mrs. Channing out of that. I don't want her annoyed. . . . I have my eye on the possible woman. . . . But I want to see another first. That Florence Fane. I'm going over there now."

"Want me to join you?"

Ryder hesitated. He knew Devlin wanted the chance to talk to a popular actress; he knew, too, that Devlin was irritated to have the investigation taken so completely out of his hands. A little cooperation now would placate him. He was tempted—for Mrs. Channing's sake. But he knew he could do better alone.

"I know her, you know," he gave back. "I think I can get a bit more by myself."

"As you say." Devlin's voice was ironically polite. "Any more suggestions, Mr. Attorney?'

Ryder ignored the hostility. "Sure I have. I want you to find out from the hotel whether La Salle was seen there at all last evening and at what time. Check up on him."

"Any little thing I can do, of course—"

"Find out when his turn is at the Palace—"

"Ten-ten," the detective shot back.

"Then can you meet me there during his act?"

"Anything to oblige," Devlin assured him. He did not sound placated. He wanted to see Florence Fane, leading woman of "Her Move," not a mere vaudeville hoofer. . . . Well, it couldn't be helped.

Now for Florence Fane. Ryder wanted to talk to Renfew, also, but that could wait. For all Renfew's living in the apartment he had had little real intimacy with Phil—

he was an older, quieter man, with his own artistic interests and Phil's liking for him did not necessarily imply
any confidences. Ryder had often been with them together. However, Renfew must be in the possession of certain
facts.

If luck held he could just catch the actress at early dinner at her apartment hotel. Luck did hold. Miss Fane was
in. No, Miss Fane could see no one. . . . Mr. Ryder? About
Mr. Darrow? Wait a moment, please. Yes, Miss Fane would
see Mr. Ryder. Ninth floor, please. Apartment 920.

He rang the bell on the door and a very pretty little
black-haired maid admitted him into a silver-tinted
living room hung with delightful blue brocade. It was
evident that Florence Fane did herself extremely well,
even to providing the right setting for her really exquisite
blond beauty.

She came to meet him from a deep-cushioned divan
beside which stood a little table with her dinner tray. He
was reminded suddenly of that tray of tea he had shared
with Virginia Channing only that noon. It seemed now
curiously remote in time.

"Oh, Mr. Ryder!"

Miss Fane, wearing, He ironically noted, a pale, dove-
gray frock of subdued implications, held out both hands
to him in a gesture that gave and demanded sympathy.

There was artifice in her carefully modulated voice,
but it had a certain quality that caressed the ear, Ryder
had to admit. He always made any favorable admissions
toward her rather against the grain. He had considered
her, on their infrequent meetings, as too shallow a little
piece of porcelain for more than passing entertainment in
her posing.

Topsy Minn had more meat in her. But it was possible
he had underestimated Miss Fane's intelligence.

Certainly he could not underestimate her beauty. She was as pretty as a picture, with great blue eyes, ash blond ringlets, and the skin of a lily. He marveled afresh at the sheer physical perfection of the creature. . . . Only, without the sparkle of intelligence, he thought physical perfection rather boring to listen to. You could always buy it in a print and contemplate a speechless loveliness. Phil's vulnerability to long eyelashes on a soft cheek was not in him.

"There are some things I want to ask you—but don't let me keep you from your meal," he said, dropping her hands rather hastily. "I know you have to get to the theater."

"Yes, the show goes on, doesn't it?" Her smile was sweetly wan. "Even when one's good friends—"

"Exactly." His voice was dry as dust. He told himself he would have to do better than that to get anything out of her.

"I don't want to upset you now by talking about things," he went on in a more human tone. "I just want to ask a few questions."

"Why, of course, Mr. Ryder!"

Her wide eyes registered a sweet pleasure in aiding him, but behind their artlessness he thought he saw a watchful speculation.

"Had Phil any enemies that you know of?"

She shook her blond head. "Why, how could he have? So kind to every one, so helpful—"

"Everybody has enemies," the man told her bluntly. "Phil was pretty high-handed sometimes. He made a lot of people mad. . . . Do you know of any quarrel he had with a man with a foreign-sounding voice?"

"Foreign sounding?" She looked prettily thoughtful. "Dear me, I *don't*—"

"Eat your dinner while you think," he admonished.

Apologetically she smiled toward the chop and salad, taking a dainty bite. "I suppose one has to. But I had no heart for food to-night—as you see—"

He was brute enough to consider the meagerness of her meal dictated by the requirements for slenderness but he merely nodded.

"A foreign-sounding man," she reflected.

Then suddenly her face cleared. It revealed a bright perception. "Do you mean Luigi—the man who wrote some music for him? I know he was having a frightful time about that! It was one of my songs and it happened to be a great success and Luigi wanted to go back on the contract—"

"Tell me who Luigi is."

Between skillful bites of chop and salad Miss Fane told him. Luigi Crimonti had written the music for several of her songs. She had made him change some of them—this particular one, in fact. She thought the changes were responsible for a good deal of the success. It was "Teach Me to Love"—did Mr. Ryder remember it? And Luigi had wanted more money for it. Phil had said he wouldn't be held up. It was something over the distribution rights. Yes, she believed she had Luigi's address somewhere—could get it from the manager.

But Mr. Ryder didn't believe that Luigi—their Luigi, quite a nice young man, really—could have done anything so horrible—? Of course, he was foreign and temperamental—but surely, over a song—?

"I don't believe anything," Ryder told her. "Not yet. I am just trying to find out things. And this is in deep confidence, of course."

He didn't care whether it was or not. He was going to be on Luigi's trail by morning. Benson could get it from the manager.

She looked immensely confidential. "Of course, Mr. Ryder."

"And another thing. You are not to be offended because a man will be taking fingerprints of you ladies in the play. We have to check up on everybody who was near Phil."

"Of course." But she looked delicately doubtful. "Only don't you think that's so horrid and vulgar? I mean, it's such poor publicity—"

"It's just a form. It's not my idea, but you know what a public prosecutor's work is."

"I know," she sympathized.

"And aside from this Luigi—*is* there anything you could suggest? I know you and Phil were great friends."

"We were very great friends," she said trippingly, as if she had the lines well conned. "We had always enjoyed our association in his work. It was a privilege to be in his company."

"Well, you know," said Ryder, eying her thoughtfully, "I sometimes thought you a bit more than friends?"

Miss Fane was ready for that. She had evidently thought this thing out.

"In his position we could hardly have been more, could we?" she gave deftly back. "He was not in a position to offer marriage, you know how it was, Mr. Ryder." Delicately she sighed. Pensively she glanced at the square emerald ring she wore, then, obliquely, at her diamond wrist watch.

"You've time yet," Ryder told her. "I'm sorry to keep you—but there's another thing. Some one will be sure to ask you where you were last evening so you might as well tell me."

"Last evening? The evening of the mur— Oh, Mr. Ryder, you don't mean that any one would—?"

"As a formality," said Ryder patiently.

He was marveling afresh how Phil could have spent so much time with this lovely moron. Then the moron surprised him.

"I'd really rather not," she said firmly. "I was spending the evening with a friend—a friend who was in trouble and has reasons for not wanting it known she was here."

"You won't tell me?"

"I'm afraid I mustn't, Mr. Ryder." She smiled sweetly at him.

"Oh, my dear girl, you'll have to. If you won't tell me you'll have to go down to the office and tell Headquarters."

"I may have to go down, Mr. Ryder, but I don't have to tell. Not if I don't think it's right."

"You want to leave it at that?"

She took a sip of the black coffee the maid had brought.

"I could say I'd spent the evening here with Marie. She would do anything for me. But I don't like to say untrue things. And I'm sure no one would ever think I had done anything out of the way."

"Well, you may have a chance to find out," he told her a little blankly.

Without the slightest animosity she turned to him. "There's something I want to ask you," she mentioned with pretty confidence. "It's about some money of Phil's. He was here yesterday morning—just yesterday—" her eyes widened in mournful recognition of the date—"and he wanted some money. Quite a lot. A thousand dollars. He said he had an appointment with his brother-in-law for luncheon and had to hurry away, and he didn't want to ask him and the banks weren't open, as it was Sunday, and I said I'd get it for him here. So he gave me his check and I gave him the money. Now his check—"

"You had so much on hand?"

"Oh, I didn't, Mr. Ryder! Poor little me. . . . But I could get it from the office—I sent down my check," she said hastily. "I didn't want to endorse Mr. Darrow's—it would look so odd at the hotel. You know how careful a girl has to be about every little thing! So I just wrote my own and I have his here."

She tripped to a little escritoire and from a drawer took out a bank book from which she removed the blue slip of check.

"Here it is, Mr. Ryder."

Ryder saw that it was Phil's check for a thousand dollars made out to her.

"I took it to the bank to-day," she went on, "and they said they could not cash a—a dead man's check"—her voice shivered appropriately—"and I'd better see his executor. I suppose that is you, Mr. Ryder. I know you did his business for him. You see, I don't want to wait for the money. It's such a lot—it seems so to me—"

"I haven't any authority to pay anything over yet," Ryder told her slowly, turning the blue check about, then restoring it to her. "It's awfully too bad, Miss Fane, to ask you to wait—but I'm afraid you'll have to."

"For how long?" Her voice was a shade sharper now. Her wide eyes less artless. They watched him very attentively.

"For thirty days or so," he said easily. "Till the will goes to probate and I settle the bills of the estate. But you needn't worry. The estate will pay his debts, once the claim is validated."

"It's such a lot," she murmured, "and it seems too bad to have to wait when I was doing him a favor—"

"Yes, of course." He remained obtusely blind to the suggestion wafted in her gentle voice. "But the delay won't be serious—and it's a very minor tragedy in the case."

She sighed, as if recognizing finality, and replaced the paper carefully in her drawer.

The maid came with a wrap of chinchilla and a chiffon cap to fit over the immaculate blond hair.

"Let me take you to the theater," Ryder offered, but once he was in the car with her he suddenly remembered that he had to telephone at that very moment, and excused himself. As fast as a taxi could take him he was back at the hotel.

He sought the manager's room, where a sharp-faced young man with a pince-nez was shown his credentials and asked a question.

"Did you cash a check for a thousand dollars for Miss Fane yesterday?"

After a hurried consultation of clerks, and a thumbing of record books, the manager answered definitely in the negative. No check had been cashed.

"Did you send her a thousand—put it on the bill?"

The hotel never did that, Mr. Ryder was assured. The management only paid minor bills for parcels at the door.

"This is quite between ourselves," Ryder told the plan. "Not a word of my question, please, should Miss Fane inquire to-night. Not a word of me in any case."

So that was that! She had lied about the check. She had Darrow's check fast enough—Stephen did not doubt its genuineness—but it had been obtained for reasons other than she had given.

The tangle was increasing. A little while before there had been nobody at all to suspect and now he was edged in with possibilities. There was Topsy Minn and her revengeful fury. There was Raymond La Salle, the jealous husband. There was this Luigi, resentful and inflamed. There was the mystery of the check to Florence Fane.

And beyond them all was Virginia Channing with her dark, anxious eyes imploring him.

What a web it was, those tangled strands of a man's life! Broken threads, broken so abruptly, leading back— who knew where? He felt them slippery and elusive in his grasp. . . . If he could untangle them wisely, tracing them back. . . .

Chapter Eight
Overheard

An hour later he was in the green-paneled drawing-room of Mrs. Channing's apartment with Mrs. Channing opposite him. It was important, he had told himself, to see her, to tell her exactly what he had told his colleagues, and have her conversant with every detail. She must remember that he had said he was an old friend, that he had known her for years.

It was important, too, to see her again and renew those earlier impressions of her sincerity. The impression had not paled, but he had grown to wonder more and more at its power over him.

He was shocked at the change in her appearance. She looked as if a year instead of a day had passed. She had made no effort now to conceal the pallor of her cheeks and the shadows were dark under her great eyes.

"Did you get some rest?" he wanted to know.

She shook her head with a wry smile. "I tried. But my head felt on fire."

"You'll have to do better than this," he told her bluntly, "if you're not going to crack under the strain."

"I won't crack."

"You will, unless you sleep and eat. No nerves can stand it. What's your drug store? I'll phone for some tablets I know and you take two to-night and forget the world. They are harmless. You'll feel right as rain by morning."

"What do you know about tablet things?" she murmured with a ghost of raillery.

"Had an ache in my leg left over from a cut during the war so my physician fixed me up with stuff that would give me sleep but no bad habits," he grinned. "Now I'm going to phone, then tell you all that's happened."

Carefully he went over each detail and she listened intently, as if memorizing every word.

"You think it's La Salle?" she asked.

"It may be. I can tell better when I've seen him. Not that I'm psychic," his eyes twinkled fleetly into hers, "but I trust a good deal to my own impressions."

The extent to which he had trusted to them that day was apparent to them both.

"He may have been suspicious of Topsy: she may have been out with some other man and he thought she was going to be with Darrow. She may have been with Darrow before, for all we know," he said bluntly. "So La Salle might have fixed himself a disguise of whiskers and hung about the entrance, until they had come in. Then it would have been easy for him to follow them, and return to his own room and destroy the disguise. It's perfectly possible."

"But what about La Salle's alibi? At the Jigsaw?"

"Sustained by Topsy? I don't give a hoot in Hades for it. Or for the Jigsaw's corroboration—though a jury might take that into account."

"Then you may be on the right track already—"

"I may—but one never knows. Then I had Renfew meet me for a spot of dinner before I came here. He had a horrid cold, poor chap, but I wanted to talk to him out of the apartment to get a line on Dervish. We can't overlook that Dervish was the only one who knew of that hotel suite—though La Salle, at the hotel, could easily have tumbled to it. But I got nothing there. Dervish was in all evening after nine. And Renfew knew nothing of Phil's real life. He could only suggest that Phil often called an Atwater number—"

"That's mine," Mrs. Channing murmured.

"And he corroborated Dervish's statement that Dervish was back in the apartment at nine that night. He said the phone rang and he asked who it was and Dervish said, 'Mr. Bartlett for Mr. Darrow—it's just nine o'clock sir, isn't it?' And he says Dervish was about the rest of the night, bringing in an electric pad and some fresh water and things."

"But why would it be Dervish—what possible motive—"

"I think Dervish is out of the picture," Ryder admitted. "I don't know why I feel a little distrustful of him—too darn perfect, perhaps. He's bound to have a weak spot. But there's no motive for his doing himself out of a good job. There is with La Salle."

He looked at his watch. "I must start soon. But I want to ask you another thing. Why didn't you tell me you had planned at first for a pick-up dinner at Phil's flat?"

"At the flat?"

"Yes. Dervish told me Phil had ordered some stuff for the ice box and was planning to stay in till Renfew came back."

"Oh, that! Why I—I didn't think it was of any importance."

"The exact details are of extreme importance," he insisted. "For instance—please think back. When did he tell you he wanted you to go to a hotel instead of his apartment?"

She closed her eyes as if she were thinking but he had a curious conviction that she was shutting out his gaze.

"Why is it important?" she wanted to know.

"Because if he phoned you and mentioned the hotel some one might have overheard and known where to look for you. If he only told you at the restaurant—"

She was silent for a long time. Then she said in a curiously flat voice, "I don't remember."

"Good God, can't you recall a thing like that?"

"Not—not positively. I think—I feel sure—it must have been at the restaurant. But I can't swear to it."

He stared at her in baffled perplexity.

Of course, her nerves were playing her tricks. She must feel utterly done in. But he would have thought that a woman would have remembered, with shocked vividness, when a man had first mentioned *that* to her.

"One more thing," he said. "Can you think of any way the Fane woman could have got a hold over Phil? She got that thousand out of him for herself. . . . What about it? Had they been intimate—could he have been bribing her to keep her from telling you?"

"I think they had been intimate," she said gravely, "but I am sure that was years ago. I know, when I spoke of her, not long since, he blurted out that he was sick to death of the little fool. I remember his words. . . . Yes, it's quite possible that he did pay her to keep the facts hidden. She may have guessed it was especially important to him just now. . . . That's possible."

She spoke consideringly, a little absently, as if her thoughts were circling far afield.

"That would explain the check." He frowned. "But I don't see that it gets us any farther along on the real problem, unless—unless you think she was so infatuated that she'd follow him to the hotel and kill him for having let some one supplant her?"

For the moment, in his absorption with the problem, the man had forgotten that he was talking to the supplanter, then her quick, distressed breathing reminded him.

"I *can't* think it—I don't see how any woman—or any man could have done that! But it was done!"

"It was done, and we've got to find the one who did it. I hate to keep dragging you over these things," he said, gruff-sounding in his sympathy, "knowing how you feel about Phil—"

"How I feel about Phil?"

"Yes," he said soothingly. He added, curiously against the grain, for words of sentiment came hard, "How you loved him."

"Loved him?" Some cord of restraint snapped in her. Her words came in a tumultuous crescendo.

"Oh, I think I hate him, I hate him!" She cried out mockingly, *"Safe as a saint, Jinny dear!"* and then put her head down into her muffling hands and choked with tearing sobs.

He could only sit and watch her. She would be better, he thought, for having given way. She was under a ghastly strain. Her words meant nothing but tortured nerves—and a fury against Phil's lack of stability. . . . A woman must have her resentment against a man who rushed her into that sort of thing, who played on her feeling for him against her other feelings. She must feel sick with humiliation at her plight. He had let her in for shame and danger. . . . Of course, he had not known. . . . And she had loved him and lost him forever. . . . His dead face must be haunting her. . . .

She choked back her sobs, not eased by them, as he had hoped, but strangling her emotion in fierce shame of it, fighting desperately back to self-control.

"I won't do that again!"

"You go to bed," he advised very gently. "Those tablets have come—I saw the maid put the package on the hall table. Take two of them now. Let me see you do it. I'll get the water."

He left her wiping her tear-stained face, and went down the hall toward where he judged the kitchen was. He was light on his feet and moved silently. A swing door opened inward on a butler's pantry and he was within it when the sound of voices from beyond the second door made him hold himself motionless.

A man was talking—evidently to the maid. A quiet, persuasive voice was saying, "You'll never be without one, once you've used it. I'll show you how it works in a moment." He knew that quiet, persuasive voice. Benson! So Devlin had sent him here, instead of to the theater; Devlin, then, had had his own suspicions of this widow whom Ryder was protecting, this friend to whom Darrow had left all his fortune.

"Listen to this, now," said the mild voice. It added casually, "You need something to take your mind off what's happened. The elevator boy was telling me this Darrow that's been killed was a great friend of the family."

There was the sound of quick stepping feet as Ellen went from table to sink.

"People are always talking," she said crisply. "I'm surprised he let you up here to sell anything. He's careful about peddlers in this building."

"Oh, I didn't tell him I was selling," the voice admitted humbly. "But a man's got to make a living. I'm buying my little girl a dress with this over-time work. . . . Sure, people'll talk. It's the big excitement—when a well-known fellow like that, a big writer, gets bumped off. And leading a double life always makes a big noise when it comes out. . . . It must have been an awful shock to his society friends. Did they telephone your lady?"

"She never knew a word about it till she saw it in the paper she brought in with her in the morning," said the girl excitedly.

"In the morning—? I thought she was at the theater—the elevator boy was telling me that."

"She got in from that. Then the phone rang and she went out to a sick friend. She wasn't back till morning. She came in as smiling as you please, poor lady—not that it's such a loss to her at that," said the girl darkly.

"That's what I say. A married man's got no call to be hanging about—"

"And I've no call to be standing about talking—"

"You're going to let me show you the new alarm, aren't you? My little girl will feel pretty disappointed if I don't sell enough for that new dress."

Ah, the persuasiveness of Benson's conciliatory voice. How natural-seeming his harmless garrulity!

"It begins just as soft," he was saying. "You'd hardly notice it, No shock. Nothing to make you jump. . . . Just that soft buz-z-z-z. I'll let you listen to it in a moment. Then—if you don't come to for that—it gets just a little louder—not much, but a little, all the time—but you get awake before it has a chance to rouse the whole house the way an ordinary alarm does. . . . And you say you never knew it till you saw it in the papers? What time was that, now?"

"Oh, after seven. . . . How much, did you say—?"

"I'll set it off for you now. It won't disturb anybody, will it, if I let it ring to its loudest? Who's her company?"

"Oh, just the man that came this morning," said the inadvertent girl.

"What sort of looking fellow was this Darrow? Handsome, like the papers said?"

"He was that."

"Never looked as if he was under the shadow of death, I suppose. Well, we never know. Did he look worried when you saw him last?"

"Worried?" From the skeptic tone Ryder could imagine the toss of Ellen's head. "Not him! He was as smiling as you pleased when he"—she broke off.

"When did you see him—toward the last?"

"Look here; I've got these glasses to put away and a date to keep. If you want to show me your little clock—"

"Mrs. Channing wants a glass of water," said Ryder pushing through the door.

He glanced over at the shabby little man placing his alarm clock so carefully on the table. Very deferentially the man looked up and said, "Good evening." Steady actor, that Benson. . . . Ryder wanted to wring his neck.

"I don't think Mrs. Channing needs any clocks to-night," he said abruptly.

"Oh, all right. But this young lady here—" He glanced at the girl who plainly resented any infringement on her rights.

"She won't be having any, either," said Ryder and stood there while, without a sign of recognition, save a meekly rebuking look from the mild, nearsighted blue eyes, Benson repacked his clocks in a little bag and left the kitchen by the service door.

Ryder took the tray with the glass of water from the maid.

"That fellow is a reporter," he told her in a confidential tone. "I recognized him. He wants to get a story from you."

"A reporter?" Her hand flew to her mouth. "From the papers?"

"You haven't said anything—not yet. But you'll have to be on the lookout. You don't want Mrs. Channing in the papers."

"That I don't!" she replied heartily, her manner mollified.

He brought Virginia the water. He watched her take the tablets. Then he said, "Devlin's pet detective was out in the kitchen trying to sell your maid a new alarm clock. He was questioning her and I overheard her tell him that you were out to the theater, then came back, answered the phone, and went out again to spend the night with a sick friend. . . . How about that coming back? You never mentioned that?"

He stood inexorably over her, staring down on the still, tensing mask of her face. She shut her eyes away from him, as if in their dark depths were sudden alarms flying to cover. They were expressionless when she looked up.

"What else did you hear?"

"Nothing more. But I want to know about this return."

"Is that so very important?"

"If you think the truth is important," he said savagely.

"Don't be angry with me," she said with bewildering gentleness. "I know it seems very upsetting to you. But it was just that—that I had forgotten something I needed for the hotel—and came back here for it."

"You and Phil together?"

"No. He waited at the restaurant. I took a taxi over and back. The phone that Ellen heard was Phil phoning to know why I was so long. Then I told Ellen I was going to a sick friend and went out."

"How could you return to him? I thought you didn't know the name of the restaurant."

"I didn't. Phil put me in the taxi and told the man to take me to my address, then bring me back. I didn't pay any attention to the place."

"What was it you went for?"

"My bag."

"But you told me—that when you went out, *alone* you said—you were carrying your bag."

"I wasn't thinking of when I started for the theater," she said faintly. "I went out alone each time. The details didn't seem so important."

"Where was your child during all this?"

"I told you she'd left for a house party on Long Island. The Sergeants' party. But she had a headache and came

back after I left. I had thought she would be away all
night."

"Then you hadn't made up your mind to go to the hotel
when you first left the house?"

She looked down at her clasped hands. "N-no—I suppose not. No, I only told Ellen I was going to the theater."

"But you don't remember when Phil first mentioned
the hotel to you? Over the phone—or at the restaurant?"

"It *must* have been at the restaurant," she murmured.
"Anyway, it was then he got me to agree."

"Is there anything else," Ryder harshly wanted to know,
"that you thought was unimportant and so failed to tell
me?"

"Nothing. Nothing."

He looked down at her bent head in sharp and bitter
bewilderment. He did not know what the devil to make of
her. She must realize the seriousness of every detail! With
her life at stake, her child's security involved, it seemed
unthinkable for her to be inaccurate about details—when
he was groping so desperately for clews to save her.

But women were inconsequential. And this matter of
the return might have sincerely seemed to her unimportant.

"There are just two ways—barring fortuitous accident—in which you and Phil could have been discovered
at that hotel," he summed up for her. "Either he was overheard telephoning, naming the hotel, or the restaurant,
where he was to meet you—or he was followed from his
house to the restaurant and then to the hotel. The spy
must have been puzzled when you left the restaurant but
evidently kept Phil in sight and saw your return. . . . It
would help a great deal if I knew definitely what had been
said over the phone."

"That I can't tell you," she said in a troubled voice. "I
simply can't trust my memory."

"Then we will have to keep both suppositions in mind. It's extraordinary you don't recall if he named the particular hotel," he could not forbear telling her.

She was silent.

"I hardly think Phil would be so rash as to name the hotel over the phone," Ryder went on, thinking aloud. "He may have thrown out suggestions. . . . What I have to think is, that either he named the restaurant to you and the spy took up the trail there or he was followed from the house. He certainly must have been shadowed, for the man to enter the hotel so quickly after you."

"It looks like it."

"And there are two kinds of jealousy that could have prompted the murder. A woman's jealous anger against Phil—and that includes Topsy Minn and Florence Fane—or a man's against him. And that includes Raymond La Salle, assuming he supposed Topsy to be the woman in the room—or any unknown man who might have been in love with you and furious against Phil."

"That last you can leave out," she said quickly. She had evidently been thinking it over. He remembered her surprise and secret reflection that morning.

"There is no one in love with you?"

"No one likely to go to such extremes," she answered with a faintly ironic smile.

"I think you owe me complete frankness as to any possible man."

"I do. And I have thought about it," she confessed. "There are two or three good friends who might like to be something more—but there is no desperate wooer. But aren't you forgetting Luigi?"

"Luigi has a possible motive of another sort. But I can't understand why he should go to so much trouble to track Phil and shoot him down when he was with a woman. He could easily have arranged less dangerous opportunities.

He would not have wanted the woman as witness to his crime."

"Unless he thought that woman was Florence Fane and wanted revenge on her, too."

"That's a thought. I won't forget it. I'm having Luigi shadowed. As soon as I left Florence Fane I phoned Headquarters to get his address and keep him covered. . . . Now you get to bed or you won't be in time for those tablets to get in their good work."

He left her, torn between the strange strength of his compassion for her and the pulling of a new uneasiness.

He wished he had not thought of something. He wished his imagination had not suggested that she had quarreled with Phil at the restaurant, returned for a revolver, gone on to the hotel with Philip.

He knew perfectly well that he ought to have Ellen sounded out on the presence of a thirty-two revolver in that apartment. But he would *not* distrust her. In spite of those curious reticences of hers, those lapses of memory, he *did* not distrust her. There was something about her, that indefinable quality of character, that compelled belief.

Or was it her charm that constrained him? Was he believing in her sincerity because she had a nun's brow and dark, troubling eyes and a low, moving voice?

He had always been a man rather impervious to women. He had been caught once by glamour, in the adolescence of his early college years, and the resultant long engagement, with the glamour sunk in satiety, had been a galling fetter. Too responsible a nature to slough off lightly any duty even to a pretty, pettish girl, he had floundered along, until increasing exasperation and a deepened knowledge of his own nature had made him snap away.

Ever since then he had taken his liberty seriously and women rather lightly. He was careful with them—as with creatures capable of taking hurt—but more careful with himself. Even the war, following closely on his graduation from Law School, had not swept him off his feet about them. He had gone in at once for the Royal Flying Corps, and his continued existence had been a sustained miracle. Only one bad smash had threatened him—the accident that had given him the wound in the leg he had mentioned to Mrs. Channing.

After the war he had returned to New York, and started in a law office, and after an exceptional success in prosecutions, he had left his firm to accept that position of Assistant District Attorney, on whose responsibilities Darrow had so often rallied him.

He reflected now, as he drove to the theater, that after all, for all his thirty-eight years, for all his thunderings at the bar, his examinations of witnesses, and those fleeting brushes of sentiment, whose consequences he so promptly and expeditiously evaded, he was probably curiously innocent of actual knowledge of women.

And now he had staked himself, his entire career, on his belief in one whom he had known but for a few hours.

What, he wondered, had she meant by that outcry of hers, *"Safe as a saint, Jinny dear"*?

Phil had undoubtedly promised her that—safe from publicity in his hidden rooms. And then his death had exposed her to this terrible publicity. Still she could not hold his death against him—poor Phil! But women's nerves were unaccountable.

And it was unaccountable that she had been so confused about their plans. Well, that had no bearing on her innocence of the murder. She was under a terrific strain, and naturally any woman would hate to bring out all those details—her hesitations, Phil's persuasions, her going back for the intimate detail of the bag. . . .

But then she had said she had taken a dress for the cleaner's in the bag. She had certainly given him to understand that she had taken the bag when she had gone to the theater.

He ought to cross-examine the maid, the doorman. And yet he would not. If he believed her, he believed her. On that belief he had staked himself.

Yet, she had lied before. . . .

Chapter Nine
The Suspect

Sergeant Devlin was waiting for him at the stage door and together they strolled into the wings and leaned against the scenery to watch La Salle and Leser in their singing and dancing act. Leser was a brisk little girl with amazing blond hair; La Salle was a good-looking boy with a gleaming smile he turned frequently on an audience that seemed to like it, and a very neat and lively pair of feet.

"I got news," the detective reported, a touch of excitement stirring his ordinarily casual voice. "La Salle was seen coming into the Highgate at nine-thirty last night, and he wasn't seen going out. The Jigsaw won't fix the time he came in there. . . . They say Topsy Minn was there first, waiting for him."

"Yes?"

"I got it figured out," the other went on, his cynical glance on the young actor now busy delivering the wise-cracks whose cues the little Leser was giving him. "He may have been about and got a glimpse of Darrow getting in the elevator with some dame. He thinks that's Topsy. Maybe he didn't like to show any interest before the clerk so he fixes up some disguise—he's an actor, you know—and walks to the doorman with his phony questions about who has gone in."

"The doorman said the man came in immediately after Darrow."

"Well, the man may be wrong about that 'immediately.' Anyway this boy is quick—look at him changing there in the wings."

"So make hay—
While your baby's sunshine smiles on you,"

shrilled Miss Leser, her checked overalls and suddenly donned sunbonnet monopolizing the spotlight.

"Hates it, don't she?" chuckled Devlin and Ryder wondered anew at the man's power of detachment.

He, himself, was tense with excitement as he felt the chase narrowing down.

"Then," the detective proceeded, "he went around the side way, went up in the elevator, got rid of his disguise, got out the little thirty-two, saw to the silencer, and went down to shoot Darrow, full of holes. . . . Now either he saw the woman or he did not. I figure not—that hand on the bedroom knob might mean she was hiding there when he broke in. Anyway, he goes out to get himself an alibi and rushes to the Jigsaw and there sits Topsy Minn. . . . So now she's protecting him. We know she wasn't the dame in the room because that woman was seen coming out after one o'clock—and Topsy's got her alibi for all that time."

He fitted an unlighted cigarette carelessly in the corner of his long, loose lips. "Anything against that theory—except that I invented it?" he negligently wanted to know.

"Not a thing," Ryder returned. He reminded himself that La Salle could not possibly identify Virginia Channing. If they got the murderer they would have no reason to track down that unknown woman. . . .

"Or else," said Devlin, "it wasn't this guy at all, but the jane who got away."

La Salle was in the spotlight now, urging loudly, through his nose, his need for lo-o-oving, and Leser ran on in lacy peignoir and frilly cap to tell him she was his, and then, peignoir abandoned, they finished with a busy little dance that brought them almost as many curtain calls as they took.

Off into the wings they ran at last, this time on the side where the two men were waiting.

"Just a moment, brother." Devlin put his hand on the boy's shoulder. "You're wanted."

Ryder could see nothing but surprise in the look that La Salle gave them.

"What's the big idea?"

"We're coming down to tell you. The manager is putting the other fellows into another room so you can have yours to yourself. Lead on."

On his heels they followed down the spiral iron staircase into the subterranean depths, turned into one of the cubicles and shut the door.

"Say, what is this?" La Salle demanded uneasily.

"I'm Sergeant Devlin from the Homicide Bureau and this is Mr. Ryder, the Assistant District Attorney. And we want to know all about how you bumped off Philip Darrow."

La Salle's hand stopped in the act of lifting a cigarette to his mouth. He stared from one to the other.

"Are you eggs crazy?"

"Thought Topsy Minn was in that room, didn't you?"

"Like hell I did. Why we was out together."

"Yeah—afterwards. No, we got you dead to rights, boy. You were seen at the hotel that night. . . . Checked out next noon didn't you?"

"Sure I checked out! No rule against leaving a hotel is there?"

"No, but there's lots about killing a man you're jealous of."

"I didn't do any killing, I tell you," said the actor heatedly. "Why the hell should I? . . . I hadn't a thing against
Darrow—"

"Except he was sweet on your girl. And you'd warned
him to lay off. And you thought she was sleeping with him."

"That's a lie. And I never said a thing to Darrow."

"Well, you did to Topsy. And she's come clean. . . .
How she waited for you at the Jigsaw till after ten-thirty
and you told her to say it was nine-thirty o'clock when you
come in—"

"I can prove it by the waiters—"

"You were seen at the Highgate at nine-thirty o'clock."

La Salle hesitated. Then, "I just ran in for a minute. I
wanted to get some more jack before I met Topsy."

"You met Topsy a little after ten-thirty."

"It was earlier! I got witnesses!"

"No, we have," Devlin taunted. "Topsy's come clean."

"She never. Why if there was anything to tell she'd never snitch—"

"You come down to Headquarters and we'll read you
her story."

La Salle looked about at Ryder, standing silently regarding him. His full-blooded, rather common good looks
were slackening into terror.

"You're sweating under your grease paint," Devlin's
cynical voice reminded him. "Wipe it off and come along."

"I want a lawyer—"

"You'll get a lawyer when we're through with you. . . .
Better stop lying, fella," Devlin advised with an easy shift
to a confidential tone, "and get it over with. Otherwise
we'll all be against you. We got it on you, anyway."

"I tell you I—"

"Get into your street clothes and come along."

"Oh, damn you to hell," said La Salle furiously. "All
right—I'm coming."

With the actor's quickness he hurried into his clothes
and between the two men left the building and entered a
taxi.

All the way down Devlin hammered at him. "What did
you do with the gun?"

"I never had a gun."

"You got a good defense—you thought it was your wife.
Sure, you got a swell case before any jury. . . . Any fellow'd
go off his nut when he thought his wife was sleeping with
another man." Even in extremis La Salle remembered the
possibilities of Leser's jealousy.

"I never said I was married," he answered cautiously.

"You'd better say so—before the jury. It will help a lot.
. . . You are married, aren't you?"

"Maybe I am. Maybe not," the young actor informed
him noncommittally.

Inspector Ascher, according to arrangement, was waiting at the office, and for an hour the three officials plied
La Salle with questions in accusation after accusation; but
nothing could shake his denials, even Devlin's insistent
asseverations that Topsy Minn had betrayed him.

"She couldn't of. She knows I didn't," he repeated stubbornly.

He admitted checking out of the Highgate because he
didn't want to be mixed up with the thing. Topsy had told
him to do that.

Devlin pounced again and again on that, but in vain.

"You *knew* you'd be suspected—your jealousy of Topsy
would make you suspected—"

"I didn't have to be jealous of Topsy. I knew where she
was all the time."

That was all they could get out of him.

"Lock him up," said Devlin disgustedly. "Maybe he'll
tell the truth in the morning."

"I won't say a thing more till I've seen a lawyer," La Salle blustered as he was led away.

Devlin stood up and stretched his long, loose-jointed frame. "I could do with some sleep myself," he yawned. "Three o'clock this morning this thing broke, didn't it? And now it's midnight. . . . Well, we got this guy locked up. That's something."

"You think he did it?" Ryder asked slowly.

Devlin gave him one of his slant, swift-stabbing looks.

"Him—or the jane. . . . I'd feel better to get him identified by her."

But the morning brought no identification.

The chambermaid and the elevator boy were positive they had seen La Salle in the hotel at about nine-thirty that evening. But Jim, the doorman. confronted with the hotel's former guest, could only say uncertainly that he didn't believe the fellow could fix himself up with whiskers so he wouldn't recognize him—and then again he might.

But Jim stuck to his story that the mysterious stranger had inquired about Mr. Deering just after Deering went in. He was sure he had looked to see if Deering had gone up. Of course, a few minutes might have elapsed—he couldn't say. But it was just after or thereabouts.

All that was sure was that La Salle had been in the hotel about nine-thirty. He might, or might not, have had any connection with the mysterious stranger. It wasn't necessary that he had—opportunity for the crime was furnished by the fact that he was at the hotel at all, but opportunity was hardly enough evidence on which to charge him with the murder.

A search of his new rooms, conducted by the enterprising Devlin, produced no evidence. No bloodstained garments, no false whiskers, no revolver.

"Naturally he's got rid of everything," said Devlin bitterly. He gave the impression that Ryder had been so preoccupied with other things that he had procrastinated in running down La Salle. And in the depths of his harassed soul Ryder was not sure but there was some truth in this.

By noon La Salle had seen a lawyer who promptly applied for a writ of habeas corpus, but the judge, on hearing the evidence from the District Attorney's office, continued the hearing for twenty-four hours.

In the meantime La Salle, under guard, was allowed to go down to the theater to fulfill his contract there— Devlin wanted no publicity-making suits for damages later. He hoped, too, to pick up something on La Salle, from watching him and perhaps overhearing something.

There was no difficulty in hearing what Topsy Minn had to say. That young lady was raising Cain. Her vivid testimony before the judge at the preliminary hearing was remembered for many a day.

"Say, he wasn't worrying about me and Darrow," she asseverated vigorously. "I wasn't taking any nights off—we wasn't through honeymooning yet—if you know what I mean!"

Her report of La Salle's confidence in her so much contradicted the report she had given Ryder the day before that he had to offer his testimony and produce the letter, regretful as it was to see it given to the papers. It could not implicate Topsy herself for she produced alibis for her evening. People she had talked to in the Jigsaw testified she was there before ten.

But the letter did suggest an affair with Darrow and substantiate the theory of La Salle's jealousy.

The headlines that afternoon bristled with sensation.

ACTOR ARRESTED
Suspected Bride Was Darrow Companion?
Mystery Woman Still Eludes Police
Net Tightening About Jealous Actor

Ryder telephoned Virginia Channing hopeful reassur-
ances, carefully framed for any ears that might be listening on the line. But he was far from hopeful himself. The
evidence was not even circumstantial. Unless something
turned up they hadn't enough to found an indictment on.

In his eagerness to save Virginia Channing he didn't
want to send an innocent man to the chair.

Of course, La Salle might break. They were hammering
at him steadily. And Devlin was rounding up his associ-
ates. Some one might know something.

And there was still Luigi Crimoni, the musician who
had threatened Darrow by telephone. From the preliminary hearing before the judge Ryder hurried to an interview with him, to come away practically convinced of
Luigi's innocence.

The man was an excitable little Italian who told a story
of playing at a friend's party all Sunday evening, and produced unnumbered friends to substantiate it. He made no
secret of his animosity against Darrow: "That song make
a fortune—his fortune," he insisted belligerently, but he
stuck to his alibi.

His friends stuck to it, too. Ryder spent hours examining them and at nine that Tuesday night returned to the
office for a conference with his two colleagues.

"I think the fellow's telling the truth," he reported. "At
any rate he's got enough witnesses to man the *Mayflower*."

"Then it's La Salle—or the jane," Devlin summed up.
"Gee, I'm sore that Keever's fingerprints of all the acto-
rines didn't fit. I certainly want that jane. . . . Either she
did it or she saw who did it. . . . And either we charge
La Salle in the morning or we'll have to let him go. . . .
Which is it going to be?"

"We haven't got enough for an indictment," Ryder told
him.

Devlin shot a guarded glance at Ascher. "I guess we concentrate on the jane."

The telephone on the table jingled, and Ascher picked it up, spoke, listened, then looked across at Ryder.

"Well, Ryder, here's another friend of yours in trouble. They picked up a body on the sidewalk—suicide, the cop thinks—with a card that says in case of accident notify Philip Darrow, — East Forty —. The poor boob's been trying to notify Darrow—didn't remember that he was the famous fellow that's bumped off. So much for publicity." He chuckled genially.

"Who is it?" said Ryder tartly.

"Oh, some old fellow, he says—not a thing on him but the card. One of Darrow's ham actors, maybe, out of luck. Says he was soused. What do you think?"

"I think I'd better go see who it is," said Ryder rising. "Probably some old actor—nobody I'd know—but it's my business to find out. Tell them I'll be right down."

Ascher transmitted the message. "He says can they take the body over to the morgue—the medical examiner is all through and they have photographed the place—or do you want it taken to the Station house?"

"Why, no, the morgue. I probably won't know the chap," Ryder stretched his big shoulders a little wearily.

He did not hear, as he left the office, that Devlin lifted the receiver, and called quickly an Atwater number.

Chapter Ten
Death Comes Again

Ryder always loathed a visit to that dark block of buildings stretching along the river at Twenty-ninth. The amazing casualness of the place was a grewsome note to one
entering—on his own feet—through the receiving room.

"This way, Tom—a floater? Over here." And from another stretcher bearer to his load, "Whoa, there, Sallie,
wait till I let you off."

The receiving room, Ryder felt, was not a place where
one cultivated the more sensitive emotions. In the war
the whole state of things had inured to horror. You expected nothing else. But it was a shock here to step from
a lighted taxi into a room where chatting youths balanced
a dripping body on a stretcher while pausing to borrow
cigarettes. And a business-like man pulled off covering
blankets and methodically noted grisly details.

His taxi had been slower than the patrol wagon and the
body he sought had been already ensconced in the identification chamber. The room to him had always a horrible
suggestion of a department store, with its air of guarded
merchandise behind the handled drawers.

The attendant hurried ahead to pull out the particular
receptacle of the latest comer and Ryder walked slowly
after him and once the vault-like drawer was extended
stood looking down.

He had formed no definite expectation, for any old actor, conscious of Darrow's charity, might have carried his card about with him, but what he saw held him speechless with astoundment. He was staring into the stiff forbidding face of Dervish.

He could hot credit it. The little man he had last seen yesterday afternoon, polishing the silver in Darrow's apartment, turning on him that resentful, vaguely accusing look of injury at his last words.

Dervish dead.

Found on the street by a policeman at nine-thirty that night on East Sixty — Street.

The policeman who had brought the body in was waiting to make his report to Ryder. He had thought the case exceptional because of Darrow's name on the card.

"He was lying on the sidewalk close to the houses there. I thought he was a drunk, when I bent over him, there was such a smell of liquor coming off him. I started to haul him up, but he just hung limp. Then I thought he'd been hit on the head—I didn't see the bullet hole over his heart at first, for there isn't much light there—it was just back from the corner. I had my hands in the sticky stuff before I knew it was blood."

He added, "Ever see him before, sir?"

"Oh, yes," said Ryder slowly. "He's Darrow's house man. . . . Let's see the clothes."

He found a small hole had been drilled neatly through the coat, waistcoat and underwear just over the heart. The stiff bloodstains were hardly dry. In the coat were powder marks. Examining it, Ryder got a rich smell of liquor from it. He sniffed curiously, then looked down at the still face of Dervish, and bent closely above that.

When he straightened he looked more puzzled than ever.

"Here's the gun," the officer said. "It was at his feet."

The revolver was of small caliber, a thirty-two. A silencer projected from the muzzle.

A thirty-two. The same caliber that had been used against Darrow. . . . Master, then man. . . .

"I suppose you've handled this?"

"Well, yes, sir, but careful-like. I knew about them prints."

"Tell me again just where he was found."

Again the officer went through the recital.

"See any one as you got up to him?"

"Not a soul on the street."

"Any sign of a struggle? How was he lying?"

"Slumped in a heap. Nothing like the look of a fight. Looks like he killed himself, don't it, sir?"

"You never can tell." Ryder was sniffing the coat again. Then he bent again low over the dead face. Then he stood and looked down into it, as it stared up at him from its ridiculous receptacle. Already death was revealing its strength and its weakness. The beak nose jutted belligerently from the sunken cheeks; the weak chin sagged helplessly, exposing rat-like teeth. The eyes held a queer, secretive glare beneath their glaze.

Gently he closed them.

"Here's the papers he was holding in his hand. Not a thing in them—they went through them with the other stuff. Here's the lot, sir."

Attentively Ryder noted the turn-out of the pockets— the old-fashioned English gold watch, with initials, the change purse, with its contents, a linen handkerchief, a stub of pencil, a knife, a bunch of keys, a wallet. In the wallet had been found the card asking to have Darrow notified in case of accident. It was a worn card, apparently carried for some time.

He turned to the papers. A long, white envelope—no distinguishing marks. Within, a bulky fold of stiff white paper, ordinary typewriter bond." Not a line on anything. The envelope had been slit for examination. The flap was tightly sealed, with tape paper for additional security.

Everything had been handled but there was hope of a few prints besides those of the morgue attendants. Keever would have to take all of these, to check up. Carefully Ryder stowed the collection in a box to take with him. The envelope was crumpled in the middle where Dervish's dead hand had gripped it.

"You say he was holding this?"

"Yes, sir. Had it in his hand."

"Which hand?"

The officer rubbed his gray head. "Well, now," he said slowly, "the right, I think. Yes, it was the right, for I got hold of him by the left arm. Then when he sagged on me, I put my other hand on his chest to straighten him and got into the blood."

In his right hand. Gripped with his dying strength. . . .

Once more Ryder stooped and drew the shroud more decorously about the lean turkey throat of the little Englishman. He felt the affront that Dervish's bitter pride would feel in lying there, unclothed and unowned, exposed to the common view.

"Take him to Sill's mortuary," he ordered. "Tell them I'm responsible for everything. I'll be round in the morning. . . . Now phone Headquarters and ask Mr. Keever for some of his men to be there to take prints for me as soon as I can get back."

In the taxi he pondered. Two murders. Within forty-eight hours. Sunday night. Tuesday night. . . . With the same weapon? By the same hand?

This could be no coincidence. Whoever had shot Darrow down had fired that other shot into Dervish's heart.

Back at the Criminal Courts Building, his box under his arm, he took the private elevator to the District

Attorney's rooms; then, hearing sounds through the opened doors, he walked toward Ascher's office.

Devlin met him at the threshold. His expression was of mingled defiance and covert triumph.

"You're just in time, Mr. Attorney. Since none of the ladies at the theater matched those prints we've sent for a friend of yours to come down and have hers taken."

"You've sent—?"

"Sure. Why not?"

"Mrs. Channing? . . . I told you," and Ryder's voice was hot with anger, "I told you not to annoy that lady. I am accountable for her. She is utterly out of this."

"Sure, I know. She was at the theater with friends. The Garlands. Only the Garlands don't know it. I wirelessed them and got the answer back this afternoon."

"Rot! They gave the tickets to a cousin—it was all in the family," lied Ryder stoutly.

But terror gripped him.

"No need to get hot and bothered over a little matter of routine, is there? Anyway, the lady's here now. We won't detain her but a moment," Devlin said and gave way before the charge of Ryder's entrance.

Virginia Channing was at the table, across from Inspector Ascher and beside Keever, who was arranging, with business-like deftness, a dark, thin roll of printer's ink on a smooth glass before her.

At Ryder's sudden appearance she looked up and gave him a gallant smile, the smile of one at the journey's-end, who faces the ultimate disaster with hopeless courage.

Everything that was in him went out to her, helpless to help.

"Virginia, I never knew of this—"

"It doesn't matter, does it?" she gave back quietly, with stiff lips.

"Just spread out your finger, Mrs. Channing." Keever had coated his glass with a thin enough film of ink, and now he put his hand over hers, grasping the thumb delicately.

"Just roll it like this—lightly," his intent voice counseled. "Toward the little finger. That's it. Now roll it like that—lightly—on this glazed paper here. Fine!"

With enthusiasm he surveyed the resultant print. His eyes never lifted above her hands, the black glass and the white paper.

"Now the index the same way—roll always toward the little finger. Easy, now."

Delicately he directed the downward pressure and roll, first on ink then on paper, of each of her digits in turn. Then of her hands.

And Ryder had to watch, in utter helplessness, the obedience of that still woman, so defenseless, so utterly undone. He was in agony of spirit.

"That's excellent, Mrs. Channing!" Unconscious of irony, Keever was surveying the damp, completed prints with admiring eyes. "Those pores are dandy."

"Couldn't be better," Devlin concurred.

From across the table he whipped the pile of photographs of the prints from the hotel room and outspread them like cards before them. For a frantic moment Ryder thought of launching himself upon them and destroying them—but that was insanity. There were negatives.

"Here we are." Devlin's voice was sharply eager. "Now, just to inform ourselves—by a comparison—"

Chapter Eleven
Fingerprints

Devlin laid the largest of the hotel prints between the two damp ones of Virginia Channing's right and left hands. Intently he stood studying them. Then, with a jerk of his hand, he thrust the three into view.

Eagerly the others bent over them. The prints were utterly dissimilar. Neither right nor left hand of Mrs. Channing corresponded to the record left upon the knob of the bedroom door of Room 700 of the Highgate Hotel. The swirls of lines, the pores in the ridges, were completely different.

Nor was a single likeness found between any of her fingerprints and those obtained from the hotel room.

"Well, that's that," said Devlin in a flat voice. Then he looked at Mrs. Channing. "Congratulations, Mrs. Channing."

She said nothing. She merely gazed, with controlled interest, at the prints, as at any curious exhibits. Ryder could not credit the thing. He could not understand.

Keever, his sharp, practiced scrutiny over, was uncorking his bottle of cleaning preparation.

"Permit me, Mrs. Channing." Deftly he wiped the staining ink from her slender hands.

She looked now at the four men about her. "Is that all you want of me?" she asked quietly.

Inspector Ascher spoke with embarrassed heartiness. "Nothing more, Mrs. Channing. Sorry to bring you down so late. We were just obliged to check up, as I explained. Thank you for obliging us."

A faintly rallying smile touched her very lovely lips. "I don't deserve much credit—I hadn't much choice, had I?" she gave back in her low and curiously moving voice.

"Mr. Ryder here tells us that you know nothing which throws any light on the case," Ascher went on, hastening to hold her small black jacket for her.

"Nothing at all, I am sorry to say."

"Then that's all. And good night."

"Good night," she returned, her composed, half-smiling glance touching lightly on them all. Devlin's slant-angled gaze never left her. There was something close to contrition in it. Now that she was innocent, her personality, her high-bred beauty, had its effect on him. But if those prints had matched he would have been on her like a worrying dog on a cat.

Keever was methodically putting her records under the light to dry.

"I almost feel as if I were in the Rogues' Gallery," she said very lightly, and again, "Good night."

She had not looked at Ryder. He had not dared let his eyes touch hers. Now he said, with elaborate casualness, "I'm taking you home," and held open the door Devlin had closed behind him not so long ago. He followed her out as if he were awaking from a nightmare.

In the taxi he put his hand over hers.

"Virginia—for God's sake—"

She smiled tensely, as if her lips still held the rigidity of that awful hour.

"You must have been frightened," she said.

"Frightened! Good God! And you—"

"I thought I was done for," she said simply.

His grip tightened. "But how—how did it happen? How could that *not* be your print—that one on the bedroom door? And the others?"

"I don't know," she said faintly. "The chambermaid's, I suppose."

"No, they checked up on the chambermaid. No, it was some one's else. You weren't there, Virginia!" He felt her hand quiver in his. "What are you hiding from me? Tell me—tell me."

"I *was* there. I *have* told you."

"Everything?"

He caught her hesitation. Then, "Everything," she said almost fiercely.

"And you were there?"

"Oh, I was there! I was there!" She added bitterly, "That night clerk would know me. . . . Oh, I was *there!*"

The despair in her voice went through him. And his grasp on her hand relaxed; he went slack under the sudden horror of his thought.

She had gone to the restaurant with Darrow. Then she had returned home alone. Afterwards she had gone out again. . . . Suppose—suppose she was indeed the woman who had left the hotel at one o'clock—but not the one who had gone in with Darrow?

They might have quarreled at the restaurant. . . . He might even have taunted her with his plans. She might have followed him in mad fury.

His mind, like a searchlight, without his least volition, swung its white light of inquiry on the tragic scene. And he looked down at her with something near to terror in his eyes.

She had taken off her black hat and was resting her head against the upholstery. The dark hair strayed in soft disorder across the low, wide brow. Her eyes were closed, in exhaustion after the strain. The light was not too dim for him to be unaware of the spirited outlines of her clear-cut features.

A woman capable de tout. A woman deeply in love—deeply resentful. What had she cried out? "Oh, I hate him, I hate him!" A woman of fire and passion, of tragic impulses, of reckless folly. In love and jealousy everything was possible.

His voice was just audible.

"What am I to think?"

Without unclosing her eyes she murmured wearily, "Whatever you like, Stephen."

It was the first time she had used his name. She had spoken it almost unconsciously—how often she had heard Phil use it to her—but at the sound a current seemed to run through the hand that was still resting on hers. Sharply he drew it away.

If he went on touching her, he would crush her to him, try to smother his hideous doubts. . . . He sat stiffly, staring away from her. . . . She had got to him, that was it. From that first hour he had never been his own man. And now it was as if the very substance of pain had entered into him and he would never be free again.

Love? He supposed that was the name for it. It seemed almost too slight a name for this passion of concern. He had gone through hells of apprehension in that very hour. He had put her before everything, before his career, his reputation, everything he had lived for.

And who was she? What did he know about her? Nothing—less than nothing. He was racked with uncertainties. He couldn't even say whether he believed her guilty of murder or not.

But he knew that he had got to save her if he could. To protect her—against everything. To spend himself, without hope or happiness, for her.

But the uncertainty was tearing him. He almost groaned. "Tell me—tell me!"

"That I didn't do it?" Her dark eyes opened, and smiled, almost clairvoyantly, into his thoughts.

"Yes."

"I did tell you."

"It doesn't make any difference to me," he said rapidly. "I don't care what you've done—even to Phil. I'm in this to save you now. But I must know the truth. I'll go crazy if I don't. I have to know what to think."

"And if I did it—?"

"I'd save you just the same," he said desperately. "You've got to be saved. Only tell me the truth about this wretched business—everything—everything. I'll fight for you—to the end—"

"You dear, you dear!" Her words were a breath of sound. Impulsively she turned and clasped his arm, her face pressed childishly against it. "I didn't know there were men like you, Stephen.. . . . I *do* tell you. I didn't do it."

"But you have some suspicion—something you are not sharing. There was some one else got in—you think you know—"

"Oh, no, no."

"But you are hiding something?"

She was silent.

The taxi drew up at the curb before her house.

"Won't you come up, Stephen?"

"Will you tell me?"

"I tell you I don't know."

He turned away into the night.

He was behaving, he told himself, some minutes later, as he swung along the street, exactly like a moronic sophomore. His feeling for her had sent him back into the moods

350 Mary Hastings Bradley

of adolescence. But her refusal to confide in him had stung him to the quick.

What could she be keeping back? Not her own guilt—he believed her absolutely there. He told himself he had never doubted her. Not the guilt of any one she knew. She said she didn't know. And he believed *that*. But she had suspicions that she was not sharing. Suspicions that she was not, perhaps, definitely acknowledging to herself. His old thought of an irate suitor of hers came back to worry him.

But would she hide the man—with so much at stake for herself? She might—perhaps for interested reasons. The man, if discovered, would disclose his motive for the crime. And probably she was not *sure* the man had done it. She was hoping some one else would be turned up. La Salle. Or Luigi.

Then suddenly, passers-by on the street were amazed to see a tall, hurrying man stop violently short, fling back his head and give a sound of almost laughter.

Dervish! He had forgotten Dervish. In his preoccupation with this woman, her fingerprints, her reticences, her strange personality, he had completely forgotten that second murder that had sent the manservant, within twenty-four hours, to follow his master into death.

Decidedly, that murder linked with the first. But how? He would know more about it when he looked through Dervish's belongings in the morning. And he had not said a word at Headquarters.

He called the office. Devlin and Ascher had gone home. He made a brief report. He would get Devlin in the morning. That could wait. But he could not wait to call Virginia Channing.

Her voice, at the sound of renewed friendliness in his, came with relief.

"I was so afraid you were angry at me!"

"I am. But it doesn't last. . . . No, what I called about—it's Dervish. Darrow's man. This other matter of yours put it completely out of my head. But Dervish is dead. Killed by a bullet through his heart. Like Darrow. And from a gun of the same caliber."

"Dervish—dead? When?"

"To-night. I had come from seeing him at the morgue when I burst in on you at Ascher's. That put it out of my head. He was shot about nine to-night."

Tersely he recounted the circumstances.

"That's near the Bartlett house," she said excitedly. "Do you think—do you think he could have been coming to give Bartlett some information—to talk things over before he told the police—and been followed and shot down?"

"I wish I knew. There's something there. If I could only find it! I'll be busy to-morrow. But if anything comes up I'll let you know."

"Oh, do."

"Good night."

His exhilaration—the exhilaration of hearing her voice again—died as he hung up the phone. He was farther than ever from a solution. He might be convinced there was a connection between the two crimes but he was utterly in the dark as to what it was. The only thing of which he was increasingly sure was that there was not sufficient material on which to indict La Salle. They would have to let him go—under surveillance. Behind bars, at nine that night, he could hardly have been instrumental in this new killing.

Meanwhile the night was yet young—for an actress. Florence Fane must be returning from her performance. Heaven send she wasn't dallying at a night club!

Heaven must have heard him, for his call, downstairs at the desk of her apartment hotel, brought the response that Miss Fane had just come in and would see Mr. Ryder at once.

Up he went to that blue brocaded sitting room he had
visited the day before. It was empty now, but Miss Fane
soon made her appearance. She was wearing a *robe d'in-
terieur,* he supposed she'd call it, of gray-blue velvet, with
misty gauzy sleeves; a trace of mascara was still height-
ening the effect of her amazing blue eyes, and a hint of
make-up gleamed on the purity of her skin. The effect was
dazzling.

It would have been simpler, he told himself bitterly, to
have fallen under the spell of this young porcelain fool than
to have handed himself over, mind and heart and soul, to
that desperate, dark-eyed woman, with her heart-breaking
courage, her tumultuous past and her dangerous present.
He'd done for his peace of mind very nicely!

Miss Fane was delighted to see Mr. Ryder again. It was
so good of him, she said, in her flute-like voice, to come.

"You may not like what I've come to say," said Stephen,
seizing with positive joy on an occasion to be disagreeable.
"It's about that check you cashed for Philip Darrow."

"Yes?"

"I've no doubt in the world he gave you the check," he
told her bluntly. "But you didn't cash it. You didn't send
any check of your own to the hotel management, and they
put no such sum on your bill. Phil was making you a donation. Now I am asking you—why?"

Miss Fane lowered her blue-tinted lids and looked down
at her lovely hands—adorned with that square-cut emerald
that had been one of Phil's donations.

"I'm afraid I did fib a little to you, Mr. Ryder," she
confessed. "A girl in my position has to be so careful. . . .
He *was* making me a little present. He thought I'd been
too generous to some friends—one sees so much hard luck
among one's friends, you know—and he wanted to make it
up to me. You know how generous he was. And he felt that
so much of his success comes from my acting. It doesn't

at all, poor little me!—but that's what he used to feel. He was always doing lovely things for me."

Ryder made no comment. "And have you decided to tell me where you were Sunday evening?"

She looked him unexpectedly in the eyes. Her gaze was both shrewd and direct. "I can if I have to—later, Mr. Ryder. But it would just make me trouble. You see there is a gentleman who would like to marry me—he is a very wealthy man, a very *lovely* man—but he hasn't got his divorce yet. And, of course, his being out with me would be misconstrued. He has to come into court with clean hands."

She recited the legal phrase glibly.

"We can prove *anything*," she declared. "But you see how awfully embarrassing it would be."

Ryder saw. "You are prepared to produce this gentleman and his testimony—and the testimony of others—should occasion require?"

"I could."

Well, that took care of Florence Fane. Or did it? He wasn't satisfied about that check.

"Suppose I make a bargain with you, Miss Fane. Suppose I report that you are accounted for on Sunday night—and suppose you tell me the complete truth about this money?"

"Oh, Mr. Ryder, I did tell you!"

"You forget I was Phil's friend as well as Assistant District Attorney. I knew a lot about his life." He let his determinedly meaning smile bore into her widened eyes.

"I suppose you think you know a lot!" she said with sudden pettishness.

"My dear, I do. I was his closest friend. . . . You and Phil had left sentiment long ago. He was impulsively generous—but not to the tune of a thousand dollars. You had something on him from auld lang syne."

Her eyes flickered an infinitesimal second. Uneasiness pricked their self-confidence. Then the glaze of blue was expressionless.

"I don't see why you say that, Mr. Ryder."

He was wasting his time. He rose.

"Think it over. My bargain will hold till morning. But I rise earlier than you, and I shall put all the facts into a morning conference. Even if your fingerprints didn't tally with those in the hotel room—that's what you're going to say next—we aren't sure that clears any one. The murder might have been done by some one coming in—for revenge. The first woman fled in panic. . . . So it is important to know where all Phil's friends were that night— especially those to whom he donated casual thousands for mere friendliness. It may embarrass you to produce your alibi—I don't doubt you have one—but we shall have to know about it."

"I think you're horrid to me," said Miss Fane. She tried an instant of brimming eyes and quivering mouth, then decided that was a blind alley. Ryder looked as malleable as adamant.

"Of course there were other reasons—he knew I'd been doing him a great favor," she began hesitantly.

"What favor?"

"Well, you know he wanted a divorce—-that wasn't any secret. Years before I used to ask him why he didn't get one, but he always said he couldn't. Not in New York. Then lately he talked about going out of the state to get one and I guess his family got anxious."

"His family? You mean his brother-in-law?"

Reluctantly, "Y-yes, that's the one I talked to," she admitted. "And of course he wanted to prevent him."

"You talked to Bartlett? And Bartlett wanted to prevent him?"

"That's the one. He thought if he could find out that Phil ever had an affair, he could prevent his getting the divorce anywhere. You know, about coming into court with clean hands. And so he came to me, but of course I wouldn't tell him *anything* about Phil. Not for all he— you'd be surprised at all he offered me, Mr. Ryder! So when I told Phil—I had to warn him his family was acting like that—why he didn't want me to be the loser by it—he wanted to make it up to me, you know—and just insisted on my taking the check. . . . It's perfectly good, isn't it, even if he is dead?" she questioned anxiously.

"Perfectly."

"But I have to wait thirty days—really, Mr. Ryder?"

"I'm afraid you do. But now that I know what it's all about there will be no dispute about its validity. . . . By the way, have you any paper, any writing from Bartlett at all, that implicates him in that matter?"

She shook her blond head. "Why, he's a *business* man, Mr. Ryder—he wouldn't write anything! We just had a little talk up here."

"When was that?"

"Hm," She pursed her lips thoughtfully. "About two or three weeks ago, I guess."

"And then you told Phil?"

She nodded. And Phil, he conjectured, had been a little slow in coming across. Then she'd probably put the screws on. . . . He remembered her letter to Phil that she would have to see him.

"Thank you so much, Miss Fane. You've made me understand completely. Forgive me for asking so many questions but I am quite sure that you understand."

She registered perfect understanding and forgiveness. Then she smiled the smile of the arch conspirator. "And you won't breathe a word to any one—?"

"I shall be discretion itself."

"About my friend?"

"I shall not even permit myself to envy him." With which cryptic speech Stephen Ryder took himself from the lovely presence and told the taxi driver to keep driving while he smoked.

In his own mind he ruled Florence Fane out. The stuff of passion was not in her. And she had other fish to fry— that unknown wealthy citizen fronting hopefully the divorce court.

Cupidity she had in plenty. Undoubtedly she had bled Phil, delicately but astutely, to keep her from selling her information to Bartlett. It had probably been going on longer than she admitted. This may have been Bartlett's second attempt. The emerald ring may have marked the failure of the first.

Of course, she would rather sell to Phil, even for much less a price, still it was thinkable that enough of Bartlett's money might actually have tempted her to sell herself out. Though Ryder thought that unlikely. But with the possibility she had kept Phil uneasy enough to make him try to sweeten her.

Pretty shrewd of old Bartlett! Determined *to* keep Phil bound. Determined to keep Phil in the family. Even if Phil changed his will, the old boy figured that if he were still Ethel's husband there was a good case to go into court. But plainly the old boy had counted on Phil's *not* changing his will.

That new will had hit Bartlett hard. And a good thing, too. If that old trouble-maker hadn't kept Phil tied to his crazy sister Phil wouldn't have run amok, dragging the woman he loved into disgrace, and getting himself murdered.

At any rate Florence Fane was out of the picture. So much for this night's work. Luigi Crimonti was out. La

Salle—? He wanted to believe in La Salle's guilt, but his mind sheered away from the conclusion. And La Salle had nothing to do with Dervish.

Who else, then? Some one he had failed to divine? Some clew that had eluded him?

Was it Dervish? No Dervish could not have shot Darrow—if he wanted to—for Dervish had been back in the apartment by nine o'clock, so both Renfew and Bartlett testified, and had remained in for the rest of the evening.

And Dervish had not shot himself. That bullet had entered from the right and Dervish's right hand had been grasping those papers.

Those papers! Ryder's mind went back to them again and again. Why should a man go out to walk, grasping an envelope of empty papers?

There was a clew, he thought, if only he could get hold of it.

He looked at his watch. Long past midnight. His lean, hard body was tired but his goading mind would not let him rest. Every hour was precious. Regan would be off duty at night. Renfew might not be in. But he had separated Dervish's keys from the things he had left in the box in his office, and he had them in his pocket. He could let himself in.

Chapter Twelve
Blown Straws

To Darrow's apartment then.

The hall was as dark as a bat's cave. The long windows of the drawing-room, that usually admitted pale rays of the city's light, were still shrouded in the dark curtains that Dervish's now dead hands had drawn.

"Hallo!" called Ryder to the darkness, lest Renfew might be in and take him for a burglar. He clicked on the hall lights. "Hallo there!"

"Huh? Huh?" Renfew's door, down the hall, was open. His voice struggled up from the depths of sleep. "Who's there?"

"It's Stephen Ryder."

"O-h!" The sound of a prolonged yawn. "What time is it?"

Now what did that make him think of? Oh, yes—Dervish answering Bartlett's phone call, the night of the murder, and Renfew's calling out to know the time. "Nine o'clock, sir."

He heard Renfew turning over in bed, evidently clicking on the light on the stand, for light sprang out the door, Ryder walked in. The architect was sitting up, blinking drowsily. He was a pleasant-looking man, with bushy, graying hair, and small, near-sighted hazel eyes. Evidences of his cold were on him and a pungent odor of preventives.

He reached for his glasses, on the stand, and Ryder sat down on the edge of the bed.

"Sorry to give you a shock, Renfew, but you'd better prepare for one. Dervish was killed about nine this evening. Shot down on East Sixty — Street. The body was found by the officer on the beat."

"Dervish?" Renfew's jaw literally dropped, his face slack with amazement.

Tersely Ryder went on to give the information.

"It simply bowls me over," said Renfew at last. "I can't pretend to much personal emotion—I never liked the man much, and he resented my being here. But—but somehow we were so intimate in a mechanical sort of way. . . . And then, following the other. Why, Ryder, it's—it's horrible!"

"It's damn puzzling," said Ryder. "There ought to be a connection, and if I were worth my salt I'd see it—but I feel as if I had blinders on. Groping round in the dark. Hoping to bump into something. . . . Now tell me everything you can think of. What time did the fellow go out?"

"I've no idea. I dined at the Century Club with Westcott and the place was empty when I got in. I don't know what's the idea of putting a policeman here daytimes and taking him away nights."

"Regan was just to prevent callers faking some excuse and making off with anything before we had a chance to examine it," said Ryder absently. "No one's going to break in at night."

Renfew looked severely at him through his glasses. "How do you know? Perhaps they knew of something somebody wanted. This is getting pretty thick. Both of them gone. Darrow and Dervish."

"Look here," said Ryder abruptly, "do you suppose Dervish had been getting away with funds—wanted Darrow out of the way before he found out?"

"That's a thought!" Renfew spoke eagerly. Defective works were his favorite pastime. "Let me see—he might have got a female accomplice to lure Phil to a hotel and then slipped in—"

His face fell. "No—Dervish was back here at nine. I asked him what time it was when the phone rang. And he was in the rest of the evening."

"You're sure of that?"

"Positive. I wasn't nearly so sleepy as I had been. He kept coming in with things. I must say he was unusually thoughtful. He came in several times of his own accord."

"Did Dervish have any enemies?"

"My dear chap, I have no more idea how many enemies he had than how many pairs of boots. I should think it extremely likely. I've often wanted to kick him into the middle of next week. He knew how to insult to perfection, without an open sign. . . . But I feel sorry for his death. Shot down. And you say he'd been drinking?"

"That was a funny part of it. The officer said he thought he was a drunk, for he smelt liquor on him. And his coat reeked of it. But not his mouth."

"Can you be sure?" said Renfew squeamishly. "When a man's dead, perhaps—"

"I've seen dead drunks," said Ryder shortly. "My life has not been sheltered. No, I'll swear he hadn't had a drop. . . . Then why the liquor on his coat?"

Renfew was on his hobby again. His eyes glistened through the glasses. "Perhaps he was carrying some of Phil's stock he was going to sell. Then a bandit sees him and shoots him for it. The bottle smashed as Dervish fell."

Renfew lay back triumphantly.

"But the revolver," Ryder objected, "a Smith and Wesson, thirty-two. The same caliber that was used on Phil. With a silencer."

"The world is full of thirty-twos. . . . And I should think all thugs would provide themselves with silencers. I am inclined to consider that coincidence. Coincidence, you know—"

"Was there ever a gun like that about the place?"

Renfew shook his head. "I wouldn't know a thirty-two from a seventy-five. I've met them only in fiction. Darrow had an old revolver, I know—"

"A Savage. Forty-five. It was there yesterday."

"But I had no idea what Dervish possessed, if anything."

"I'm going to look now."

Ryder rose, and Renfew struggled out of bed, carefully putting on his slippers and Jaeger robe, and followed after him. Dervish's room opened off the kitchen, and as the two men opened the door, Renfew said nervously, "To think that everything in this place—but mine—belongs to some fellow that is dead! . . . I think I'll move over to the club, tomorrow. It's a horrid queer feeling."

He watched Ryder opening the dresser drawers. "I'd just got schooled to the idea that Darrow wasn't coming home—and now Dervish. . . . I wish you'd stay the rest of the night. You can take some of my things if you don't want to use Phil's. . . . You don't think there's a sort of vendetta on against the place, do you? Some crazy janitor they discharged or anything?"

Ryder listened with the top surface of his mind. The rest was intent upon the search.

Shirts neatly piled. Ties stretched smoothly. Handkerchiefs in a precise corner. Socks folded ready to be put on. Underwear folded. . . . Ryder had known he would find things like that. The order was a replica of the order that Dervish had always maintained, against odds, in Phil's chest of drawers.

Nothing unusual in the bureau. In the closet the little man's suits hung in order. Neat pepper and salt for the street. Much like the one that only this night had been drilled through by an assassin's gun. The afternoon coat. Trousers. The perfect butler's evening uniform. . . . Folded on a shelf the green baize apron that Ryder had last seen him wearing. . . . Boots in trees in neat rows. Small feet, the man had. But then, he was a small man. Methodical hat boxes. Overcoats.

Up on the shelves boxes of old clothes. Old suits Darrow had evidently given him put away in camphor cakes. Odd socks tidily ironed and folded. "Must be saving for a rug," Ryder muttered. A book of snapshots—mostly of the liner he used to be on. An old Santa Claus suit Ryder remembered having seen Darrow wear at the last Christmas party. A package of summer suits.

Nothing in the table drawer but letters. An uncle, in England, penning the stereotyped phrases of the infrequent letter writer. "We hope this finds you well as it leaves us." Ryder noted the address. He must look up the next of kin. A post card, also from England. Carefully checked bills. These were for the house. A check book. A bank book of a neighborhood bank. Dervish's entries were regular. Careful saver, that fellow. Month after month. Year after year.

Rapidly Ryder's glance skimmed the pages. Then he stopped short. On Monday, the day before, Dervish had deposited a thousand dollars to his account.

Renfew had long returned to bed and slumber but Ryder dragged him remorselessly up again.

"What do you know about this? Did you hear of his getting any thousand?"

Renfew surveyed the entry in astonishment. "Not a thing."

"Any thousand lying round he could have got his hands on?"

"Lord, no. Fact is, Phil asked me for some extra cash that night before he went on. Came into my room and asked me. It was Sunday, you know, and he hadn't got a check cashed."

Ryder reflected. If Florence Fane had stuck to her first story about cashing a check for a thousand for Darrow then he could have believed that this was the money and that Dervish had appropriated it. But she had wiped that story away.

Where in the world had Dervish come into a thousand dollars? Had Phil given *him* a check, too, for keeping his mouth shut? No, for Dervish could never have cashed it after Phil's death. Then— And then Ryder suddenly struck his hand to his head. "Oh, my God, what an ass I am! What a double-barreled, sea-going ass!"

Renfew sat up anxiously. "Look here, you aren't feeling ill, are you?"

Ryder was pacing the room as if it were a hurricane deck. "Man, don't you see? No, of course—you don't know. . . . I've been stumbling round in a fog. But if you keep going, round and round, always clutching, why you touch something—you run into it if you keep on and on. I've just run into it."

"Look here, old fellow, it's two o'clock. You haven't had proper sleep for three nights. Suppose you lie down—"

"I've *hit* something, Renfew! In my mind, . . . See here, when Dervish told you it was nine o'clock, that night Bartlett called up, Sunday night, did you look at your watch and confirm it? Or did you take his word for it?"

"Why—his word, of course. Why shouldn't I?"

Ryder did not answer. He was standing stock still, his head thrown back, his eyes gray, narrowed slits. He seemed to be looking at something a long way off. . . . Back, along a slender thread of light. . . . .

He did not answer when Renfew spoke. He seemed literally unhearing, wrapped in his tense concentration.

Then he walked quietly out of the room and Renfew heard him pulling the boxes about in Dervish's closet.

A rum chap, Renfew reflected. Going out of his head over this business of poor Darrow's. . . . What the deuce could he have hit in his mind, as he expressed it? . . . He'd gone wild with exultation, then frozen to attention like a pointer dog. . . . However, it wasn't his case. *Somebody* had to get some sleep. And drawing the blanket over his ears to shut out the sounds of Ryder's rummaging, the weary architect slept.

In Dervish's room, the sound of ransacking had stopped. Ryder was standing by an opened box; looking down at a neatly folded suit of scarlet. He took it out, unfolded it, laid aside the carefully wrapped boots, pushed aside a black leather belt and a red cap, ran his hands through the tissue paper in the box.

Nothing there. His face was blank with disappointment. Then, swiftly he unwrapped one boot after the other, and thrust a hand within., In the second boot his hand struck something. When he drew it out he was looking down at the white wig and beard. The beard had been very neatly trimmed to modern proportions.

Swiftly he examined it. It had been made to fasten on over the ears, in casual, Santa Claus fashion, but now it had been remade, and lined with adhesive for close adherence, and that adhesive, though dry, was only freshly dry.

In his mind's eye Ryder could see Dervish's sloping cheeks and receding chin muffled in that quiet, scholarly beard. . . . And then in memory he saw again that still, remote face he had gazed on in death, only a few hours ago. If only those dead lips could speak—that strange, inaccessible heart give up its secrets . . .

Chapter Thirteen
A Mad Plan

Some time, presumably, in the remainder of that gray morning, Stephen Ryder slept, for when Renfew rose belatedly he found that the living-room couch had been slept on, the bath tub washed in, and Darrow's dresser palpably ransacked for fresh linen.

Ryder was gone. He had gone with a package that he guarded carefully while he bolted a hasty breakfast and scanned the headlines of the morning press.

ANOTHER MURDER RAFFLES POLICE
DARROW'S BUTLER DEAD IN STREET
SUICIDE HINTED

Almost casually he skimmed the columns of conjectures with which the reporters were keeping the sensation of the mysterious deaths vivid to their readers, then hurried to his office and locked his package in a desk drawer.

He telephoned Devlin, then turned the box of Dervish's effects over to Keever's men to be gone through for fingerprints. He sent a man to the morgue to bring back the prints of the attendants there and of the policeman who had found Dervish's body.

He called up Sill's mortuary, to make arrangements for the private burial on the next day. Phil had wanted no funeral, and under the circumstances Ryder was eager to keep the curiosity seekers at bay. Sill reported his place stormed by them, morbidly eager to see the dead playwright who had been murdered in circumstances of such scandal.

On Ryder's desk was a message from Bartlett, received the previous afternoon, asking to be consulted, as the closest member of Darrow's family and the wife's representative, in whatever arrangements the executor was making for the funeral. Ryder telephoned Bartlett at his house and made an appointment for two o'clock.

Devlin was down by that time, anxious to talk over this latest murder with him. Ryder gave him the facts he knew, up to the finding of that mysterious beard. He said nothing of that piece of curious evidence, which he had locked in his desk drawer. Together the two men examined the revolver and looked at the reports from the prints.

These reports were exactly what Ryder had expected. Not a print on gun or envelope but those of the morgue attendants and the policeman. Keever declared the weapon had been carefully wiped with an oiled rag, then used with gloves. There was not a print of any kind on the handle or the trigger.

Ryder stared grimly at that revolver, on his face the same look of strained intense concentration it had worn since his explosion to Renfew the night before, then he dropped it in his pocket. A sharp line of worry was cutting deeper and deeper between his eyes.

"We gotta get hold of this man's intimates," Devlin was insisting. "Can you help us there?'

But Ryder, with a brusque negative, shook his head. "I've got a theory," he began and then, "I'll tell you tonight. Give me to-day to line it up."

Abruptly he went out and back to the fingerprint department. While he waited there he phoned the bank that

Dervish had patronized and learned that the thousand dollars had been deposited in cash. Bills of large denomination, the teller remembered. When Keever had finished, Ryder hurried out, going first to one shop of sporting goods and then to another, on a quest so unsuccessful that the lines of worry tightened on his lean face.

Two o'clock found him still searching. Then he looked at his watch and hurried to Bartlett's home. The housekeeper remembered him from the other evening and admitted him but she said that Mr. Bartlett was at his office—he always was at that time.

"I have an appointment—there must be some misunderstanding," Ryder stated. "I will phone his office."

The woman indicated a back hall phone but he shook his head. "I'd rather speak more privately," he said, and paying no attention to her speech that there was no one there but the cook in the kitchen he made his way directly to the library on the upper floor.

There he telephoned and found that Bartlett was waiting for him at his office.

"My mistake," said Ryder. "Sorry—I can't get down town just now. Will eight o'clock be all right at your house?"

Bartlett told him that it would.

"I'll just make some memoranda of that," said Ryder aloud, conscious of the shadow of the housekeeper in the open door, and pulling out some paper from a drawer he made some hasty jottings.

"I suppose you heard what happened on your street last night?" he said casually to the woman without looking up.

"You mean that man's death?"

"Yes, poor Dervish. You must have seen him here, haven't you?"

"Indeed I have not. He has never darkened these doors."

"You speak as if the poor chap cast a very black shadow."

She pursed her lips. A thin, flat-bosomed, respectable woman—the housekeeper one would know Bartlett would employ.

"Like master, like man," she said remotely.

"Oh, Dervish was a very good character," Ryder said good-naturedly. "I'm sure Mr. Bartlett would tell you that."

"Mr. Bartlett never mentioned him to me until this morning. But a drunken man isn't a good character."

"Dervish wasn't a drinker."

"It was in all the papers. The smell of liquor on him. The policeman thought he was a drunk. And Mr. Bartlett says it must have been this man he saw reeling along as he went out to post his letter—he mentioned it to me when he came in."

"You mean he saw Dervish?" Ryder's voice was carefully expressionless, his lowered gaze occupied with the lines he was scrawling.

"Not to know him. But he told me he'd seen a drunk out there. The city was getting to a fine state, he said when he came in. . . . When he saw the papers this morning he said that must have been the man. Shot himself in his cups, he said."

"What time did he mail this letter?"

"The usual time. Just before nine o'clock. . . . Mr. Bartlett was quite excited about it this morning. He said undoubtedly this man was concerned in his master's death."

Like most repressed women whose duties have silenced them, the housekeeper was loquacious when she got under way.

"Well, I never knew Dervish drank," said Ryder absently. He folded his papers and put them in his pocket. "Tell Mr. Bartlett I'll be here at eight."

Outside the house he walked slowly toward the west. The mail box was ahead of him, on the corner. A quiet corner. No stores. No bright lights, evidently, at nine.

Old residences. . . . It must have been in the shadows of those buildings there that Bartlett had seen Dervish. Reeling, he said. Ryder could not imagine Dervish reeling. Yet he must have reeled and collapsed when that fatal bullet found his heart. Poor little devil. . . .

There were no curious loungers about. People passed the spot obliviously, on business of their own. An ordinary city street.

He turned the corner and from the nearest telephone booth called Headquarters.

"La Salle has been discharged—under surveillance," Inspector Ascher reported. "Devlin is working on that end of it—trying to dig up some of the fellow's friends. . . . But I'm inclined to think this Dervish murder is linked up with the first. Remorse, you know, and suicide. The doc thinks that wound *might* have been self-inflicted—but the photo they took of the body shows papers in the right hand."

"God be thanked!" said Ryder fervently.

"What's that?" Ascher asked in surprise. "Look here, you got anything up your sleeve?"

Ryder answered obliquely, "May I see you and Devlin at four o'clock?"

"At four? Sure, we'll be here. But where are you going now?"

"Get me at the Metropolitan if you want to reach me."

"The Metropolitan—?"

"The museum."

A sound of incredulity came over the wire. "Damn it, Ryder, is this a time to look at the pretty pictures?"

"Not pictures, Ascher—Spanish armor," said Ryder suavely. "Get me care of Breck if anything breaks. But it won't. And I'll be back at four."

"That bird is nuts," Ascher took the trouble to report to Devlin. "He's been reading detective fiction—dissertations on high-brow art between flashes of God-given inspiration. . . . He's looking at Spanish armor. At the Metropolitan. And the papers hounding us like hell."

"Two murders, a vanished woman and not a damned clew," Devlin summed up gloomily, "and the Assistant District Attorney goes to the museum. . . . I wonder if he took the pretty widow with him?"

Devlin's suspicions would have been justified if he had heard Ryder's next phone call, asking Mrs., Channing to meet him at the museum.

She came quickly but had a long wait in the entrance hall before she saw Ryder's tall figure, advancing with its swinging stride, a box clasped under the arm.

"I want you to do something for me," he said abruptly.

"Anything!"

"Wait till you hear. You won't like it."

He was speaking jerkily, his eyes staring ahead. He looked queerly intent and remote, as if he hardly saw her. She felt suddenly small and a little frightened.

"What is it, Mr. Ryder? Of course I'll do it."

"I want you to go to Bartlett's house to-night at six o'clock. Here is the address. Usually he is home at six but to-night I will arrange to have a caller detain him in his office. Represent yourself as coming from one of his societies—say the Watch and Ward. Say you have papers to give into his own hands. The housekeeper will probably keep you waiting on that seat in the hall."

"Yes?"

"At six-five there will be smoke pouring out from the basement. Don't worry. I want to get the fire department there. The firemen will keep the housekeeper distracted. When you get a chance in the confusion slip up the stairs to the big library that runs across the front of the house on the second floor and hide yourself behind a tall carved oak screen in one of the corners. That room will not be disturbed by the firemen. You stay behind that screen."

"And then—?"

"Then," said Ryder, staring very far ahead, "you just stay there till I come in at eight o'clock with Bartlett. When I call on you, come out and identify him as the man you saw in the room at the hotel."

"The man *I* saw—you want me to say—?"

"That you were there. Yes. Say you saw him through a crack in the bedroom door. . . . I wouldn't ask you to do this if I did not feel it was safe," he said slowly, not seeming to look at her, but mindful of her draining color, her aghast eyes.

"Your fingerprints are different—that will let you out afterwards," he reminded her.

"The—the clerk—won't be there?"

"God, no. You'll never see him again, I hope. . . . And you may not have to say a word. I only want you in case I have to put on extra pressure."

"But—Bartlett? You think it's Bartlett?"

"I can't explain the connection. It's too long a story. You'll have to take me on trust."

"As you did me," she said. "Yes, I'll do it."

"I'm sorry to ask you. . . . But I'm staking everything I've got on to-night. . . . Are you afraid?"

"Horribly."

"I must warn you," he said, "that Devlin and Ascher will be hiding in that room, too, and hear you. But I shall tell them that you are doing it at my request. The difference in the fingerprints ought to clear you of their suspicion."

She looked at him with a strained smile. "But suppose he turns on me—and denounces me? He might suspect me—if he suspects about the will! And if he brought in the night clerk—"

"I won't call on you unless I have to," said Ryder slowly. "And I'll protect you from his suspicion afterwards.

The whole thing is a gamble. I'm staking everything on it. Will you—if you have to?"

"If you want me to," she answered. Ryder took her quiet courage for granted. He had no idea how her heart lurched in sick terror at the thought of playing the role he asked, of thrusting herself into the noose of the suspicion she thought she had evaded.

Tersely he went over the plan again and she listened with desperate attention.

"If you feel you'd rather not—after thinking it over," he said finally, "just go away. I shan't blame you. I shall understand."

"I won't fail," she promised. "I'll hide there if it's humanly possible."

He did not see the frantic fear that grew in her eyes as he put her into her taxi for home.

Four o'clock found him with his colleagues at his office.

"Well, Mr. Ryder," said Ascher, betraying his impatience. "We are anxious to get into touch with you on this—you have been keeping us rather in the dark."

"The Inspector has got it all doped out," Devlin announced. "Suicide. A guilty conscience. Dervish bumped off Darrow, for reasons best known to himself, then turned the gun on himself. . . . Maybe this Dervish was married and it was his girl Darrow was fooling with. . . . We're looking to you, with your intimate knowledge, to give us the clews."

"That's at least a tenable theory," Ascher insisted.

"Oh, it's fine, it takes care of everybody," Devlin conceded. "Until some hysterical jane blows in confessing she killed Darrow and a stool pigeon reports that some thug bumped off Darrow—and then had no chance to rob him. Or until Topsy Minn gets mad and spills the beans on La Salle. But if nothing turns up you're okay and no

more trouble. . . . What do you say, Ryder? What gems of
thought have you brought us from the museum?"

Ryder drew a chair to the table and across that table he
leaned toward the two men, facing him in their very evident ironic antagonism. His face was haggard; his eyes under their narrowed lids were bright with nervous alertness.

"I *know* I'm on the right trail," he said. "I can *see* it. I
haven't got a damn bit of proof—but I'm going out to get
the proof. Will you help me?"

"Sure," said Devlin laconically. "It's our business, ain't
it? But d'you mind confiding just who and whom your
suspicions *see?*"

Ryder looked from one to the other.

"I'll tell you at half past eight to-night," he said. "You'll
hear for yourselves if you'll do what I ask you."

Swiftly he recounted his plan for an alarm of fire at
Bartlett's house. "I want the engines there at six-fifteen—I
shall instruct them exactly what to do. They must run that
hose—the nozzle shut off—up the front stairs. I want you
two, in rubber coats like the men, to mingle with them,
then watch your chances and slip into that front room.
I've asked Mrs. Channing to hide herself behind the screen
in case I need her later. I want you each to dive under a
davenport—there are two big ones there, back against the
walls, with overhanging valances, but with space enough
for a man to hide. I looked to-day."

Ascher stared, dumfounded. Devlin's casualness was
unimpaired.

"That's a nice idea," he said genially. "And what are the
servants doing?"

"Another hose at the back door will distract them.
There are only two women in the house. You can watch
your chance—then take up your positions there—"

"Squads flat," murmured Devlin.

"And wait for about two hours and a half. Till I—"

"In the rubber coat?"

"Give that to the men to carry out. At eight I'll be there to see Bartlett. I have an appointment."

"Suppose he takes you to another room?"

"I'll see that he doesn't. If necessary I'll say I'm afraid of a dictaphone planted and insist on the room he didn't suggest. But I don't think that will happen. That is his receiving room."

"And then—"

"Then," said Ryder grimly, "you'll know the rest. Don't come out till I ask you to. Will you do this?"

Ascher said heatedly, "This looks to me both theatrical and—and undignified. Henry Bartlett is one of our most respected citizens—an influential man—not one I'd like to tamper with without cause. And you have given us no cause. If you have reason to think he was implicated in anything, if you have hope of any words passing between you, in what he assumes to be confidence, surely there are other ways, other arrangements—"

"I'm going to plant two men there," said Ryder stubbornly. "I'll take full responsibility for this afterwards. And I'd rather have you two in on it than any one else."

"If you can pin anything on Henry Bartlett—and make it sticky" said Devlin lyrically. "Boy—I'll roll a peanut from here to eternity. . . . But it looks like a damn fool stunt."

"Suppose you give us the facts that have led to your conclusions," Ascher very reasonably urged.

"I couldn't convince you. . . . I may have fooled myself. . . . But I'm taking the one way to find out."

"And if it fails?"

"It *won't* fail," the other insisted. "God, I can't be wrong! I see it, all pointing, pointing. . . . I can't argue. I've got to get Bartlett's caller primed. I've got to give the fire department their instructions. I've got to see to the smoke bundles. Don't waste my time talking," he said, with the sudden passion that shook him. "Chance it blind. I tell you—I tell you I *know!*"

The two others looked at each other. "Look here," said Devlin abruptly. "I think we owe you one for last night. I admit we were suspicious of that widdy. All right, I'll go under the sofa for you. But if you fail, and this coup doesn't come off, then I suppose you know that you are going to be left high and dry—?"

Ascher was looking as if he could bear that prospect. "It's melodrama," he said disgustedly. "I still insist that we follow the usual procedures—"

"And get nowhere. No, Mr. Ascher, I take full responsibility. I know it's a smash if I fail. . . . And whatever Mrs. Channing says, if I have to call on her, please remember that she has been primed by me. I shall go ahead in any case, but I do ask your support."

"Sure, let's come in on the credit for us," said Devlin jocosely. He winked casually at Ascher. "This is going to be good. Come on in, Ascher—the ground floor is fine."

But when Ryder left them, their consent given, he had no great doubt as to their reasons for acceptance. They were not unwilling that he should ride to a fall. And that they should be there to see it—even at the risk of an unbecoming situation for themselves.

For the consequences of the fire, for possible damage to the house, if his case failed, he assumed full responsibility. And Ascher's last words echoed mockingly m his ears.

"Ryder—you're mad as a hatter. Mad."

14

A Shining Mark

At six that night, a loquacious little man was arguing insistently with Mr. Bartlett as to the best possible use to be made out of the large donation he was considering bestowing upon one of Bartlett's pet fields of work. Uncertainly he balanced between various causes, but Bartlett was very patient and affable with this earnest citizen from up state. Mr. Bartlett was never impatient with donors.

At six o'clock, at Mr. Bartlett's residence, a lady in a black suit presented herself, saying she had papers for Mr. Bartlett alone. The housekeeper assured her he would be in at any moment and established her upon a sofa in the lower hall where she could keep an eye on her through the dining-room door.

At six-three a cleaning man poked negligently in the area depths before the front windows, then trudged off down the street. At six-five a boy chased a cat into the Bartletts' back yard and stooped into another area way after her.

Three minutes after each incident smoke was pouring from the area ways. At six-ten the shrill, prolonged scream of sirens heralded the clanging arrival of red gleaming fire engines. A hook and ladder drew up to the front of the house and the first fireman off it rushed to the area window, crashed the glass and—but this was not observed from the sidewalk—threw in another bundle between the bars.

After that things became chaotic. Fire engines drew up by the water plug; a hook and ladder reared its trellises against the back of the house. A swarm of men in rubber coats and helmets dragged a heavy serpent of hose up the front steps and in through the door that the excited and protesting housekeeper opened for them.

Dense smoke was pouring up from the basement. A gang of men with axes, followed by the housekeeper, rushed down the basement stairs. The men with the nozzled hose dragged it up the front stairs, then, inexplicably, dragged it down again, shouting to the cook, who appeared below, that the fire was in the basement. The cook was in no condition to observe that in the upper hall two men had swiftly divested themselves of their rubber coats and fled into the front room.

No one remembered about the lady in the front hall. Afterwards they considered it not surprising that she had gone.

At six-twenty the hose was between the bars of the basement windows pouring a drenching stream and firemen within were busily smothering a smoldering blaze. Curiously enough some of the men carried out bits of charred rags. At six-thirty they reported the fire out, and with their miraculous swiftness recoiled the hose, replaced the ladders, sprang into position and with more screaming of sirens and clanging of brass the red terrors of the streets were gone.

The housekeeper and cook were left wringing their hands over a drenched basement, and talking anxiously of crossed wires.

At six-forty-five they were explaining to Mr. Bartlett, who telephoned electricians, spoke suspiciously of cleaning fluids, and thanked heaven the rest of the house was untouched. The cook took a good deal of credit for keeping them from upstairs.

At seven-fifteen Mr. Bartlett was sitting down to dinner. At eight Mr. Ryder was announced.

He was shown upstairs, into the apparently empty front room. Very carefully he looked about it. It was furnished in heavy oak, the walls lined with books. Two large overstuffed davenports, covered in dark English chintz, stood near two of the walls, and in another corner a large oak screen hid the ugliness of a wall safe. In front of the fire, at the end opposite from the davenports, was the big table desk, with a desk chair on one side and a lounging chair on the other.

In a few moments Mr. Bartlett came in and greeted him with geniality.

"I am sorry to keep you waiting—a threat of fire in the basement rather upset the domestic machinery. . . . I trust now, after reflection, that we can talk things over in a more friendly spirit. I suppose it is on the matter of the will that you have come?"

For a moment Ryder's heart inexplicably sank. This big genial man, with his silver hair, his florid face, his pompous assured manner—this man of established position, of iron principles—could this be the man he planned to implicate? Was he not mad, as Ascher had said, following a wild goose chase that would bring him to ridicule and defeat?

He thought of those two men under the davenports, waiting with some curiosity, some hope, but a not unreasonable expectation of witnessing his discomfiture. But his thoughts dropped away from them. He was preoccupied with the feeling of Virginia Channing's presence behind that screen. He had been mad, indeed, he thought, to ask her to risk herself on this venture. It seemed unthinkable that he had been the one to place her seclusion, her safety, again in jeopardy. He had been too intent on his project. . . .

He wished with all his heart that she were safe away.

But she was not. She was there. And he must win her safety. He was a gambler, with everything depending upon the turn of a card.

Now to play his hand.

"I have come about a good many things," Ryder answered, after that perceptible pause. He drew the large chair toward the desk table and looked across it to Bartlett.

"Unusual things have been happening," he went on. "Dervish's death, for one thing. Here on your street."

"Extraordinary, that," said Bartlett readily. "I must have seen the man a few minutes before he killed himself—I suppose there is no question but what it was suicide? I mentioned to my housekeeper that I had seen a drunken man against the buildings."

"You think he was drunk?"

"He gave every evidence," said Bartlett, in surprise at the question. "He was lurching—I didn't look too narrowly at him, however—and I thought I detected liquor on the air. I suppose now he had been drinking to nerve himself for the final shot. Do you know, Mr. Ryder, I am inclined to believe it was not the first shot this man had fired—that he might have been guilty of Darrow's death. Perhaps this is the solution."

His voice sounded quietly satisfied, and he looked across at Ryder with grave conviction. "Perhaps it's all we'll ever know," he said, thoughtfully.

"You give no great credit to the police."

Bartlett arched his brows. "Ah, we don't ask the impossible of you! And this man took his secrets to the grave."

"On the contrary, he left a number behind him."

Ryder waited. Then, "Mr. Bartlett, I have come here alone, without the knowledge of my colleagues who, I do not hesitate to say, would hardly credit the conclusions I have come to. They are unaware of my presence here this evening. . . . You may think my procedure very strange, but I am going to ask you to let me take your fingerprints."

For a moment Bartlett stared. Then he gave a genuinely ringing laugh of contempt. "By all means, Mr. Ryder. But may I ask why?"

"Perhaps some papers of Mr. Darrow's have been tampered with."

He was watching the other keenly and thought, as he threw out that suggestion, that he saw an expression of covert relief flit through the hard, watchful eyes.

"If you refuse, I need hardly remind you that I could enforce the request—"

"Take them now, by all means," Bartlett spread out a large hand. "Which finger, if you please?"

The humor in his voice betokened unanxiety. He had the air of playing almost benevolently with the situation.

Ryder took out the flat glass plate he had brought and began rolling thinly on it a sheer coating of printer's ink. "Each hand and each finger, if you please."

"By all means," Bartlett assented again. Unhurriedly he complied with Ryder's directions, subjecting each finger in turn to the ink and then rolling it lightly on the glazed paper the other provided. When ten prints lay in moist black-and-whiteness before them he looked across the table at his caller.

"Anything else, Mr. Ryder? I imagined this was to be a colloquy upon the subject of the funeral arrangements— and the will."

"That enters into it." Carefully Ryder arranged the prints at one side. Then from his pocket he drew out a revolver and laid it carefully between them.

"That is the revolver found beside Dervish's body. A Smith and Wesson thirty-two. It was a bullet from a thirty-two which killed Darrow. I believe that to be the gun from which it was fired."

Bartlett gazed upon it with merely polite attention. "Very likely—if my theory of Dervish's guilt is correct," he returned.

"You will observe," said Ryder, "that it has a silencer."

"Is that the meaning of the apparatus which projects?"

"Exactly. . . . This revolver is precisely as it was when it came into my possession, with the exception that the empty cartridge, which had not been ejected, has been taken out. Every other chamber—these are all loaded—has been untouched. . . . The assassin had been most careful to wipe it off with an oiled rag after loading, and when he fired at Dervish he was evidently wearing gloves for no prints were found upon it."

"I presume this leads to something," said Bartlett with just sufficient courtesy. But his eyes were intent.

"I said, it had been wiped off *after loading,* Mr. Bartlett. *But*—the man who loaded it used his fingers to insert the cartridges in the chamber. Only one cartridge, I think, he put in. Into a chamber just vacated. And the reason I have not disturbed the others is because this one cartridge he put in is enough for my purpose. He left a clear print of what is evidently his right forefinger on that cartridge. It has been photographed. I have it with me."

Without taking his eyes from the still face across from his, Ryder drew out of his pocket an enlargement from the negative, a brilliant black and white print.

"Some of it is blurred—but enough is distinct for my purpose," he stated.

Quickly he laid that enlargement before the print of the forefinger of Bartlett's right hand; he took a hard, sharp look, then drew a deep breath. He pushed the two pieces of paper toward the other man.

"They coincide, Mr. Bartlett."

As if against his will Bartlett stared down at those prints. Little flecks of deep red were spotting the ruddy mask of his face. But he gave no other sign of emotion.

"I cannot see," he said, stiffly, "what you are trying to deduce."

"My deductions are finished. I am confronting you with the *proof.*"

"Proof of what, sir?" The rasp of Bartlett's voice seemed to sound a genuinely indignant impatience. And Virginia Channing, behind her screen, unable to see the little pieces of paper which confronted those two men, felt her hopes sink beneath the dominating assurance of that frigid voice.

"That you are the murderer of Philip Darrow and of his man, Dervish."

Through a crack in the screen Virginia dared eye the men. She saw that Bartlett's face was reddening, his eyes contracting to pin points of attention.

"Rubbish, Mr. Ryder. Rubbish," his frigid voice said contemptuously. But a change had come into that voice. It sounded like a shield, like the man's still bulk, behind which his secret thoughts were scurrying up dark corridors of thought.

"It is *proof,*" said Ryder. "I came to you alone with it, before taking my colleagues into my confidence, because I wanted the pleasure of hearing from your own lips your confession of your crime. . . . I plan to surprise them with it. They know nothing as yet of this print. It was entirely my idea."

His voice rang triumphantly. The other was silent.

The big room grew very still. A clock ticked slowly away in its corner, opposite the wooden screen. Bartlett's

heavy breathing was heard as rhythmically. . . . The sound
of the world outside, of rolling motors and horns honking
on the Avenue, was muffled by the heavy draperies drawn
across the windows. An atmosphere of solitude and isola-
tion in which two men sat confronting each other, in their
implacable hostility.

When Bartlett spoke there was a new note in his voice,
a quiet, considering hesitation. "You say you have not
taken your colleagues into your confidence? Have you
said enough to know what their opinion of this ridiculous
accusation would be?"

"I have said nothing at all," said Ryder promptly. "They
have no inkling that you are implicated—not even in my
slightest thought. Alone I arrived at this result. Alone I
made the deductions."

He seemed to harp tauntingly upon that.

"I have told no one. I shall astonish them all. They do
not know that I am here to-night. If they did they would
only suppose that I came to confer about the will. I even
brought the will in my pocket—in case the print was a
failure. But it has been a success. *My* success."

From her crack Virginia saw something flicker across
Bartlett's watchful face; then that face seemed to set, to
harden. . . . A sense of danger worked upon her excited
nerves. What folly of Ryder to taunt him there alone, un-
guarded—to leave that revolver lying between them.

"You insist," Bartlett was saying, temperately, "that it
was I—*I* who fired this—this weapon?"

His hand, appropriately, gestured to it, and remained
hovering as if in inquiry. . . . She wanted to shriek out,
in her sudden terror. Was Stephen blind, that he did not
see—?

With his hands carelessly on the arms of his chair
Ryder was rising, as if to end the interview.

"I have the *proof*. I, and only I. . . . I am waiting to give your confession to the world."

And then Bartlett's big hand moved, with desperate speed. He gripped the gun and leveled it at Ryder's heart.

He fired. There was a muffled report, and then the body of Ryder crumpled back into the chair, swayed forward and his head fell heavily upon the table.

Chapter Fifteen
Virginia Speaks

A little smoke wound silently out of the muzzle of the silencer.

In a blue mist it dissolved over Ryder's down-dropped head.

Out from her screen, hurling it aside with a crash, came Virginia Channing, her eyes sick with horror. Past Bartlett, standing astounded at the apparition, his smoking revolver in his hand, she flew to Ryder's side, clasping her arms about his sagging shoulders.

"Oh, Stephen, Stephen—dear God, *Stephen*—"

It is a slower process to crawl out from a sofa than to spring from behind a screen, but both Devlin and Ascher accomplished it in extraordinarily quick time, though presenting a somewhat curious spectacle had there been detached-minded spectators about. Tousled and disheveled, they rose to their feet to find themselves confronted by Bartlett's gun, and his big face set in murderous resolve.

"Back! Or I shoot!"

It was the woman who flung herself, with unexpectedness, upon his outstretched arm, knocking it wild, and giving the two men their chance to pinion him. Devlin seized one wrist, Ascher another. The revolver fell to the floor.

"You'll swing for this, you thug," panted Devlin.

The big man slacked in their grip as if the words smote him with bitter realization. There was a click, and the expert Devlin snapped a handcuff over one of Bartlett's wrists.

"Put the other over," he commanded, and Ascher made the gesture for their captive. Bartlett was motionless. Both wrists were now encircled by the bands of steel linked with chain.

He stood still a moment, then sank suddenly into the chair from which he had risen.

"You watch him, Inspector," said Devlin sharply. "Here—"

Mrs. Channing had fled back to Ryder, bending beside his chair, her arms supporting him. His head had fallen sidewise against her shoulder. Devlin came to the other side.

"Right over the heart," he muttered, his fingers finding the tiny hole in the cloth charred by the powder marks.

"I saw him aim," said Virginia dully. The room whirled blackly about her; she heard a rushing, as of winds, in her ears. She had a feeling as if her life blood were draining from her wrists.

"Look out—she's going to faint," a voice at a great distance was saying.

With every effort at her command she mastered herself.

"No, no—I am all right. But get a doctor for him, *quick!* There must be something—oh, Stephen, Stephen—"

"Not a chance," said Devlin soberly. "Let me take him, Mrs. Channing. You'll swing for this," he said savagely to Bartlett's mottled face.

"Stephen, Stephen," she was whispering under her breath. Her arms refused to relinquish their burden to Devlin. It *could* not be. Like that. Stephen—*dead.* But Phil had died—like that. To herself she was sobbing, "No, no—dear God, *no!*"

And then in her arms Stephen stirred. She felt the motion.

"He's alive! A doctor—"

Her hands were at his coat. Ripping open the buttons. Feeling within.

Devlin's hands sought with her, to find the wound and stanch it. But his hand stopped. A puzzled look came over his face.

"What the—"

Ryder's lips stirred. His eyes opened, lighted with slow consciousness.

"Steel jacket," he said heavily. "Don't worry—Jinny."

Briefly his eyes lifted to hers.

He managed a spasmodic smile. Then he said, in a stronger voice, on a note of surprise, "But it knocked me out."

"I'll say it did! Man, you knocked *us*—cold." Devlin turned to the Inspector, voluble in excitement. "He's got a steel jacket on. He was daring him to do it!"

"Why hadn't you changed the cartridge? I thought that was your play," said Ascher. His own face was rather white and his lips felt thick and stiff. It's a nasty thing to see a man you know drop before another's gun. "When you dropped—"

"Wanted it real," said Ryder. "Assault with deadly weapon. Intent to kill. No loophole."

He straightened up. Strength was coming back to him. The blow over his heart had been terrific, beyond his expectation, but the bullet had not penetrated that steel mesh in which it had spread itself ineffectually.

"And I've got him right," he added grimly.

He looked across at his adversary.

"You've answered all my questions," he told him. "Going to dispose of me and my suspicions, weren't you? Awkward little accident, of course—you'd have to explain me

away. You couldn't leave me in a hotel room, like Darrow—or on a sidewalk, like Dervish. . . . Annoying, to
have it happen in your own house. But what could be more
natural? I'd come on a friendly little visit, over the will.
We were discussing the latest crime, wondering whether
the shot could have been fired from the right or left side—
and as I pointed it, to demonstrate, the gun went off in my
hands. . . . You'd wipe the gun clean, put it in my hand,
and call in your household."

"I shot you as I would a madman," said Bartlett hoarsely. "You were threatening me."

"That isn't what you'd have told the police. Just a re-
grettable accident. No motive! Nothing to connect you
with it—or with the previous crimes we had just been discussing. No more than if I'd made the slip in my own
office. Nothing on earth to damn you. . . . You made up
your mind to it in an instant. You're a resolute man, Mr.
Bartlett. I knew that about you. I sized you up. But I had
to test you out. To know how far you would go."

"You scoundrel!" said Bartlett furiously. His face was
livid. With an immense effort he controlled himself to a
measure of coherence. "I was not myself. Your monstrous
accusations—the fear they'd be believed—my reputation
smirched—"

"Save that for the jury," Devlin callously advised.
"You'll need it."

"Mr. Ryder, I congratulate you," said Inspector Ascher
very earnestly and formally. "I congratulate you on your
powers of penetration."

"Yeah. And on the steel jacket." Out of the tail of his
eye Devlin flicked a glance at Mrs. Channing.

"Among other things," he added casually, and fitted a
cigarette into the corner of his mouth.

"I hope it annoys you to see me smoke," he mentioned
politely to Bartlett.

Virginia was still standing by Ryder's chair, her hand pressed on his shoulder. He was alive. The world was going on again. . . . He was alive. His gray eyes had smiled at her. His strength and will had taken command of the situation. He was alive. . . .

His eyes had smiled at her but briefly. His attention now was all for Bartlett, for that big-faced man with the silver hair whose vicious will and ruthless determination had sent Phil Darrow out of his gay tumultuous life into the frozen silence of the beyond. Because of this man Phil was dead. . . . And his little English servant was dead.

"All right, Bartlett," he said. "You can give it to us now—your confession. I said I came to get it. . . . How did you kill Darrow?"

The big man was silent. His face was a mottled mask. Behind it he seemed to be trying to summon powers of concentration of denial.

Ryder leaned across the table. "Why did you? You had him there, with the woman in the room. Evidence enough to stop the divorce. In your hands. . . . Why did you kill him? Why did you fire that shot? Why did you do murder?"

Methodically the efficient Ascher had taken paper out from the drawer in the table—white, ordinary typewriter paper it was. As he smoothed it, he looked curiously at it, his attention concentrated.

Ryder gave him a slight nod. "Yes, that's the paper that was in Dervish's hands. I got a sample to-day. It all fitted in. . . . Come on, Bartlett. Why did you kill? . . . I'll tell you. You went there to kill. You may have told yourself you took that gun for self-defense—risky thing breaking into a man's room, finding him with a woman. But you had murder in your heart. You were thinking of the will—there was always the thought that if Phil should die, before he changed that will—"

Bartlett stared. immovably, his face unchanged. Ryder's eyes were blazing fury.

"Come on, what can you say for yourself?" he challenged. "You shot like the coward you were—seizing your chance, with the woman out of the room."

Bartlett raised his hands as if to wipe the sweat that poured down his face; the tug of his chains reminded him and he let his hands sink, with a click into his lap. Dumbly he stared down on them.

"I'll tell you," went on Ryder's inexorable voice. "I'll tell you the whole thing, step by step—"

"Yeah—tell *me*," insisted Devlin. "How did you know it was *him?* How did you know it wasn't LaSalle?"

"La Salle!" Ryder flung that aside contemptuously now. "That didn't click, Devlin. He didn't act guilty. I haven't had much experience tracking down criminals but I've seen guilty men in my work. And had to make up my mind about them. . . . And then came Dervish's murder when La Salle was safely locked up."

He addressed his adversary again. "Dervish did for you, Bartlett. . . . That bold stroke wasn't so successful, after all. Even with the gun wiped clean."

Inspector Ascher looked up from the paper on which he had been making a neat row of triangles.

"How did you get onto it?" he demanded. "What gave you the slant?"

"I tried to think the damn thing through," said Ryder. "I looked for motive—and opportunity. La Salle didn't fit in. He had motive, perhaps—opportunity, perhaps—but he didn't click. I can't explain it. Luigi—? Motive—but not sufficient—and a hundred alibis. And *Fane?* She said she had an alibi. I didn't look it up. She wasn't the sort to go off the deep end over a man. Too much at stake. But there was her thousand from Phil, paying her for keeping her mouth shut about herself and Phil. To pay her for the

money she might have made by selling herself out to Bartlett."

He added, *"That* set me thinking. The first thread,
winding back, Bartlett. I'd seen you, when you heard that
will was changed. That money meant a lot to you. Keeping
Phil in the family meant a lot. I pried into your affairs.
Like most busybodies you had neglected your own business. Nothing much put away. You counted utterly upon
that money for your future. Perhaps you were even more
immediately embarrassed for money than I knew."

Speechless, heavily breathing, Bartlett listened without
a word. Once he ran his tongue furtively about his dry
lips. His eyes never left Ryder's face.

"You counted on handling that money for your sick
sister. You were frantic at the thought of losing it. You'd
go to any lengths to keep it, to keep Phil where you could
have a hold on him. . . . Very well—whom else would you
tamper with? Who could give you information that would
prevent Phil's getting that divorce?

"Dervish, of course. An old servant, loyal enough—but
who doesn't want money? Something you can get without
advertising the fact. . . . It might have seemed to Dervish
that there was small harm in revealing his master's philan-
derings. No harm, that is, compared to the good it would
do Dervish's bank account. . . . Dervish was a proud little
chap. I daresay he longed to return to England in his sort
of affluence."

"I'll bet he planned to pose as a duke!" Devlin interjected.

"There was a thousand dollars deposited by Dervish
the day after the murder. Where could a thousand dollars
have come into that little man's hands? The market? Not
a sign of that among his papers. Now, the day he deposited it, the morning after Darrow had been killed, you had
come to see him at the apartment, Bartlett. Very natural.

Very proper. But what passed between you? The bank said Dervish had deposited that money in cash. I say, that a thousand dollars cash had passed between you. In payment for Dervish's services the night before."

Ascher was taking hasty notes. He looked up now. "The night before? But what did Dervish do—?"

But Ryder was steadily addressing Bartlett. "When you came first to Dervish, with your proposition, he hadn't any facts to give you. He had never spied on Darrow— never put down dates and people. But now, he started out to earn what you promised him. When Phil planned to have company in his flat that night—that was his first plan, I am aware—Dervish thought his chance had come for easy money, and tipped it off to you. Then Renfew came and spoiled that. He probably telephoned you it would be off. You told him to keep his eyes open. Phil would be meeting the lady somewhere. So Dervish planned—and listened. He heard Phil telephone the change of plan. He heard the name of the restaurant—possibly he heard Phil telephone the restaurant for reservations. I rather think that was it. Then, when Phil went out, Dervish followed. He was seen, going out. After that, I conjecture that he went to the restaurant, saw Phil and his companion at a table, and trailed them to the hotel. Or, knowing of Phil's private suite, he went directly to the hotel and hung about."

"But, look here, the chap who did that had whiskers," Devlin objected.

"Dervish had whiskers on. There was a Santa Claus suit among his effects—neatly folded in moth balls. Relic of an old party. I nearly passed it by. And then—then I thought of that thousand. Of Florence Fane and her hush money. . . . And of how Dervish could have earned his thousand. I went back to that suit. And the whiskers were there, in a boot, neatly trimmed to every-day proportions. And they had been worn recently, too, not in Santa Claus

fashion, but in close, actor's carefulness. . . . Then I *knew*.
I knew that somewhere on his way to that restaurant or
hotel Dervish had fitted those whiskers on. He wasn't taking any chances on having Phil recognize him. Then, when
he found that Mr. Deering and a lady had gone in, he
either telephoned you at once or—suppose you enlighten
us on that, Bartlett?"

Bartlett tightened his hard lips.

"That's negligible," said Ryder. "I am inclined to think
he telephoned you then, and asked you to ring him up
later at the apartment—"

"Rubbish," said Bartlett harshly, speaking for the first
time. "I rang him up, of my own volition, at nine o'clock.
Renfew will verify that. Darrow and his companion did
not enter the hotel until ten."

Ascher held his pencil poised, regarding Ryder. Devlin
drew on his cigarette, his eyes intent.

"Yeah," he said slowly, "Dervish could hardly have seen
them go in—"

"How did Renfew know it was nine o'clock?" said Ryder
impatiently. "Dervish told him. It was undoubtedly after
ten. But ten o'clock or nine o'clock were all the same to
a man in Renfew's condition, in bed in the dark; sick and
dopy with cold and fever. He did not look at his watch.
. . . After that, he says Dervish came in rather often of his
own accord. Registering his presence in the apartment.
. . . You and Dervish set that time to protect yourselves,
Bartlett. I remember you were very exact and careful about
it in your account to me."

Bartlett merely made a noise in his throat. His small,
intent eyes never left Ryder's face, as if he were waiting,
waiting for those words of conclusion to come.

"And then you went out, taking that revolver with you.
Thoughtfully fitted with a silencer. . . . You had the room
number from Dervish. He knew it—he lied to me there. It

was easy to gain access to the elevators at that hour without passing by the desk. You probably got off at a higher
floor and walked down. The signs over the stairs are lighted. And then you came to seven hundred."

Every eye was on Bartlett. Every eye was beholding him
twofold: there, stertorously breathing in that chair, and
beyond, three nights back, in that hotel corridor outside
the door of that fatal room.

"You must have bent first to listen at that door," went
on Ryder's voice. It was a disembodied thing, painting
picture after picture for them. They could see Bartlett
waiting and listening outside that door.

"You had one hand in your pocket where that revolver
lay—for safety's sake, let us say. You had some reason to
know what rages Phil could be roused to. Then you went
in. Perhaps the door was unlocked—a boy had just delivered ginger ale—perhaps you knocked and Phil thought it
another boy with the ice water. Anyway, you walked in on
Darrow."

"Liar!" said Bartlett heavily.

"He was in the living room of his suite, his working
place," went on the detached, inexorable voice. "Suppose
we say that his companion was in the bedroom and he was
alone. And in that instant, the advantage of your opportunity rushes over you. No witnesses! The woman out of the
way—yet there enough to bear the brunt of the crime! One
quick move—and no more chance of his changing the will.
How much better, instead of evidence to keep him from a
divorce, how much surer and swifter—to kill! . . . And you
let him have it."

"It's a lie," said Bartlett harshly. "A lie—a lie! I was
never there. My housekeeper will swear I was never out of
the house."

"She never heard you go out—her rooms are at the
back. That is no evidence."

"You can't connect me with it," said the man, assurance returning. "It's all a lie. I was never there."

"Virginia," said Ryder, without looking at her.

She drew a deep breath. Then she spoke in a low, clear, steady tone, "I saw you, Mr. Bartlett. I looked through the door. And I identify you."

Chapter Sixteen
Cornered

Bartlett's big head jerked around to her. His eyes blazed.

"That door was shut," he said thickly. Then he made a furious, strangled noise in his throat. "It was self-defense," he gasped out. "He sprang at me. I could not hold him off. I fired only in self-defense."

Rapidly Ascher was writing.

"And then?" prompted Ryder's quiet voice.

"Then I turned out the lights," said Bartlett mechanically. Again he made that impotent motion to wipe the sweat away. "I shut the door behind me. I found the stairs and went down them. At a floor below the stairs seemed to end, there were people in the hall and I mingled with them and came down in the elevator. I walked home."

"You can call the wagon, Devlin," said Ryder quietly.

Bartlett rose convulsively to his feet, and in the same breath the men rose, too, alertly. He thrust his great bulk forward across the table and made a gesture with his chained hands at the woman.

"You—you identify me, do you?" he gasped. "You ruin me, will you? You—Darrow's paramour! I'll drag your name down with mine! I'll trail you in the filth—I'll make you a scorn and a byword—"

"Wrong again, Bartlett." Ryder cut peremptorily into the raucous threats. "Mrs. Channing was not the lady. She has a complete alibi. Her fingerprints are not those of the unknown lady who stood listening—and then fled. That lady, unfortunately, was not here to identify you, but we were so sure of you that Mrs. Channing gave us this aid. . . . You are trapped out of your own mouth, Bartlett. About Darrow. . . . And trapped by your fingerprint on the cartridge of the bullet that killed Dervish."

"Dervish," said the man, as if he had forgotten him. Then he spoke contemptuously. "He was a rat—and a blackmailer."

He went on heavily, "I took Darrow's life in self-defense. I regret the necessity-—but self-preservation is justifiable. And it was an unworthy life."

He turned his heavy head and looked at Ascher's racing pencil. He had stooped to write again.

"Sure," said Devlin ironically, "they are all unworthy lives that stand in your way. . . . I suppose this little Dervish was unworthy of living, too?"

"He was a rat—and a blackmailer," said Bartlett in the same voice. "I went to that apartment that morning and gave him that thousand. I had promised him only five hundred for his information, but I told him I did not want it known that I was seeking proof. I told him that I had not acted on his information—that I was shocked at the murder. I assumed with him that it was the woman. But of course he suspected."

Ryder thought of the little man, polishing his silver that afternoon, turning things over and over in his mind.

The heavy voice went on, as if speaking were automatic. "He was avaricious. He saw the way to make a lot of money. He thought he had a fortune in his grasp. But he felt he must strike quickly. Before the woman was found. . . ."

"I had no idea," Bartlett broke off to explain, almost righteously, "of having the woman suffer for what she did not do. But even if she were found, any jury, without proof, would let her off. You remember," he said punctiliously to Ryder, "that I told you she was probably innocent of the murder and had fled. I trusted she would never be found. Guilty as she was of sin, it would have been a strange judgment on her to have to suffer for a sin she did not commit—"

"Yeah, and you're the boy who would let her do it," said the sardonic Devlin. "Saying to yourself, for heart balm, that she had it coming on other counts. . . . Yeah, you're a pillar of righteousness. With your hands red."

Curiously Bartlett looked down at his hands and continued staring at his manacled wrists.

"Then Dervish—?" Ryder prompted.

"Dervish called me up, from outside the apartment, and asked twenty-five thousand dollars for his silence," Bartlett said, still looking down. "I had not that much money available. I am not a rich man. I told him ten thousand. I told him that was all I could raise. We had to talk guardedly over the phone as if it were a business deal, but I could see the man was utterly determined. He reminded me that my life was at stake—that his knowledge would send me to trial if not the chair. Finally we compromised on fifteen thousand. He was insistent about having the money at once, and I told him I would get it that next day. He did not want to come to the house, and I told him to meet me at nine that next evening—Tuesday—near the mail box on the corner of my street. I asked him not to move till I recognized him."

"Might be people about, at first," said Devlin conversationally.

"But I swear to you," said Bartlett earnestly, "that I did not at first intend—it was only that next morning when I was turning over possible ways of getting the money that

the idea came. . . . I even thought of taking the money
from a possible donor, who came in, at six that afternoon,
and turning it over to Dervish."

Ryder remembered that pseudo-donor.

"But that would have been defrauding my societies,"
Bartlett went on, with discriminating righteousness. "And
I had no assurance that this Dervish would keep his word.
He was a menace as long as he lived. I saw my whole career
threatened—my life, my name. And then—since my other
act, that evening, had not proved disastrous—"

"Yeah, you got away with murder once and found out
how easy it was," said Devlin. "It works that way. Until it
quits working."

"I am not a man to be intimidated," said Bartlett, pur-
suing his own analysis. "I considered this man a menace
to me and to my work, and I saw no more reason to hesitate putting him out of the way than I would a venomous
reptile. I meant to run no undue risks but depend upon
circumstances. If the street were crowded, if Dervish and
I were seen together, then I would simply talk with him
and plead inability to raise the money, asking for time. I
prepared an envelope of blank paper to give him, however,
in case—in case I should have opportunity for the plan I
considered the most necessary."

He stared ahead of him, nodding judicially at the word.
"The street proved deserted. I walked toward the mail box,
with the envelope of blank paper in my left hand. He would
think it the money. I went to the mail box and clanged the
lid, in case any one should happen to be observing from a
distance, then I turned about and walked past Dervish. I
had seen him there, in the shadow of the building, waiting
for me. I hardly paused; I turned a little and gave him the
papers with my left hand, then as he took them I thrust
the revolver against his side and fired. I was away from
him before he fell, I think. I did not look back."

"But the liquor—you threw that liquor over him?" Ryder demanded.

"Oh, the liquor." Bartlett made as to pass a hand over his forehead but at the tug of chains his hand fell back limply. He moistened his lips again. "Yes, yes, I had forgotten the liquor. I threw that quickly as he reeled—I had the flask in my pocket. . . . How did you know?"

"You were so damned anxious to have him thought a drunk. I suppose you thought that if people saw him staggering, after you left, the smell of liquor would make them put it down to drink, then think he had shot himself in a drunken souse. But that liquor was another of the threads reaching back to you, Bartlett. I smelt it on his coat. But not on his mouth. Nor on his shirt. Only blood on that, Bartlett. . . . So some one wanted him thought a drunk. And why?"

Ryder's voice sharpened. "I walked the floor over that. I figured that you figured that you might just be seen on the street passing close to him and you'd better speak of it first. You'd better speak of seeing a drunk out there. You did speak of it to your housekeeper, and to me. But you overreached yourself there, No one had seen you. . . . The breaks were for you but you gave yourself away. You were too cunning—taking care of every contingency. Of course, if you *had* been seen it would have been wise. . . . But another thing. When you spoke to me of passing a drunk, spoke with your righteous indignation, do you suppose I believed that you would *pass* a drunk? Not you! You'd have had him arrested, called an officer, and taken him off to jail. You'd have invoked every power of your enforcement leagues to get the poor souse behind bars. *Pass* a drunk, Bartlett! You'd have arrested our Lord at the wedding of Cana! And a poor drunk on the sidewalk—you let your foot slip when you spoke of passing him!"

"Yeah, and you'd had him giving up the name of the fella that sold it to him and got your snoopers after him," said Devlin righteously. "Ryder, you certainly had this bird dead to right. Pass a drunk!"

Explosively he added, "Throwing liquor on him to make him a suspicious character. Where'd you get the liquor, Bartlett? I'll bet it was the best, too." Half unconsciously he glanced about the room.

"You hoped that death would be taken for suicide," Ryder went on, "for you threw the gun at his feet. But you were flurried—all the self-justification in the world could not make even those nerves of yours shock proof. You did not stop to consider the implication of those papers in the right hand. And the shot entered from the right. A natural way—for a suicide. But the right hand held those papers. Those papers that he thought were a fortune. . . . But not a print of yours on them. Nor on the gun. You thought you'd seen to everything. But you forgot the cartridge."

"We all forgot the cartridge," said Inspector Ascher thoughtfully. "All but you, Ryder. You were shrewd to think of it."

"And lucky to find it. That print was all the proof, all the honest-to-God proof I had. And that wouldn't carry me far. Prints have been fakes—as perhaps you don't know, Bartlett. And it didn't connect you with Darrow. But I knew that if Bartlett had killed Dervish it was to silence Dervish because he knew too much. And if Bartlett was the man to strike down Dervish, in cold blood swiftly, relentlessly, then I could provoke him to strike me—before witnesses. It was a chance. But it was a fighting chance. And it worked." Devlin had telephoned. Through the curtained windows now they heard the clang of a bell, then the screech of suddenly applied brakes. Then the doorbell peeled through the silent house.

No one moved. From her room on the third floor the housekeeper was heard, slowly descending the stairs. Bartlett raised his head, listening acutely. For the first time he seemed to realize his situation, to visualize himself, standing there for the last time in his house where he had been so bulwarked with comfort and position . . . standing there, waiting, while his housekeeper, all unknowing, was creaking down the stairs, to admit upon him the supreme disaster of his deeds.

His face set in granite lines. His eyes stared bleakly ahead. Stiffly he turned, fronting the closed door.

"We might as well meet 'em halfway," observed Devlin, the unconcerned. "Coming, Mr. Inspector?"

Ascher was folding his papers very neatly. "This is a remarkable piece of work, Mr. Ryder," he said earnestly. His voice was still enthusiastic but a hint of envy had crept into it. "You did some interesting thinking."

Ryder turned quickly to him. "I gave you fellows no chance. I felt you wouldn't be with me—and I had to work it out in my own way. But we were all in on this to-night. You gave me a vote of blind confidence when you agreed to my mad plan. We are here together—that's all anybody needs to know."

"Wel-l-l, we'll give you the edge on it, Mr. Attorney," said Devlin, nonchalantly. "Are you coming?"

"You don't need to come down with us," Ascher said hastily. "We've got everything. We'll just lock him up and start things going in the morning. You take care of yourself. That blow may have done more than you know."

He turned to Mrs. Channing, "And I want to thank you, Mrs. Channing, for the assistance you have given. Not only in words—you were very quick in blocking that revolver. You didn't see that, Ryder. He had us covered. There might have been another shot—and Devlin and I didn't have any steel jackets on. We are much indebted to you."

"Yes—and we'll see that this bird doesn't mention your name in this—not if the court knows itself," said Devlin. "You can count on us."

For a moment, with unusual openness his slant gaze
dwelt on her, on her clear, high-bred look, the loveliness
and courage of those dark eyes that were now so shadowed with strain. There was admiration, there was liking,
there was faint envy and a curious contrition in his look,
remembering how his thoughts had. brushed her. Then,
with a sudden jocose twinkle, he flicked Ryder a knowing
glance and turned to their prisoner.

"Well—let's go."

An excited colloquy had silenced in the hall. The feet
of the oncoming policemen were heard now on the stairs.

And Bartlett went. But at the door he stopped, straightened his shoulders defiantly, and said, in set, arrogant
words, "I have done nothing—that was not justified," then
he went on.

Chapter Seventeen
Unguessed

"That's what he thinks, too," said Ryder grimly.

They were in the taxi, then, side by side in its solitude. A dim light shining down from the top. Ahead, the bulk of the driver's back, beyond the glass barrier. Outside the flashes of street lights and the interposing shadows of passing taxis.

"Devlin was right," he went on. "Any life that got in his way was an unworthy life. He was the act of God."

Relaxed, Virginia Channing leaned back against the upholstery. She took off her casque of a hat and ran her fingers smoothingly over her banding hair.

"I feel as if I'd lived a million years," she murmured.

He drew a long breath. "God, it's over! I can hardly realize it. . . . And you are safe."

"Safe," she said after him. It was a beautiful word. She had never known a word so good. She liked to hear it. "Safe!" Then, "I feel as if I'd been afraid forever," she told him.

His hand made a motion toward her, then drew back.

"Forget it now," he said a little curtly. "Never think of it again if you can help it. Forget it."

"You think I can?" Her lips smiled.

"I think you are strong. Too strong to brood."

"How do you feel?" she asked suddenly.

"Right enough."

"You took a dreadful chance. Suppose he had aimed for your head?"

"I had to take that chance. But I knew he'd figure that a shot through the head couldn't be explained away as well as one through the heart. He would have explained that I'd been pointing the gun at myself—picturing Darrow or Dervish. Oh, I counted on his firing for the heart. And I rose a little, to give him the better aim."

"Where in the world did you get that jacket?"

He grinned triumphantly. "At the museum. It's a valuable relic. I had a devil of a time getting them to part with it. . . . They won't be pleased when they see that bullet in the mesh. But I'd looked all over town first."

"Is your heart really all right now? Does it hurt?"

"Like the devil, if you want to know." The corners of his mouth quirked ironically. "But not from that bullet."

He was astounded when he heard himself saying that. *"What are you saying, you fool?"* he asked himself roughly. This was Phil's love. The woman who loved Phil. Only so few days ago.

"I'm not going to worry you," he said hurriedly. "Not now. But it's no good pretending it hasn't happened. I'm a fool about you. . . . No good telling me I don't know you," he said almost angrily, though she had made no move to speak. "I know you more from these days than years of normal living could tell me. . . . You know I'd have died to keep you safe."

To himself he added, "And I damned near did."

Aloud he insisted, "And it's no good saying I don't want you. I do. I want to take care of you more than anything in the world. . . . Perhaps—some day—you'll let me."

Now he had done it, he thought. Made a mess of everything.

He wasn't looking at her. He was staring straight ahead. He felt her eyes lifting to him.

"Stephen, you—you're *sure?*"

"Sure? Oh, good God!" He made a violent gesture.

"In spite of—everything?"

"There are no 'in spites,'" he said steadily, still looking fixedly in front of him. "You are you. I love you for what you are. What you did with your life before you knew me—that's your affair. You—loved Phil." He brought it out with difficulty. "Well, I hadn't a chance to win you then. You didn't know me. I didn't know you. But I know you now. And some day—"

"But I didn't love Phil!" She flung it out on a sobbing breath that brought his eyes sharply to her. "Oh, Stephen, I can tell you now! I never meant to tell a human soul. But you—you have to know—"

"I don't want to know anything you'll be sorry for having told me."

"I won't be sorry. You must listen. Then never, never let her know. . . . It was my child, Stephen. Little Nina—Phil loved her. Oh, back in the beginning, when I was first a widow, he was fond of me, but I turned that aside and he stayed a friend. Never anything more. At times—some years— we didn't see so much of each other. But always friendly. Then—then Nina grew up. And last June, when she came home from school—so changed, and so beautiful—he fell suddenly, terribly in love with her. And she with him."

Her voice broke. "She was just a *child*—thinking herself so old, so sophisticated. Just a child—mad with infatuation. You know what Phil was—what he could be. He enchanted her. I was helpless. He was frantic for a divorce. He couldn't keep away from her. I did everything to hide it—I went everywhere I could with them. Finally I begged her to go away for a year—abroad—and then, if she still wanted to, and he had his divorce—

"Now you see why he was so wild for it. Well, they consented, and Phil planned to get his freedom while

she was gone. . . . Then, when Bartlett opposed him and
finally threatened him so definitely, Phil must have gone
utterly mad. Nina was going to a dance that night; her last
night before she sailed. Out on Long Island. She said she
wanted excitement—to help her keep going. Planned to
stay all night and come home in the morning. Phil wasn't
asked. These were youngsters—of her own age. But he had
begged to take her to dinner first and drive her out. He
swore he'd not make her unhappy. Only a good-by! *'Safe
as a saint, Jinny dear,'* he promised when they went away
together. *Safe as a saint!*"

She was sobbing wildly. "The child didn't mean any
wrong. She wanted only to see him alone. They meant first
to go to his own place and have dinner together. I think he
meant to take her to the party. She had her evening dress
with her in her little bag—she was going to dress there.
But when he found Renfew was staying in—he must have
felt desperate with frustration. And then he asked her to
his rooms at the hotel. I suppose she didn't think that it
made much difference, his rooms, either way. His studio,
he probably called it. Perhaps he didn't mean any harm to
her, even then. Only a good-by. They were so crazily in
love. And she was going away."

The mother sat up straighter, pushing the hair from her
wet eyes. Her voice steadied. "She didn't realize what she
was doing," she insisted again. "She was scarcely seven-
teen. Full of modern notions of freedom and courage—all
the old romance in fresher words. Defiant of convention.
. . . So she went. And—and it all happened, just as I told
you. About the going into the next room. And hearing the
noise. And coming out to find Phil there—dead."

She added, dully, "Those were her prints on that bedroom door."

Ryder caught his breath. "And you—?"

"I was out at the theater with a friend—"

"You were actually at the theater? You had a genuine alibi?"

"Only for the first part of the evening."

"But for God's sake, why didn't you give it to me—at the beginning? When I found the key? You could have saved yourself all suspicion—gained time for arranging the sick friend alibi—if that were ever needed—"

She said slowly, "I thought of it—how I thought of it. I was at 'Journey's End' with an old friend from out of town, Cecil Garnett. He took the eleven-fifty to Chicago, afterwards. He doesn't know a thing about this, yet. But if he ever gave me the alibi he'd stick to it and save me in spite of myself. And I couldn't use the truth. I wanted to throw off suspicion—but—but I didn't want it proved that I could *not* have been at the hotel—in case Nina was suspected. I had to keep myself ready to save her."

"Oh, my dear." Ryder's voice was very gentle.

Mentally he was saying that he would give that alibi to Devlin and Ascher the first thing the next morning. Tell them casually she hadn't wanted to mention that friend to him at first. They would think it a matter of jealousy—that she had tried to hide behind the Garlands. Complicated—yes, but life was complicated. And he didn't want the breath of suspicion resting on her.

"When I got home from the theater," Virginia rushed breathlessly on, "I found that some one had been calling up, leaving no name. Then the phone rang again and I answered. It was Nina, calling from a drug store down town. She asked me to meet her. I went—I found her frantic with terror. Think of her, the child, in that horror. Terrified and trapped. . . . She had fled from that hotel, leaving her bag behind. When she thought of it, I she went into a drug store and began to call the house. She was beside herself with grief for Phil and fear for herself. I told her I would get her things. I sent her home. I made her feel safe.

I spoke as if it were nothing. *You* know, the competent way mothers speak—"

Pitifully, the mother laughed under her breath.

"I went to the hotel. There were people coming in late in the lobby and I went up with them. No one seemed to notice me. I could have gone in the side entrance that she had told me about—she had gone down the stairs and out the, side way—but when I saw the people in the lobby I thought that way was best. I got off with the crowd at the sixth floor then turned down the hall, found the stairs and went to the seventh. I had the key. She had given it to me. I shall never forget standing outside that door . . . nor when I got inside it."

Ryder said something inaudible. His mind was a chaotic series of pictures.

Nina—the girl he had seen in her mother's drawing-room, that exquisite little creature in her young dawn of beauty. He remembered her strangely troubling dark eyes, her childish curls, the heart-shaped little face sharpening to its defiant chin.

He remembered the quiet figure beside her mother in the taxi, on the way to the steamer, holding her mother's hand in silence. What thoughts had possessed them both! The girl must have been strung up to the breaking-point. But she had carried herself steadily.

He saw again that picture on Phil's dresser, that exotic beauty of Nina's in its Spanish masquerade of tantalizing maturity and seductiveness. Phil had framed that picture with care. Discarded every other one for it but that snap shot which showed the child of earlier years in his arms.

And he had never guessed! Even knowing Phil, he had never guessed.

And then he saw Virginia Channing, standing there in that hotel corridor fitting that huge key with its numbered disk into the door of Room 700. Saw her steeling herself for what she must face, stepping in, closing the door behind her.

She was saying, "You know the rest. I wound the things about me—I was afraid to carry out the bag, for fear I'd look suspicious. You see I didn't know what Phil had told the clerk—I was afraid he had registered for the night. I scratched the initials off the bag—*V. A. C.* She is Virginia, too, though she has always been called Nina. And then, because I had telephoned back to Ellen from that drug store, after I had talked with Nina, that I was going to be away all night with a sick friend—I hadn't said I'd be away all night when I went out—I felt I had to stick to it, that I would be less conspicuous coming in at breakfast time than alone at some unearthly hour. I couldn't think very sensibly. I just clung to my plan. My mind was numb."

"And Nina went home—?"

"Went home, and said she had a headache and came back. Ellen didn't see she didn't have her case. Ellen told her I was called out and that was all. Ellen said she heard her moving about very late. I daren't think what the child was going through. But she got herself together. And finally, mercifully, she slept. She looked like a sleeping child when I saw her in the morning. And she *is* a child and she *will* forget," Virginia insisted passionately. "She has no idea of all she has escaped. She will remember it only as a bad dream."

She added, "I'll wireless her to-night that the murderer has been found. I'll say something reassuring about the woman's remaining unknown—I'll say it carefully. She may be concerned about that wireless the Garlands received about the theater party with me. But Nina has strong stuff in her—I'm not afraid for her courage and self-control. She'll fight through."

"She came by it honestly," said Ryder quietly.

"Now don't you see," she went on eagerly, "why I was so vague about the restaurant? And all the plans? I've had so few details from her! I couldn't say anything definitely to you for fear it should be wrong and hinder you. I had to keep all the avenues open. When you overheard Ellen and learned I'd returned—that was when I came back from the theater—I had to say I'd come back from the restaurant. I know how idiotic it all sounded. But what could I do? It was a wonder you trusted me at all. You must have known I was holding something back."

"I thought, perhaps, you were trying to shield some man," he admitted. "Some man that might have been jealous of you. But I believed what you said about yourself."

"That was a miracle! I was so bound round in lies! I did get startled over that man, when you first spoke of it—I had to wonder if there was anybody mad enough about Nina and suspicious enough to be murderous—several boys are crazy about her. But I realized that couldn't be so. Those boys were all at the boat, just as usual."

She added, "She'll turn to some boy, later. This flare-up for Phil was just an adolescent romance, partly his charm, partly the flattery of his age and position. She half realized it herself at times."

She reverted, as if childishly anxious to exculpate herself in his eyes, "Now you understand why I was so vague, don't you? Oh, I didn't know which way to turn! At the beginning, when you first came to see me, I hadn't meant to admit anything about Phil—about his intimacy with us. So of course I denied that I was the one he wanted to marry. Then, when you told me about the will, I was frantic. I knew he'd done it for Nina—he wanted her to have the money but to have her name kept out of it. Then I was so afraid that you would suspect that I had to pretend that I was the one he loved."

She added, shivering in remembered fear, "I was so afraid when you saw her. That you'd suspect. She was so lovely."

"But such a child," he told her wonderingly. "Just be-ginning beauty—nothing more."

"It was enough for Phil—more than enough. He was a child at heart, too. . . . Poor Phil. . . . But she'll get over it," reiterated Virginia passionately. "She is so young. And the child has character—see how she pulled herself togeth-er, that day, and went off to her school without a betray-ing word. Oh, she has courage—"

"Her mother's courage."

He was looking down at her, his eyes shining. He was alight with love, love that had come strangely and almost bitterly, sharp with apprehensions and weighted with heavy fears. Now he knew release from all his pain, from all the hedging inhibitions that he had thought were barriers.

She had never loved Phil. She had never known that blaze of passion and despair. The flame in her had been her love for her child. Her heart, her woman's heart, had not been through those fires. It was beating there beside him. . . .

They were all alone. The square back of the driver, out in front of the barrier glass, did not matter. He had driven hundreds of other lovers before. He did not look back.

The taxis rolling past did not matter. The shadowy forms of the trees in the park, dark against a city-lighted sky, did not matter.

Nothing mattered but the woman beside him, the fire and sweetness of her, the warmth of her dark eyes, the murmur of her low, moving voice. He put his arms about her and she leaned close to him. His arms, his love, were harbor after the storm.

About the Author

Mary Hastings Bradley (1882-1976) wrote numerous short stories, historical novels, mysteries, and nonfiction travelogues recounting her adventures in different countries. She married lawyer, explorer, and big-game hunter Herbert Bradley, joining him on some of his trips. They accompanied Mary's uncle, biologist Carl Akeley, on his expedition to the Belgian Congo in the early 1920s in search of specimens for the American Museum of Natural History. During WWII she was a war correspondent for *Collier's*. Her daughter, Alice, would go on to write science fiction as 'James Tiptree, Jr.'

DETECTIVE FICTION
SUSPENSE THRILLERS
CLUED PUZZLERS

Coachwhip offers classic mysteries
in both paperback,

CoachwhipBooks.com

and epub,

Coachwhip.com

Also Available
CoachwhipBooks.com

Also Available
CoachwhipBooks.com

Also Available
CoachwhipBooks.com

CRY MURDER

EDITH HOWIE

Also Available
CoachwhipBooks.com

MURDER
A LA
MODE

ELEANORE
KELLY
SELLARS

CLASSIC RED BADGE PRIZE MYSTERY

Also Available
CoachwhipBooks.com

MURDER ON
THE DAY OF
JUDGMENT

VIRGINIA RATH

PATTERN
IN BLACK
AND RED

FARADAY KEENE